REAVER™

CREATED BY JUSTIN JORDAN & REBEKAH ISAACS

JUSTIN JORDAN
Writer, Creator

REBEKAH ISAACS
Artist, Creator

ALEX GUIMARÃES
Colorist

CLAYTON COWLES
Letterer

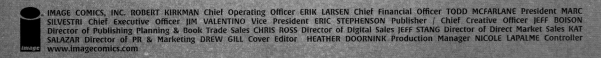

SKYBOUND ROBERT KIRKMAN Chairman   DAVID ALPERT CEO   SEAN MACKIEWICZ SVP, Editor-in-Chief SHAWN KIRKHAM SVP, Business Development   BRIAN HUNTINGTON VP, Online Content SHAUNA WYNNE Publicity Director   ANDRES JUAREZ Art Director   JON MOISAN Editor   ARIELLE BASICH Associate Editor KATE CAUDILL Assistant Editor   CARINA TAYLOR Graphic Designer   PAUL SHIN Business Development Manager JOHNNY O'DELL Social Media Manager   DAN PETERSEN Sr. Director of Operations & Events Foreign Rights Inquiries ag@sequentialrights.com Other Licensing Inquiries contact@skybound.com www.skybound.com

image IMAGE COMICS, INC. ROBERT KIRKMAN Chief Operating Officer ERIK LARSEN Chief Financial Officer TODD MCFARLANE President MARC SILVESTRI Chief Executive Officer JIM VALENTINO Vice President ERIC STEPHENSON Publisher / Chief Creative Officer JEFF BOISON Director of Publishing Planning & Book Trade Sales CHRIS ROSS Director of Digital Sales JEFF STANG Director of Direct Market Sales KAT SALAZAR Director of PR & Marketing DREW GILL Cover Editor   HEATHER DOORNINK Production Manager NICOLE LAPALME Controller www.imagecomics.com

JON MOISAN
Editor

BECKY CLOONAN
Cover Artist

ANDRES JUAREZ
Logo Design

CARINA TAYLOR
Production Design

REAVER VOLUME 1. FIRST PRINTING. February 2020. Published by Image Comics, Inc. Office of publication: 2701 NW Vaughn St., Ste. 780, Portland, OR 97210. Copyright © 2020 Skybound, LLC. Originally published in single magazine form as REAVER #1-6. REAVER™ (including all prominent characters featured herein), its logo and all character likenesses are trademarks of Skybound, LLC, unless otherwise noted. Image Comics® and its logos are registered trademarks and copyrights of Image Comics, Inc. All rights reserved. No part of this publication may be reproduced or transmitted in any form or by any means (except for short excerpts for review purposes) without the express written permission of Image Comics, Inc. All names, characters, events and locales in this publication are entirely fictional. Any resemblance to actual persons (living or dead), events or places, without satiric intent, is coincidental. Printed in the U.S.A. For information regarding the CPSIA on this printed material call: 203-595-3636. ISBN: 978-1-5343-1500-6

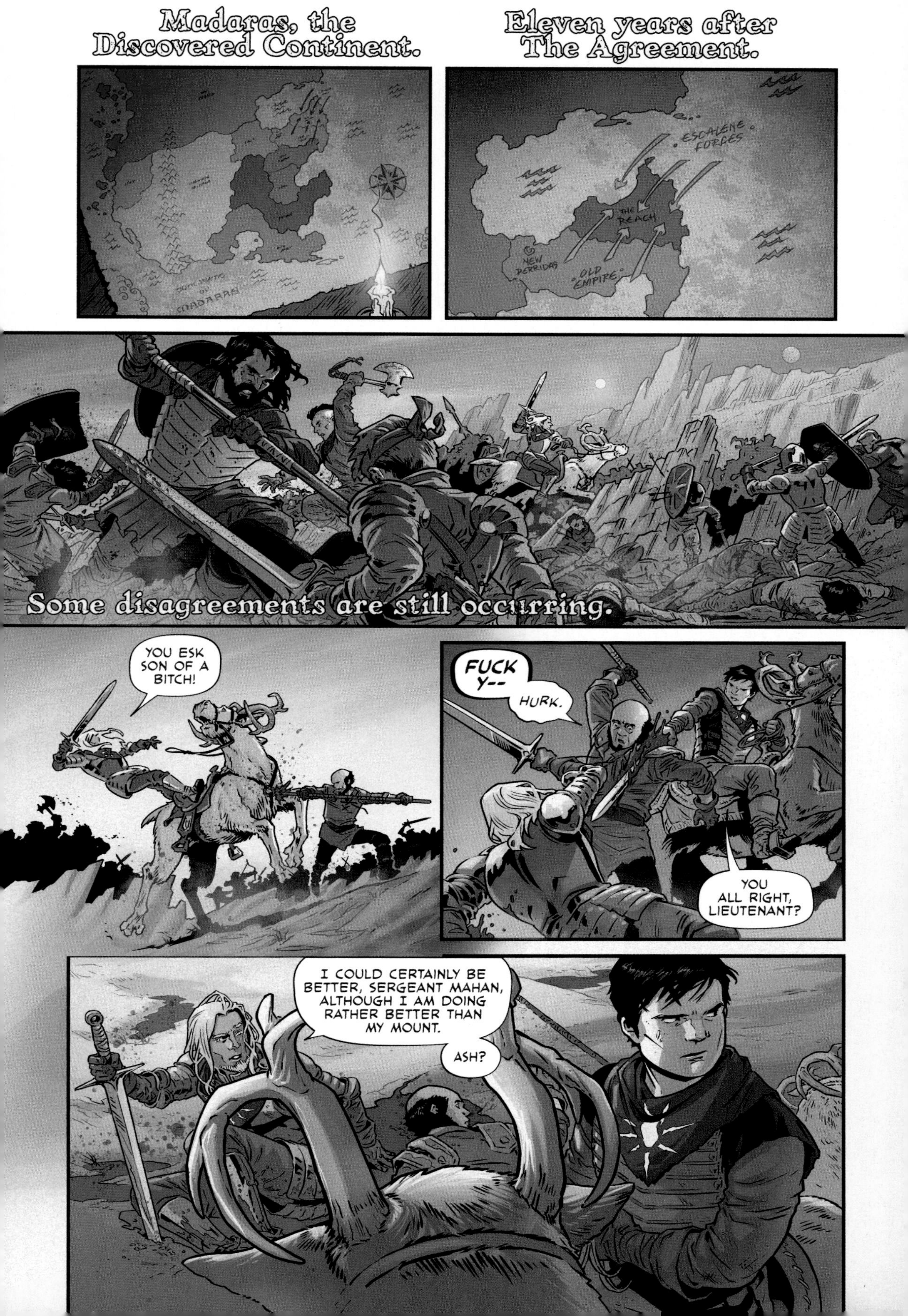

Madaras, the Discovered Continent.
Eleven years after The Agreement.
ESCALENE FORGES
THE REACH
NEW DERRIDAS
OLD EMPIRE
Some disagreements are still occurring.
YOU ESK SON OF A BITCH!
FUCK Y--
HURK.
YOU ALL RIGHT, LIEUTENANT?
I COULD CERTAINLY BE BETTER, SERGEANT MAHAN, ALTHOUGH I AM DOING RATHER BETTER THAN MY MOUNT.
ASH?

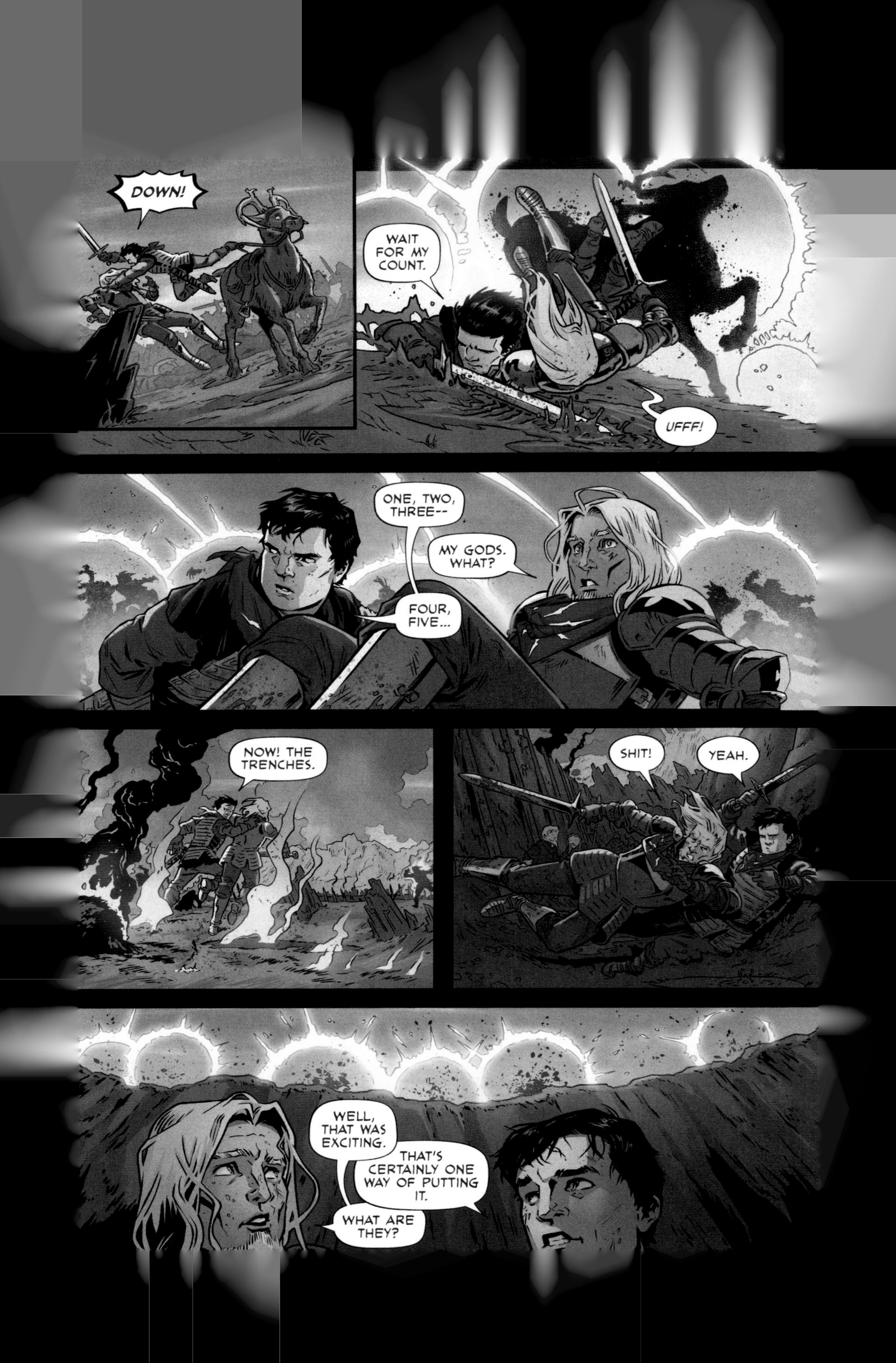
DOWN!
WAIT FOR MY COUNT.
UFFF!
ONE, TWO, THREE--
MY GODS. WHAT?
FOUR, FIVE...
NOW! THE TRENCHES.
SHIT!
YEAH.
WELL, THAT WAS EXCITING.
THAT'S CERTAINLY ONE WAY OF PUTTING IT.
WHAT ARE THEY?

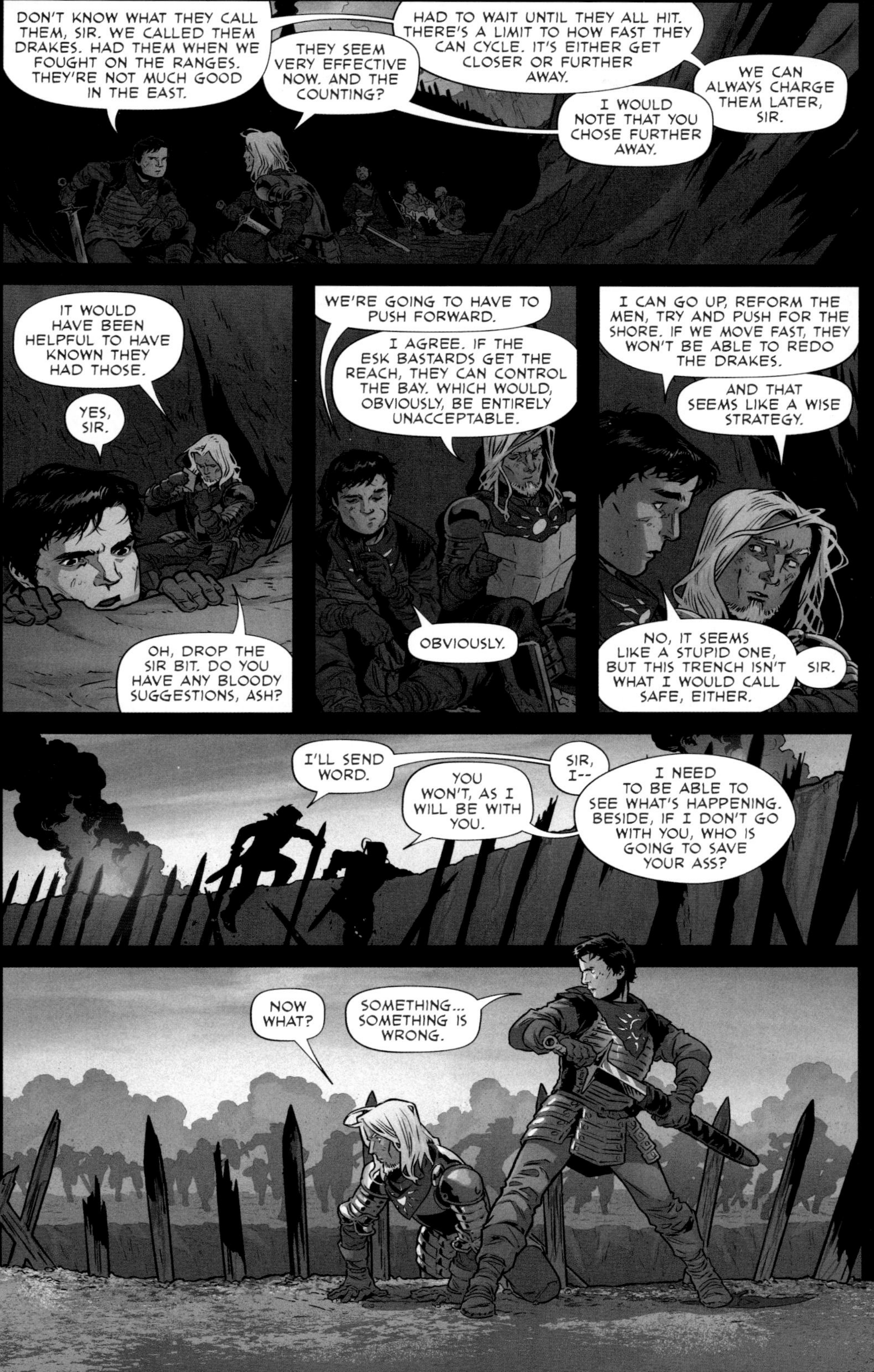
DON'T KNOW WHAT THEY CALL THEM, SIR. WE CALLED THEM DRAKES. HAD THEM WHEN WE FOUGHT ON THE RANGES. THEY'RE NOT MUCH GOOD IN THE EAST.
THEY SEEM VERY EFFECTIVE NOW. AND THE COUNTING?
HAD TO WAIT UNTIL THEY ALL HIT. THERE'S A LIMIT TO HOW FAST THEY CAN CYCLE. IT'S EITHER GET CLOSER OR FURTHER AWAY.
I WOULD NOTE THAT YOU CHOSE FURTHER AWAY.
WE CAN ALWAYS CHARGE THEM LATER, SIR.
IT WOULD HAVE BEEN HELPFUL TO HAVE KNOWN THEY HAD THOSE.
YES, SIR.
OH, DROP THE SIR BIT. DO YOU HAVE ANY BLOODY SUGGESTIONS, ASH?
WE'RE GOING TO HAVE TO PUSH FORWARD.
I AGREE. IF THE ESK BASTARDS GET THE REACH, THEY CAN CONTROL THE BAY. WHICH WOULD, OBVIOUSLY, BE ENTIRELY UNACCEPTABLE.
OBVIOUSLY.
I CAN GO UP, REFORM THE MEN, TRY AND PUSH FOR THE SHORE. IF WE MOVE FAST, THEY WON'T BE ABLE TO REDO THE DRAKES.
AND THAT SEEMS LIKE A WISE STRATEGY.
NO, IT SEEMS LIKE A STUPID ONE, BUT THIS TRENCH ISN'T WHAT I WOULD CALL SAFE, EITHER.
SIR.
I'LL SEND WORD.
YOU WON'T, AS I WILL BE WITH YOU.
SIR, I--
I NEED TO BE ABLE TO SEE WHAT'S HAPPENING. BESIDE, IF I DON'T GO WITH YOU, WHO IS GOING TO SAVE YOUR ASS?
NOW WHAT?
SOMETHING... SOMETHING IS WRONG.

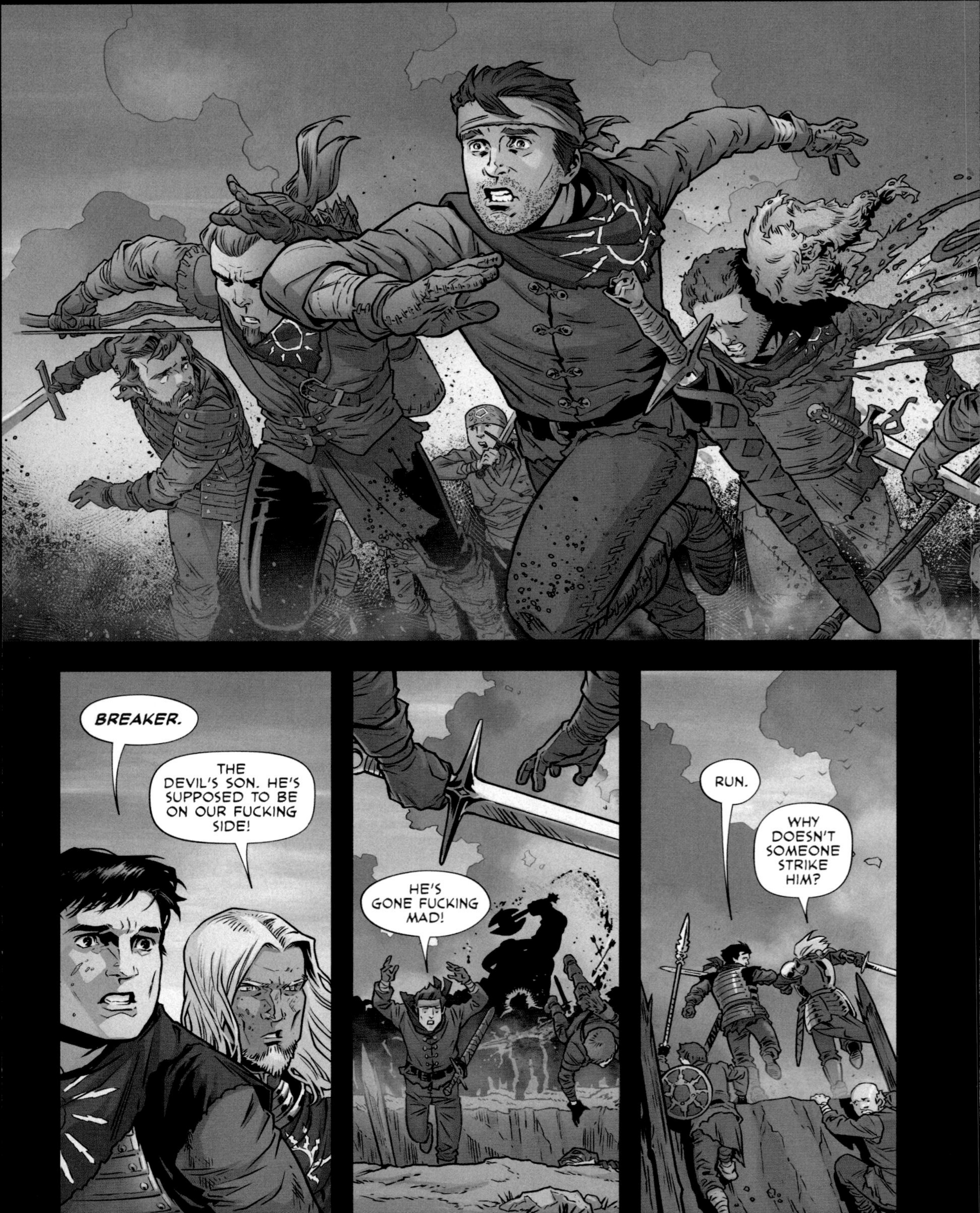
BREAKER.
THE DEVIL'S SON. HE'S SUPPOSED TO BE ON OUR FUCKING SIDE!
HE'S GONE FUCKING MAD!
RUN.
WHY DOESN'T SOMEONE STRIKE HIM?

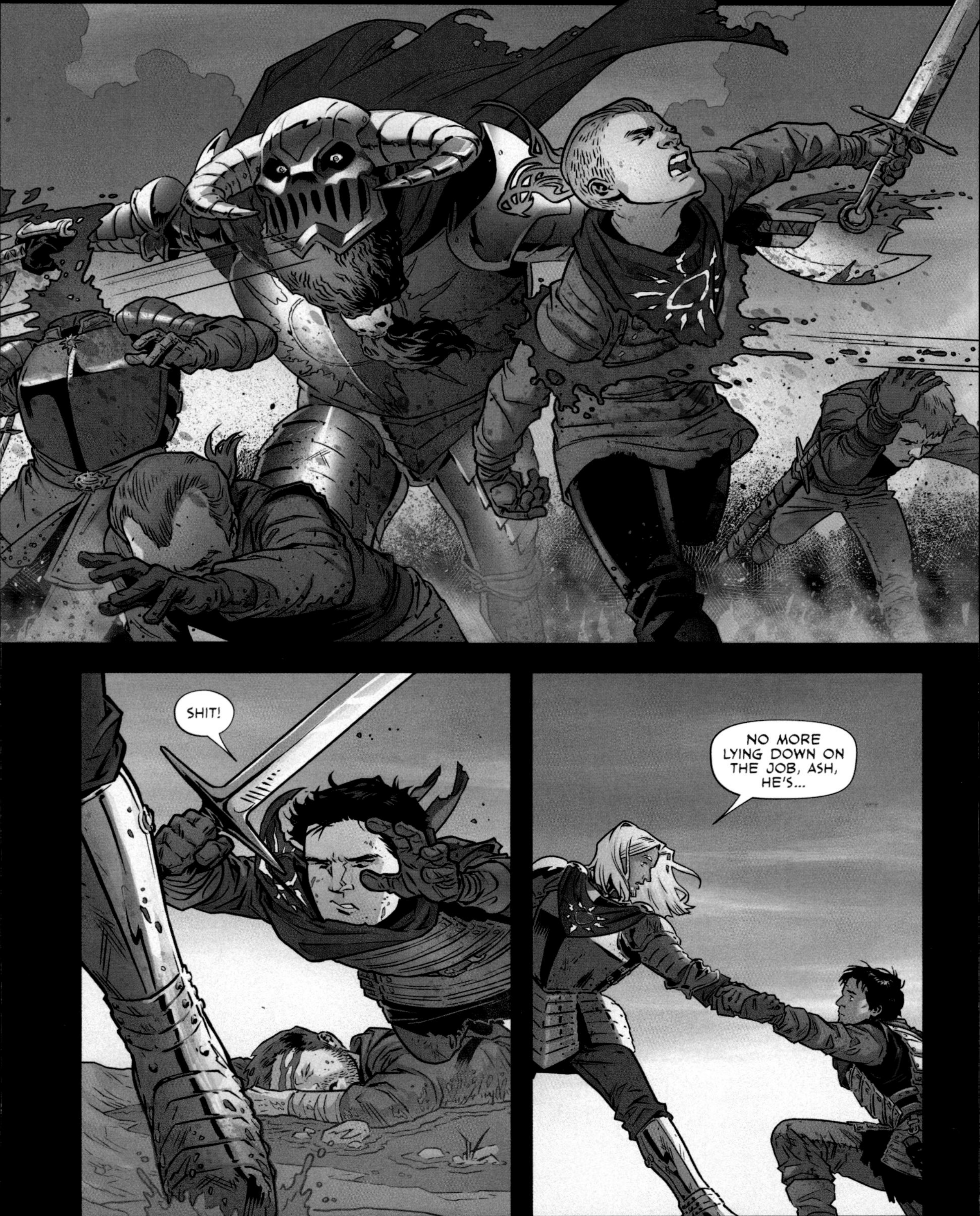
SHIT!
NO MORE LYING DOWN ON THE JOB, ASH, HE'S...

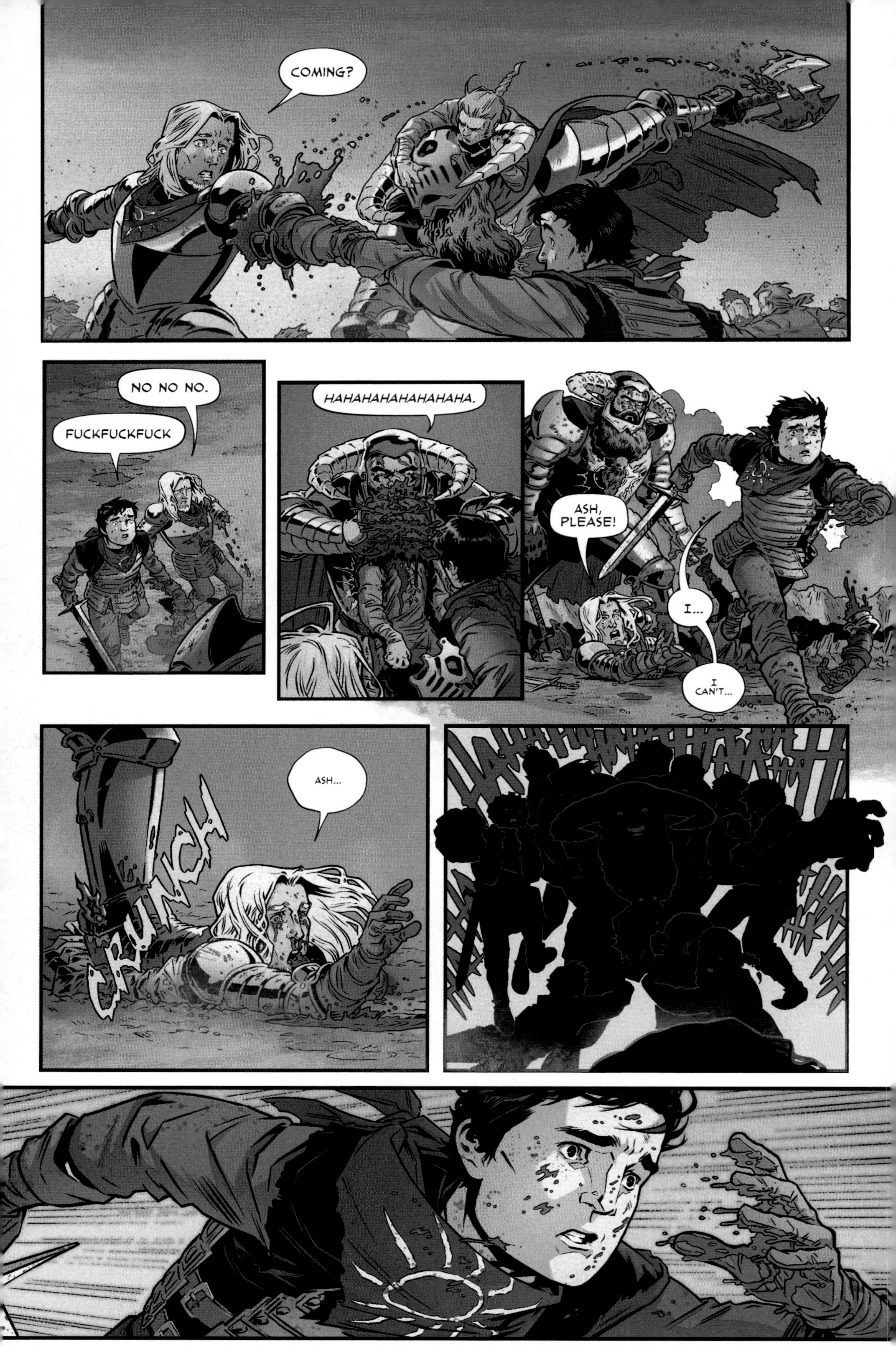
COMING?
NO NO NO.
FUCKFUCKFUCK
HAHAHAHAHAHAHAHA.
ASH, PLEASE!
I...
I CAN'T...
ASH...
CRUNCH

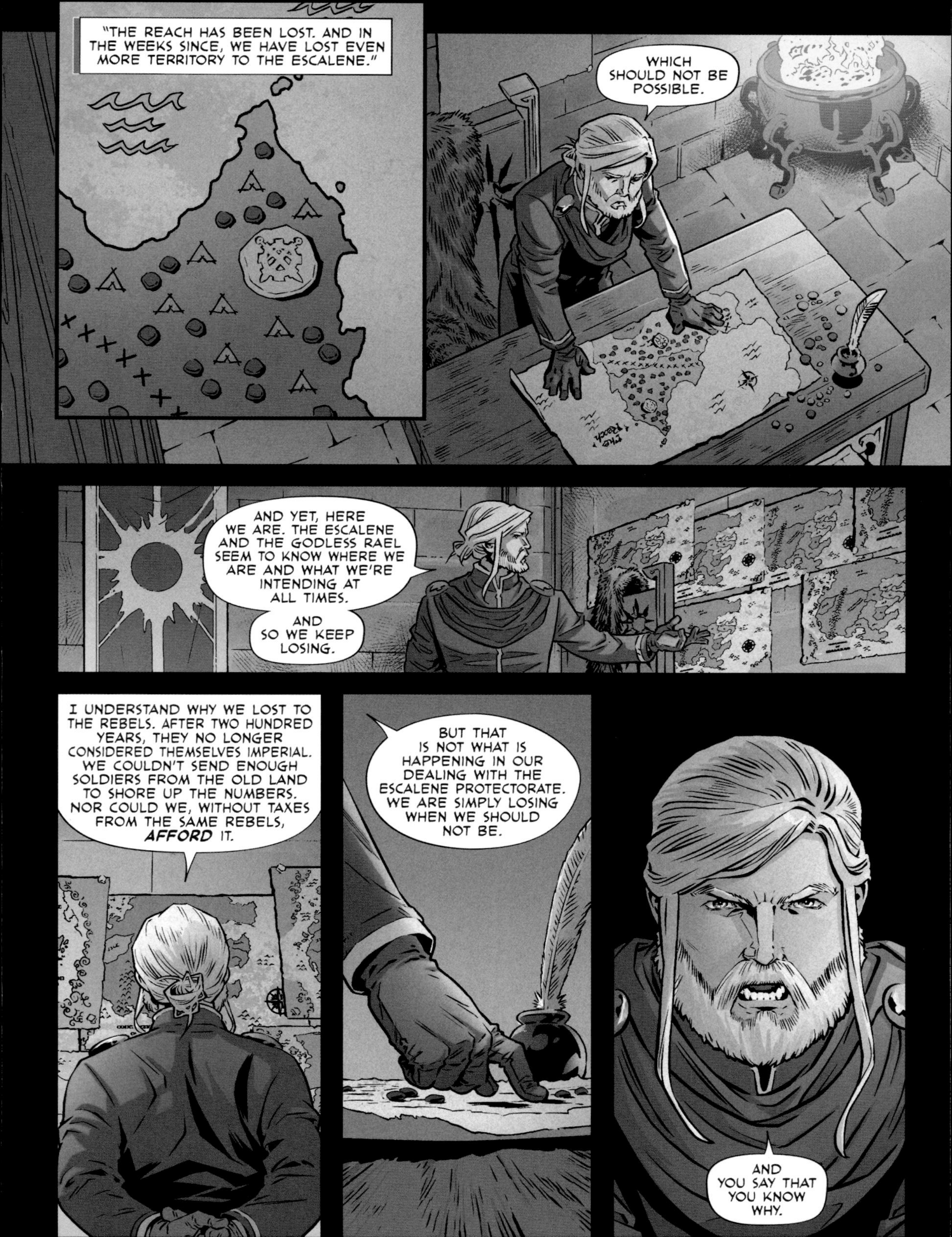
"THE REACH HAS BEEN LOST. AND IN THE WEEKS SINCE, WE HAVE LOST EVEN MORE TERRITORY TO THE ESCALENE."
WHICH SHOULD NOT BE POSSIBLE.
AND YET, HERE WE ARE. THE ESCALENE AND THE GODLESS RAEL SEEM TO KNOW WHERE WE ARE AND WHAT WE'RE INTENDING AT ALL TIMES.
AND SO WE KEEP LOSING.
I UNDERSTAND WHY WE LOST TO THE REBELS. AFTER TWO HUNDRED YEARS, THEY NO LONGER CONSIDERED THEMSELVES IMPERIAL. WE COULDN'T SEND ENOUGH SOLDIERS FROM THE OLD LAND TO SHORE UP THE NUMBERS. NOR COULD WE, WITHOUT TAXES FROM THE SAME REBELS, ***AFFORD*** IT.
BUT THAT IS NOT WHAT IS HAPPENING IN OUR DEALING WITH THE ESCALENE PROTECTORATE. WE ARE SIMPLY LOSING WHEN WE SHOULD NOT BE.
AND YOU SAY THAT YOU KNOW WHY.

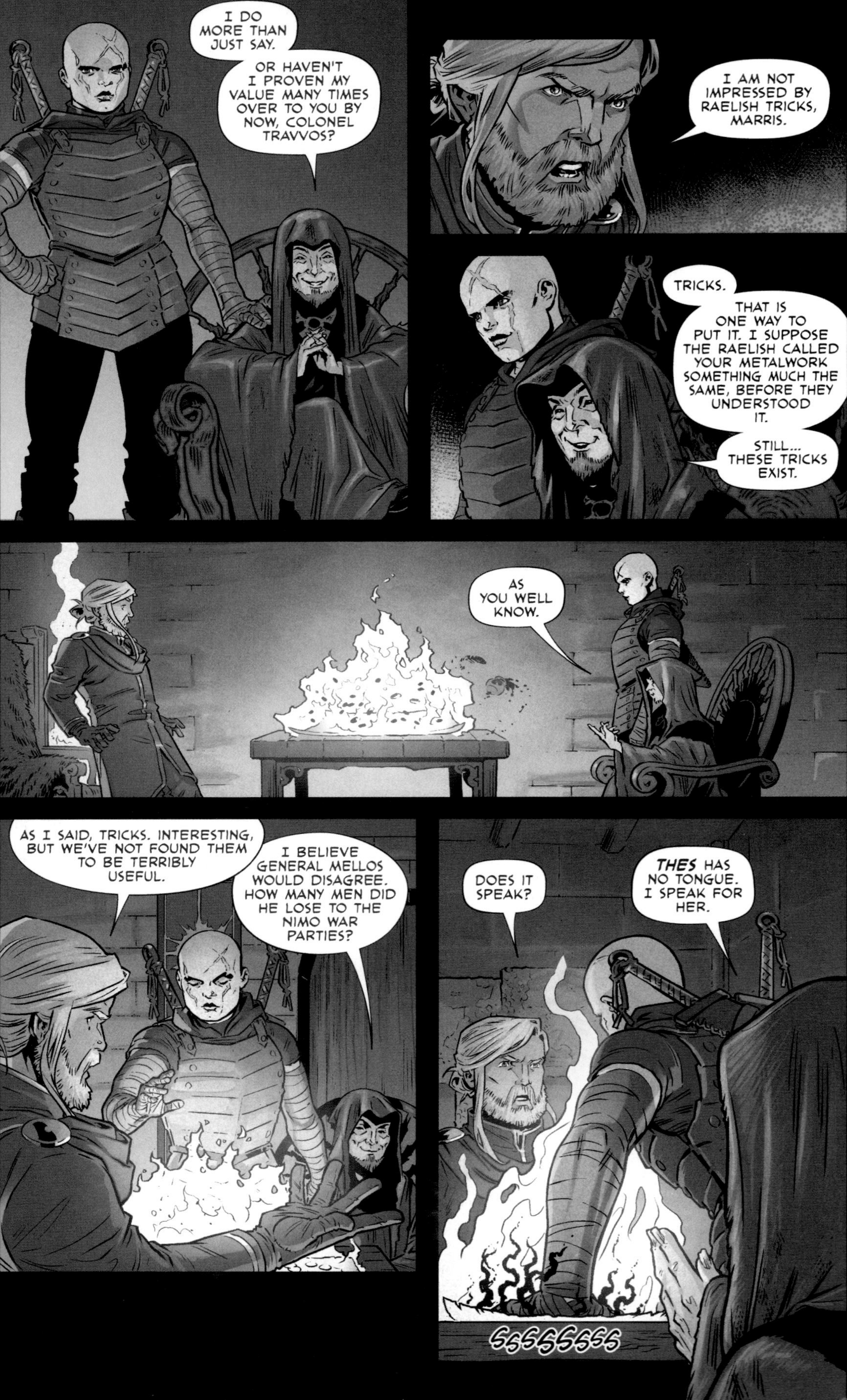
I DO MORE THAN JUST SAY.
OR HAVEN'T I PROVEN MY VALUE MANY TIMES OVER TO YOU BY NOW, COLONEL TRAVVOS?
I AM NOT IMPRESSED BY RAELISH TRICKS, MARRIS.
TRICKS.
THAT IS ONE WAY TO PUT IT. I SUPPOSE THE RAELISH CALLED YOUR METALWORK SOMETHING MUCH THE SAME, BEFORE THEY UNDERSTOOD IT.
STILL... THESE TRICKS EXIST.
AS YOU WELL KNOW.
AS I SAID, TRICKS. INTERESTING, BUT WE'VE NOT FOUND THEM TO BE TERRIBLY USEFUL.
I BELIEVE GENERAL MELLOS WOULD DISAGREE. HOW MANY MEN DID HE LOSE TO THE NIMO WAR PARTIES?
DOES IT SPEAK?
THES HAS NO TONGUE. I SPEAK FOR HER.
SSSSSSSSS

THE ANVIL.

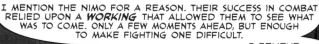

I MENTION THE NIMO FOR A REASON. THEIR SUCCESS IN COMBAT RELIED UPON A *WORKING* THAT ALLOWED THEM TO SEE WHAT WAS TO COME. ONLY A FEW MOMENTS AHEAD, BUT ENOUGH TO MAKE FIGHTING ONE DIFFICULT.

I BELIEVE THAT THE ESCALENE'S RAEL ALLIES HAVE SOMETHING SIMILAR. IT IS POSSIBLE TO GLEAN GLIMPSES THROUGH BLOOD AND BONE. BUT TO DO IT ON THIS SCALE WOULD REQUIRE A LOSS OF LIFE STAGGERING IN ITS ENORMITY. THE AKASH COULD NOT PROVIDE THIS. BUT THE ESCALENE COULD.

IF THEY HAD SUCH A THING, HOW DO WE DEFEAT THEM?

KNOWLEDGE HAS A COST. ALWAYS. POWER HAS A COST. ALWAYS. THE NIMO HAD TO SACRIFICE CHILDREN THEY LOVED TO DO IT. DOING IT ON A SCALE LIKE THIS WOULD REQUIRE ENORMOUS SACRIFICE.

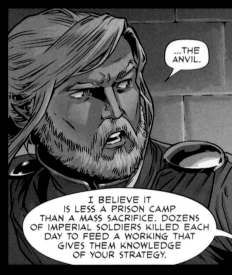

...THE ANVIL.

I BELIEVE IT IS LESS A PRISON CAMP THAN A MASS SACRIFICE. DOZENS OF IMPERIAL SOLDIERS KILLED EACH DAY TO FEED A WORKING THAT GIVES THEM KNOWLEDGE OF YOUR STRATEGY.

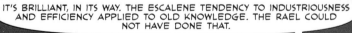

IT'S BRILLIANT, IN ITS WAY. THE ESCALENE TENDENCY TO INDUSTRIOUSNESS AND EFFICIENCY APPLIED TO OLD KNOWLEDGE. THE RAEL COULD NOT HAVE DONE THAT.

YOU HAVE A PROPOSAL, THEN? SOME CLEVER GAMBIT TO STOP THIS?

I DO.

A SMALL GROUP OF CRIMINALS WILL GO DISGUISED AS AN ESCALENE PRISON CONVOY. THIS, YOU WILL FIND, IS A PROPOSAL WITH NO DOWNSIDE FOR YOU. IF WE SUCCEED, YOU, COLONEL TRAVVOS, WILL BE PRAISED FOR THIS DARING PLAN. SHOULD WE FAIL...

I HAVE PLAUSIBLE DENIABILITY. YOU WERE ALL CONDEMNED, AFTER ALL. DAMNED. YOU ESCAPED AND TRIED TO FLEE TO ESCALENE. WELL PLAYED, MISTER MARRIS. AND I SUPPOSE YOU HAVE THESE PRISONERS ALREADY IN MIND?

OH, YES.

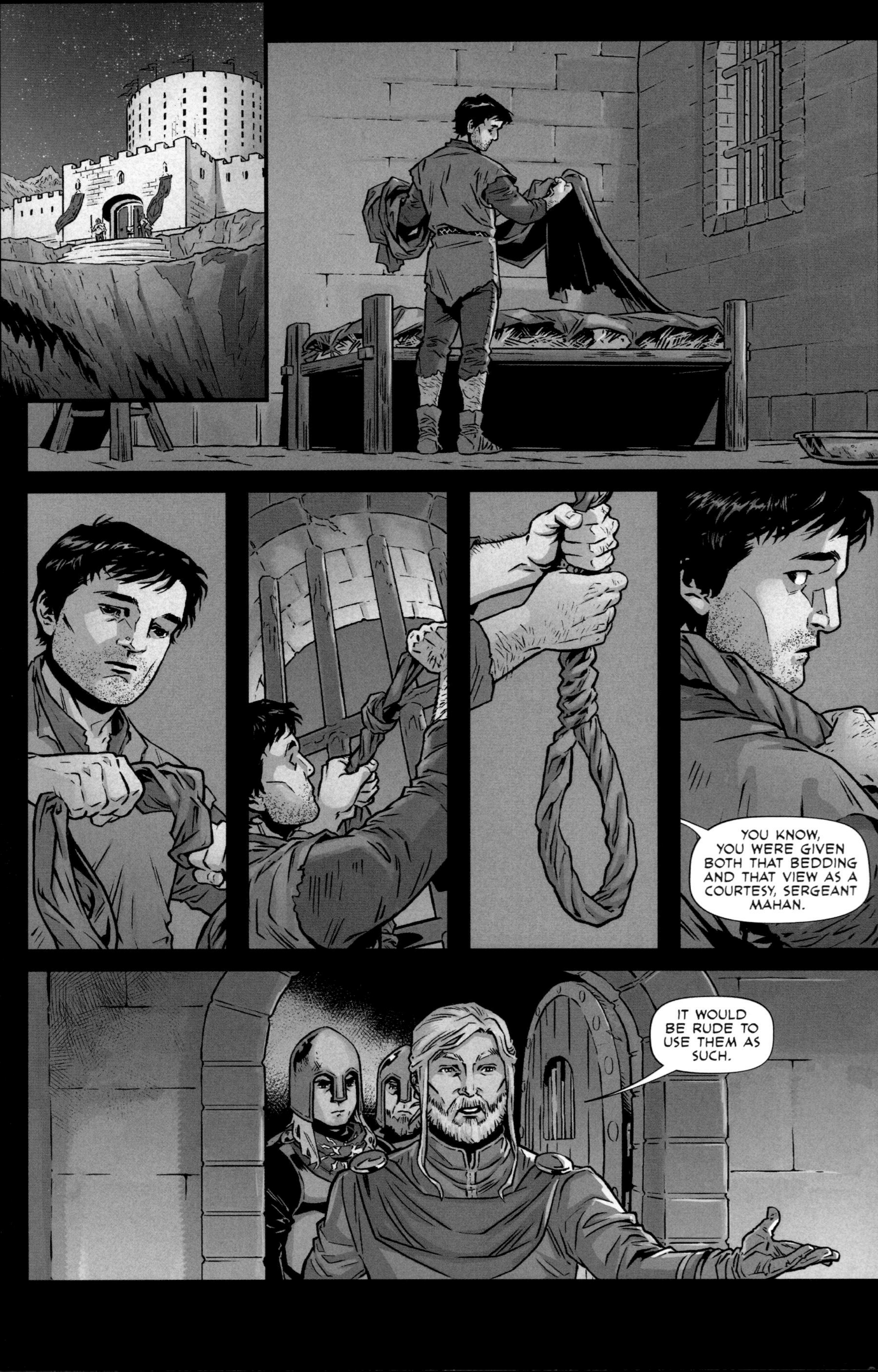
YOU KNOW, YOU WERE GIVEN BOTH THAT BEDDING AND THAT VIEW AS A COURTESY, SERGEANT MAHAN.
IT WOULD BE RUDE TO USE THEM AS SUCH.

YES, SIR.

I WILL BE FINE.

STOP THAT. YOU NEEDN'T BOTHER. NOT HERE. NOT NOW.

YOU ARE ESCALENE, ARE YOU NOT?

I AM A LOYAL SERVANT OF THE EMP--

YES, YES, I KNOW. YOUR PARENTS CAME FROM CATASI, DID THEY NOT?

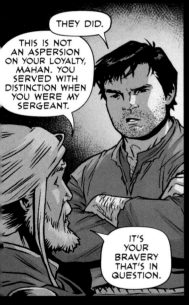

THEY DID.

THIS IS NOT AN ASPERSION ON YOUR LOYALTY, MAHAN. YOU SERVED WITH DISTINCTION WHEN YOU WERE MY SERGEANT.

IT'S YOUR BRAVERY THAT'S IN QUESTION.

I UNDERSTAND WHY YOU WOULD LIKE TO KILL YOURSELF. COWARDICE IS HARD TO STOMACH, ESPECIALLY WHEN IT IS OUR OWN.

BUT SUICIDE WOULD SIMPLY BE MORE COWARDICE. HOW WOULD YOU LIKE TO HAVE A CHANCE TO REDEEM SOMETHING OF YOUR HONOR, SERGEANT?

SIR?

I HAVE A MISSION FOR YOU. MAKE NO MISTAKE: YOU WILL DIE. BUT YOU WILL DIE IN SERVICE, WHICH IS BETTER, I THINK, THAN BEING FOUND SWINGING IN A PISS-SOAKED CELL.

ALL YOU HAVE TO SAY IS--

YES.

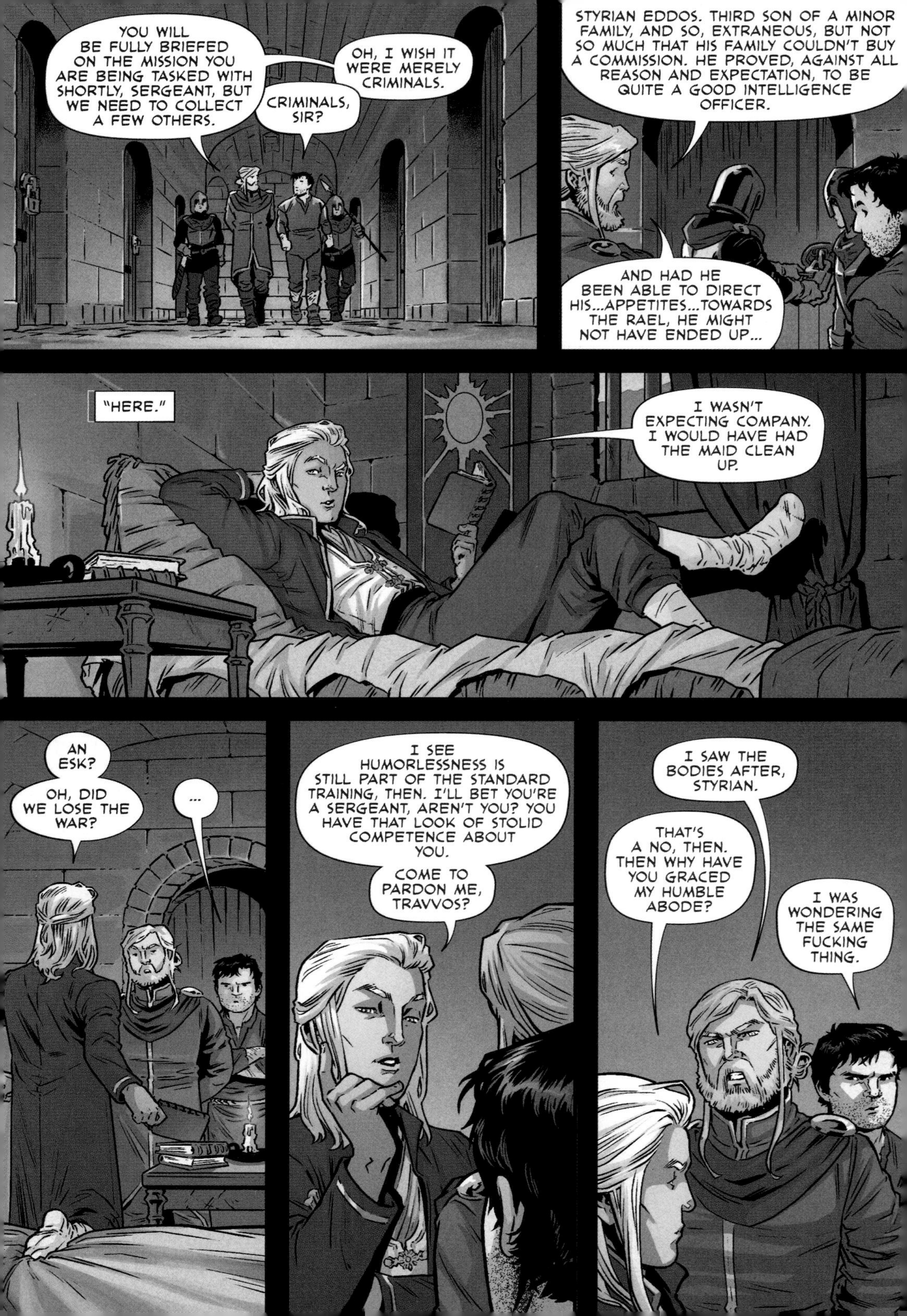
YOU WILL BE FULLY BRIEFED ON THE MISSION YOU ARE BEING TASKED WITH SHORTLY, SERGEANT, BUT WE NEED TO COLLECT A FEW OTHERS.
CRIMINALS, SIR?
OH, I WISH IT WERE MERELY CRIMINALS.
STYRIAN EDDOS. THIRD SON OF A MINOR FAMILY, AND SO, EXTRANEOUS, BUT NOT SO MUCH THAT HIS FAMILY COULDN'T BUY A COMMISSION. HE PROVED, AGAINST ALL REASON AND EXPECTATION, TO BE QUITE A GOOD INTELLIGENCE OFFICER.
AND HAD HE BEEN ABLE TO DIRECT HIS...APPETITES...TOWARDS THE RAEL, HE MIGHT NOT HAVE ENDED UP...
"HERE."
I WASN'T EXPECTING COMPANY. I WOULD HAVE HAD THE MAID CLEAN UP.
AN ESK?
OH, DID WE LOSE THE WAR?
...
I SEE HUMORLESSNESS IS STILL PART OF THE STANDARD TRAINING, THEN. I'LL BET YOU'RE A SERGEANT, AREN'T YOU? YOU HAVE THAT LOOK OF STOLID COMPETENCE ABOUT YOU.
COME TO PARDON ME, TRAVVOS?
I SAW THE BODIES AFTER, STYRIAN.
THAT'S A NO, THEN. THEN WHY HAVE YOU GRACED MY HUMBLE ABODE?
I WAS WONDERING THE SAME FUCKING THING.

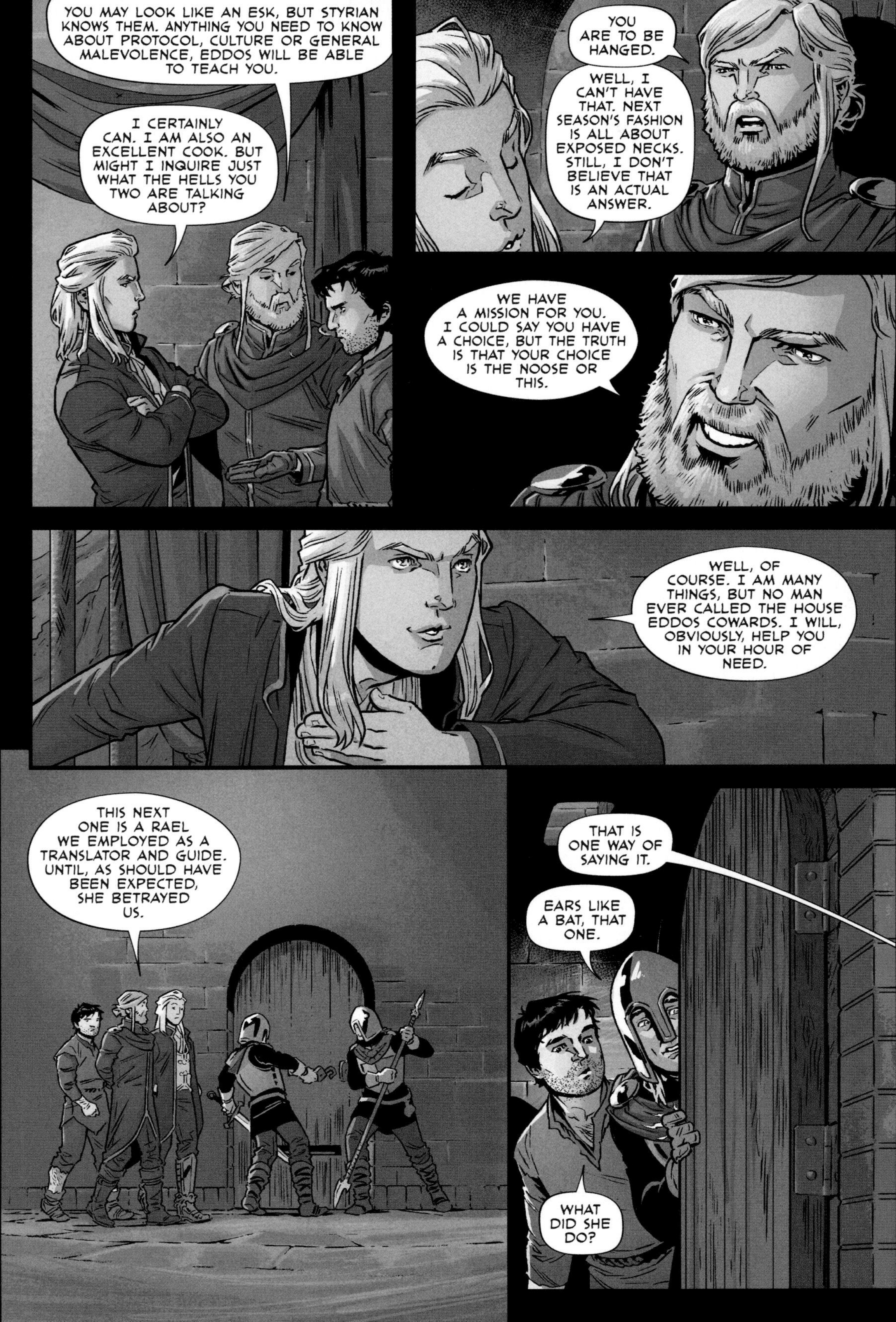

YOU MAY LOOK LIKE AN ESK, BUT STYRIAN KNOWS THEM. ANYTHING YOU NEED TO KNOW ABOUT PROTOCOL, CULTURE OR GENERAL MALEVOLENCE, EDDOS WILL BE ABLE TO TEACH YOU.
I CERTAINLY CAN. I AM ALSO AN EXCELLENT COOK. BUT MIGHT I INQUIRE JUST WHAT THE HELLS YOU TWO ARE TALKING ABOUT?
YOU ARE TO BE HANGED.
WELL, I CAN'T HAVE THAT. NEXT SEASON'S FASHION IS ALL ABOUT EXPOSED NECKS. STILL, I DON'T BELIEVE THAT IS AN ACTUAL ANSWER.
WE HAVE A MISSION FOR YOU. I COULD SAY YOU HAVE A CHOICE, BUT THE TRUTH IS THAT YOUR CHOICE IS THE NOOSE OR THIS.
WELL, OF COURSE. I AM MANY THINGS, BUT NO MAN EVER CALLED THE HOUSE EDDOS COWARDS. I WILL, OBVIOUSLY, HELP YOU IN YOUR HOUR OF NEED.
THIS NEXT ONE IS A RAEL WE EMPLOYED AS A TRANSLATOR AND GUIDE. UNTIL, AS SHOULD HAVE BEEN EXPECTED, SHE BETRAYED US.
THAT IS ONE WAY OF SAYING IT.
EARS LIKE A BAT, THAT ONE.
WHAT DID SHE DO?

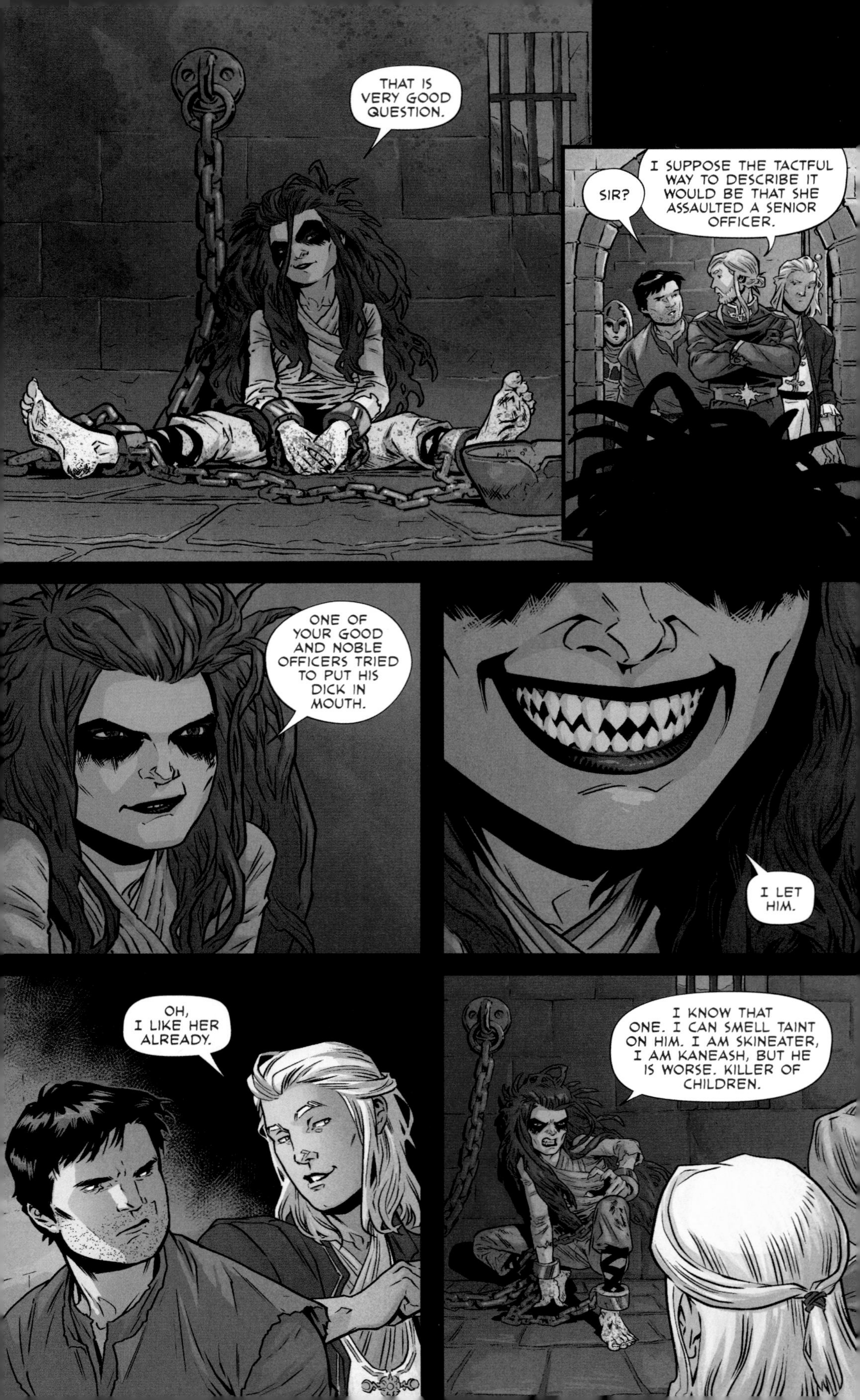
THAT IS VERY GOOD QUESTION.
SIR?
I SUPPOSE THE TACTFUL WAY TO DESCRIBE IT WOULD BE THAT SHE ASSAULTED A SENIOR OFFICER.
ONE OF YOUR GOOD AND NOBLE OFFICERS TRIED TO PUT HIS DICK IN MOUTH.
I LET HIM.
OH, I LIKE HER ALREADY.
I KNOW THAT ONE. I CAN SMELL TAINT ON HIM. I AM SKINEATER, I AM KANEASH, BUT HE IS WORSE. KILLER OF CHILDREN.

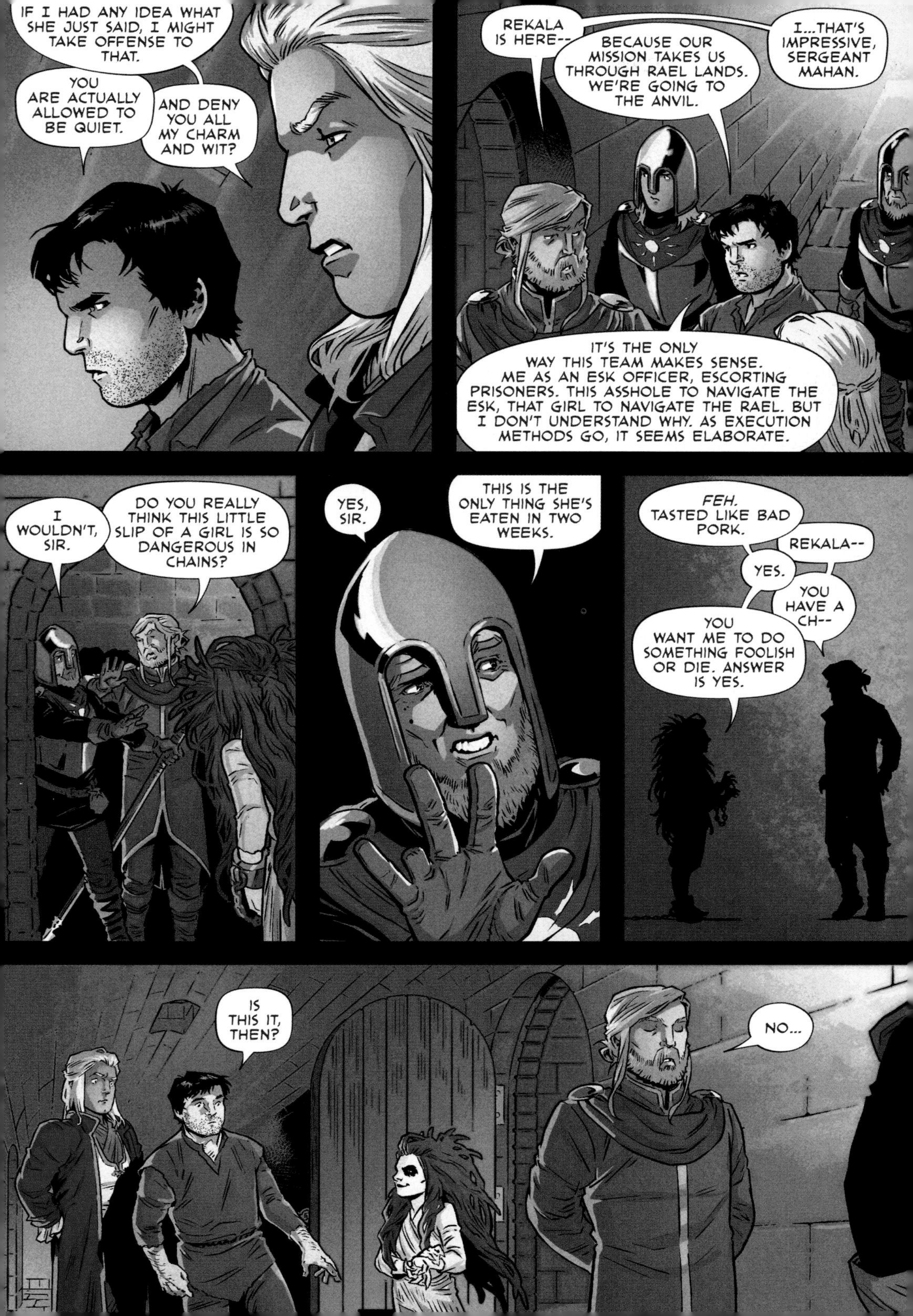
IF I HAD ANY IDEA WHAT SHE JUST SAID, I MIGHT TAKE OFFENSE TO THAT.
YOU ARE ACTUALLY ALLOWED TO BE QUIET.
AND DENY YOU ALL MY CHARM AND WIT?
REKALA IS HERE--
BECAUSE OUR MISSION TAKES US THROUGH RAEL LANDS. WE'RE GOING TO THE ANVIL.
I...THAT'S IMPRESSIVE, SERGEANT MAHAN.
IT'S THE ONLY WAY THIS TEAM MAKES SENSE. ME AS AN ESK OFFICER, ESCORTING PRISONERS. THIS ASSHOLE TO NAVIGATE THE ESK, THAT GIRL TO NAVIGATE THE RAEL. BUT I DON'T UNDERSTAND WHY. AS EXECUTION METHODS GO, IT SEEMS ELABORATE.
I WOULDN'T, SIR.
DO YOU REALLY THINK THIS LITTLE SLIP OF A GIRL IS SO DANGEROUS IN CHAINS?
YES, SIR.
THIS IS THE ONLY THING SHE'S EATEN IN TWO WEEKS.
FEH. TASTED LIKE BAD PORK.
REKALA--
YES.
YOU HAVE A CH--
YOU WANT ME TO DO SOMETHING FOOLISH OR DIE. ANSWER IS YES.
IS THIS IT, THEN?
NO...

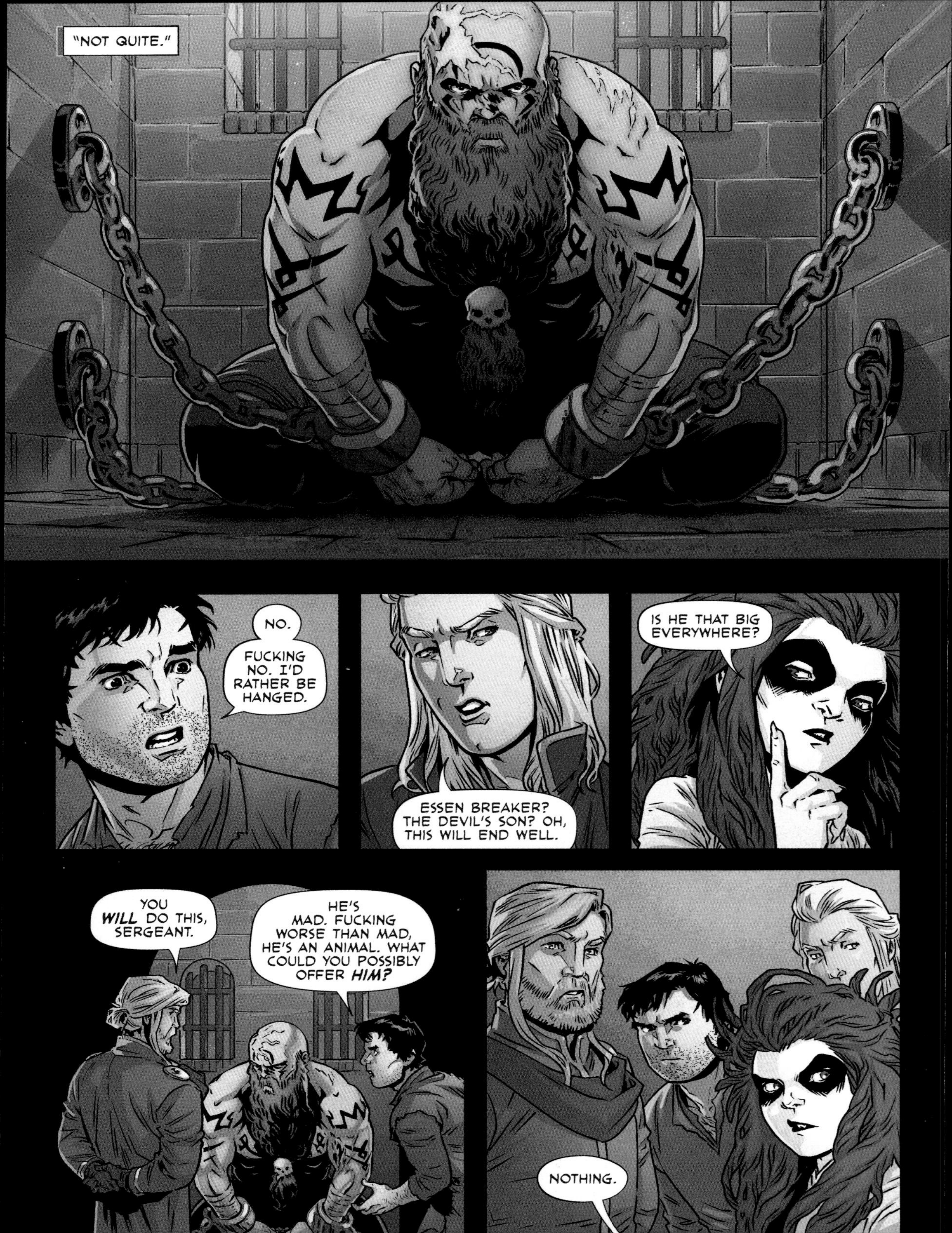
"NOT QUITE."
NO.
FUCKING NO. I'D RATHER BE HANGED.
ESSEN BREAKER? THE DEVIL'S SON? OH, THIS WILL END WELL.
IS HE THAT BIG EVERYWHERE?
YOU *WILL* DO THIS, SERGEANT.
HE'S MAD. FUCKING WORSE THAN MAD, HE'S AN ANIMAL. WHAT COULD YOU POSSIBLY OFFER *HIM?*
NOTHING.

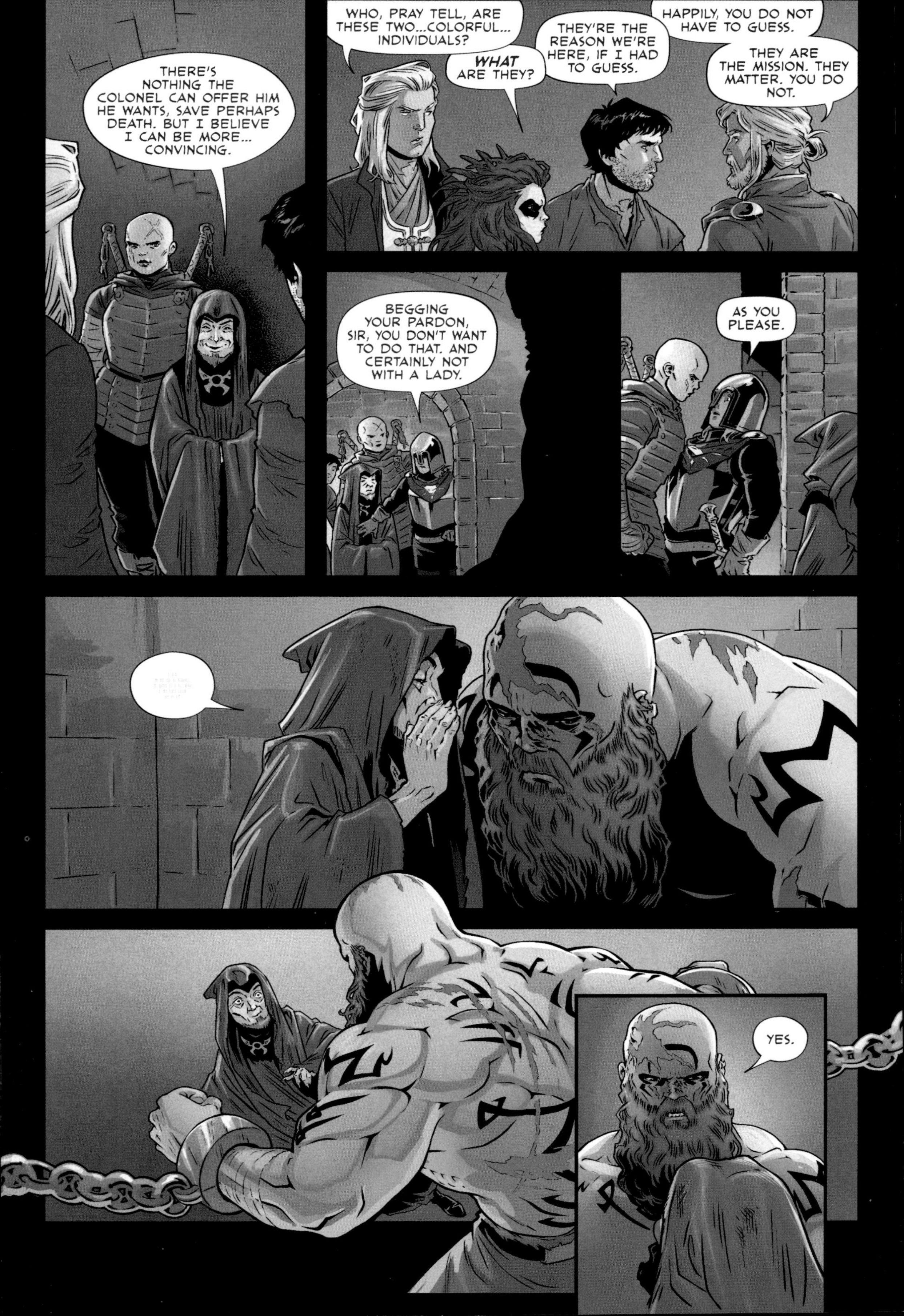

THERE'S NOTHING THE COLONEL CAN OFFER HIM HE WANTS, SAVE PERHAPS DEATH. BUT I BELIEVE I CAN BE MORE... CONVINCING.
WHO, PRAY TELL, ARE THESE TWO...COLORFUL... INDIVIDUALS?
WHAT ARE THEY?
THEY'RE THE REASON WE'RE HERE, IF I HAD TO GUESS.
HAPPILY, YOU DO NOT HAVE TO GUESS.
THEY ARE THE MISSION. THEY MATTER. YOU DO NOT.
BEGGING YOUR PARDON, SIR, YOU DON'T WANT TO DO THAT. AND CERTAINLY NOT WITH A LADY.
AS YOU PLEASE.
YES.

THERE IS ONE MORE PERSON YOU NEED TO MEET.

'ELLO.

THAT IS TONK PILS, FORMER QUARTERMASTER AND NOTABLE THIEF.

OI, AND AS THINGS GO, NOTABLE IS NOT SOMETHING A THIEF WANTS TO BE, I RECKON.

AND WHAT DOES THIS ONE ADD TO HAPPY, LITTLE BAND?

CLARITY.

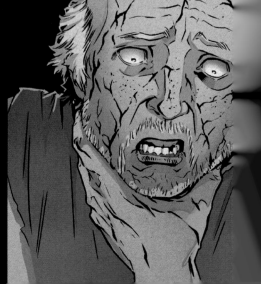

EH?

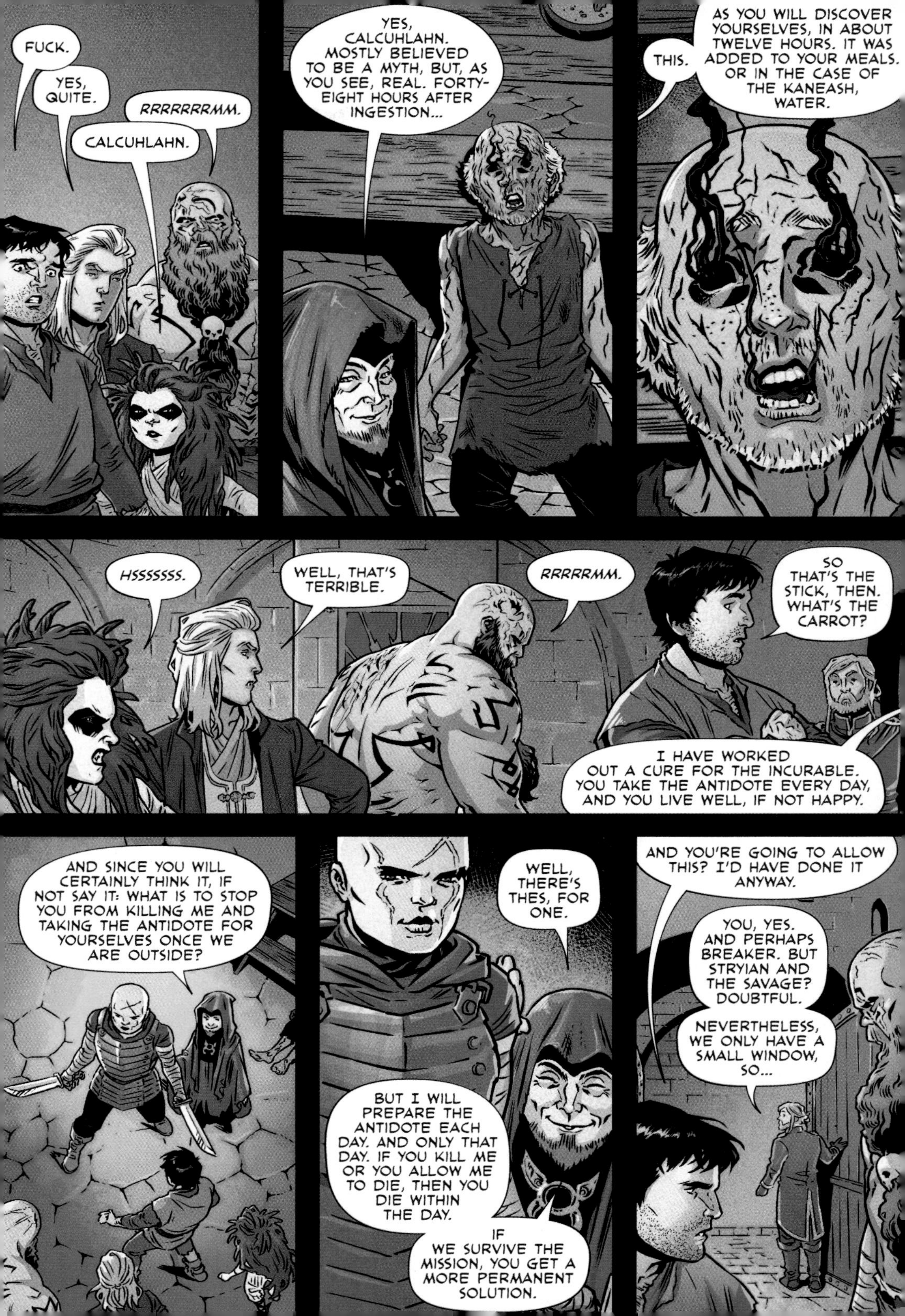
FUCK.
YES, QUITE.
RRRRRRRMM.
CALCUHLAHN.
YES, CALCUHLAHN. MOSTLY BELIEVED TO BE A MYTH, BUT, AS YOU SEE, REAL. FORTY-EIGHT HOURS AFTER INGESTION...
THIS.
AS YOU WILL DISCOVER YOURSELVES, IN ABOUT TWELVE HOURS. IT WAS ADDED TO YOUR MEALS. OR IN THE CASE OF THE KANEASH, WATER.
HSSSSSSS.
WELL, THAT'S TERRIBLE.
RRRRRMM.
SO THAT'S THE STICK, THEN. WHAT'S THE CARROT?
I HAVE WORKED OUT A CURE FOR THE INCURABLE. YOU TAKE THE ANTIDOTE EVERY DAY, AND YOU LIVE WELL, IF NOT HAPPY.
AND SINCE YOU WILL CERTAINLY THINK IT, IF NOT SAY IT: WHAT IS TO STOP YOU FROM KILLING ME AND TAKING THE ANTIDOTE FOR YOURSELVES ONCE WE ARE OUTSIDE?
WELL, THERE'S THES, FOR ONE.
BUT I WILL PREPARE THE ANTIDOTE EACH DAY. AND ONLY THAT DAY. IF YOU KILL ME OR YOU ALLOW ME TO DIE, THEN YOU DIE WITHIN THE DAY.
IF WE SURVIVE THE MISSION, YOU GET A MORE PERMANENT SOLUTION.
AND YOU'RE GOING TO ALLOW THIS? I'D HAVE DONE IT ANYWAY.
YOU, YES. AND PERHAPS BREAKER. BUT STRYIAN AND THE SAVAGE? DOUBTFUL.
NEVERTHELESS, WE ONLY HAVE A SMALL WINDOW, SO...

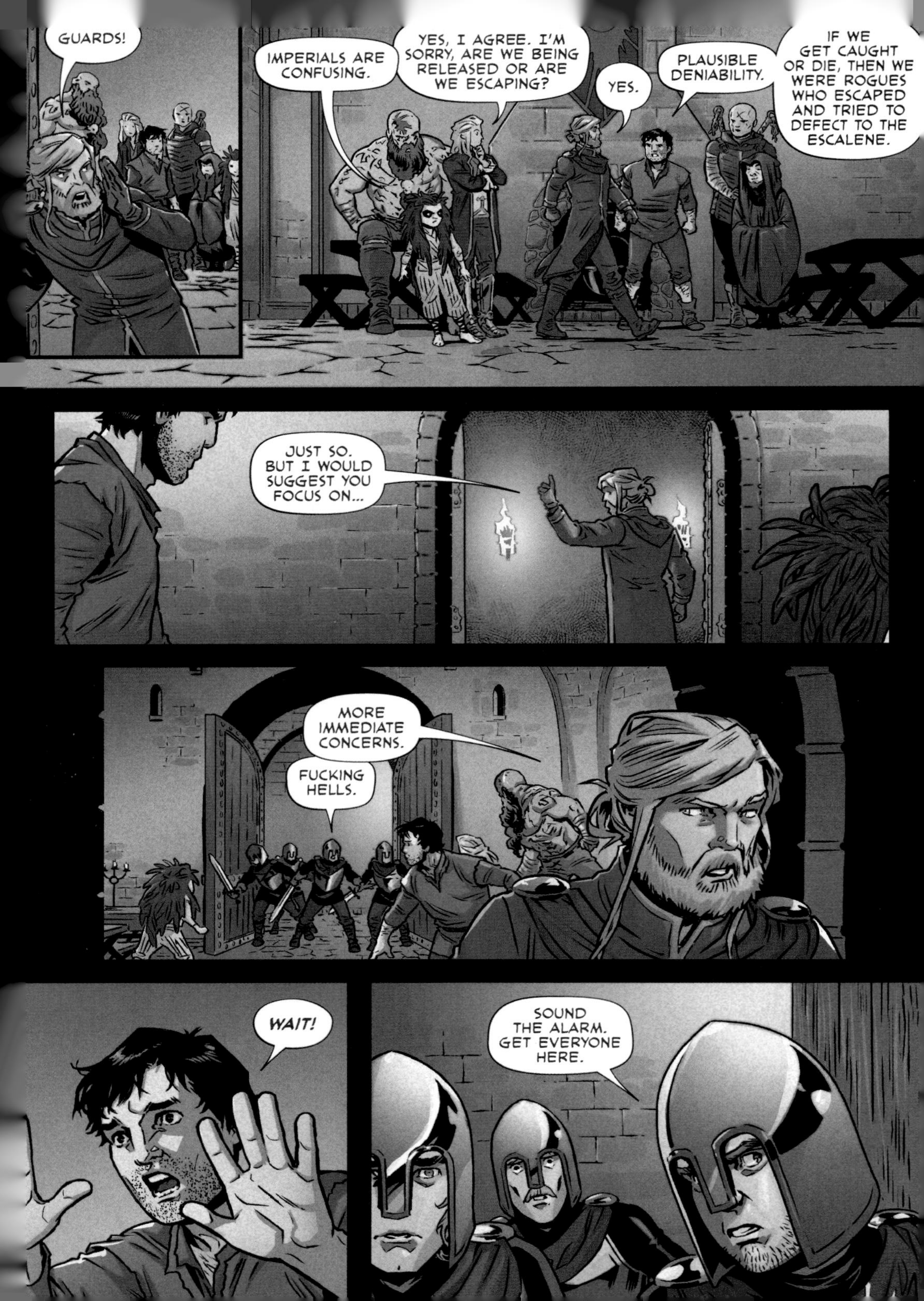
GUARDS!
IMPERIALS ARE CONFUSING.
YES, I AGREE. I'M SORRY, ARE WE BEING RELEASED OR ARE WE ESCAPING?
YES.
PLAUSIBLE DENIABILITY.
IF WE GET CAUGHT OR DIE, THEN WE WERE ROGUES WHO ESCAPED AND TRIED TO DEFECT TO THE ESCALENE.
JUST SO. BUT I WOULD SUGGEST YOU FOCUS ON...
MORE IMMEDIATE CONCERNS.
FUCKING HELLS.
WAIT!
SOUND THE ALARM. GET EVERYONE HERE.

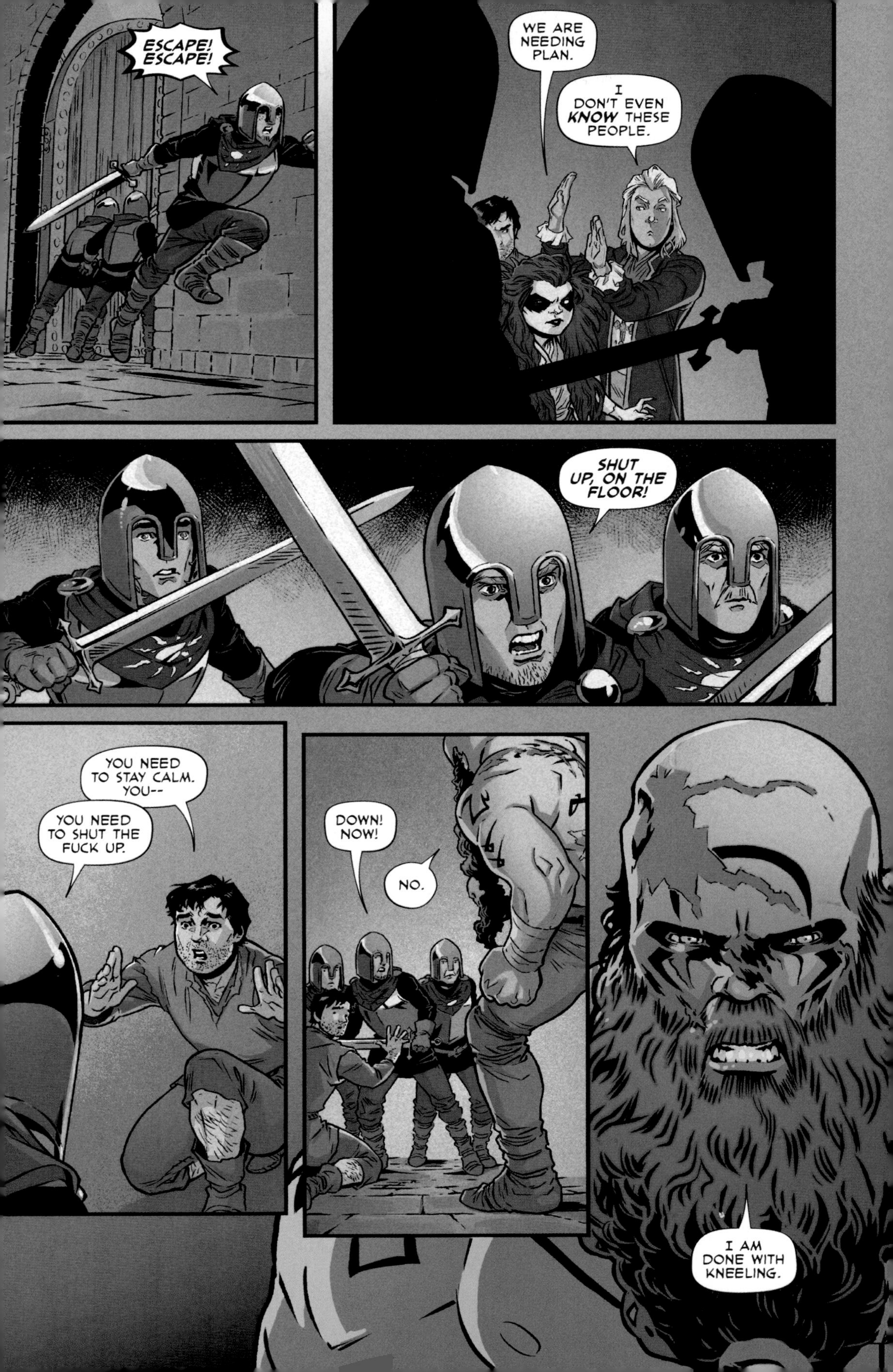
ESCAPE! ESCAPE!
WE ARE NEEDING PLAN.
I DON'T EVEN KNOW THESE PEOPLE.
SHUT UP, ON THE FLOOR!
YOU NEED TO STAY CALM. YOU--
YOU NEED TO SHUT THE FUCK UP.
DOWN! NOW!
NO.
I AM DONE WITH KNEELING.

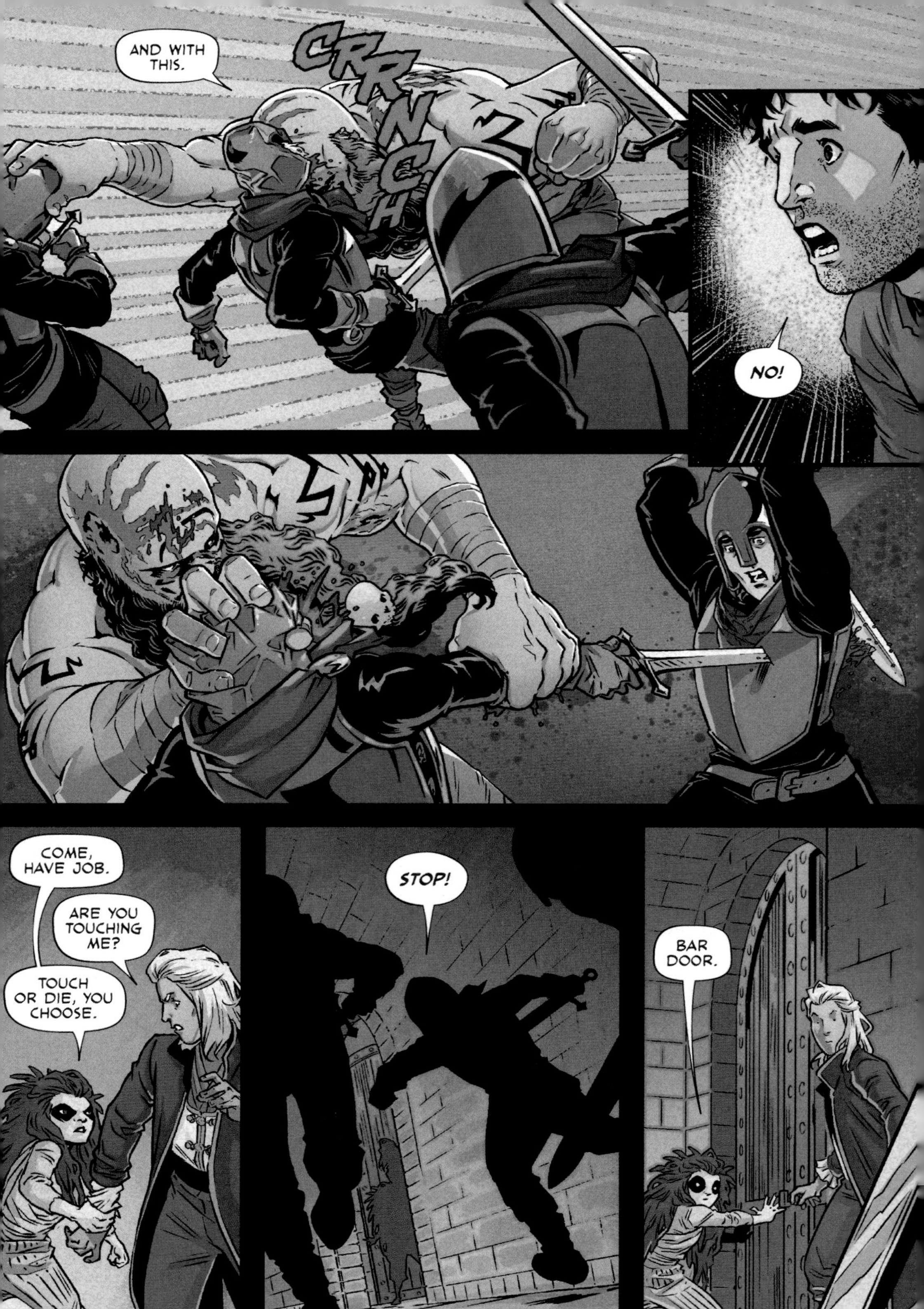
AND WITH THIS.
CRRNCH
NO!
COME, HAVE JOB.
ARE YOU TOUCHING ME?
TOUCH OR DIE, YOU CHOOSE.
STOP!
BAR DOOR.

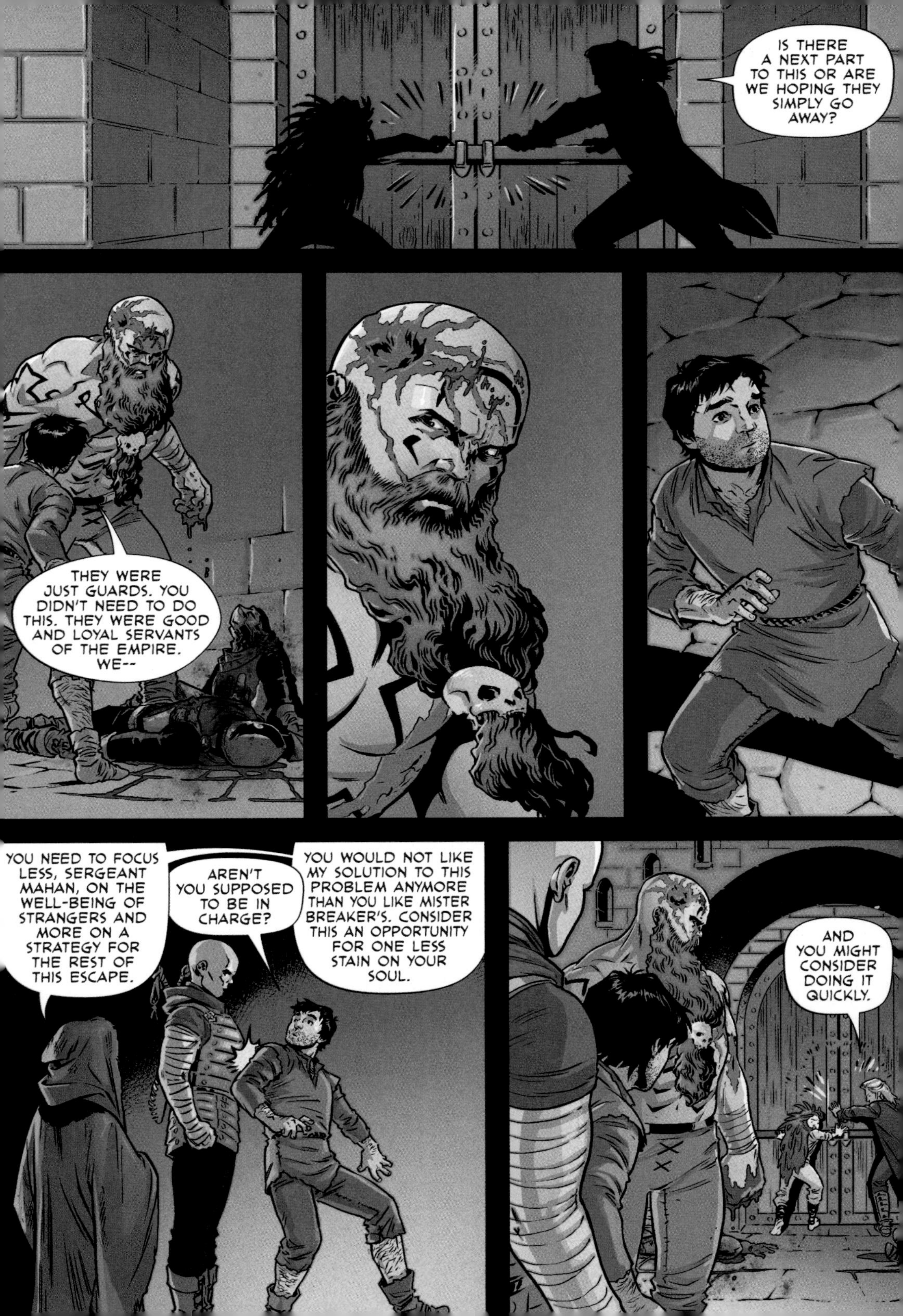
IS THERE A NEXT PART TO THIS OR ARE WE HOPING THEY SIMPLY GO AWAY?
THEY WERE JUST GUARDS. YOU DIDN'T NEED TO DO THIS. THEY WERE GOOD AND LOYAL SERVANTS OF THE EMPIRE. WE--
YOU NEED TO FOCUS LESS, SERGEANT MAHAN, ON THE WELL-BEING OF STRANGERS AND MORE ON A STRATEGY FOR THE REST OF THIS ESCAPE.
AREN'T YOU SUPPOSED TO BE IN CHARGE?
YOU WOULD NOT LIKE MY SOLUTION TO THIS PROBLEM ANYMORE THAN YOU LIKE MISTER BREAKER'S. CONSIDER THIS AN OPPORTUNITY FOR ONE LESS STAIN ON YOUR SOUL.
AND YOU MIGHT CONSIDER DOING IT QUICKLY.

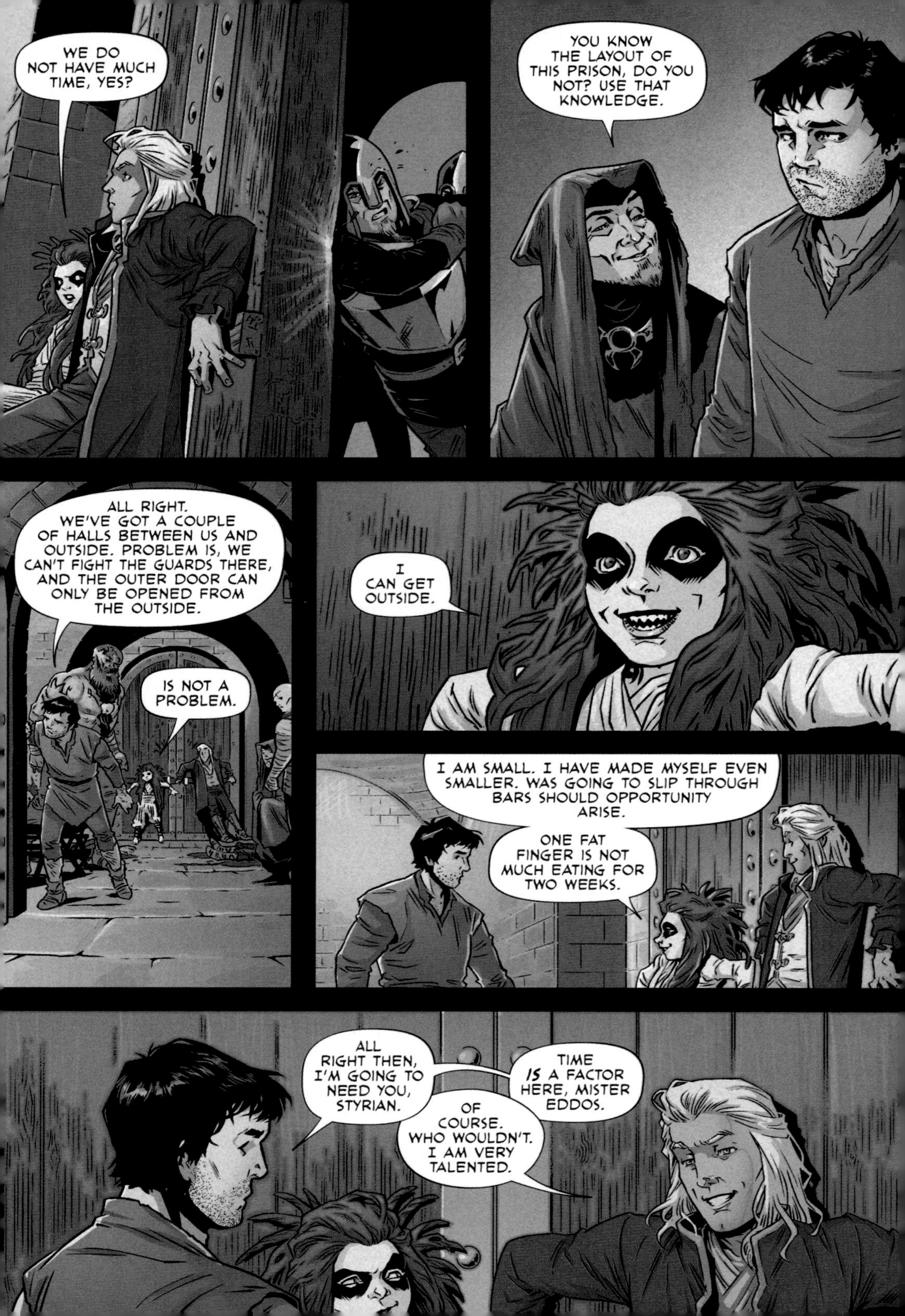
WE DO NOT HAVE MUCH TIME, YES?
YOU KNOW THE LAYOUT OF THIS PRISON, DO YOU NOT? USE THAT KNOWLEDGE.
ALL RIGHT. WE'VE GOT A COUPLE OF HALLS BETWEEN US AND OUTSIDE. PROBLEM IS, WE CAN'T FIGHT THE GUARDS THERE, AND THE OUTER DOOR CAN ONLY BE OPENED FROM THE OUTSIDE.
IS NOT A PROBLEM.
I CAN GET OUTSIDE.
I AM SMALL. I HAVE MADE MYSELF EVEN SMALLER. WAS GOING TO SLIP THROUGH BARS SHOULD OPPORTUNITY ARISE.
ONE FAT FINGER IS NOT MUCH EATING FOR TWO WEEKS.
ALL RIGHT THEN, I'M GOING TO NEED YOU, STYRIAN.
TIME *IS* A FACTOR HERE, MISTER EDDOS.
OF COURSE. WHO WOULDN'T. I AM VERY TALENTED.

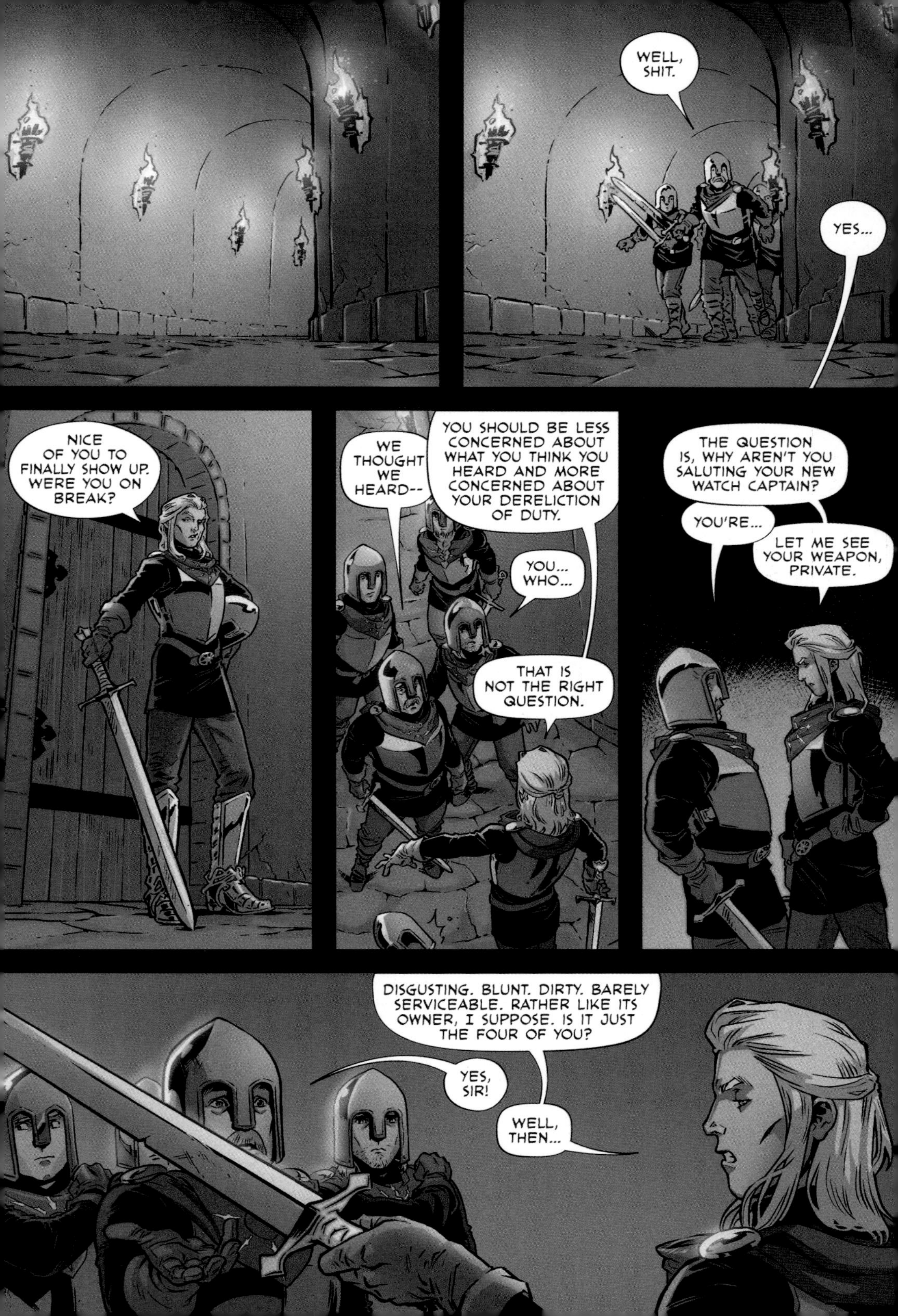
WELL, SHIT.
YES...
NICE OF YOU TO FINALLY SHOW UP. WERE YOU ON BREAK?
WE THOUGHT WE HEARD--
YOU SHOULD BE LESS CONCERNED ABOUT WHAT YOU THINK YOU HEARD AND MORE CONCERNED ABOUT YOUR DERELICTION OF DUTY.
YOU... WHO...
THAT IS NOT THE RIGHT QUESTION.
THE QUESTION IS, WHY AREN'T YOU SALUTING YOUR NEW WATCH CAPTAIN?
YOU'RE...
LET ME SEE YOUR WEAPON, PRIVATE.
DISGUSTING. BLUNT. DIRTY. BARELY SERVICEABLE. RATHER LIKE ITS OWNER, I SUPPOSE. IS IT JUST THE FOUR OF YOU?
YES, SIR!
WELL, THEN...

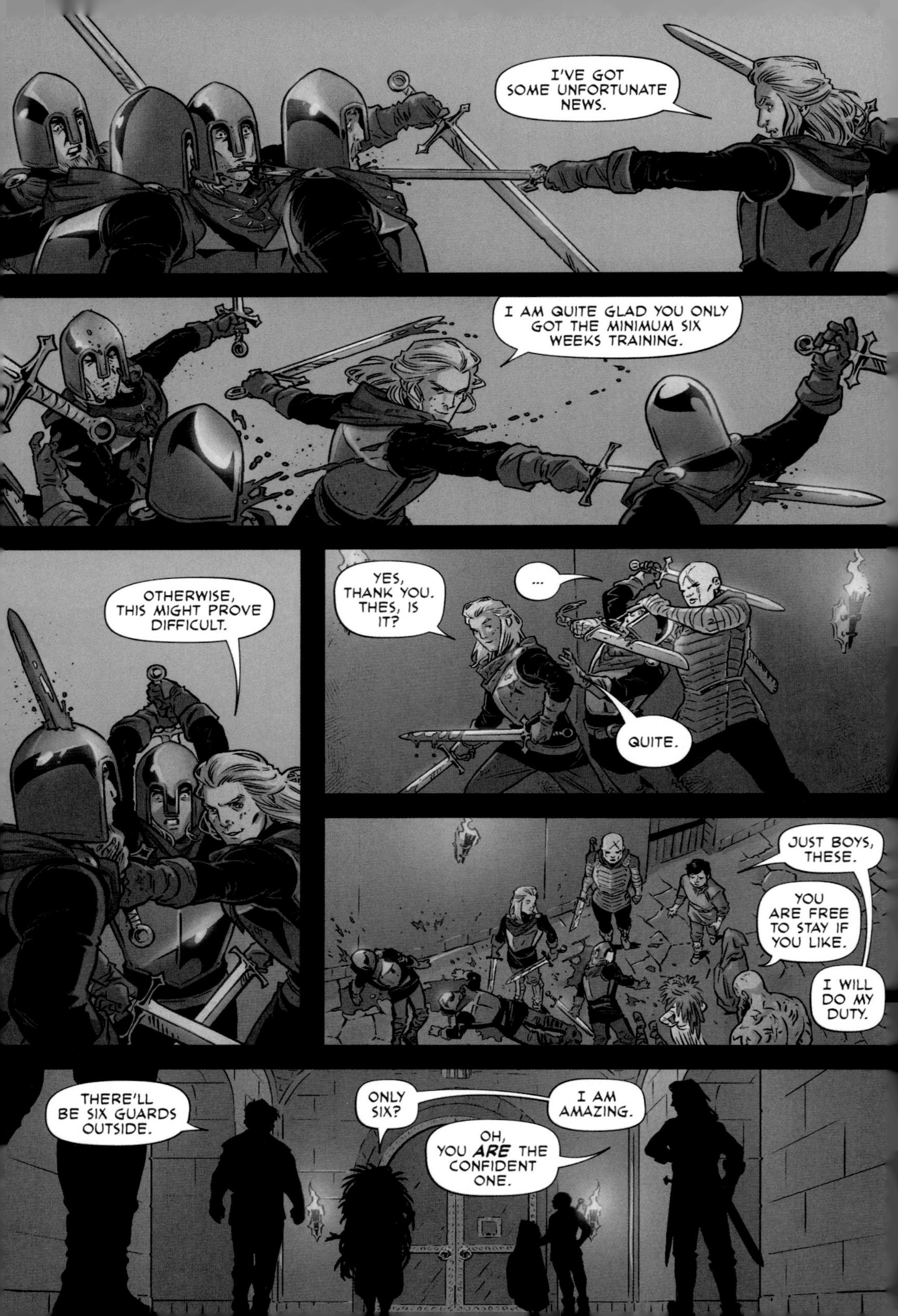
I'VE GOT SOME UNFORTUNATE NEWS.
I AM QUITE GLAD YOU ONLY GOT THE MINIMUM SIX WEEKS TRAINING.
OTHERWISE, THIS MIGHT PROVE DIFFICULT.
YES, THANK YOU. THES, IS IT?
...
QUITE.
JUST BOYS, THESE.
YOU ARE FREE TO STAY IF YOU LIKE.
I WILL DO MY DUTY.
THERE'LL BE SIX GUARDS OUTSIDE.
ONLY SIX?
I AM AMAZING.
OH, YOU ARE THE CONFIDENT ONE.

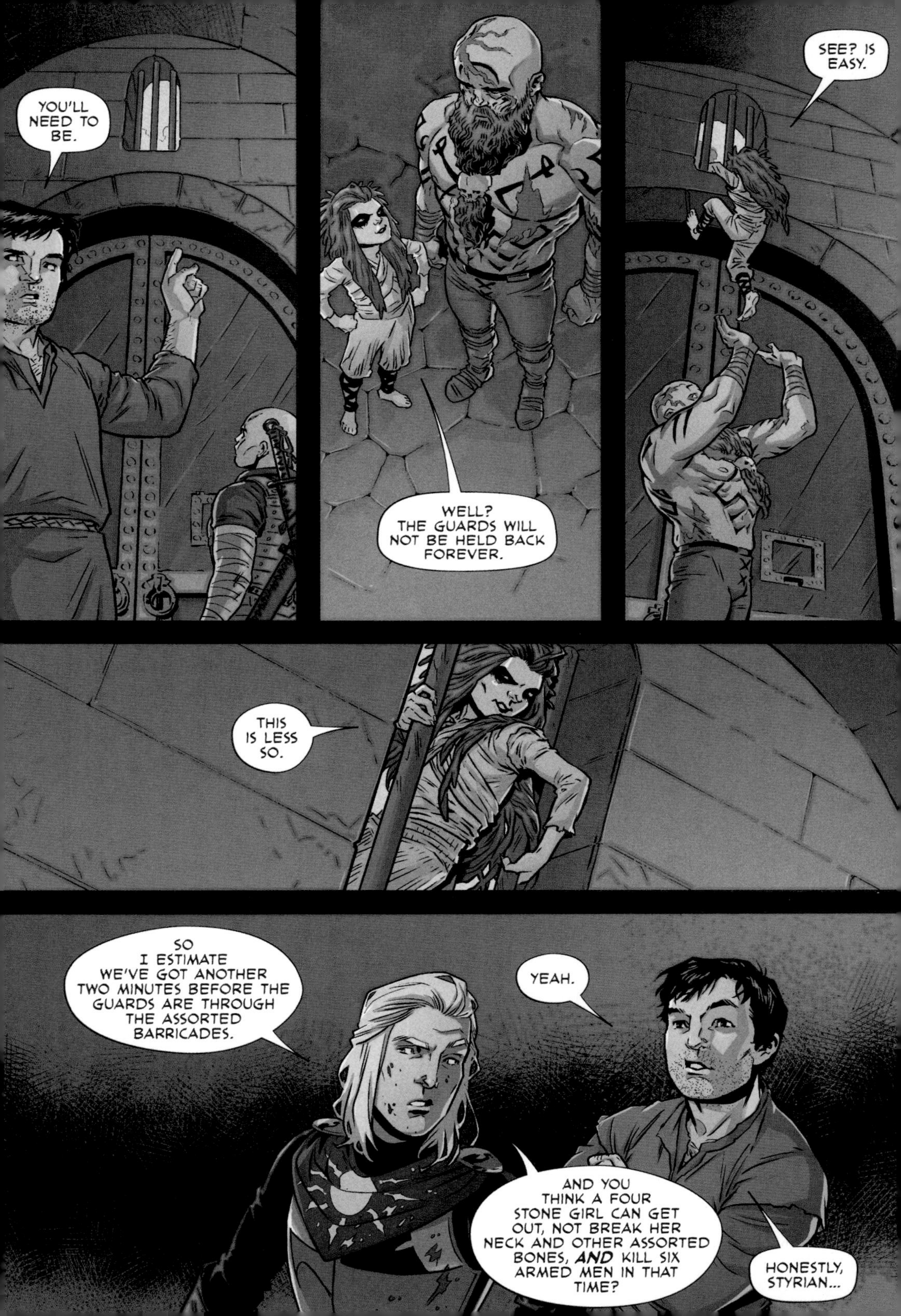
YOU'LL NEED TO BE.
WELL? THE GUARDS WILL NOT BE HELD BACK FOREVER.
SEE? IS EASY.
THIS IS LESS SO.
SO I ESTIMATE WE'VE GOT ANOTHER TWO MINUTES BEFORE THE GUARDS ARE THROUGH THE ASSORTED BARRICADES.
YEAH.
AND YOU THINK A FOUR STONE GIRL CAN GET OUT, NOT BREAK HER NECK AND OTHER ASSORTED BONES, AND KILL SIX ARMED MEN IN THAT TIME?
HONESTLY, STYRIAN...

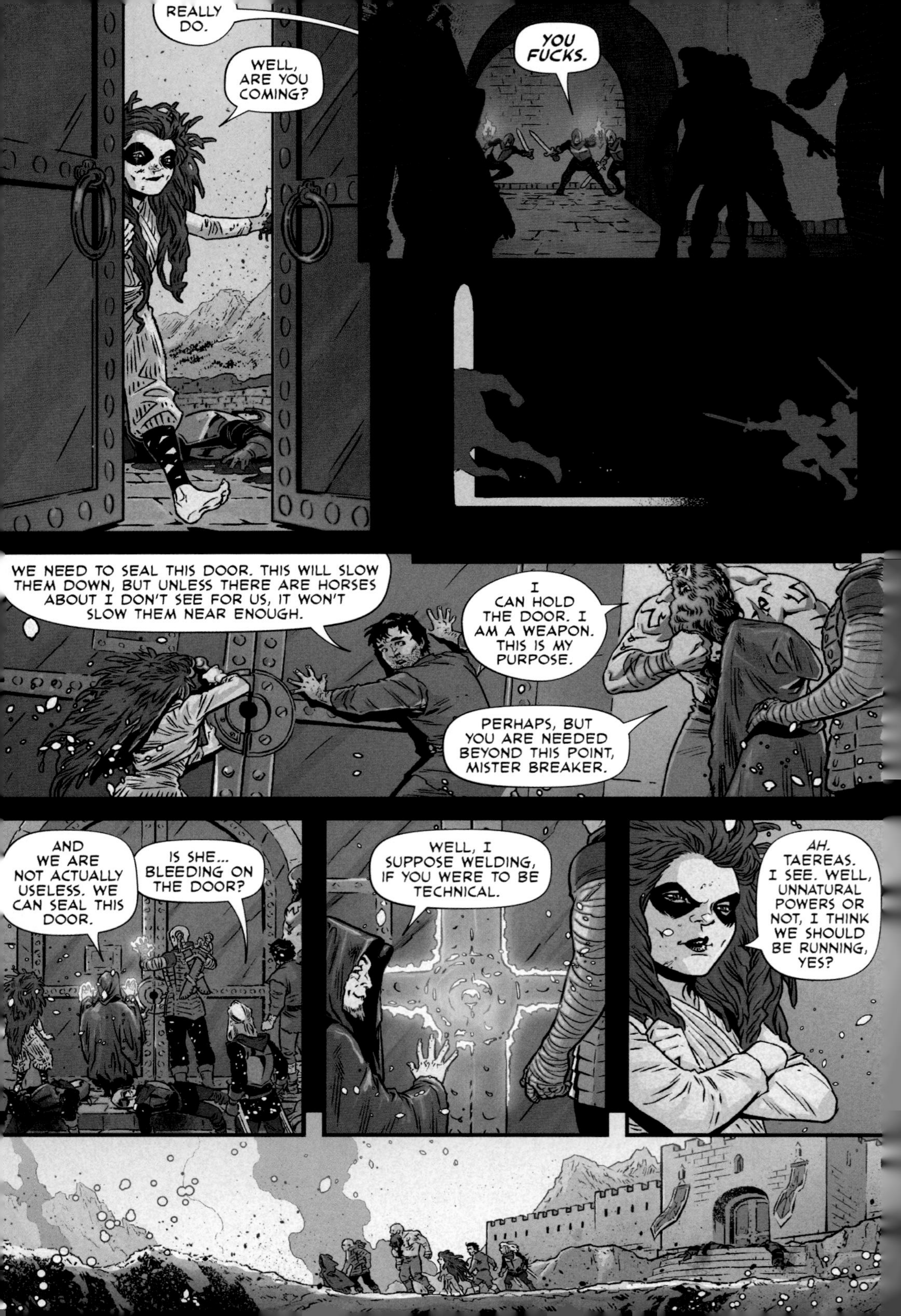
REALLY DO.
WELL, ARE YOU COMING?
YOU FUCKS.
WE NEED TO SEAL THIS DOOR. THIS WILL SLOW THEM DOWN, BUT UNLESS THERE ARE HORSES ABOUT I DON'T SEE FOR US, IT WON'T SLOW THEM NEAR ENOUGH.
I CAN HOLD THE DOOR. I AM A WEAPON. THIS IS MY PURPOSE.
PERHAPS, BUT YOU ARE NEEDED BEYOND THIS POINT, MISTER BREAKER.
AND WE ARE NOT ACTUALLY USELESS. WE CAN SEAL THIS DOOR.
IS SHE... BLEEDING ON THE DOOR?
WELL, I SUPPOSE WELDING, IF YOU WERE TO BE TECHNICAL.
AH. TAEREAS. I SEE. WELL, UNNATURAL POWERS OR NOT, I THINK WE SHOULD BE RUNNING, YES?

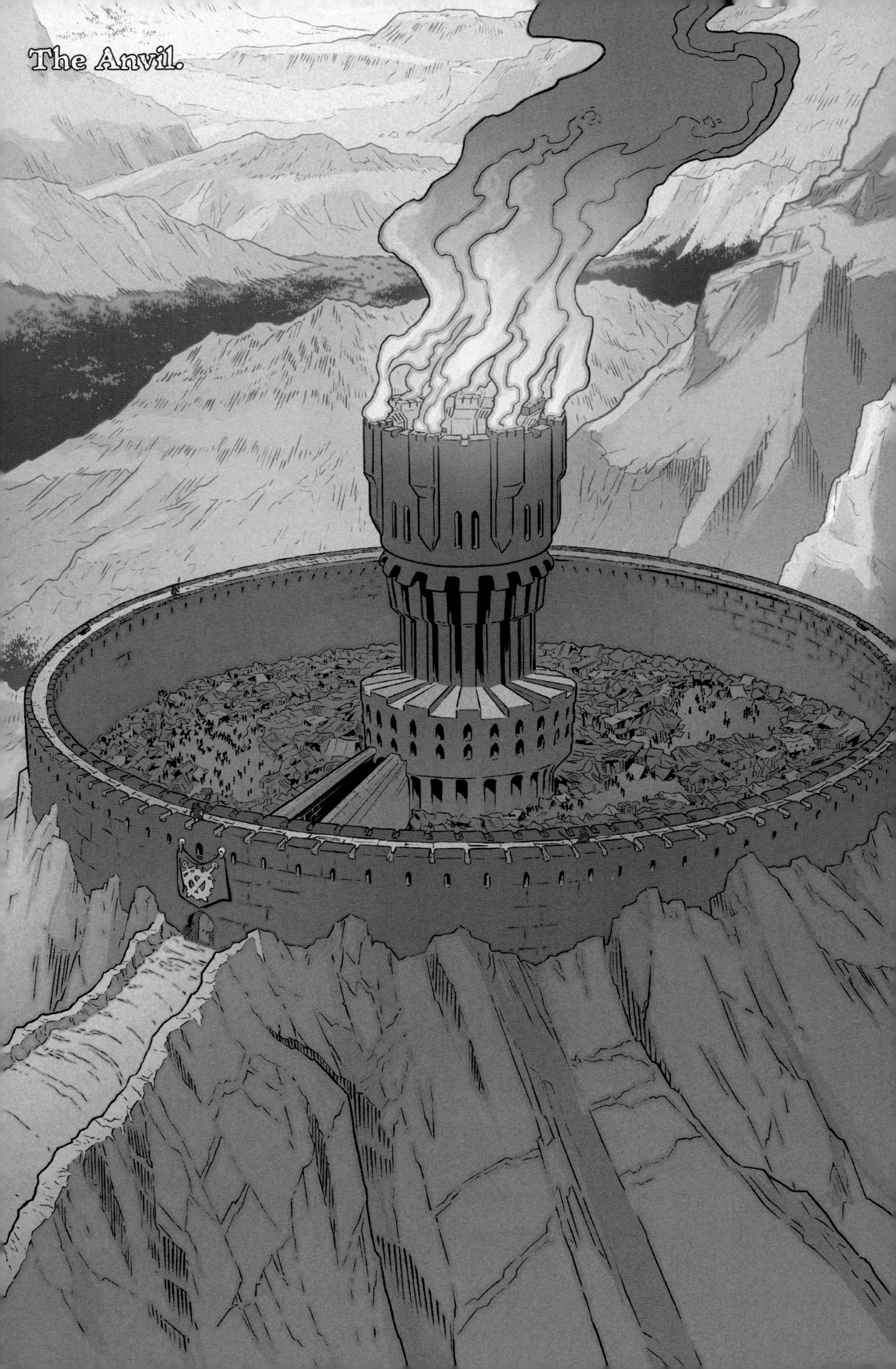
The Anvil.

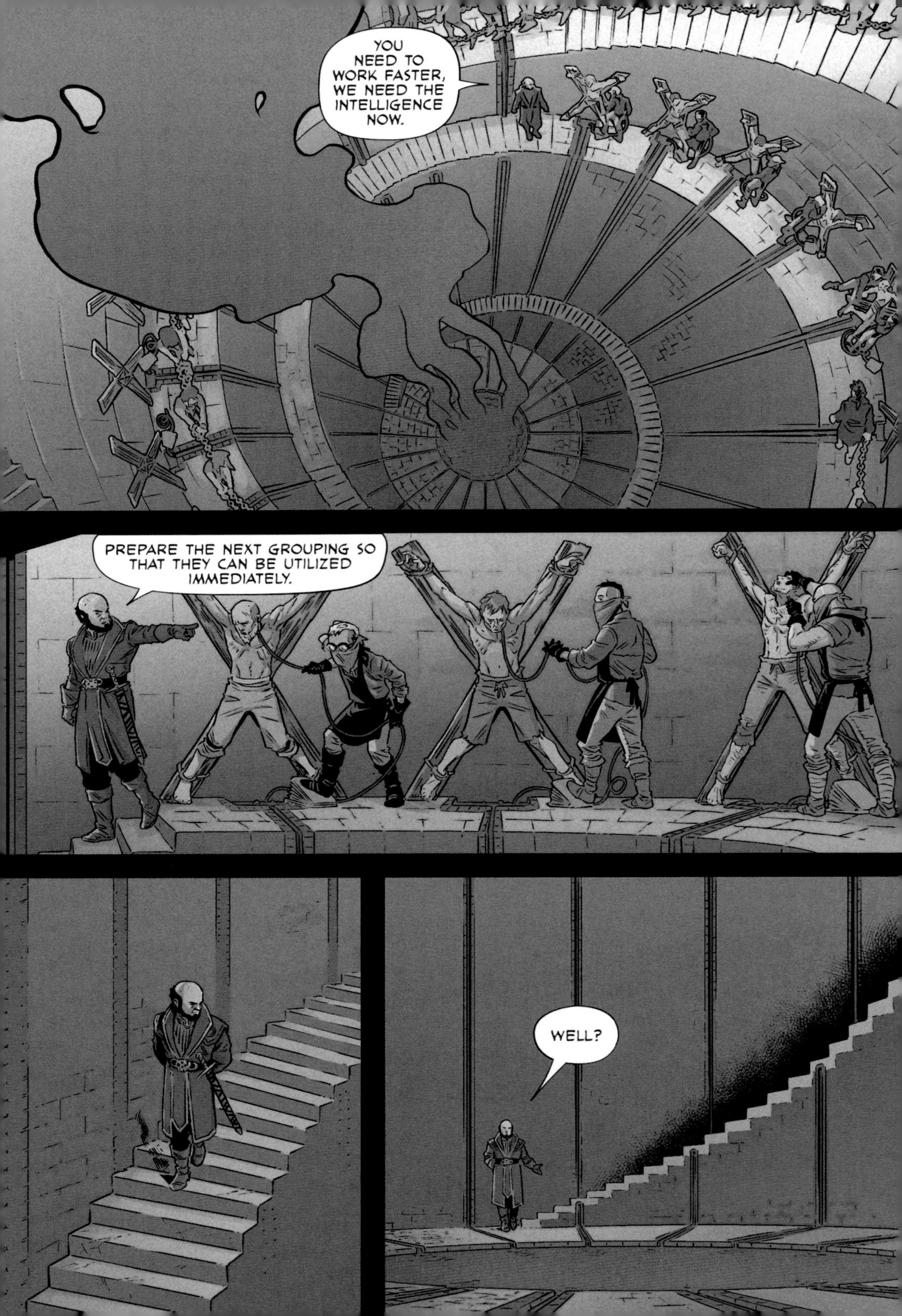
YOU NEED TO WORK FASTER, WE NEED THE INTELLIGENCE NOW.
PREPARE THE NEXT GROUPING SO THAT THEY CAN BE UTILIZED IMMEDIATELY.
WELL?

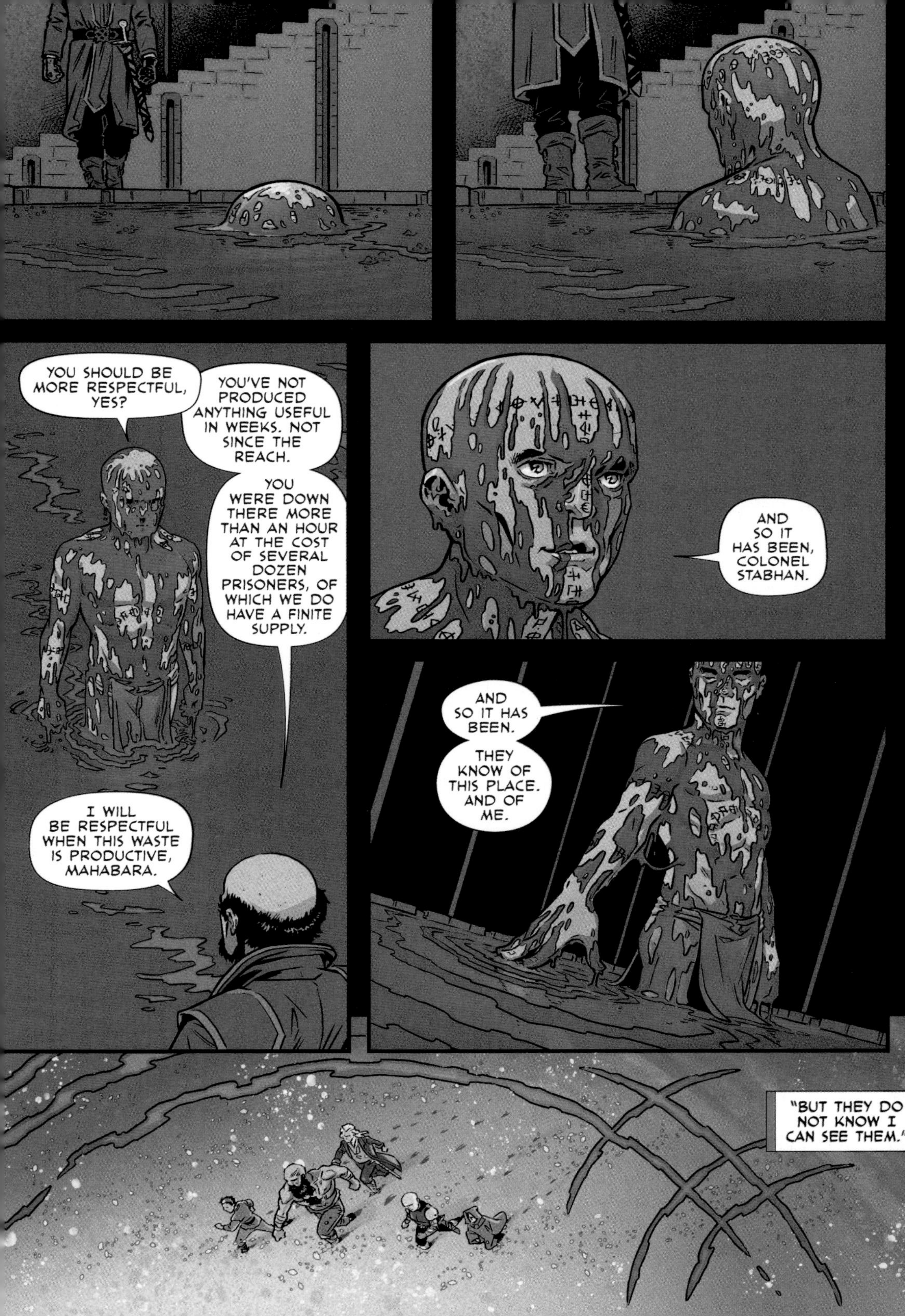

YOU SHOULD BE MORE RESPECTFUL, YES?
YOU'VE NOT PRODUCED ANYTHING USEFUL IN WEEKS. NOT SINCE THE REACH.
YOU WERE DOWN THERE MORE THAN AN HOUR AT THE COST OF SEVERAL DOZEN PRISONERS, OF WHICH WE DO HAVE A FINITE SUPPLY.
I WILL BE RESPECTFUL WHEN THIS WASTE IS PRODUCTIVE, MAHABARA.
AND SO IT HAS BEEN, COLONEL STABHAN.
AND SO IT HAS BEEN.
THEY KNOW OF THIS PLACE. AND OF ME.
"BUT THEY DO NOT KNOW I CAN SEE THEM."

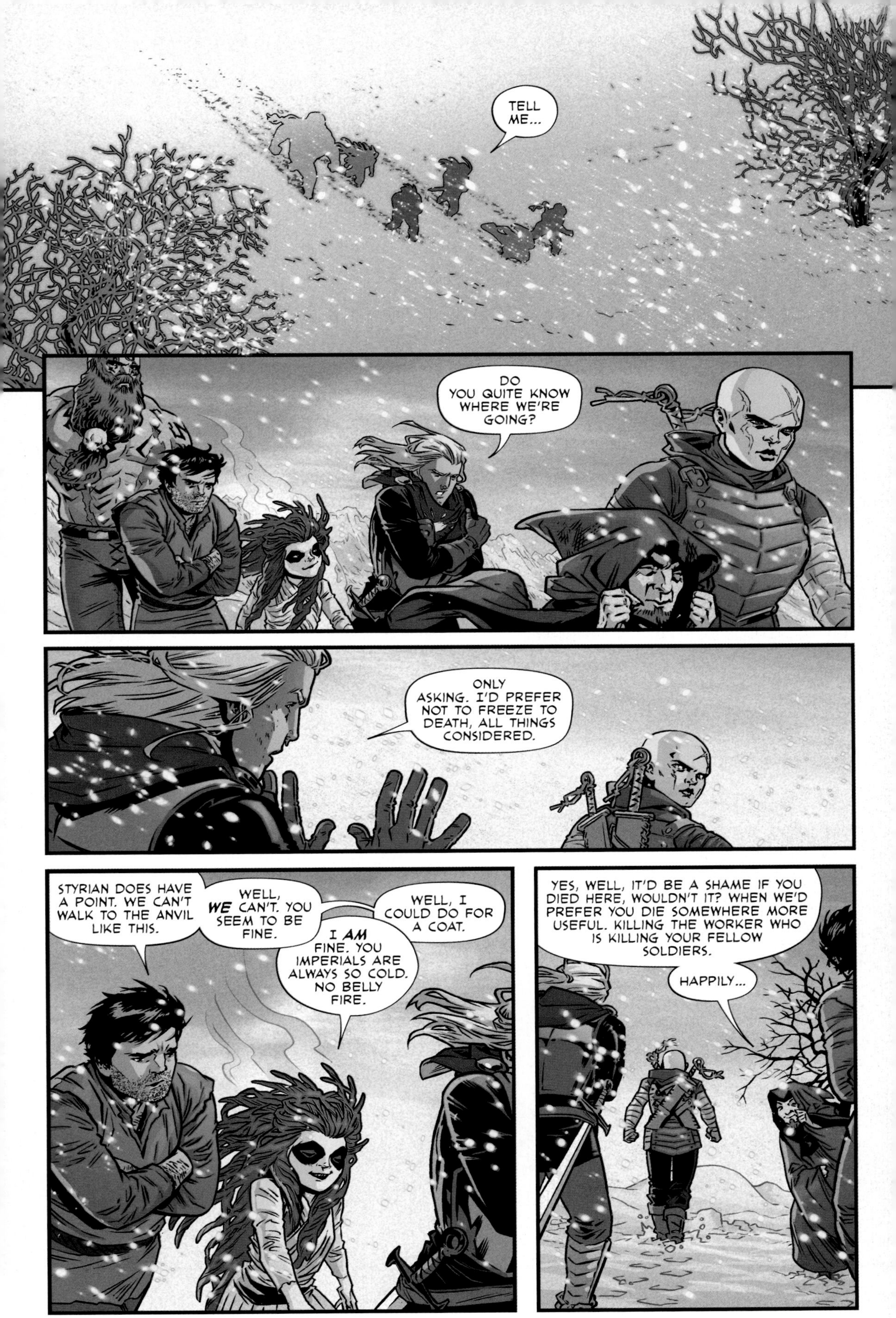
TELL ME...
DO YOU QUITE KNOW WHERE WE'RE GOING?
ONLY ASKING. I'D PREFER NOT TO FREEZE TO DEATH, ALL THINGS CONSIDERED.
STYRIAN DOES HAVE A POINT. WE CAN'T WALK TO THE ANVIL LIKE THIS.
WELL, *WE* CAN'T. YOU SEEM TO BE FINE.
WELL, I COULD DO FOR A COAT.
I *AM* FINE. YOU IMPERIALS ARE ALWAYS SO COLD. NO BELLY FIRE.
YES, WELL, IT'D BE A SHAME IF YOU DIED HERE, WOULDN'T IT? WHEN WE'D PREFER YOU DIE SOMEWHERE MORE USEFUL. KILLING THE WORKER WHO IS KILLING YOUR FELLOW SOLDIERS.
HAPPILY...

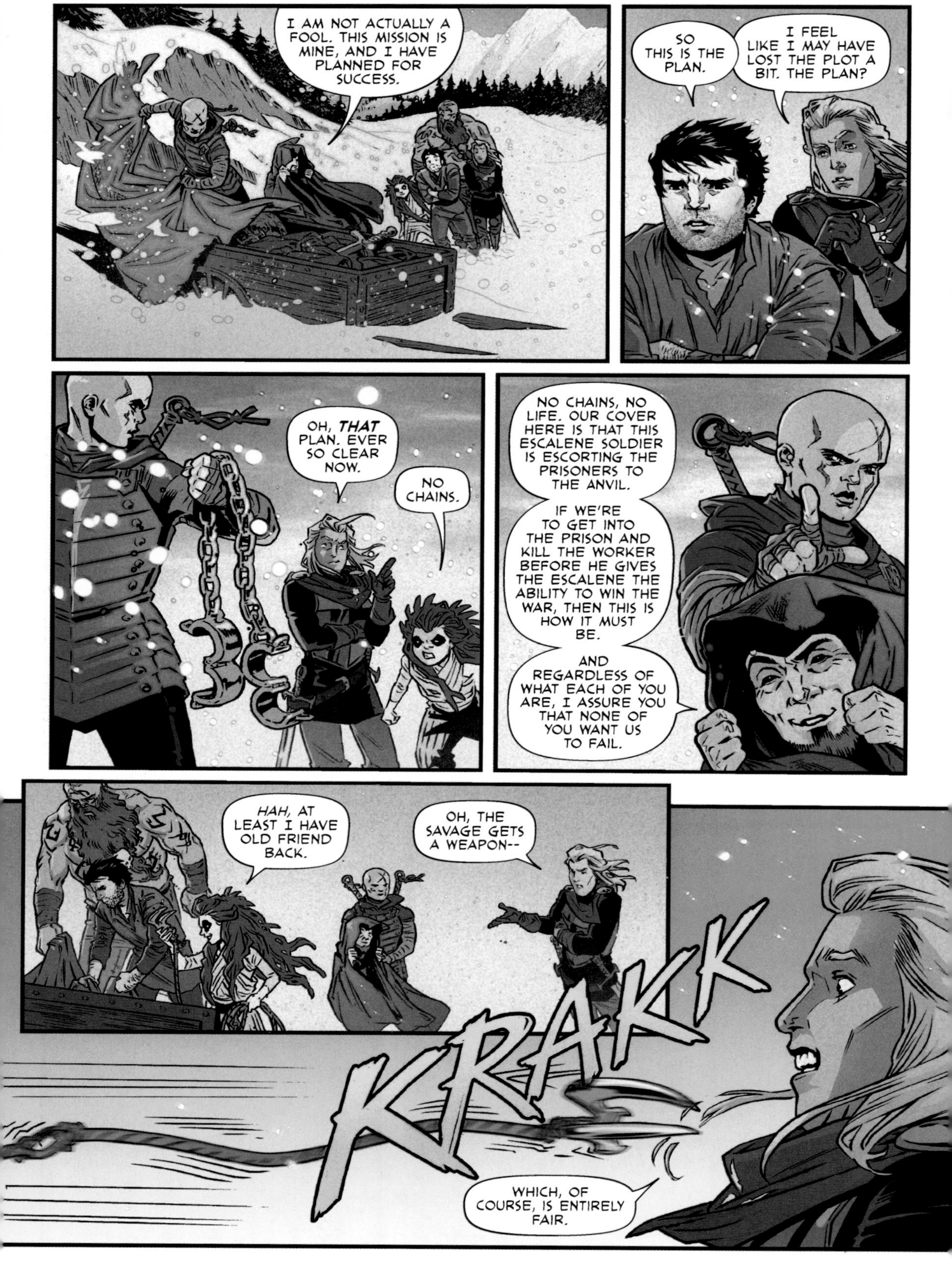
I AM NOT ACTUALLY A FOOL. THIS MISSION IS MINE, AND I HAVE PLANNED FOR SUCCESS.
SO THIS IS THE PLAN.
I FEEL LIKE I MAY HAVE LOST THE PLOT A BIT. THE PLAN?
OH, THAT PLAN. EVER SO CLEAR NOW.
NO CHAINS.
NO CHAINS, NO LIFE. OUR COVER HERE IS THAT THIS ESCALENE SOLDIER IS ESCORTING THE PRISONERS TO THE ANVIL.
IF WE'RE TO GET INTO THE PRISON AND KILL THE WORKER BEFORE HE GIVES THE ESCALENE THE ABILITY TO WIN THE WAR, THEN THIS IS HOW IT MUST BE.
AND REGARDLESS OF WHAT EACH OF YOU ARE, I ASSURE YOU THAT NONE OF YOU WANT US TO FAIL.
HAH, AT LEAST I HAVE OLD FRIEND BACK.
OH, THE SAVAGE GETS A WEAPON--
KRAKK
WHICH, OF COURSE, IS ENTIRELY FAIR.

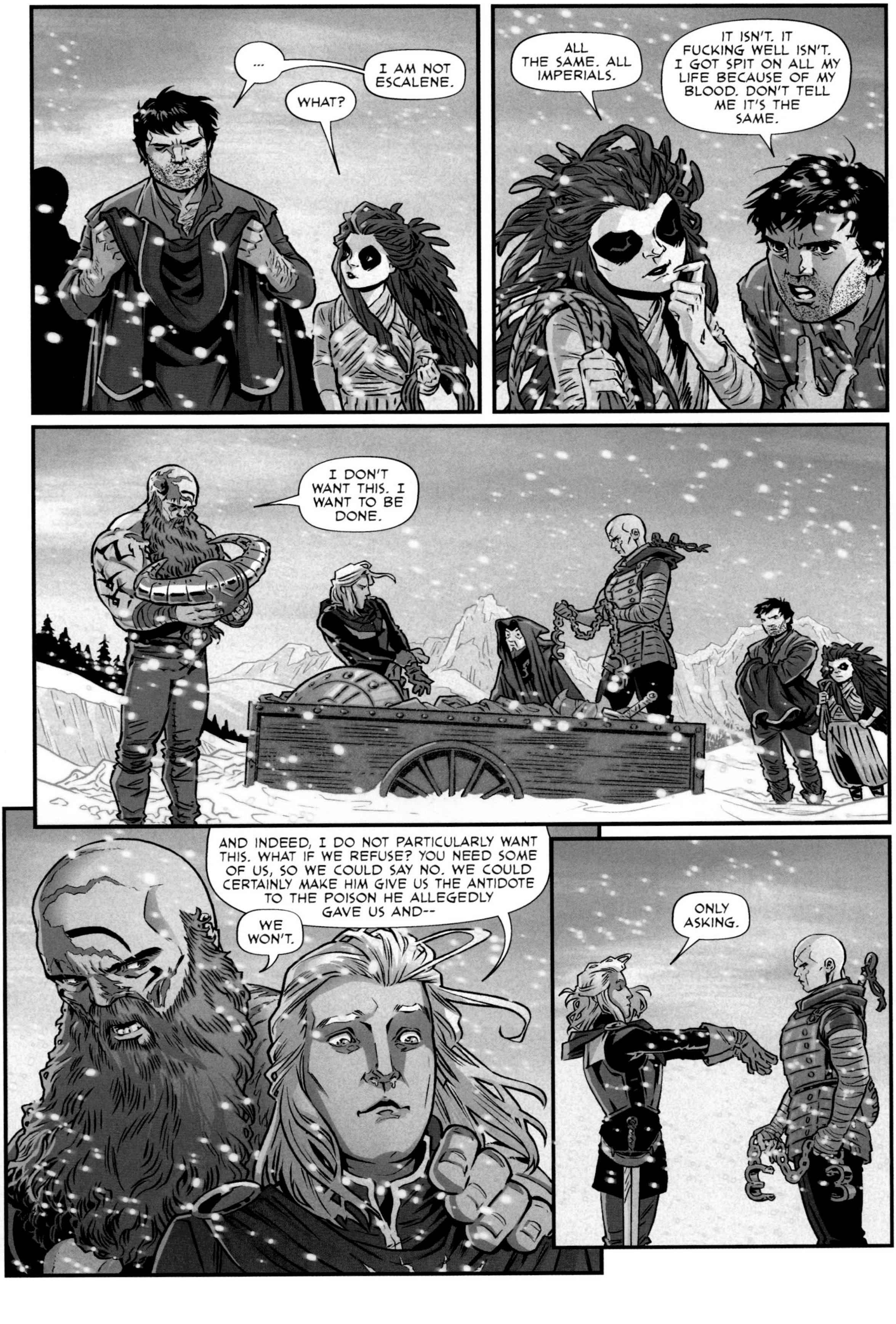
...
I AM NOT ESCALENE.
WHAT?
ALL THE SAME. ALL IMPERIALS.
IT ISN'T. IT FUCKING WELL ISN'T. I GOT SPIT ON ALL MY LIFE BECAUSE OF MY BLOOD. DON'T TELL ME IT'S THE SAME.
I DON'T WANT THIS. I WANT TO BE DONE.
AND INDEED, I DO NOT PARTICULARLY WANT THIS. WHAT IF WE REFUSE? YOU NEED SOME OF US, SO WE COULD SAY NO. WE COULD CERTAINLY MAKE HIM GIVE US THE ANTIDOTE TO THE POISON HE ALLEGEDLY GAVE US AND--
WE WON'T.
ONLY ASKING.

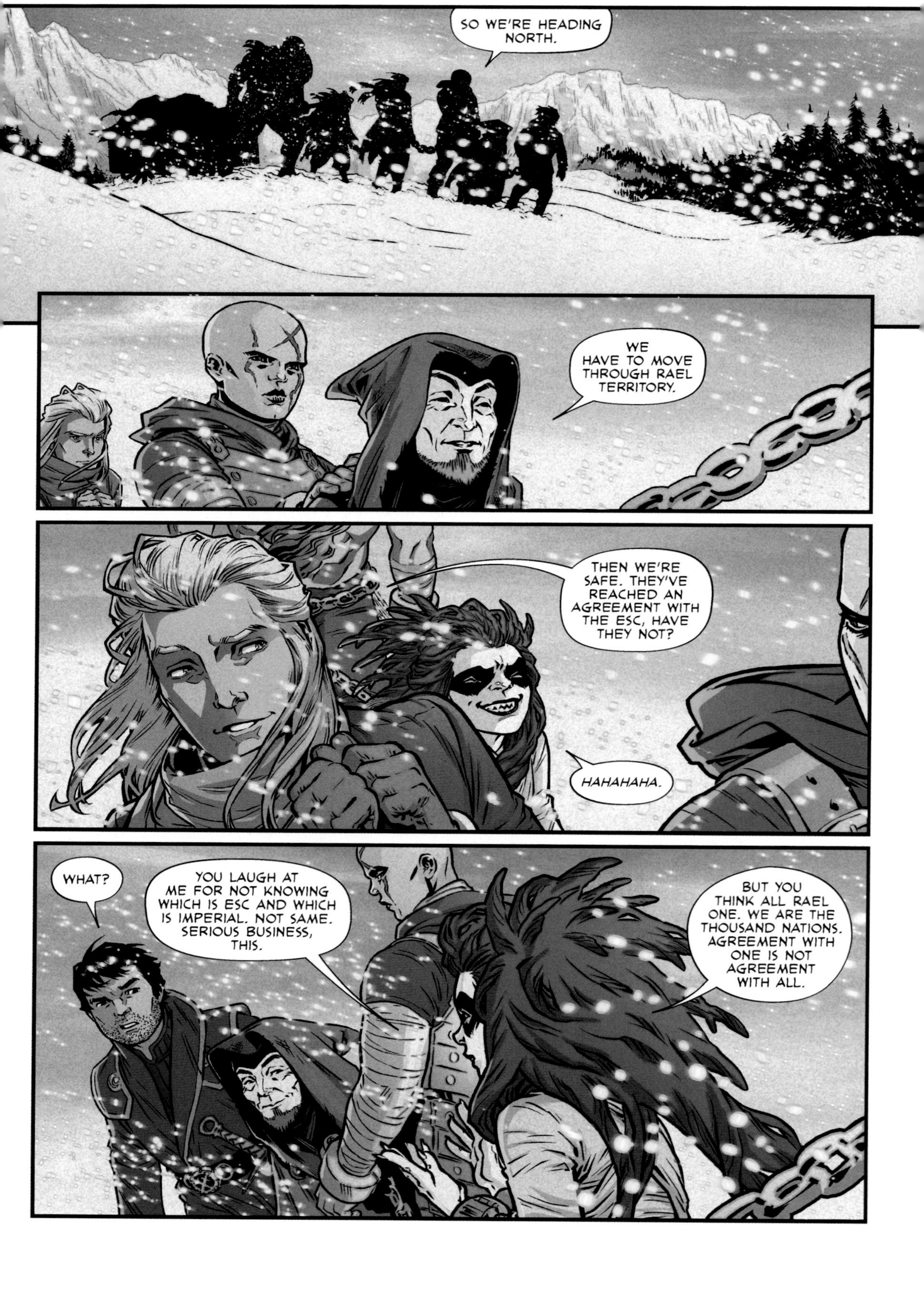
SO WE'RE HEADING NORTH.
WE HAVE TO MOVE THROUGH RAEL TERRITORY.
THEN WE'RE SAFE. THEY'VE REACHED AN AGREEMENT WITH THE ESC, HAVE THEY NOT?
HAHAHAHA.
WHAT?
YOU LAUGH AT ME FOR NOT KNOWING WHICH IS ESC AND WHICH IS IMPERIAL. NOT SAME. SERIOUS BUSINESS, THIS.
BUT YOU THINK ALL RAEL ONE. WE ARE THE THOUSAND NATIONS. AGREEMENT WITH ONE IS NOT AGREEMENT WITH ALL.

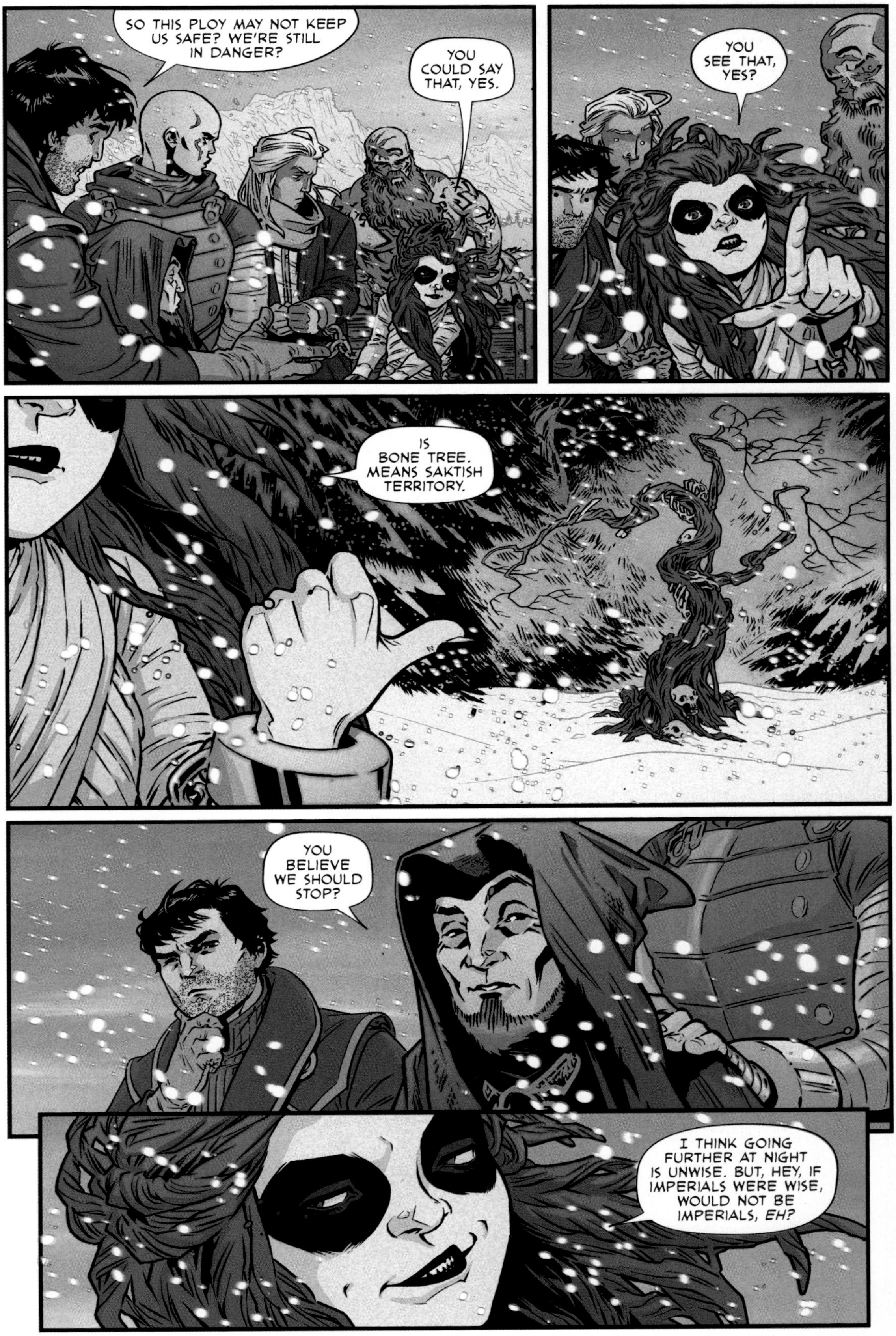
SO THIS PLOY MAY NOT KEEP US SAFE? WE'RE STILL IN DANGER?
YOU COULD SAY THAT, YES.
YOU SEE THAT, YES?
IS BONE TREE. MEANS SAKTISH TERRITORY.
YOU BELIEVE WE SHOULD STOP?
I THINK GOING FURTHER AT NIGHT IS UNWISE. BUT, HEY, IF IMPERIALS WERE WISE, WOULD NOT BE IMPERIALS, *EH?*

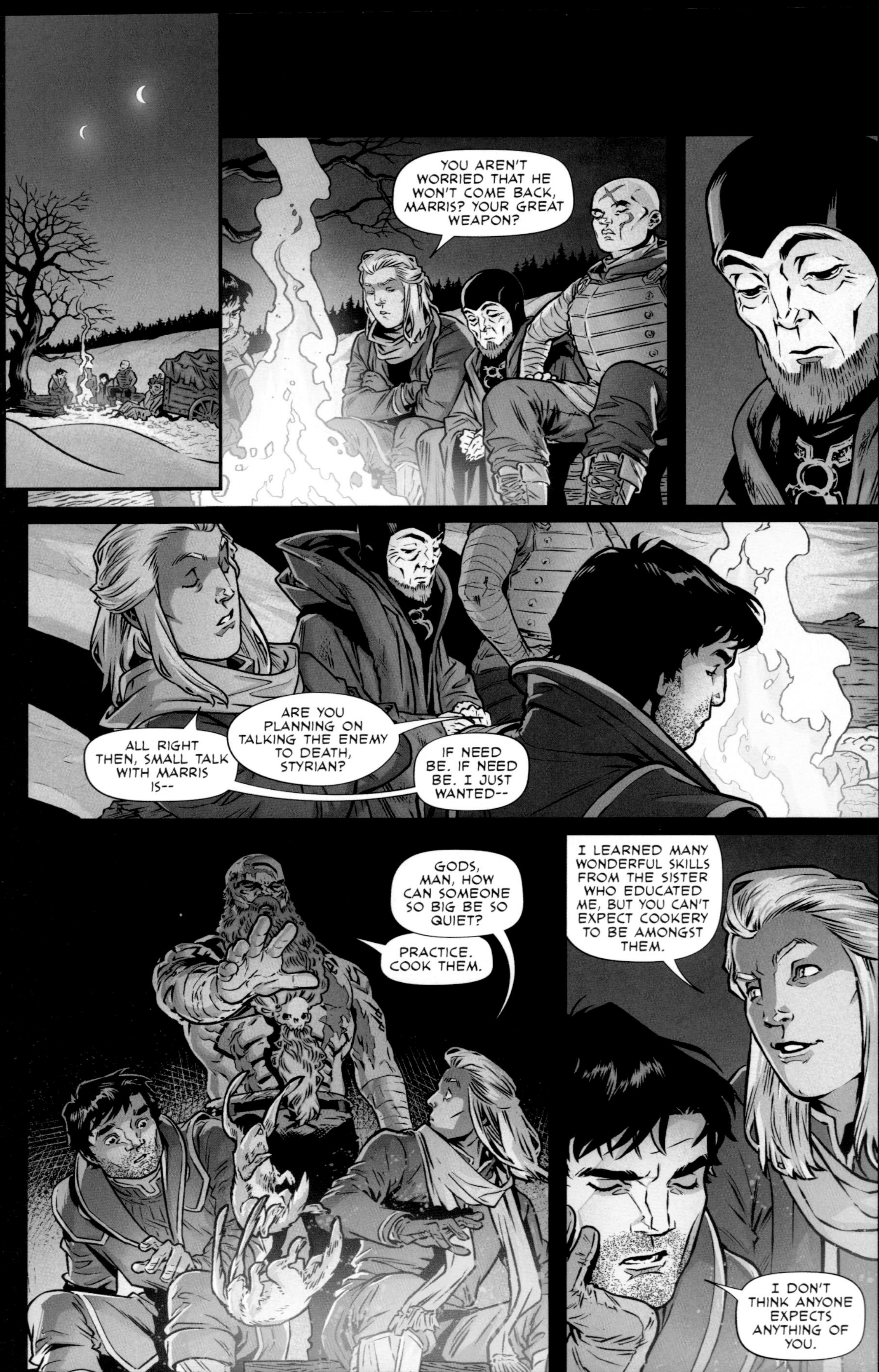
YOU AREN'T WORRIED THAT HE WON'T COME BACK, MARRIS? YOUR GREAT WEAPON?
ALL RIGHT THEN, SMALL TALK WITH MARRIS IS--
ARE YOU PLANNING ON TALKING THE ENEMY TO DEATH, STYRIAN?
IF NEED BE. IF NEED BE. I JUST WANTED--
GODS, MAN, HOW CAN SOMEONE SO BIG BE SO QUIET?
PRACTICE. COOK THEM.
I LEARNED MANY WONDERFUL SKILLS FROM THE SISTER WHO EDUCATED ME, BUT YOU CAN'T EXPECT COOKERY TO BE AMONGST THEM.
I DON'T THINK ANYONE EXPECTS ANYTHING OF YOU.

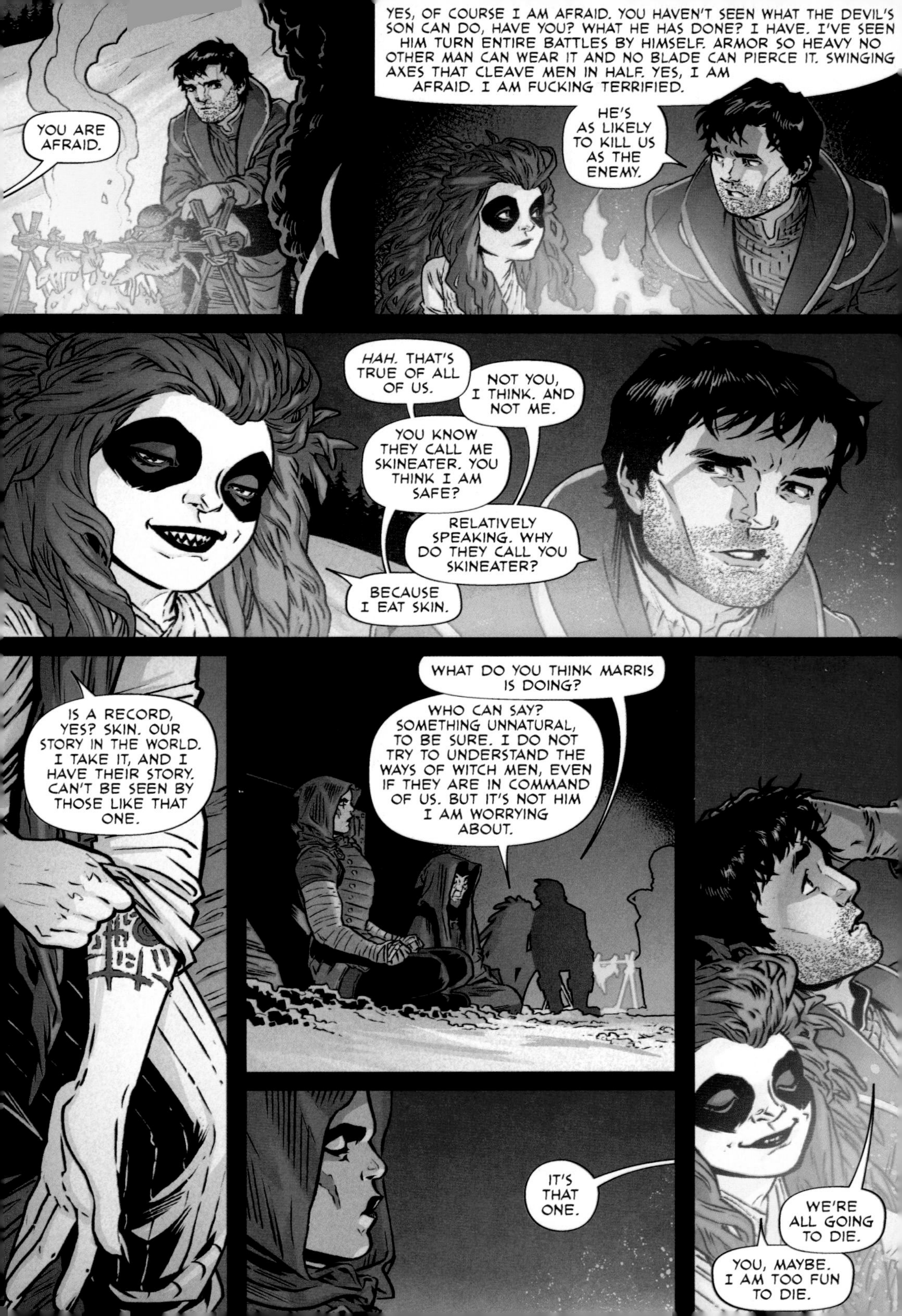
YOU ARE AFRAID.
YES, OF COURSE I AM AFRAID. YOU HAVEN'T SEEN WHAT THE DEVIL'S SON CAN DO, HAVE YOU? WHAT HE HAS DONE? I HAVE. I'VE SEEN HIM TURN ENTIRE BATTLES BY HIMSELF. ARMOR SO HEAVY NO OTHER MAN CAN WEAR IT AND NO BLADE CAN PIERCE IT. SWINGING AXES THAT CLEAVE MEN IN HALF. YES, I AM AFRAID. I AM FUCKING TERRIFIED.
HE'S AS LIKELY TO KILL US AS THE ENEMY.
HAH. THAT'S TRUE OF ALL OF US.
NOT YOU, I THINK. AND NOT ME.
YOU KNOW THEY CALL ME SKINEATER. YOU THINK I AM SAFE?
RELATIVELY SPEAKING. WHY DO THEY CALL YOU SKINEATER?
BECAUSE I EAT SKIN.
IS A RECORD, YES? SKIN. OUR STORY IN THE WORLD. I TAKE IT, AND I HAVE THEIR STORY. CAN'T BE SEEN BY THOSE LIKE THAT ONE.
WHAT DO YOU THINK MARRIS IS DOING?
WHO CAN SAY? SOMETHING UNNATURAL, TO BE SURE. I DO NOT TRY TO UNDERSTAND THE WAYS OF WITCH MEN, EVEN IF THEY ARE IN COMMAND OF US. BUT IT'S NOT HIM I AM WORRYING ABOUT.
IT'S THAT ONE.
WE'RE ALL GOING TO DIE.
YOU, MAYBE. I AM TOO FUN TO DIE.

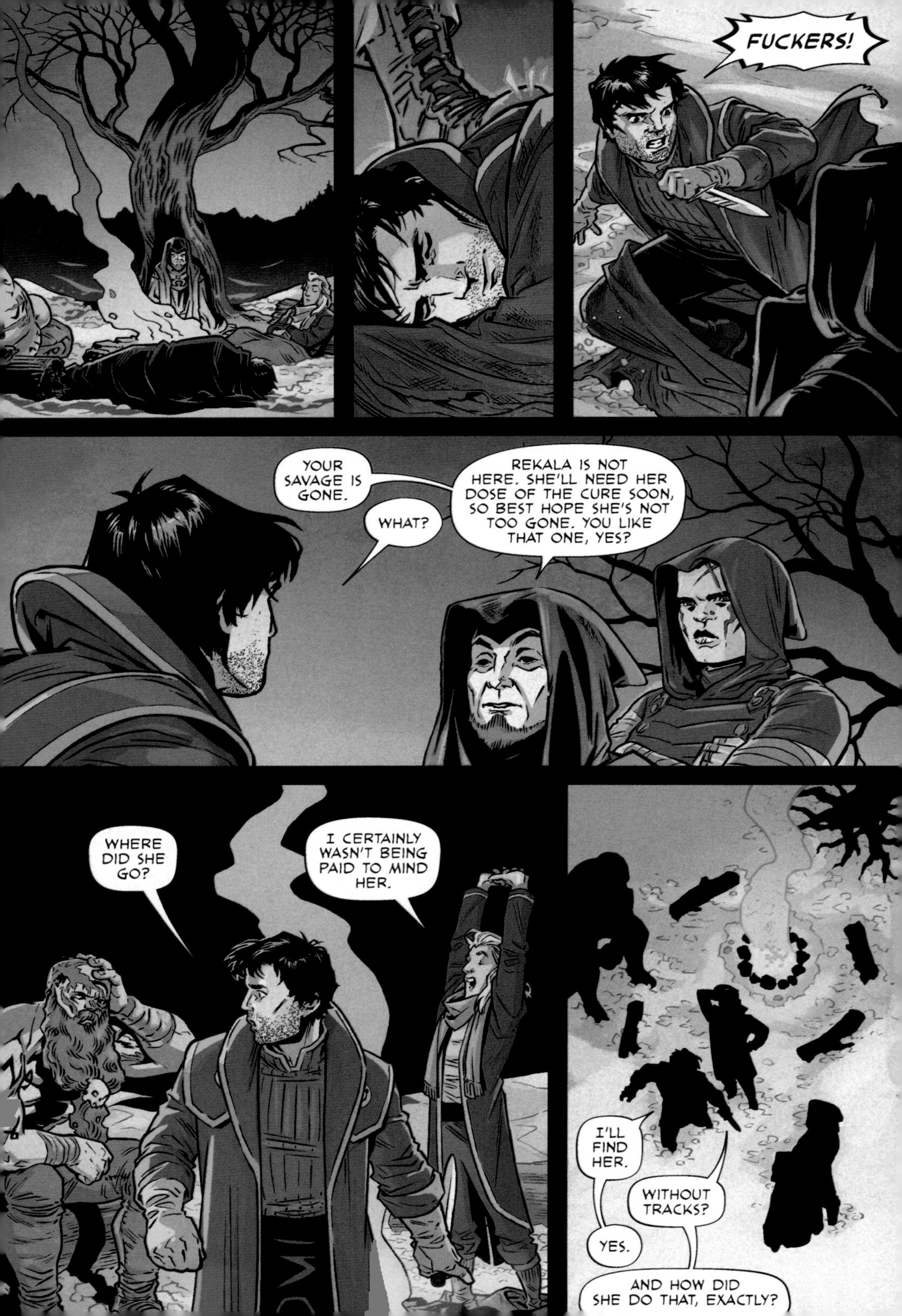
FUCKERS!
YOUR SAVAGE IS GONE.
WHAT?
REKALA IS NOT HERE. SHE'LL NEED HER DOSE OF THE CURE SOON, SO BEST HOPE SHE'S NOT TOO GONE. YOU LIKE THAT ONE, YES?
WHERE DID SHE GO?
I CERTAINLY WASN'T BEING PAID TO MIND HER.
I'LL FIND HER.
WITHOUT TRACKS?
YES.
AND HOW DID SHE DO THAT, EXACTLY?

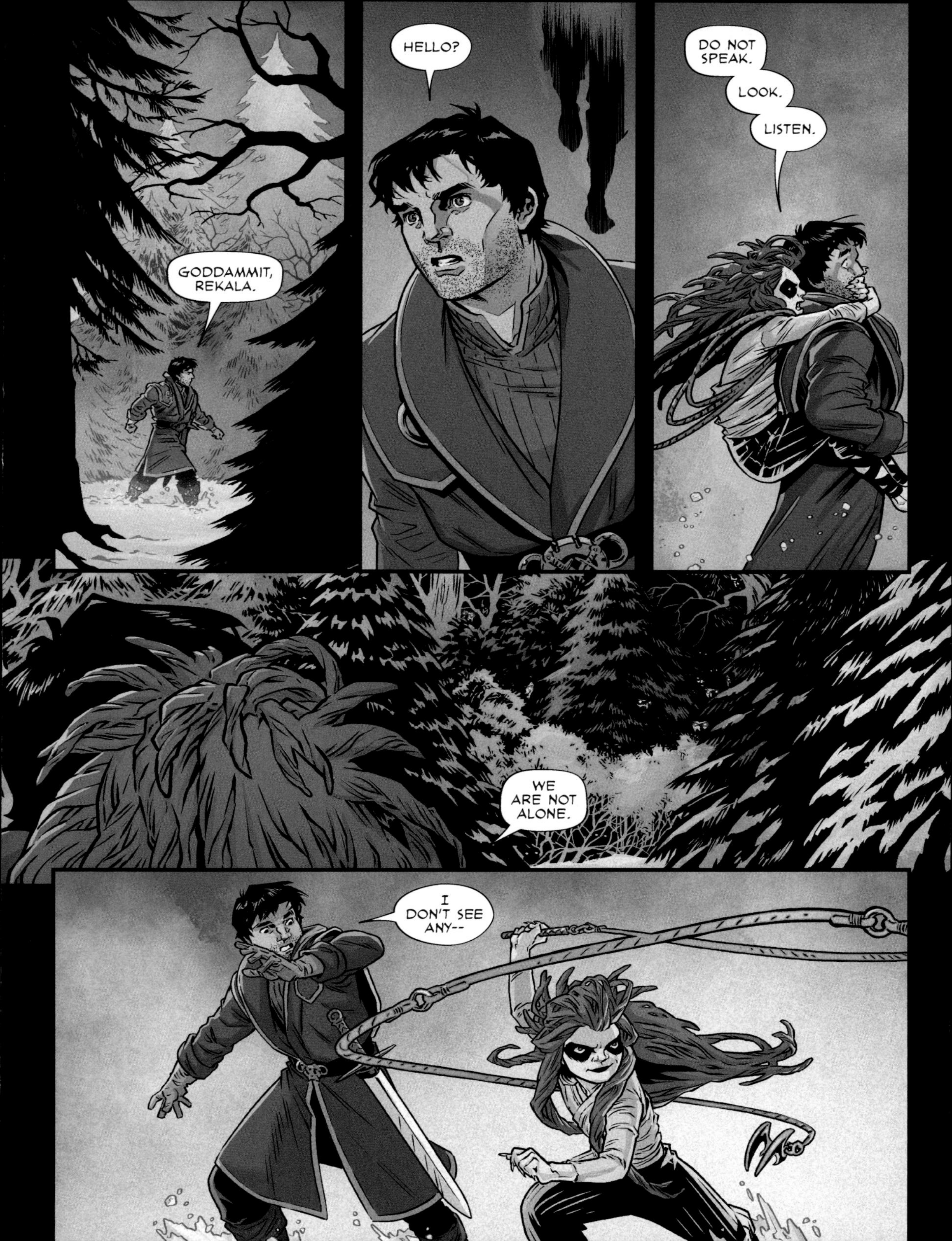
GODDAMMIT, REKALA.
HELLO?
DO NOT SPEAK.
LOOK.
LISTEN.
WE ARE NOT ALONE.
I DON'T SEE ANY--

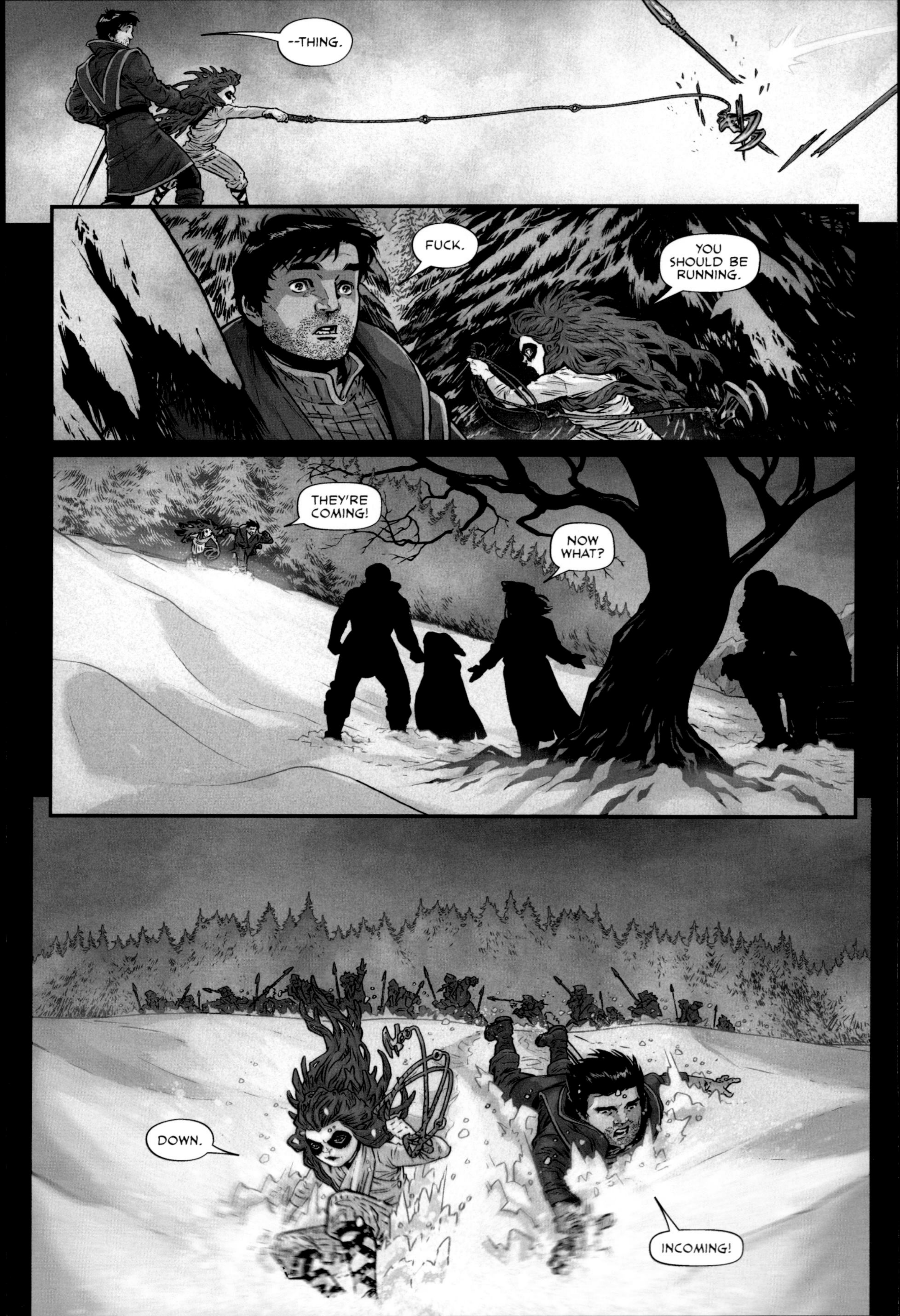
--THING.
FUCK.
YOU SHOULD BE RUNNING.
THEY'RE COMING!
NOW WHAT?
DOWN.
INCOMING!

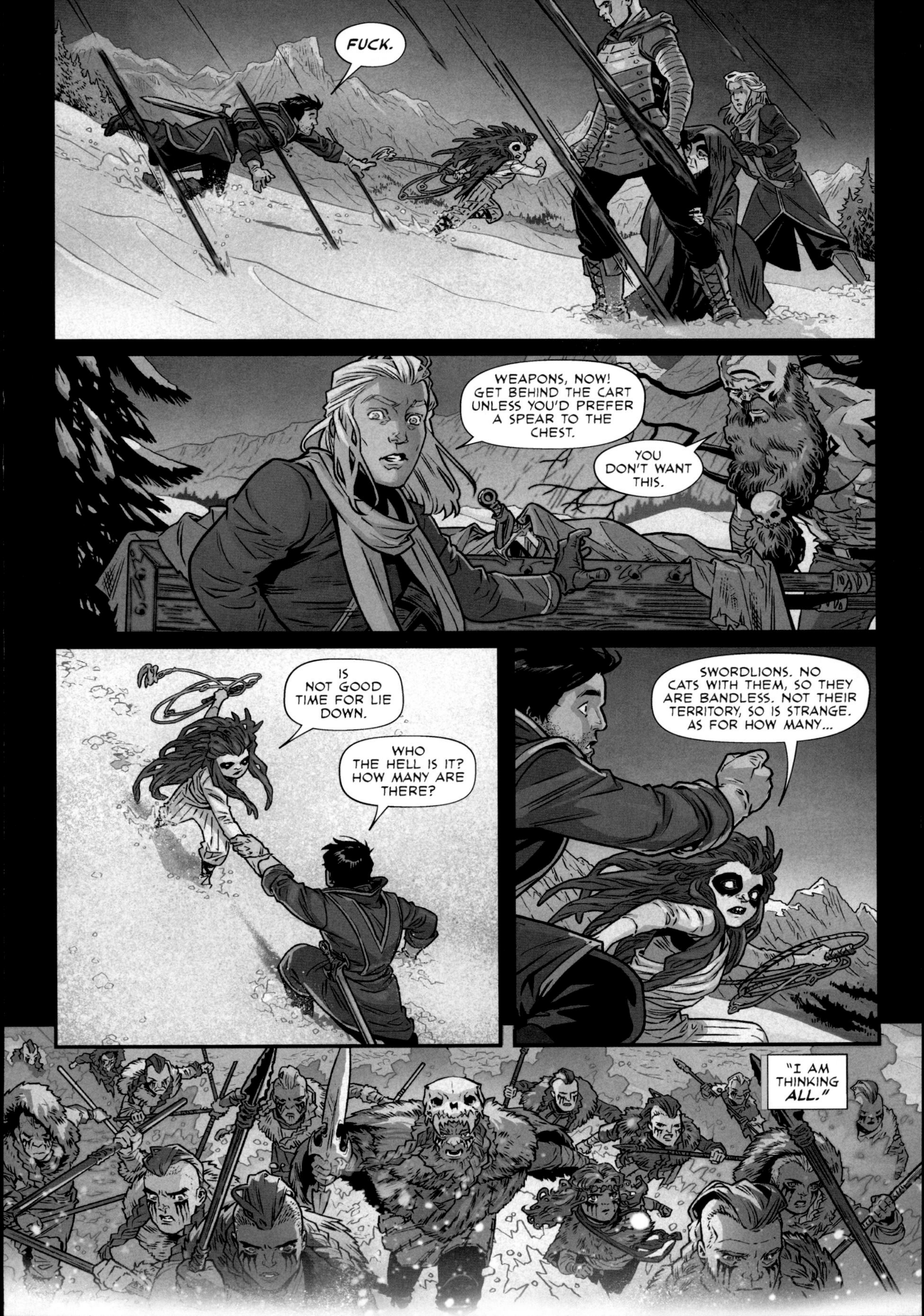
FUCK.
WEAPONS, NOW! GET BEHIND THE CART UNLESS YOU'D PREFER A SPEAR TO THE CHEST.
YOU DON'T WANT THIS.
IS NOT GOOD TIME FOR LIE DOWN.
WHO THE HELL IS IT? HOW MANY ARE THERE?
SWORDLIONS. NO CATS WITH THEM, SO THEY ARE BANDLESS. NOT THEIR TERRITORY, SO IS STRANGE. AS FOR HOW MANY...
"I AM THINKING ALL."

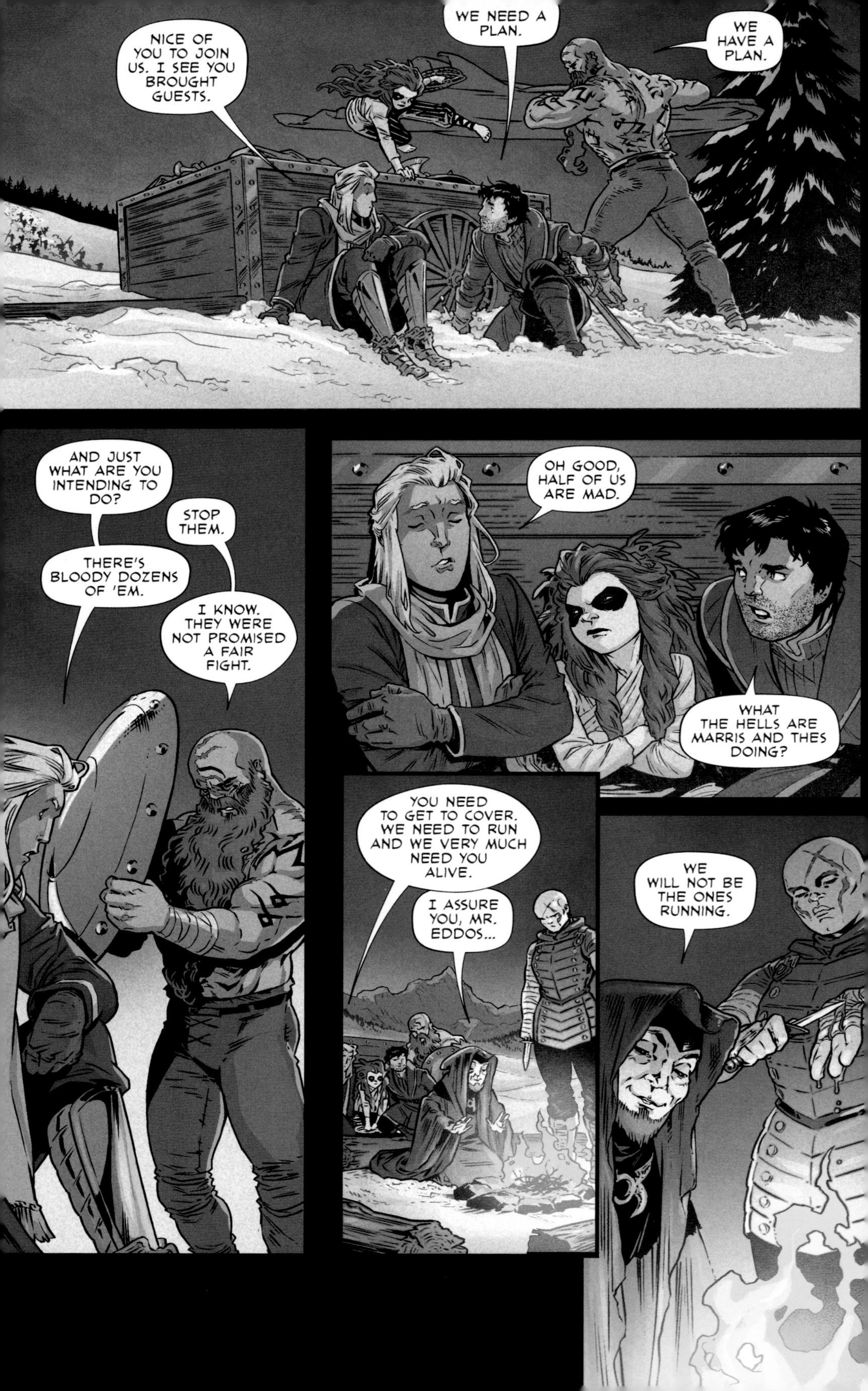

NICE OF YOU TO JOIN US. I SEE YOU BROUGHT GUESTS.
WE NEED A PLAN.
WE HAVE A PLAN.
AND JUST WHAT ARE YOU INTENDING TO DO?
STOP THEM.
THERE'S BLOODY DOZENS OF 'EM.
I KNOW. THEY WERE NOT PROMISED A FAIR FIGHT.
OH GOOD, HALF OF US ARE MAD.
WHAT THE HELLS ARE MARRIS AND THES DOING?
YOU NEED TO GET TO COVER. WE NEED TO RUN AND WE VERY MUCH NEED YOU ALIVE.
I ASSURE YOU, MR. EDDOS...
WE WILL NOT BE THE ONES RUNNING.

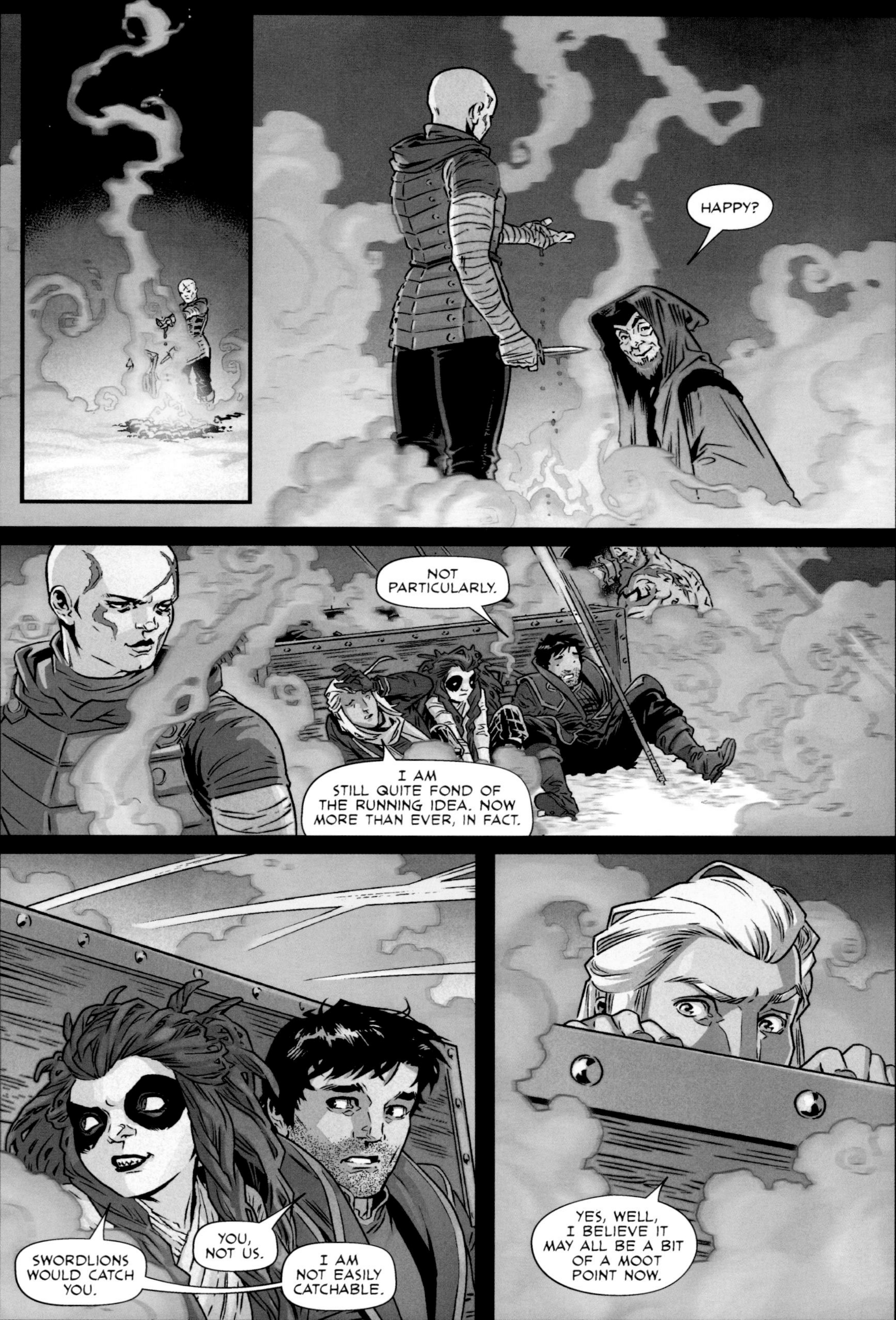
HAPPY?
NOT PARTICULARLY.
I AM STILL QUITE FOND OF THE RUNNING IDEA. NOW MORE THAN EVER, IN FACT.
SWORDLIONS WOULD CATCH YOU.
YOU, NOT US.
I AM NOT EASILY CATCHABLE.
YES, WELL, I BELIEVE IT MAY ALL BE A BIT OF A MOOT POINT NOW.

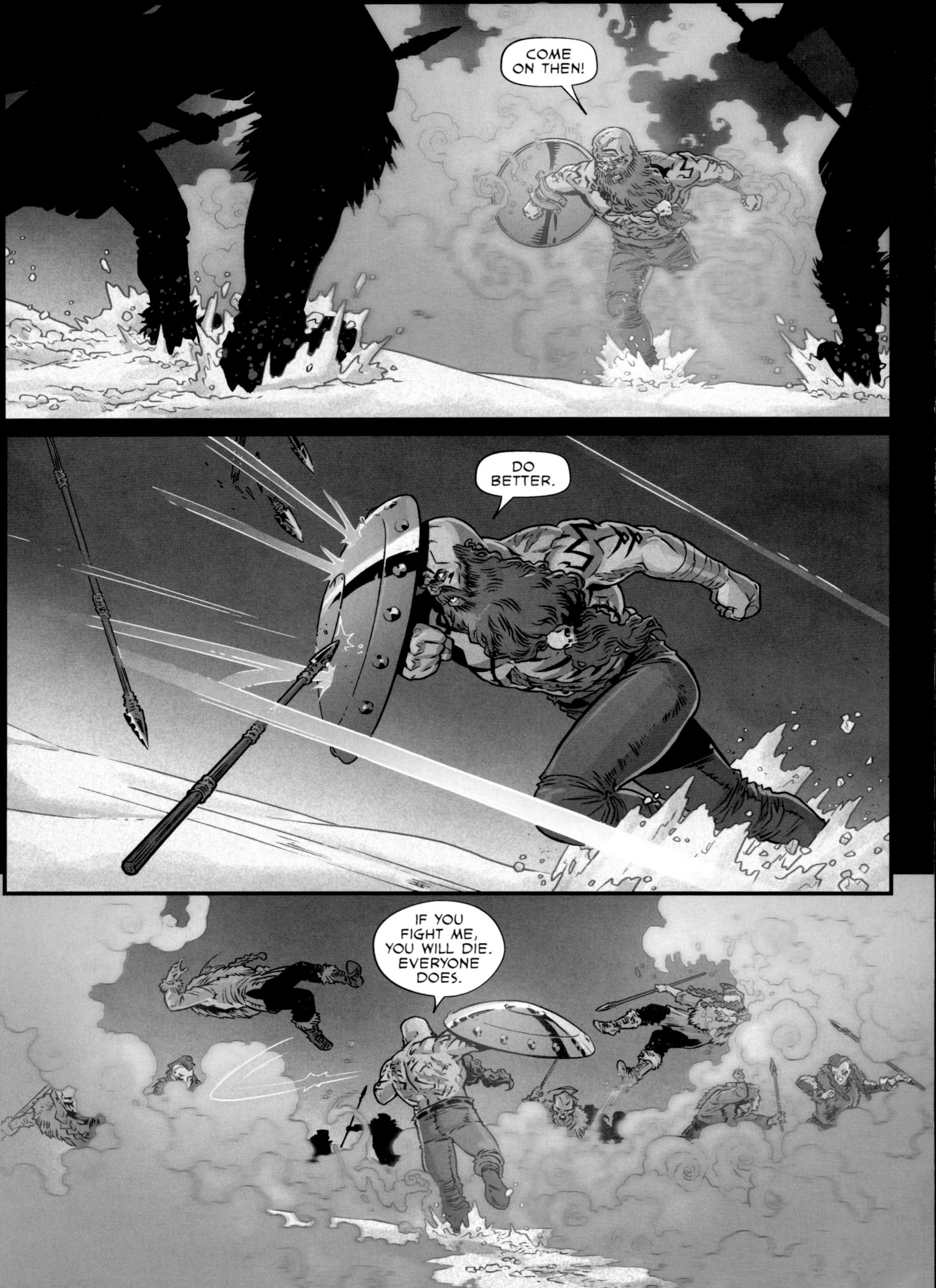
COME ON THEN!
DO BETTER.
IF YOU FIGHT ME, YOU WILL DIE. EVERYONE DOES.

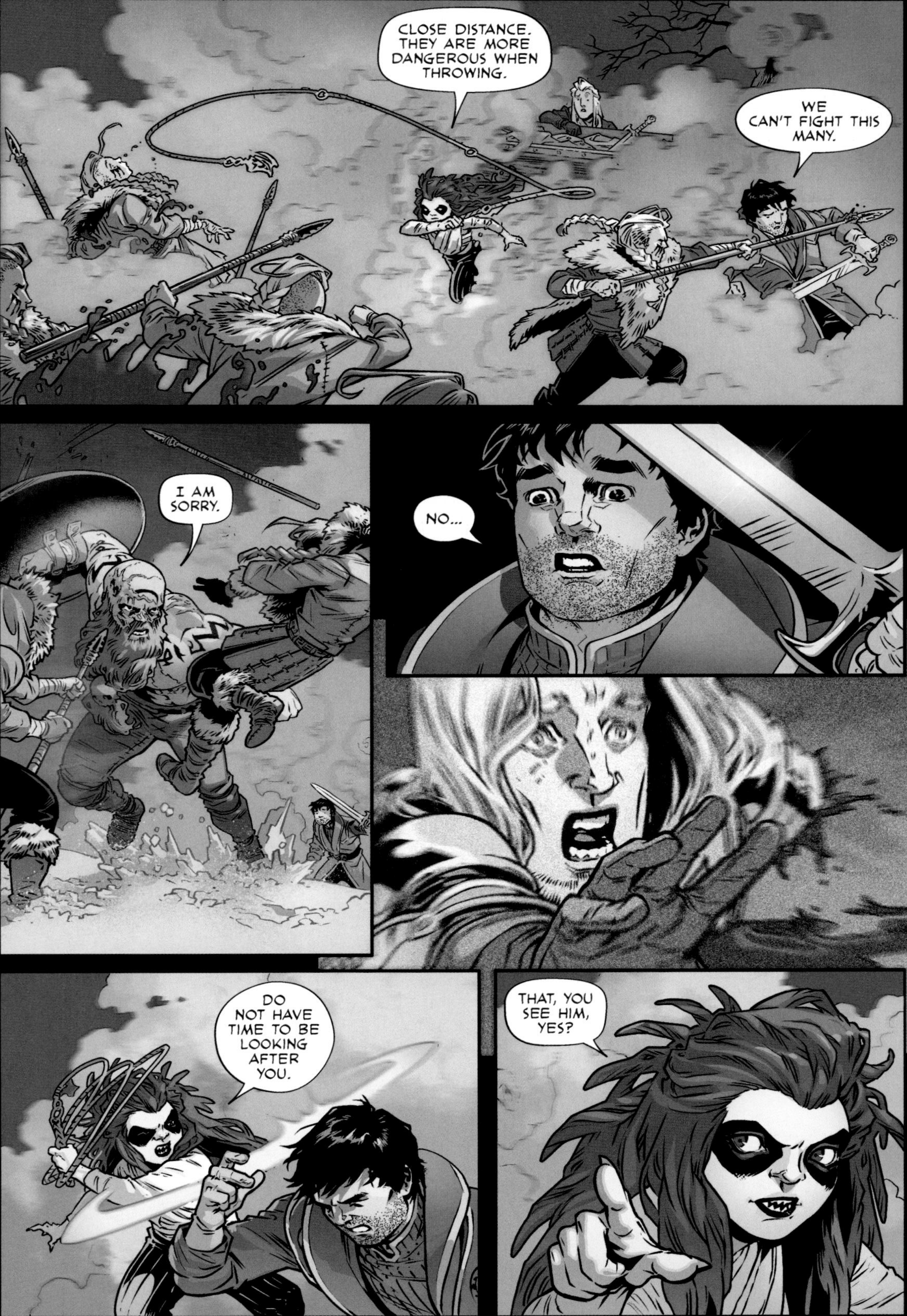
CLOSE DISTANCE. THEY ARE MORE DANGEROUS WHEN THROWING.
WE CAN'T FIGHT THIS MANY.
I AM SORRY.
NO...
DO NOT HAVE TIME TO BE LOOKING AFTER YOU.
THAT, YOU SEE HIM, YES?

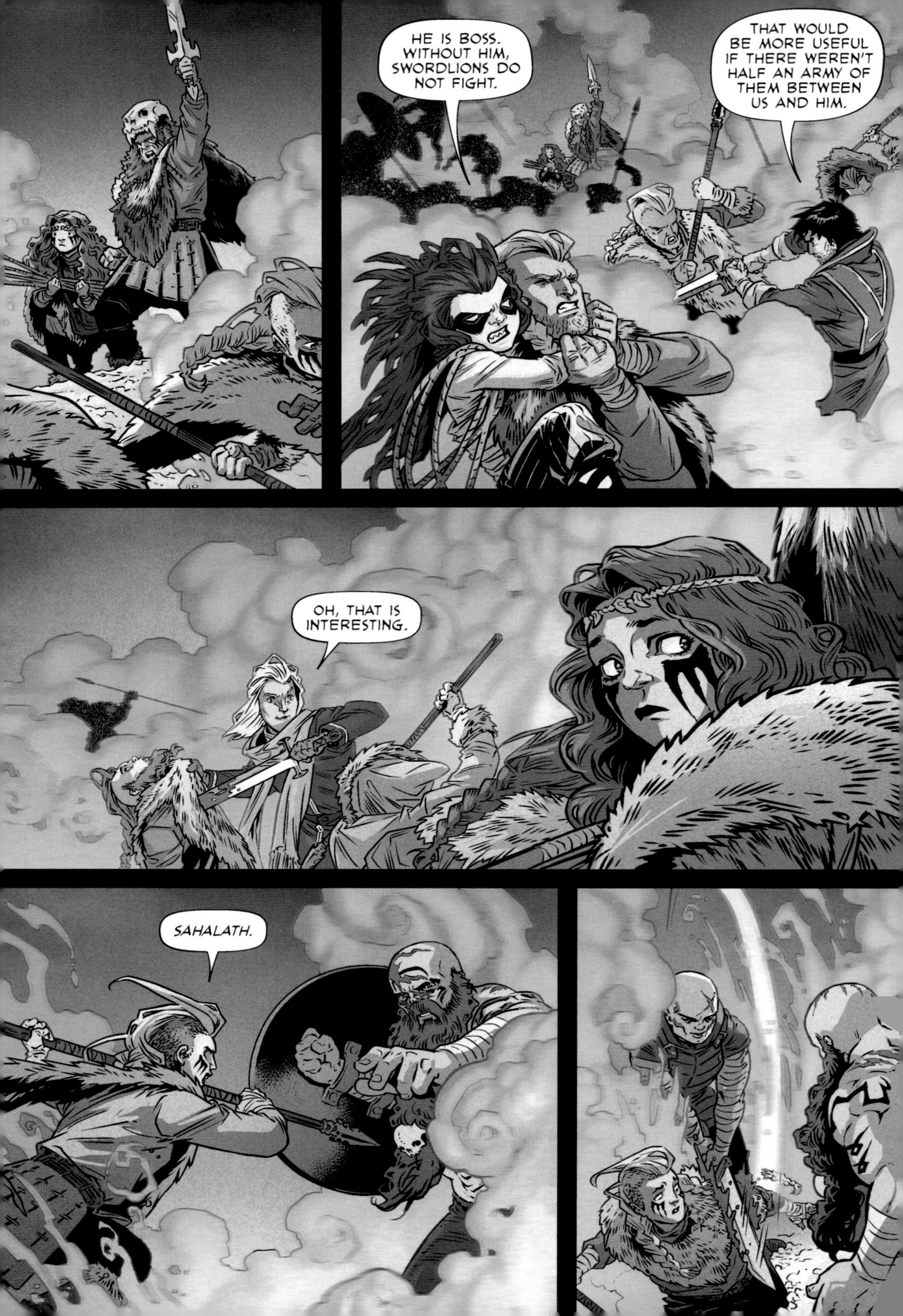
HE IS BOSS. WITHOUT HIM, SWORDLIONS DO NOT FIGHT.
THAT WOULD BE MORE USEFUL IF THERE WEREN'T HALF AN ARMY OF THEM BETWEEN US AND HIM.
OH, THAT IS INTERESTING.
SAHALATH.

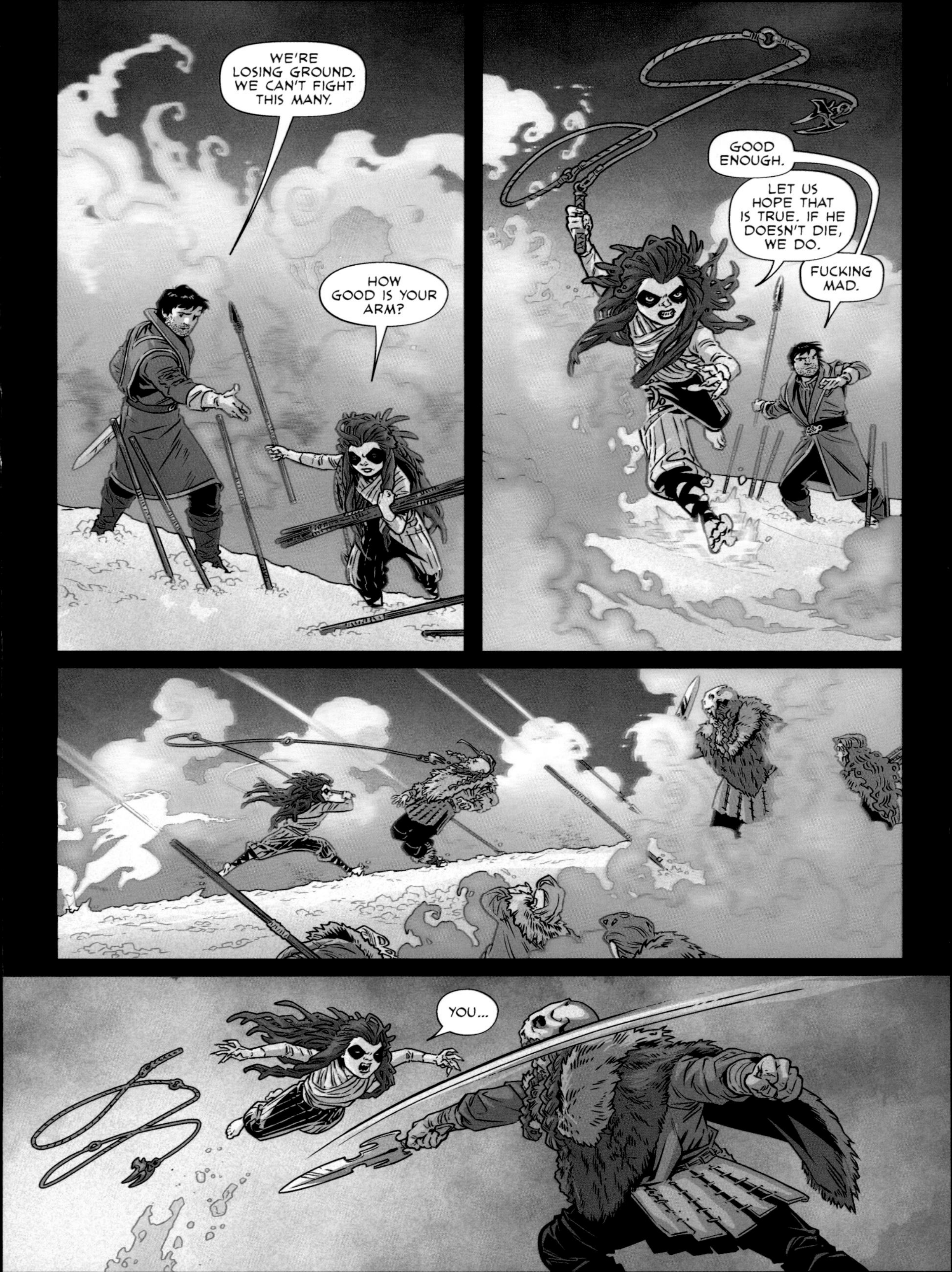
WE'RE LOSING GROUND. WE CAN'T FIGHT THIS MANY.
HOW GOOD IS YOUR ARM?
GOOD ENOUGH.
LET US HOPE THAT IS TRUE. IF HE DOESN'T DIE, WE DO.
FUCKING MAD.
YOU...

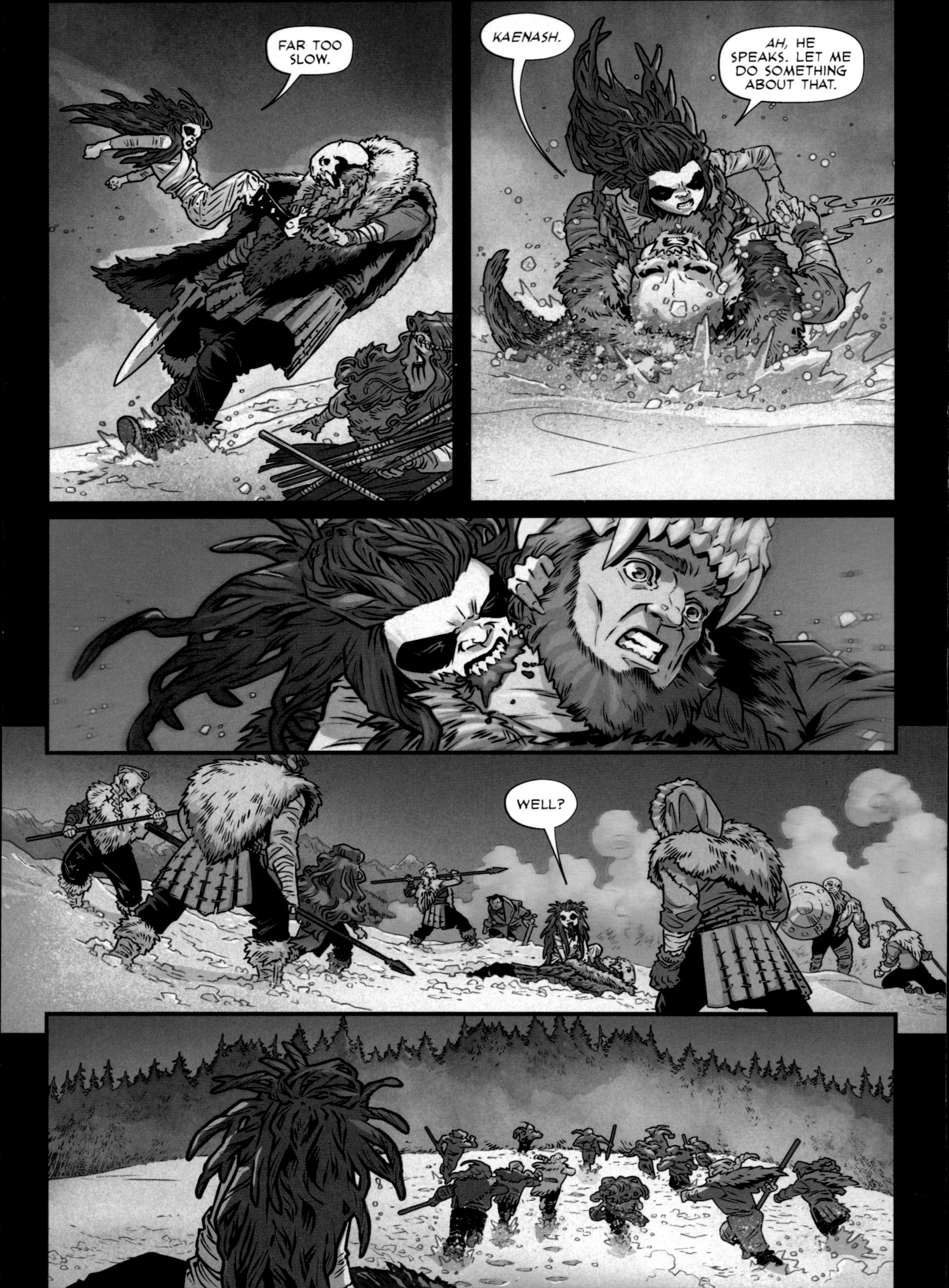
FAR TOO SLOW.
KAENASH.
AH, HE SPEAKS. LET ME DO SOMETHING ABOUT THAT.
WELL?

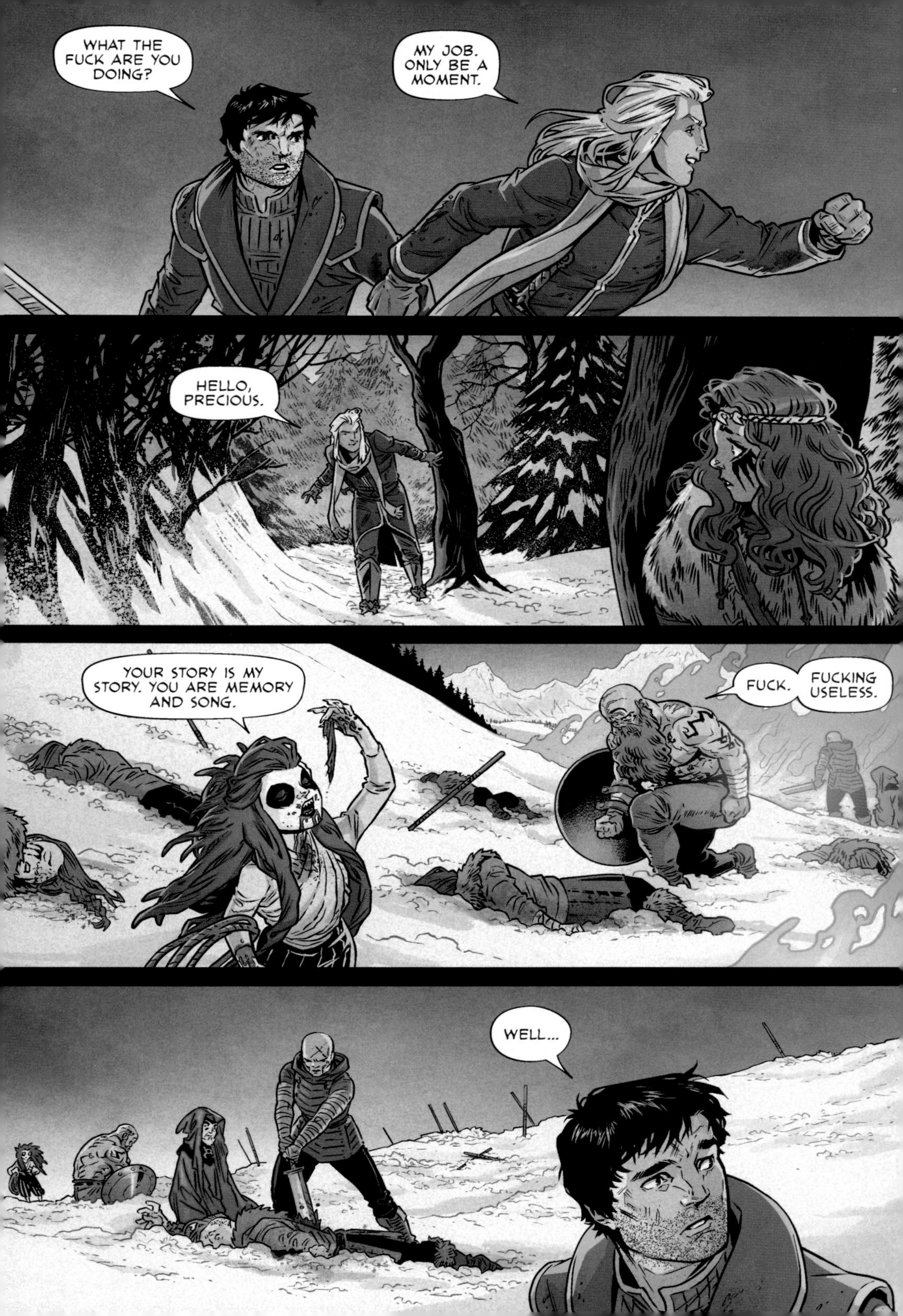
WHAT THE FUCK ARE YOU DOING?
MY JOB. ONLY BE A MOMENT.
HELLO, PRECIOUS.
YOUR STORY IS MY STORY. YOU ARE MEMORY AND SONG.
FUCK.
FUCKING USELESS.
WELL...

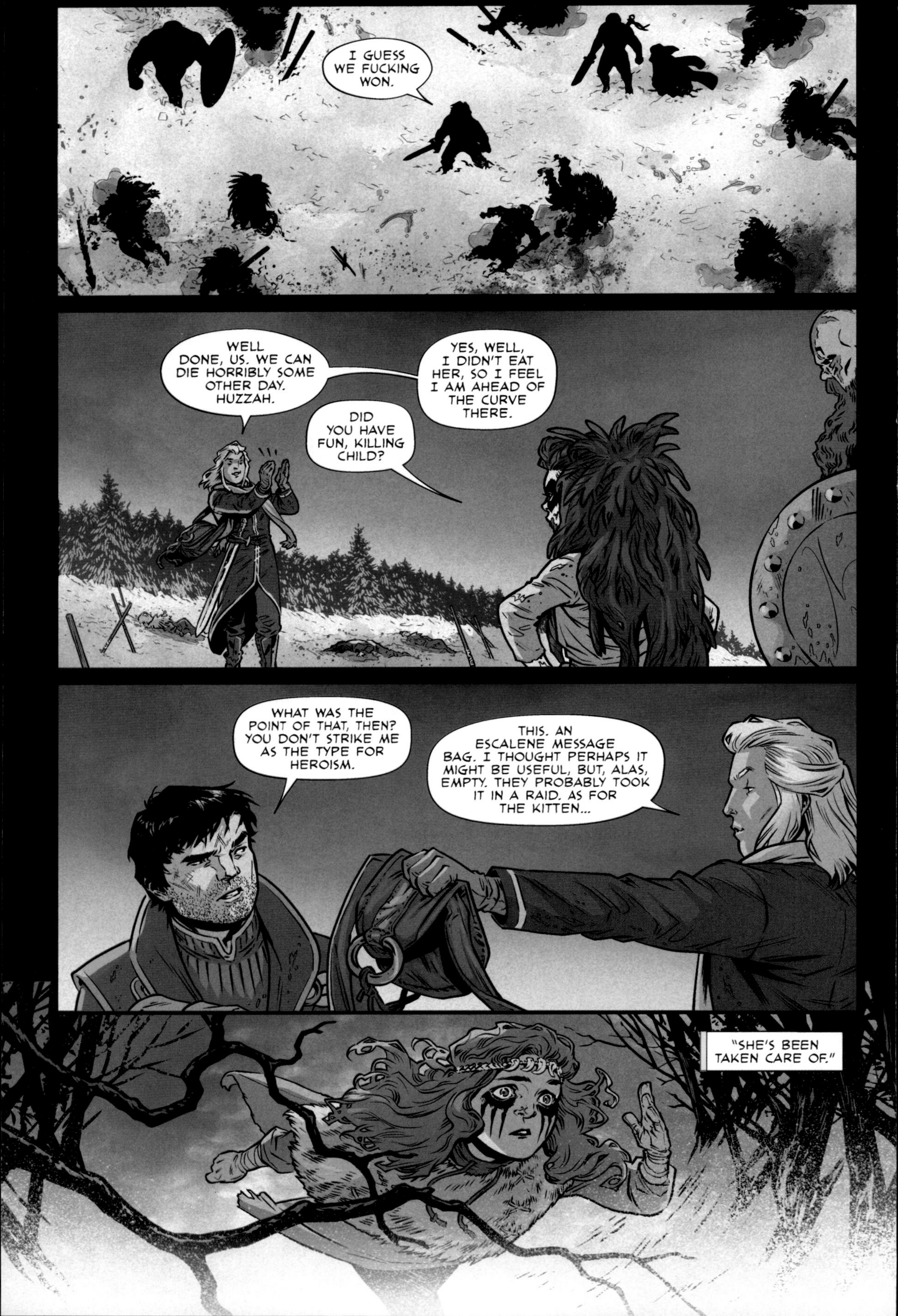
I GUESS WE FUCKING WON.
WELL DONE, US. WE CAN DIE HORRIBLY SOME OTHER DAY. HUZZAH.
YES, WELL, I DIDN'T EAT HER, SO I FEEL I AM AHEAD OF THE CURVE THERE.
DID YOU HAVE FUN, KILLING CHILD?
WHAT WAS THE POINT OF THAT, THEN? YOU DON'T STRIKE ME AS THE TYPE FOR HEROISM.
THIS. AN ESCALENE MESSAGE BAG. I THOUGHT PERHAPS IT MIGHT BE USEFUL, BUT, ALAS, EMPTY. THEY PROBABLY TOOK IT IN A RAID. AS FOR THE KITTEN...
"SHE'S BEEN TAKEN CARE OF."

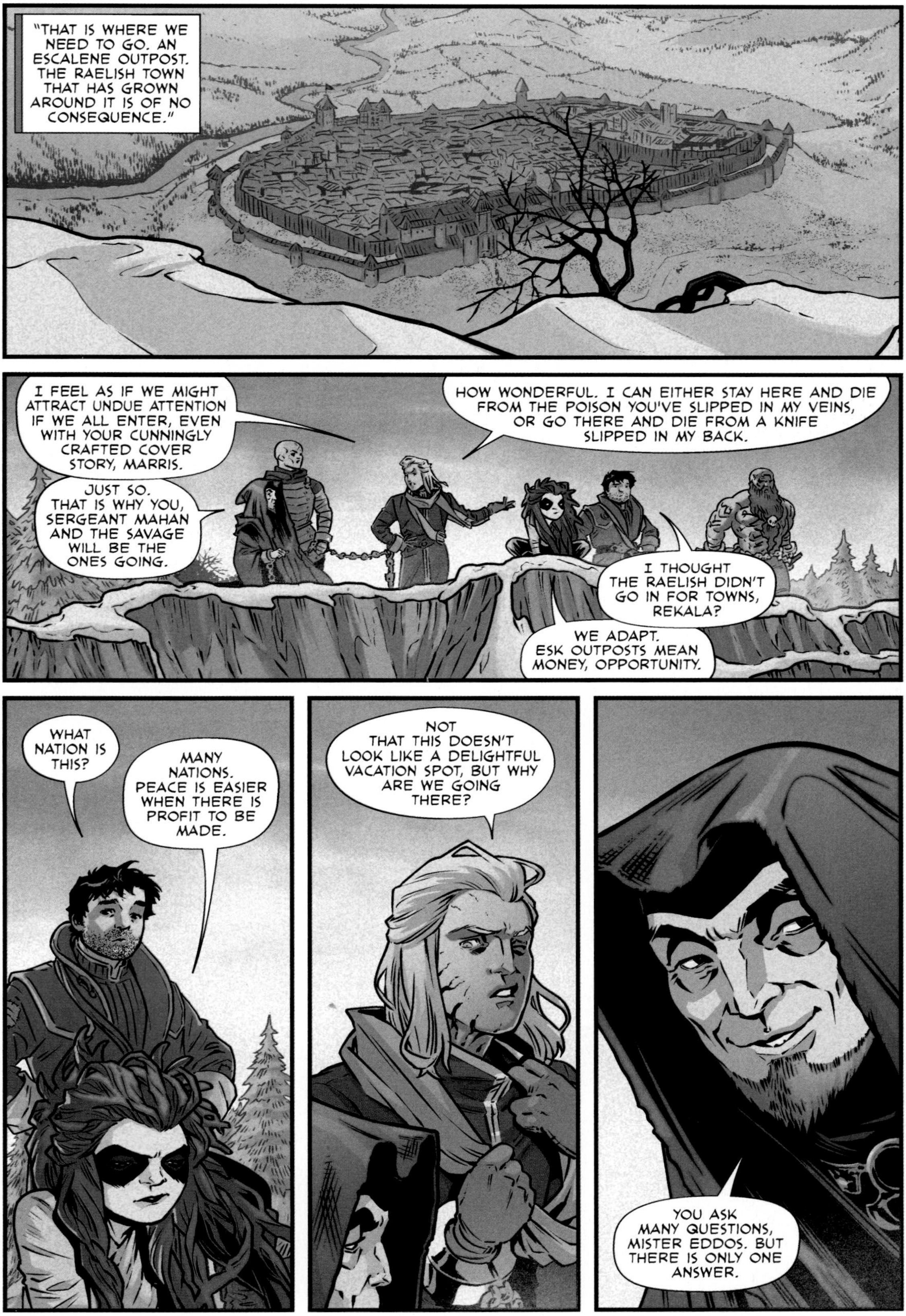
"THAT IS WHERE WE NEED TO GO. AN ESCALENE OUTPOST. THE RAELISH TOWN THAT HAS GROWN AROUND IT IS OF NO CONSEQUENCE."
I FEEL AS IF WE MIGHT ATTRACT UNDUE ATTENTION IF WE ALL ENTER, EVEN WITH YOUR CUNNINGLY CRAFTED COVER STORY, MARRIS.
JUST SO. THAT IS WHY YOU, SERGEANT MAHAN AND THE SAVAGE WILL BE THE ONES GOING.
HOW WONDERFUL. I CAN EITHER STAY HERE AND DIE FROM THE POISON YOU'VE SLIPPED IN MY VEINS, OR GO THERE AND DIE FROM A KNIFE SLIPPED IN MY BACK.
I THOUGHT THE RAELISH DIDN'T GO IN FOR TOWNS, REKALA?
WE ADAPT. ESK OUTPOSTS MEAN MONEY, OPPORTUNITY.
WHAT NATION IS THIS?
MANY NATIONS. PEACE IS EASIER WHEN THERE IS PROFIT TO BE MADE.
NOT THAT THIS DOESN'T LOOK LIKE A DELIGHTFUL VACATION SPOT, BUT WHY ARE WE GOING THERE?
YOU ASK MANY QUESTIONS, MISTER EDDOS. BUT THERE IS ONLY ONE ANSWER.

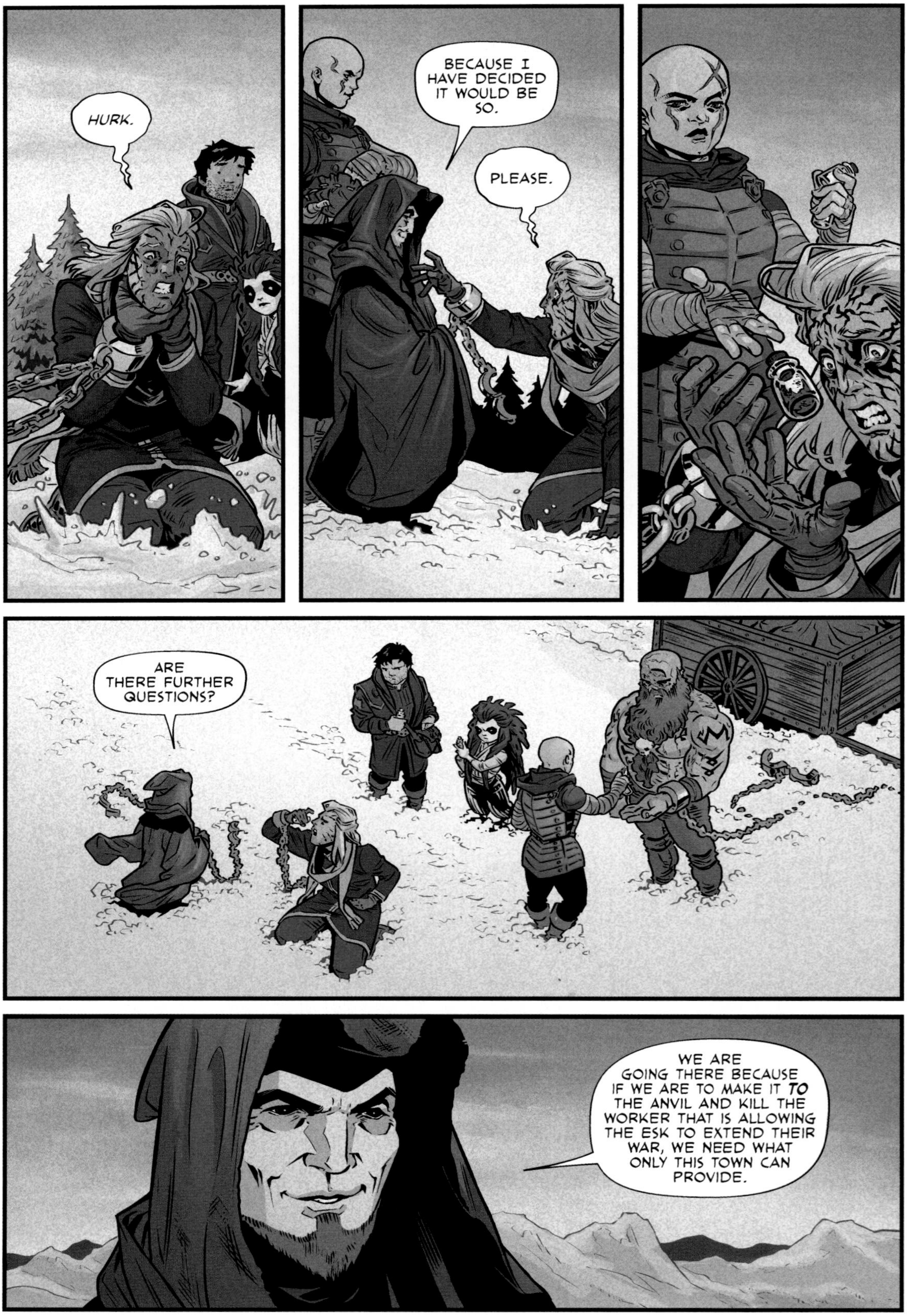
HURK.
BECAUSE I HAVE DECIDED IT WOULD BE SO.
PLEASE.
ARE THERE FURTHER QUESTIONS?
WE ARE GOING THERE BECAUSE IF WE ARE TO MAKE IT *TO* THE ANVIL AND KILL THE WORKER THAT IS ALLOWING THE ESK TO EXTEND THEIR WAR, WE NEED WHAT ONLY THIS TOWN CAN PROVIDE.

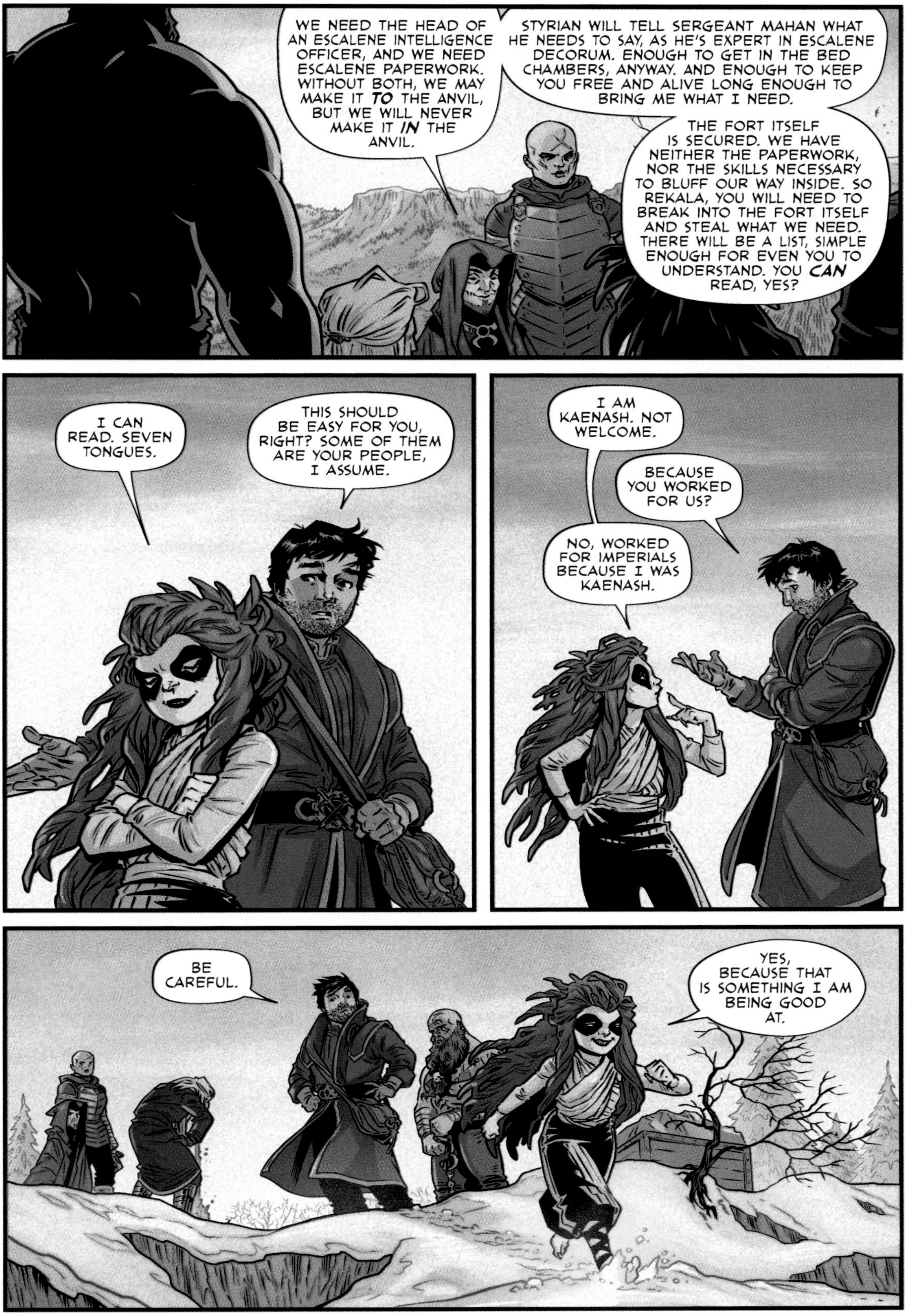
WE NEED THE HEAD OF AN ESCALENE INTELLIGENCE OFFICER, AND WE NEED ESCALENE PAPERWORK. WITHOUT BOTH, WE MAY MAKE IT *TO* THE ANVIL, BUT WE WILL NEVER MAKE IT *IN* THE ANVIL.
STYRIAN WILL TELL SERGEANT MAHAN WHAT HE NEEDS TO SAY, AS HE'S EXPERT IN ESCALENE DECORUM. ENOUGH TO GET IN THE BED CHAMBERS, ANYWAY. AND ENOUGH TO KEEP YOU FREE AND ALIVE LONG ENOUGH TO BRING ME WHAT I NEED.
THE FORT ITSELF IS SECURED. WE HAVE NEITHER THE PAPERWORK, NOR THE SKILLS NECESSARY TO BLUFF OUR WAY INSIDE. SO REKALA, YOU WILL NEED TO BREAK INTO THE FORT ITSELF AND STEAL WHAT WE NEED. THERE WILL BE A LIST, SIMPLE ENOUGH FOR EVEN YOU TO UNDERSTAND. YOU *CAN* READ, YES?
I CAN READ. SEVEN TONGUES.
THIS SHOULD BE EASY FOR YOU, RIGHT? SOME OF THEM ARE YOUR PEOPLE, I ASSUME.
I AM KAENASH. NOT WELCOME.
BECAUSE YOU WORKED FOR US?
NO, WORKED FOR IMPERIALS BECAUSE I WAS KAENASH.
BE CAREFUL.
YES, BECAUSE THAT IS SOMETHING I AM BEING GOOD AT.

I FEEL LIKE THEY'RE STARING AT ME.

YES, I BELIEVE THAT WOULD BE BECAUSE THEY *ARE* STARING AT YOU.

WHY? YOU'RE THE ONE WITH IMPERIAL LOOKS.

WELL, THAT IS CERTAINLY TRUE.

BECAUSE I LOOK LIKE I BELONG, IF ONLY AS A MERCENARY. YOU, ON THE OTHER HAND, LOOK AS IF THAT UNIFORM IS MADE OF NAILS.

WE'RE CLEARLY NOT A STEALTH GROUP. THIS IS A TERRIBLE PLAN.

OH, I DON'T KNOW. I CERTAINLY HAVE A BETTER CHANCE HERE THAN WITH MARRIS.

I DON'T LIKE THIS.

NO...

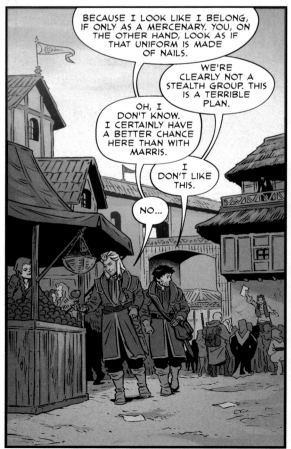

I SUPPOSE YOU WOULDN'T.

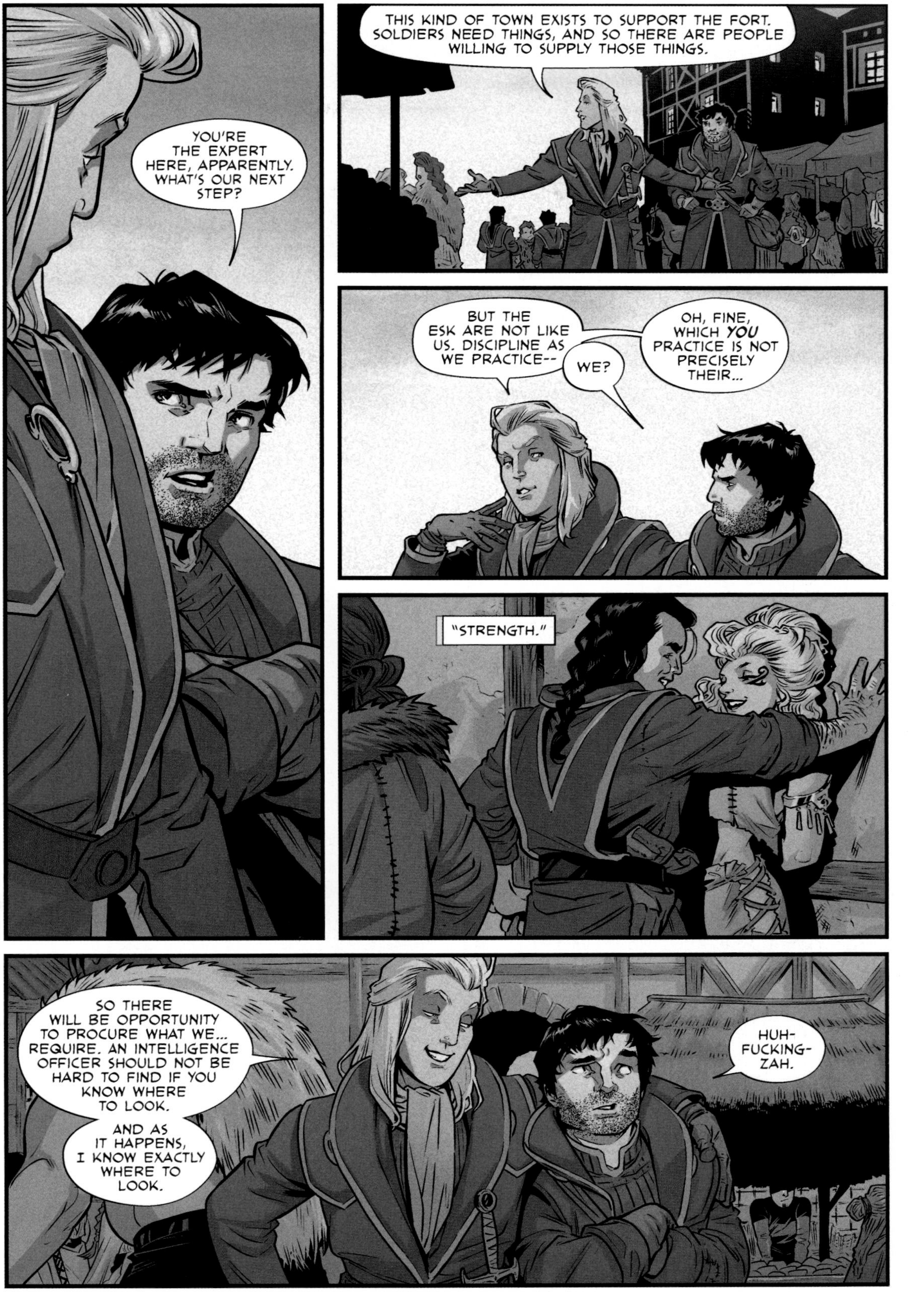
YOU'RE THE EXPERT HERE, APPARENTLY. WHAT'S OUR NEXT STEP?
THIS KIND OF TOWN EXISTS TO SUPPORT THE FORT. SOLDIERS NEED THINGS, AND SO THERE ARE PEOPLE WILLING TO SUPPLY THOSE THINGS.
BUT THE ESK ARE NOT LIKE US. DISCIPLINE AS WE PRACTICE--
WE?
OH, FINE, WHICH YOU PRACTICE IS NOT PRECISELY THEIR...
"STRENGTH."
SO THERE WILL BE OPPORTUNITY TO PROCURE WHAT WE... REQUIRE. AN INTELLIGENCE OFFICER SHOULD NOT BE HARD TO FIND IF YOU KNOW WHERE TO LOOK.
AND AS IT HAPPENS, I KNOW EXACTLY WHERE TO LOOK.
HUH-FUCKING-ZAH.

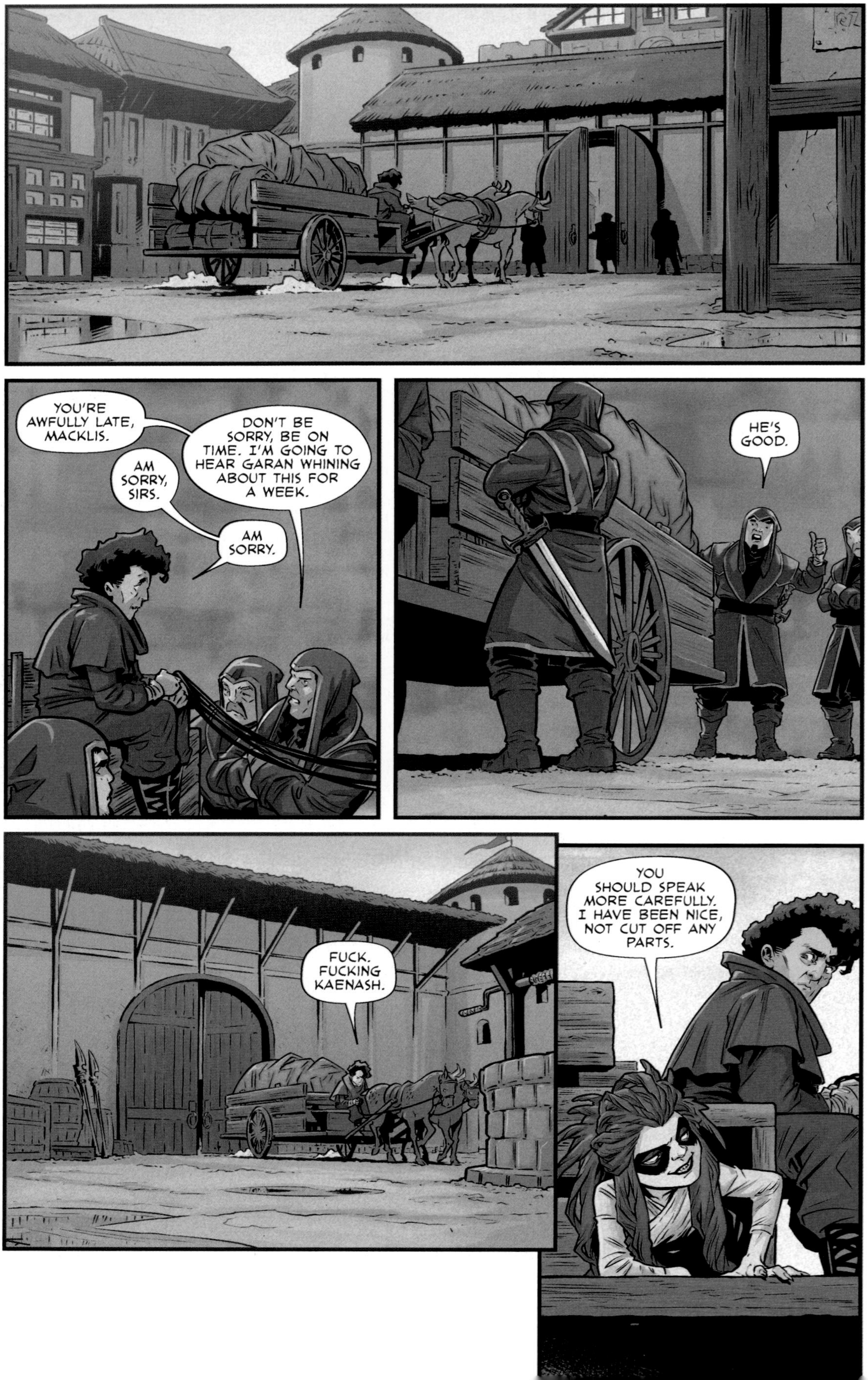
YOU'RE AWFULLY LATE, MACKLIS.
DON'T BE SORRY, BE ON TIME. I'M GOING TO HEAR GARAN WHINING ABOUT THIS FOR A WEEK.
AM SORRY, SIRS.
AM SORRY.
HE'S GOOD.
FUCK. FUCKING KAENASH.
YOU SHOULD SPEAK MORE CAREFULLY. I HAVE BEEN NICE, NOT CUT OFF ANY PARTS.

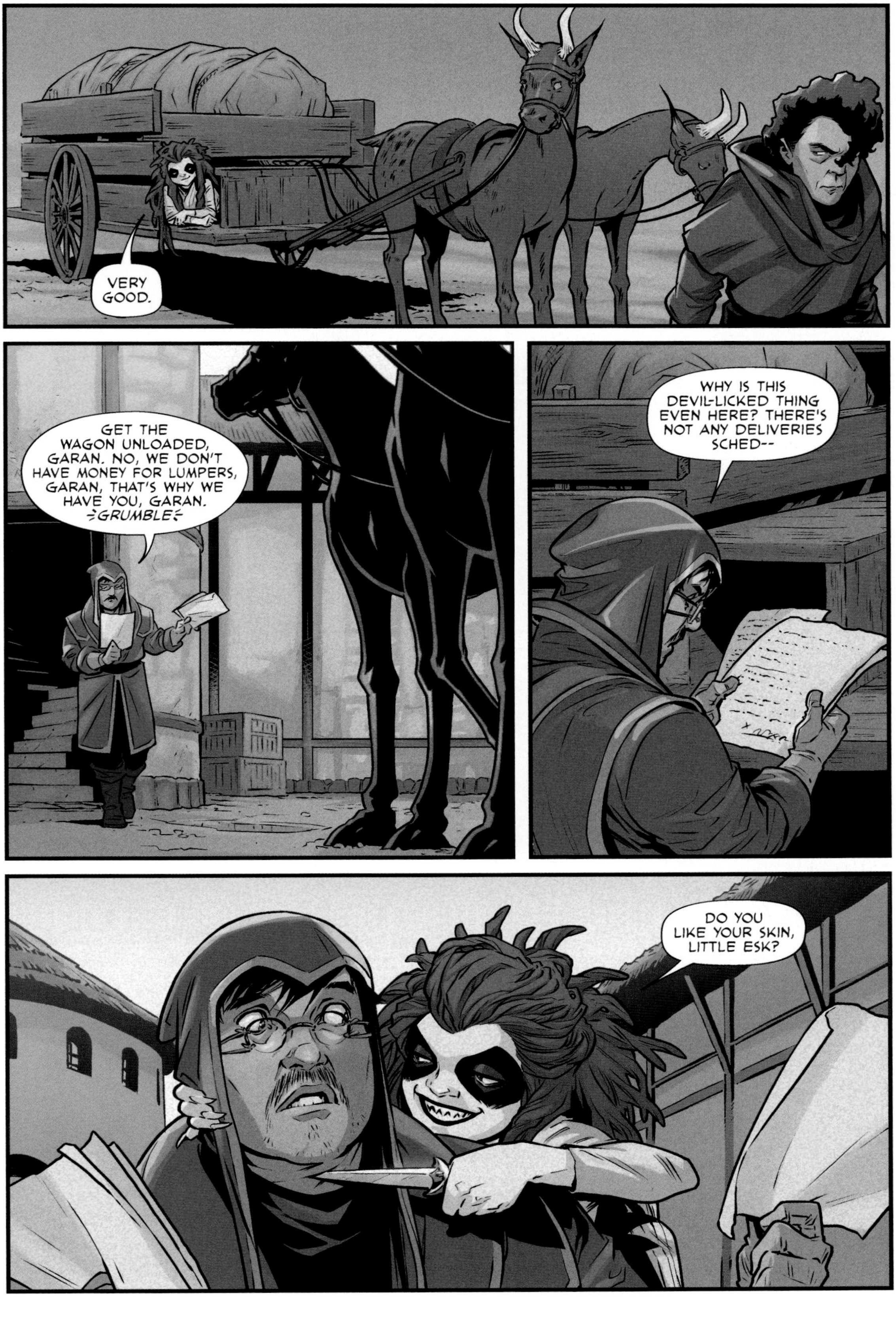
VERY GOOD.
GET THE WAGON UNLOADED, GARAN. NO, WE DON'T HAVE MONEY FOR LUMPERS, GARAN, THAT'S WHY WE HAVE YOU, GARAN. ⪡GRUMBLE⪢
WHY IS THIS DEVIL-LICKED THING EVEN HERE? THERE'S NOT ANY DELIVERIES SCHED--
DO YOU LIKE YOUR SKIN, LITTLE ESK?

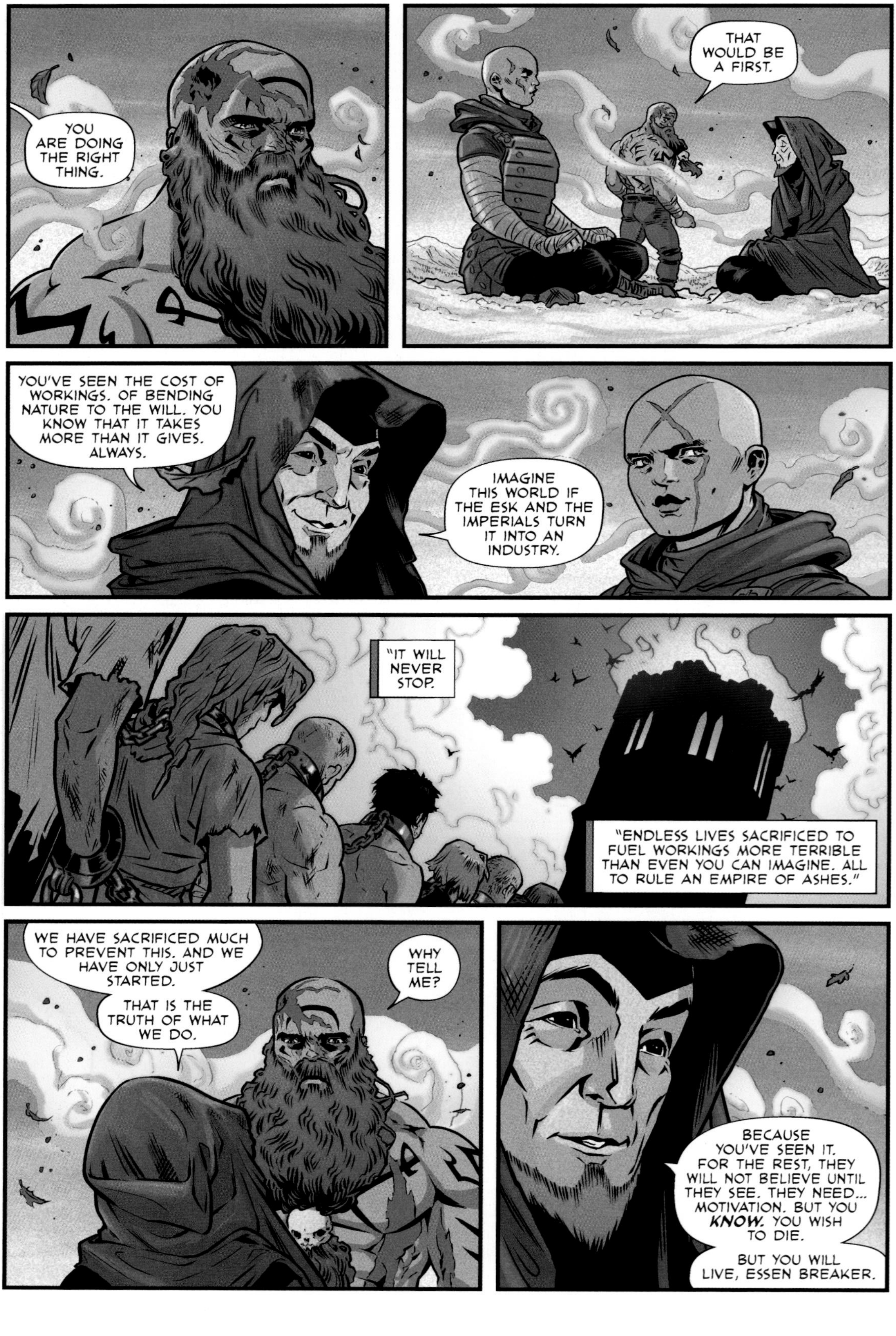
YOU ARE DOING THE RIGHT THING.
THAT WOULD BE A FIRST.
YOU'VE SEEN THE COST OF WORKINGS. OF BENDING NATURE TO THE WILL. YOU KNOW THAT IT TAKES MORE THAN IT GIVES. ALWAYS.
IMAGINE THIS WORLD IF THE ESK AND THE IMPERIALS TURN IT INTO AN INDUSTRY.
"IT WILL NEVER STOP.
"ENDLESS LIVES SACRIFICED TO FUEL WORKINGS MORE TERRIBLE THAN EVEN YOU CAN IMAGINE. ALL TO RULE AN EMPIRE OF ASHES."
WE HAVE SACRIFICED MUCH TO PREVENT THIS. AND WE HAVE ONLY JUST STARTED.
THAT IS THE TRUTH OF WHAT WE DO.
WHY TELL ME?
BECAUSE YOU'VE SEEN IT. FOR THE REST, THEY WILL NOT BELIEVE UNTIL THEY SEE. THEY NEED... MOTIVATION. BUT YOU ***KNOW.*** YOU WISH TO DIE.
BUT YOU WILL LIVE, ESSEN BREAKER.

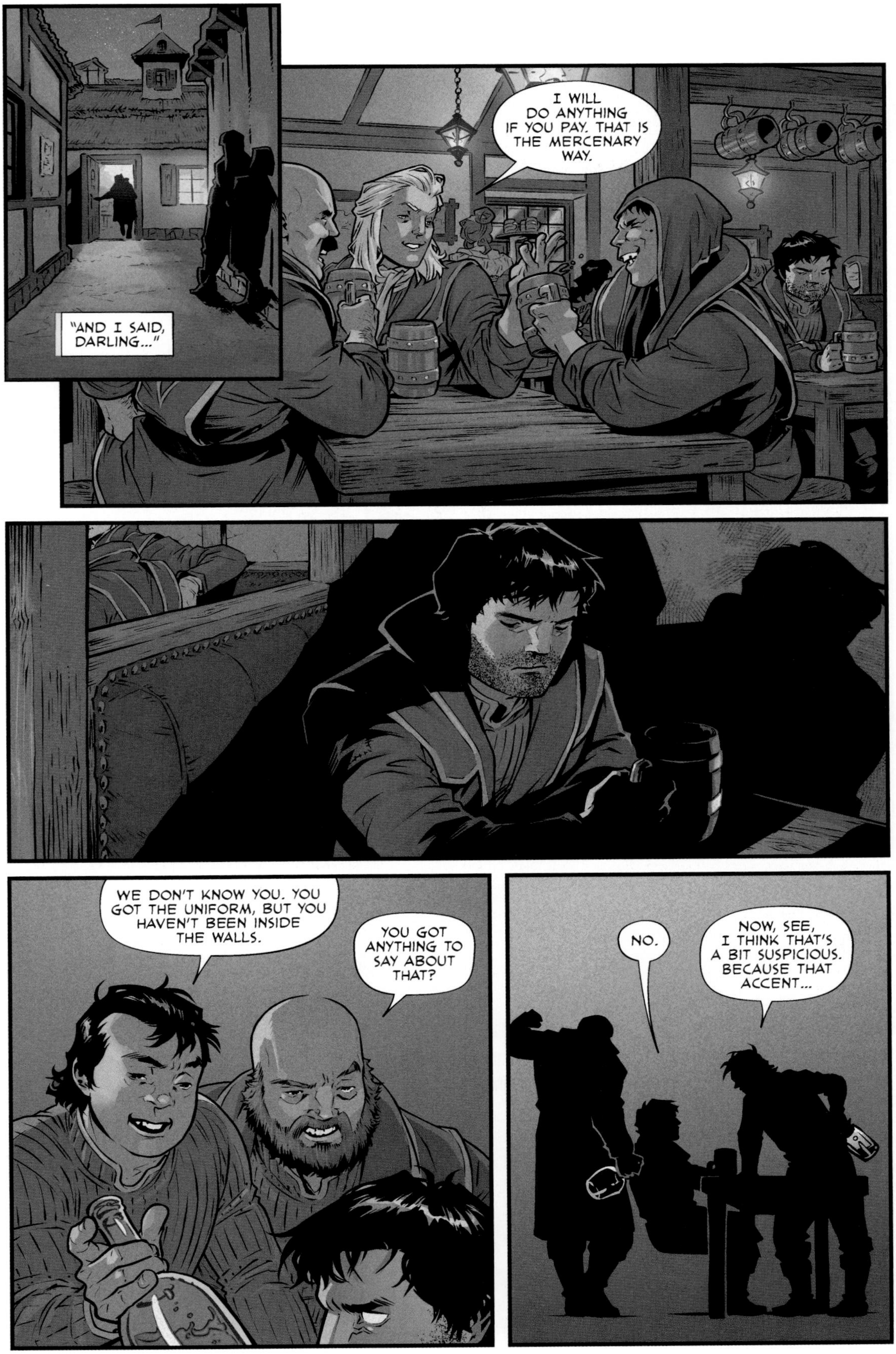
"AND I SAID, DARLING..."
I WILL DO ANYTHING IF YOU PAY. THAT IS THE MERCENARY WAY.
WE DON'T KNOW YOU. YOU GOT THE UNIFORM, BUT YOU HAVEN'T BEEN INSIDE THE WALLS.
YOU GOT ANYTHING TO SAY ABOUT THAT?
NO.
NOW, SEE, I THINK THAT'S A BIT SUSPICIOUS. BECAUSE THAT ACCENT...

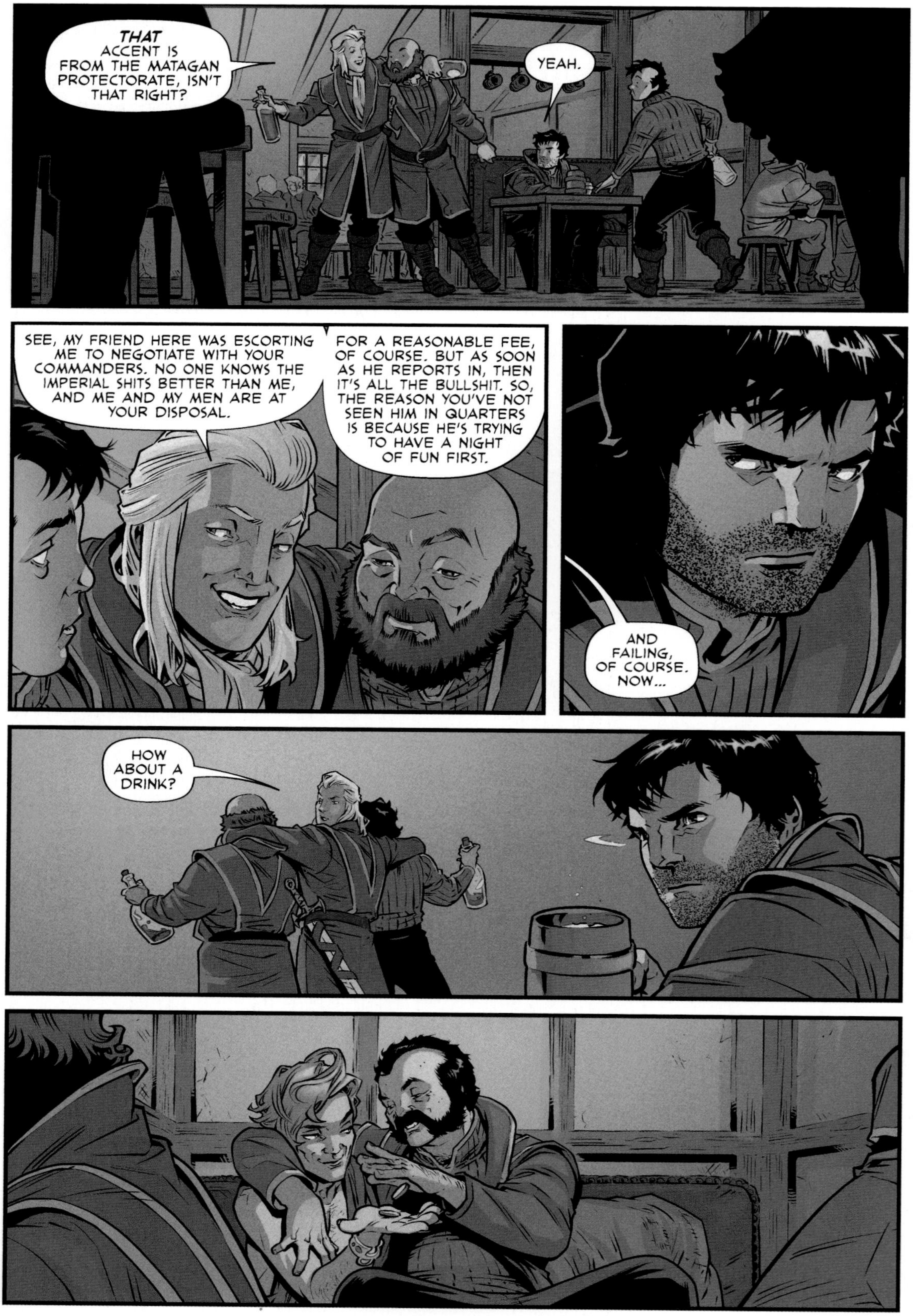
THAT ACCENT IS FROM THE MATAGAN PROTECTORATE, ISN'T THAT RIGHT?
YEAH.
SEE, MY FRIEND HERE WAS ESCORTING ME TO NEGOTIATE WITH YOUR COMMANDERS. NO ONE KNOWS THE IMPERIAL SHITS BETTER THAN ME, AND ME AND MY MEN ARE AT YOUR DISPOSAL.
FOR A REASONABLE FEE, OF COURSE. BUT AS SOON AS HE REPORTS IN, THEN IT'S ALL THE BULLSHIT. SO, THE REASON YOU'VE NOT SEEN HIM IN QUARTERS IS BECAUSE HE'S TRYING TO HAVE A NIGHT OF FUN FIRST.
AND FAILING, OF COURSE. NOW...
HOW ABOUT A DRINK?

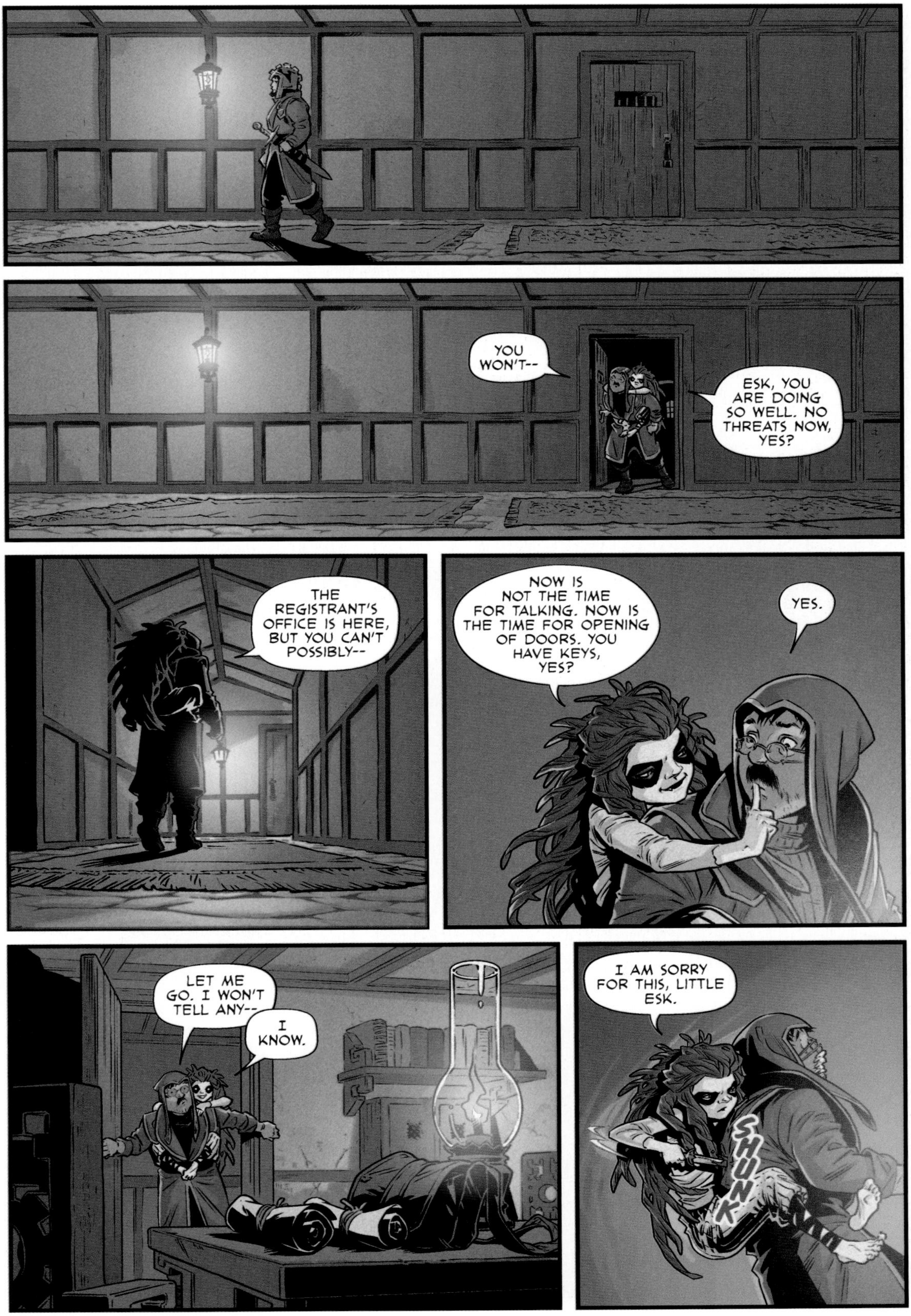
YOU WON'T--
ESK, YOU ARE DOING SO WELL. NO THREATS NOW, YES?
THE REGISTRANT'S OFFICE IS HERE, BUT YOU CAN'T POSSIBLY--
NOW IS NOT THE TIME FOR TALKING. NOW IS THE TIME FOR OPENING OF DOORS. YOU HAVE KEYS, YES?
YES.
LET ME GO. I WON'T TELL ANY--
I KNOW.
I AM SORRY FOR THIS, LITTLE ESK.
SHUNK

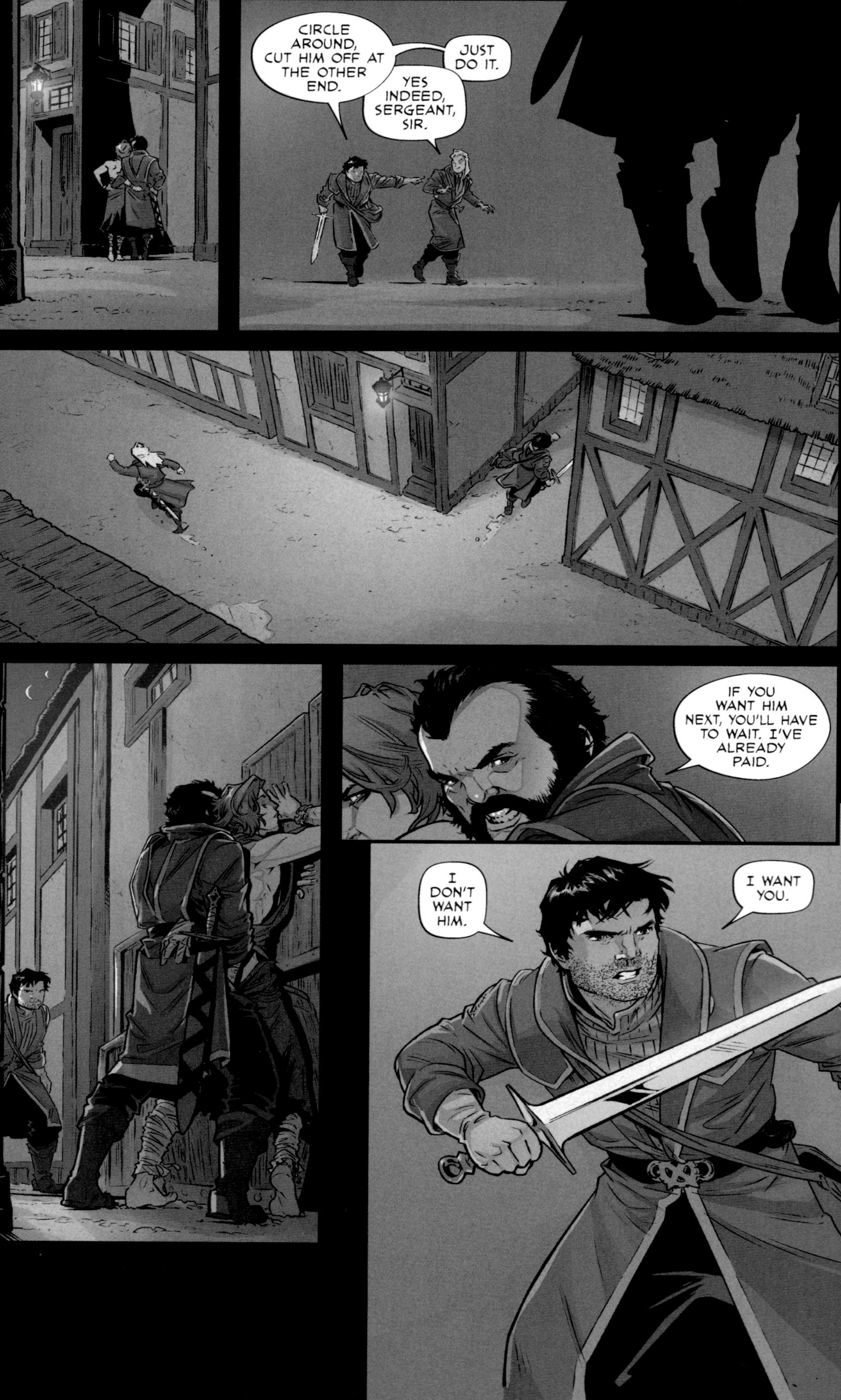
CIRCLE AROUND, CUT HIM OFF AT THE OTHER END.
YES INDEED, SERGEANT, SIR.
JUST DO IT.
IF YOU WANT HIM NEXT, YOU'LL HAVE TO WAIT. I'VE ALREADY PAID.
I DON'T WANT HIM.
I WANT YOU.

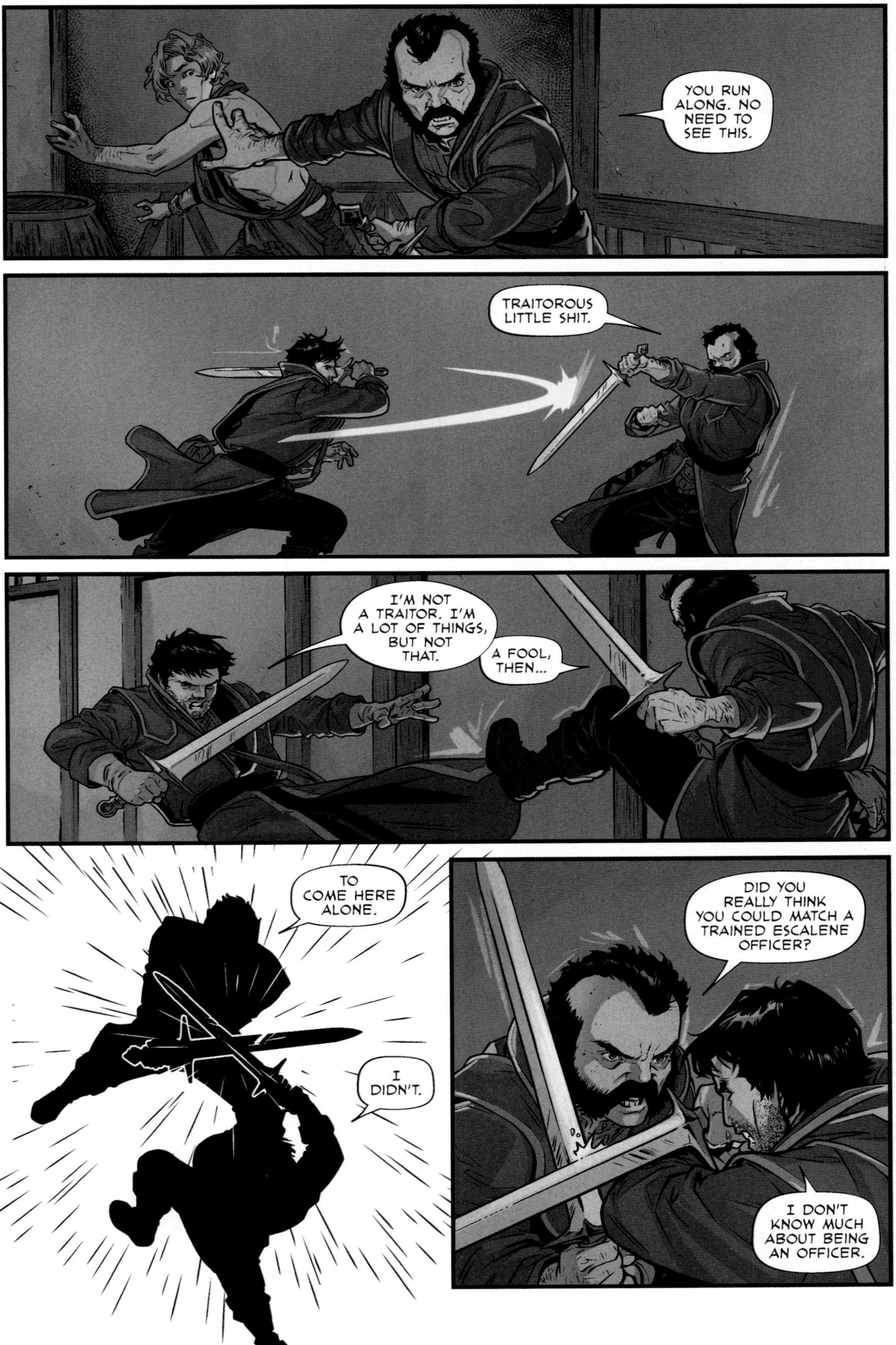
YOU RUN ALONG. NO NEED TO SEE THIS.
TRAITOROUS LITTLE SHIT.
I'M NOT A TRAITOR. I'M A LOT OF THINGS, BUT NOT THAT.
A FOOL, THEN...
TO COME HERE ALONE.
I DIDN'T.
DID YOU REALLY THINK YOU COULD MATCH A TRAINED ESCALENE OFFICER?
I DON'T KNOW MUCH ABOUT BEING AN OFFICER.

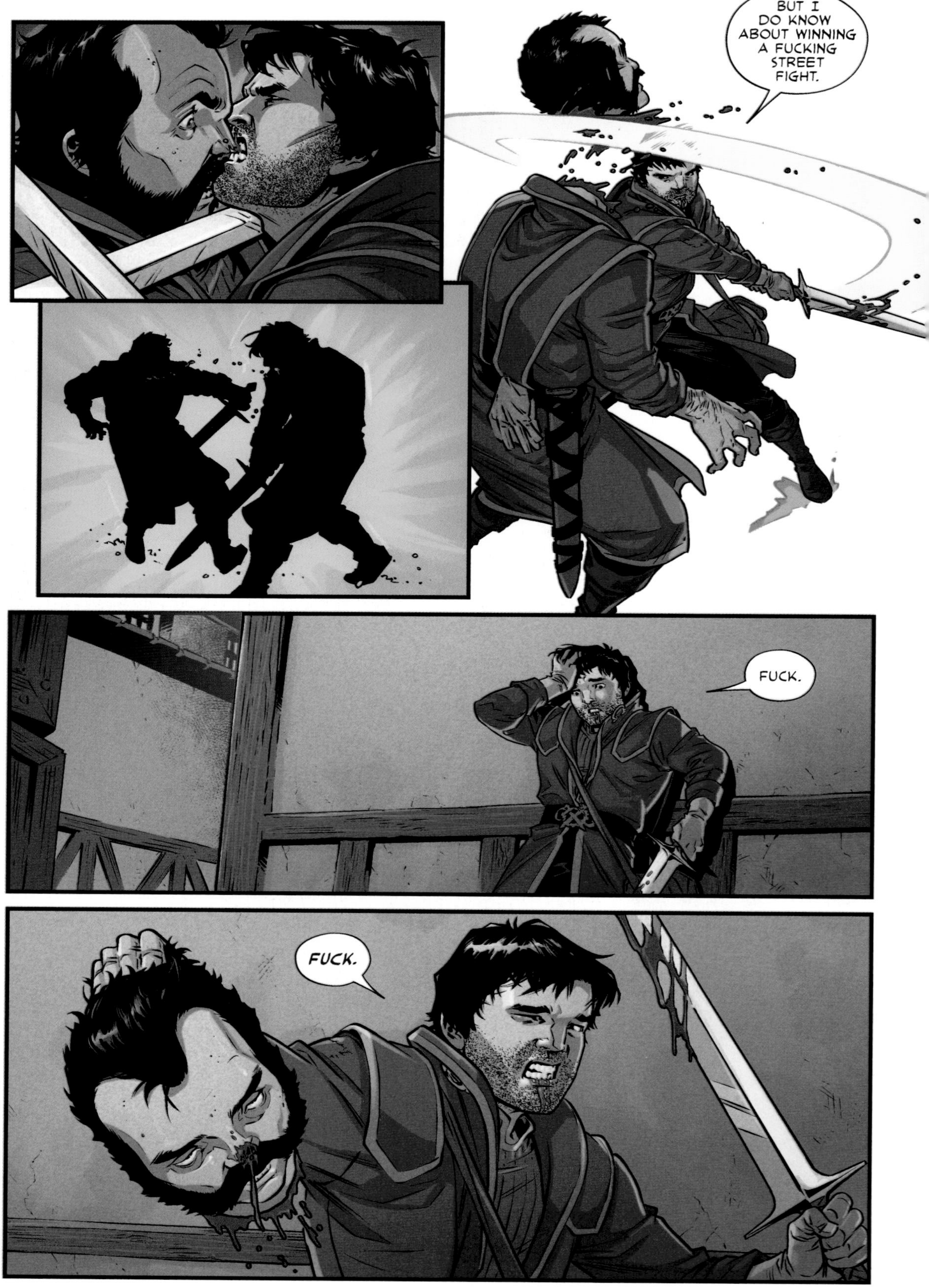
BUT I DO KNOW ABOUT WINNING A FUCKING STREET FIGHT.
FUCK.
FUCK.

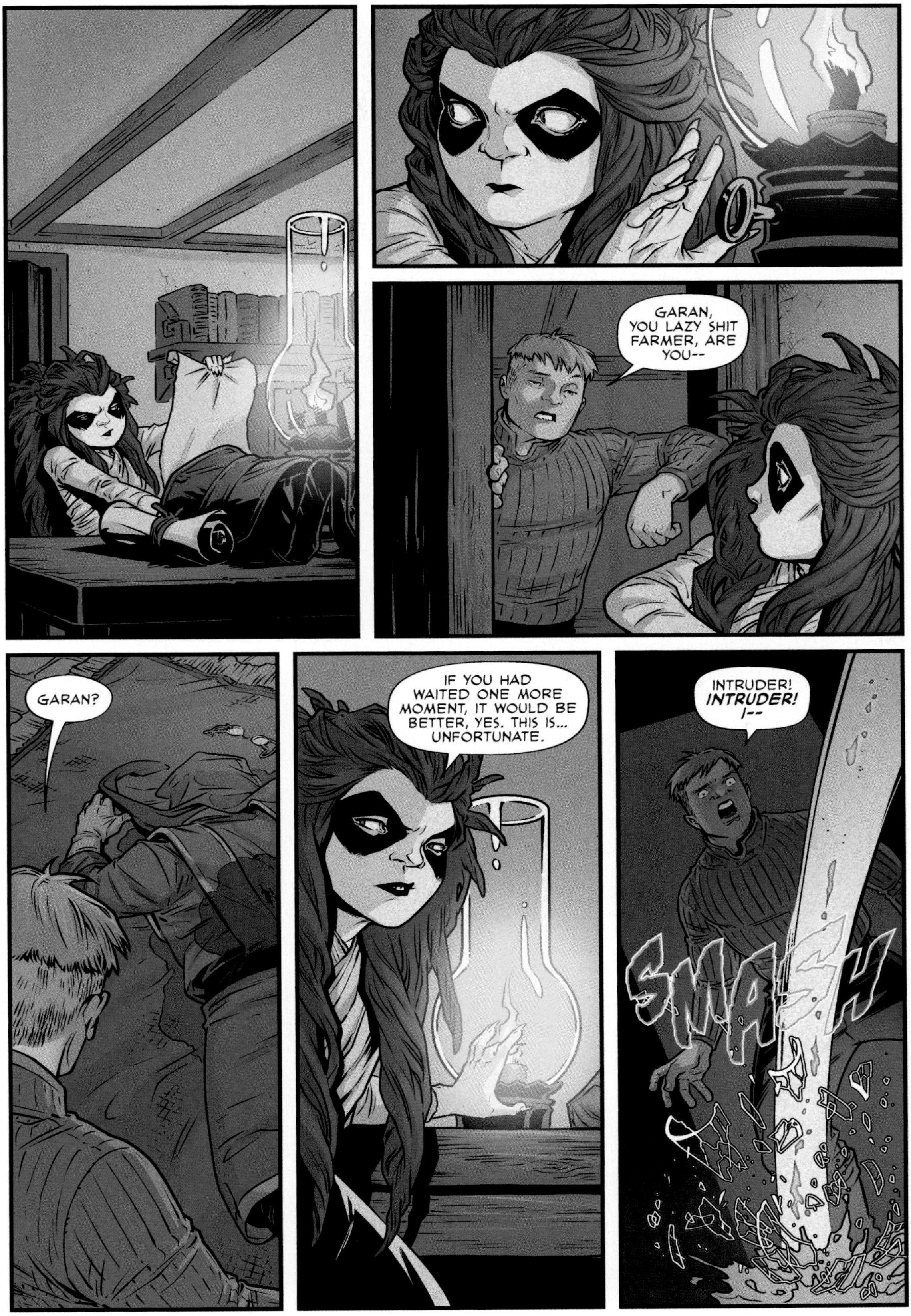
GARAN, YOU LAZY SHIT FARMER, ARE YOU--
GARAN?
IF YOU HAD WAITED ONE MORE MOMENT, IT WOULD BE BETTER, YES. THIS IS... UNFORTUNATE.
INTRUDER! *INTRUDER!* I--
SMASH

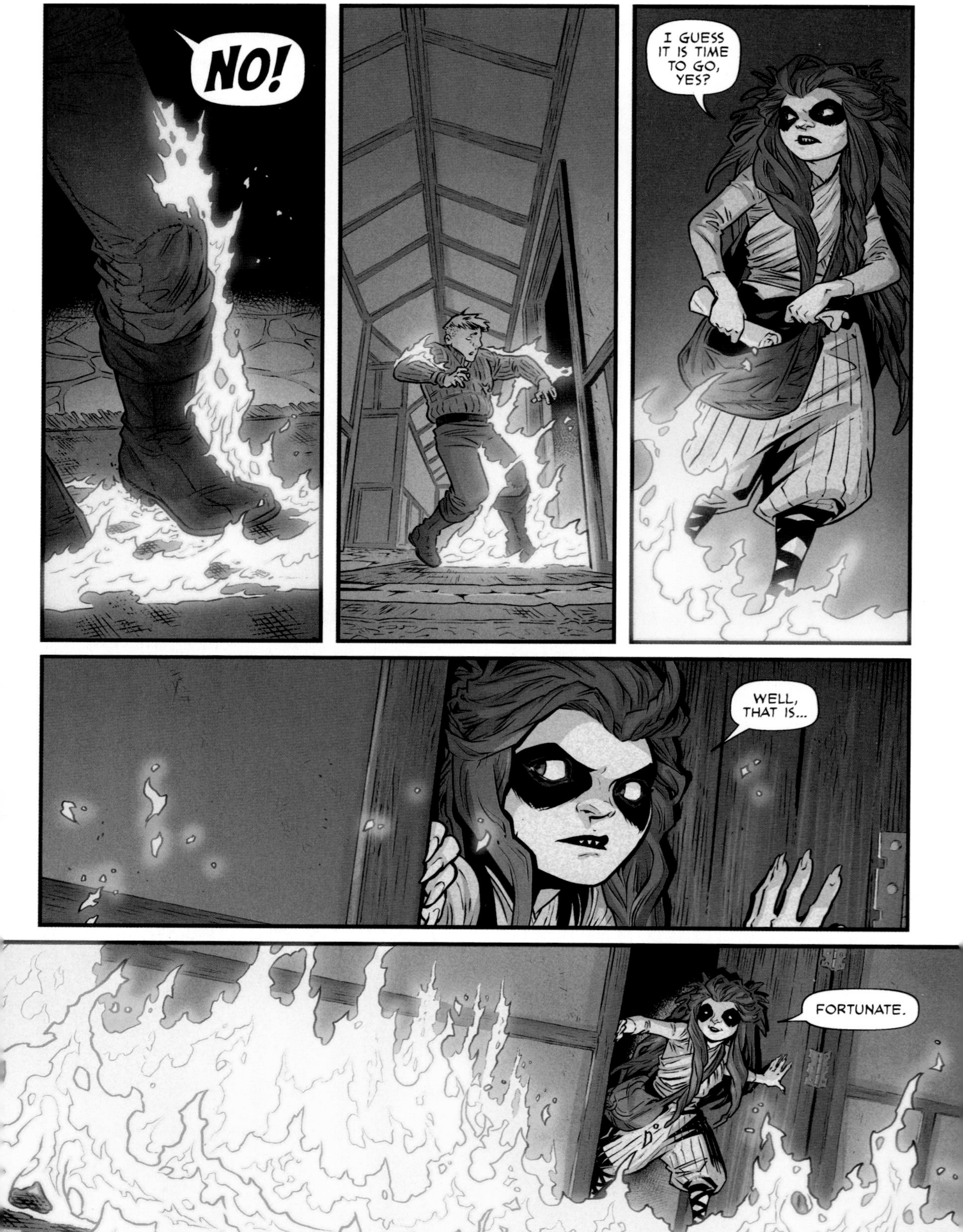
NO!
I GUESS IT IS TIME TO GO, YES?
WELL, THAT IS...
FORTUNATE.

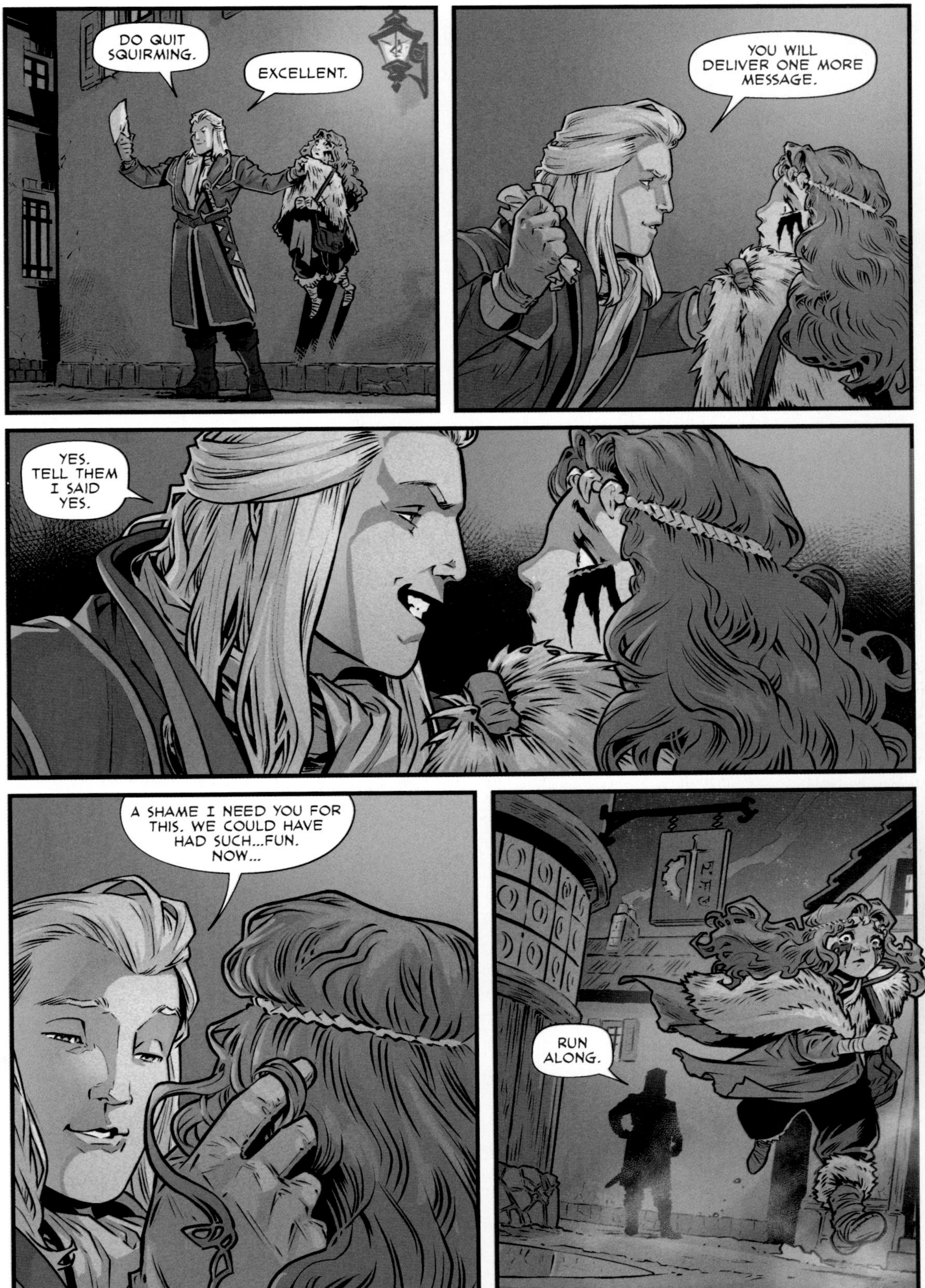
DO QUIT SQUIRMING.
EXCELLENT.
YOU WILL DELIVER ONE MORE MESSAGE.
YES. TELL THEM I SAID YES.
A SHAME I NEED YOU FOR THIS. WE COULD HAVE HAD SUCH...FUN. NOW...
RUN ALONG.

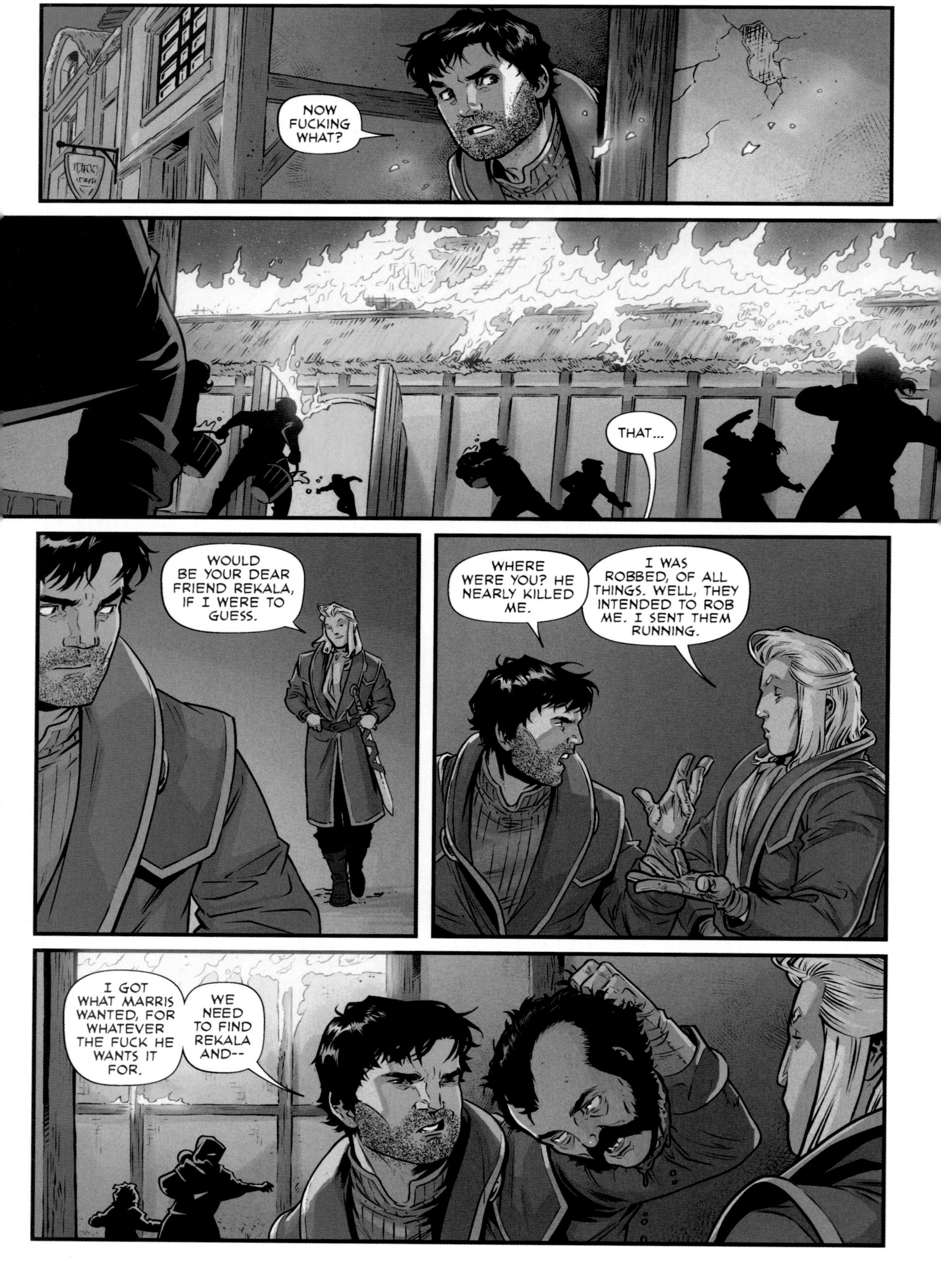
NOW FUCKING WHAT?
THAT...
WOULD BE YOUR DEAR FRIEND REKALA, IF I WERE TO GUESS.
WHERE WERE YOU? HE NEARLY KILLED ME.
I WAS ROBBED, OF ALL THINGS. WELL, THEY INTENDED TO ROB ME. I SENT THEM RUNNING.
I GOT WHAT MARRIS WANTED, FOR WHATEVER THE FUCK HE WANTS IT FOR.
WE NEED TO FIND REKALA AND--

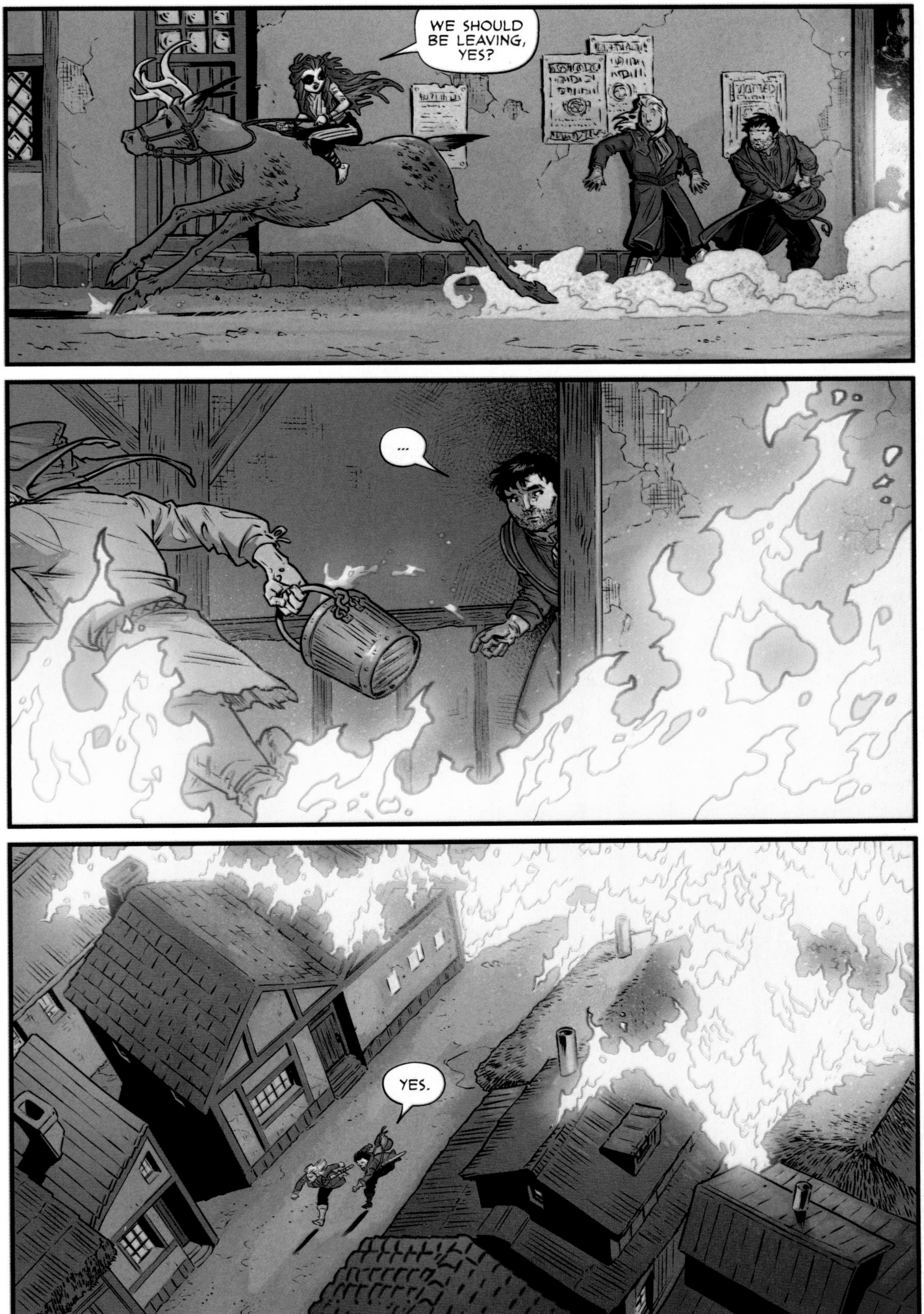
WE SHOULD BE LEAVING, YES?
...
YES.

I SEE YOU WERE SUCCESSFUL...

WHUMP

MORE OR LESS.

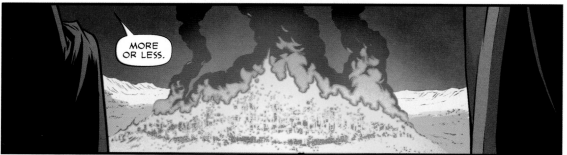

EH, MOTHER CHAOS IS OUR FRIEND, YES?

I UNDERSTAND WHAT REKALA NEEDED TO DO. BUT THIS...

WHAT THE FUCK DO YOU NEED WITH A CORPSE?

KNOWLEDGE.

EVERYTHING HAS A COST.

THAT IS THE FIRST RULE OF WORKINGS. AND, I THINK, THE WORLD.

AND THE COST WILL ALWAYS BE MORE THAN YOU GET IN RETURN. THIS, TOO, I SUSPECT, IS TRUE OF MOST THINGS.

THE ESCALENE HAVE AN ADVANTAGE BECAUSE THEY HAVE REALIZED THAT THE COST NEEDN'T ALWAYS BE PAID BY THE ONE WHO BENEFITS.

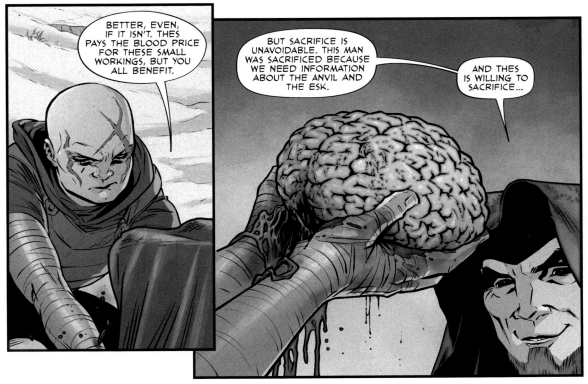

BETTER, EVEN, IF IT ISN'T. THES PAYS THE BLOOD PRICE FOR THESE SMALL WORKINGS, BUT YOU ALL BENEFIT.

BUT SACRIFICE IS UNAVOIDABLE. THIS MAN WAS SACRIFICED BECAUSE WE NEED INFORMATION ABOUT THE ANVIL AND THE ESK.

AND THES IS WILLING TO SACRIFICE...

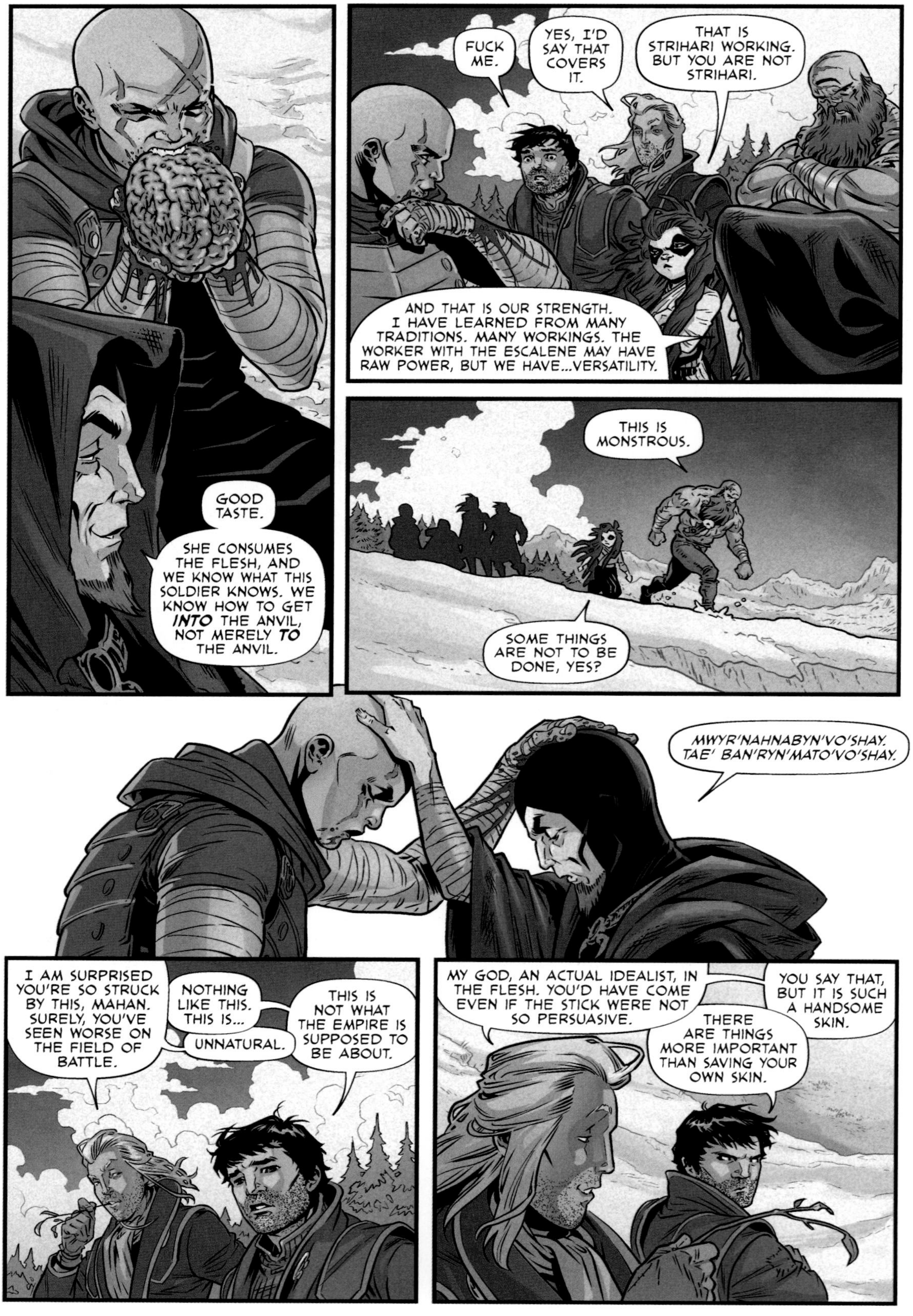
GOOD TASTE.
SHE CONSUMES THE FLESH, AND WE KNOW WHAT THIS SOLDIER KNOWS. WE KNOW HOW TO GET *INTO* THE ANVIL, NOT MERELY *TO* THE ANVIL.
FUCK ME.
YES, I'D SAY THAT COVERS IT.
THAT IS STRIHARI WORKING. BUT YOU ARE NOT STRIHARI.
AND THAT IS OUR STRENGTH. I HAVE LEARNED FROM MANY TRADITIONS. MANY WORKINGS. THE WORKER WITH THE ESCALENE MAY HAVE RAW POWER, BUT WE HAVE...VERSATILITY.
THIS IS MONSTROUS.
SOME THINGS ARE NOT TO BE DONE, YES?
MWYR'NAHNABYN'VO'SHAY. TAE' BAN'RYN'MATO'VO'SHAY.
I AM SURPRISED YOU'RE SO STRUCK BY THIS, MAHAN. SURELY, YOU'VE SEEN WORSE ON THE FIELD OF BATTLE.
NOTHING LIKE THIS. THIS IS...
UNNATURAL.
THIS IS NOT WHAT THE EMPIRE IS SUPPOSED TO BE ABOUT.
MY GOD, AN ACTUAL IDEALIST, IN THE FLESH. YOU'D HAVE COME EVEN IF THE STICK WERE NOT SO PERSUASIVE.
THERE ARE THINGS MORE IMPORTANT THAN SAVING YOUR OWN SKIN.
YOU SAY THAT, BUT IT IS SUCH A HANDSOME SKIN.

YOU ARE NOT AFRAID.

I AM.

OF YOU? NO, I AM NOT AFRAID. THERE IS FAR WORSE TO FEAR, YES? YOU ARE NOT SO TERRIBLE.

I AM EVERYTHING THEY SAY, AND WORSE THAN THAT. I'VE KNOWN NOTHING BUT WAR SINCE I WAS A CHILD.

ESSEN BREAKER. THE REAVER. THE DEVIL'S SON. I FILLED THE ENEMY WITH DREAD. EVERY SOLDIER KNOWS MY NAME. I WAS PROUD OF THAT ONCE.

AND NOW?

AFTER THE AGREEMENT, I WAS SENT WEST. TO DEAL WITH THE RAELISH PROBLEM IN THE TERRITORIES WE STILL HAD.

DURING THE WAR, I BELIEVED. I BELIEVED IN THE EMPIRE. I BELIEVED WE WERE BETTER.

AND THEN I SAW.

I SAW WHAT WE DROVE THEM TO DO. THE AKASH KILLED THEIR CHILDREN TO TRY AND STOP US FROM KILLING THEM. AND THEN...

YOU SAW YOUR OWN SIDE TRY TO LEARN THIS, YES?

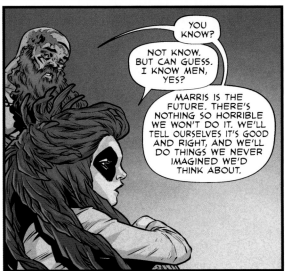

YOU KNOW?

NOT KNOW. BUT CAN GUESS. I KNOW MEN, YES?

MARRIS IS THE FUTURE. THERE'S NOTHING SO HORRIBLE WE WON'T DO IT. WE'LL TELL OURSELVES IT'S GOOD AND RIGHT, AND WE'LL DO THINGS WE NEVER IMAGINED WE'D THINK ABOUT.

THEN WHY FIGHT? YOU COULD HAVE DIED ALREADY. MANY TIMES. BUT STILL, YOU FIGHT.

HABIT?

IS NOT AN ANSWER.

I OWE A DEBT. THERE WERE MEN WHO BELIEVED IN ME. MEN I BETRAYED. I KILLED. SO I OWE. AND I WILL PAY...

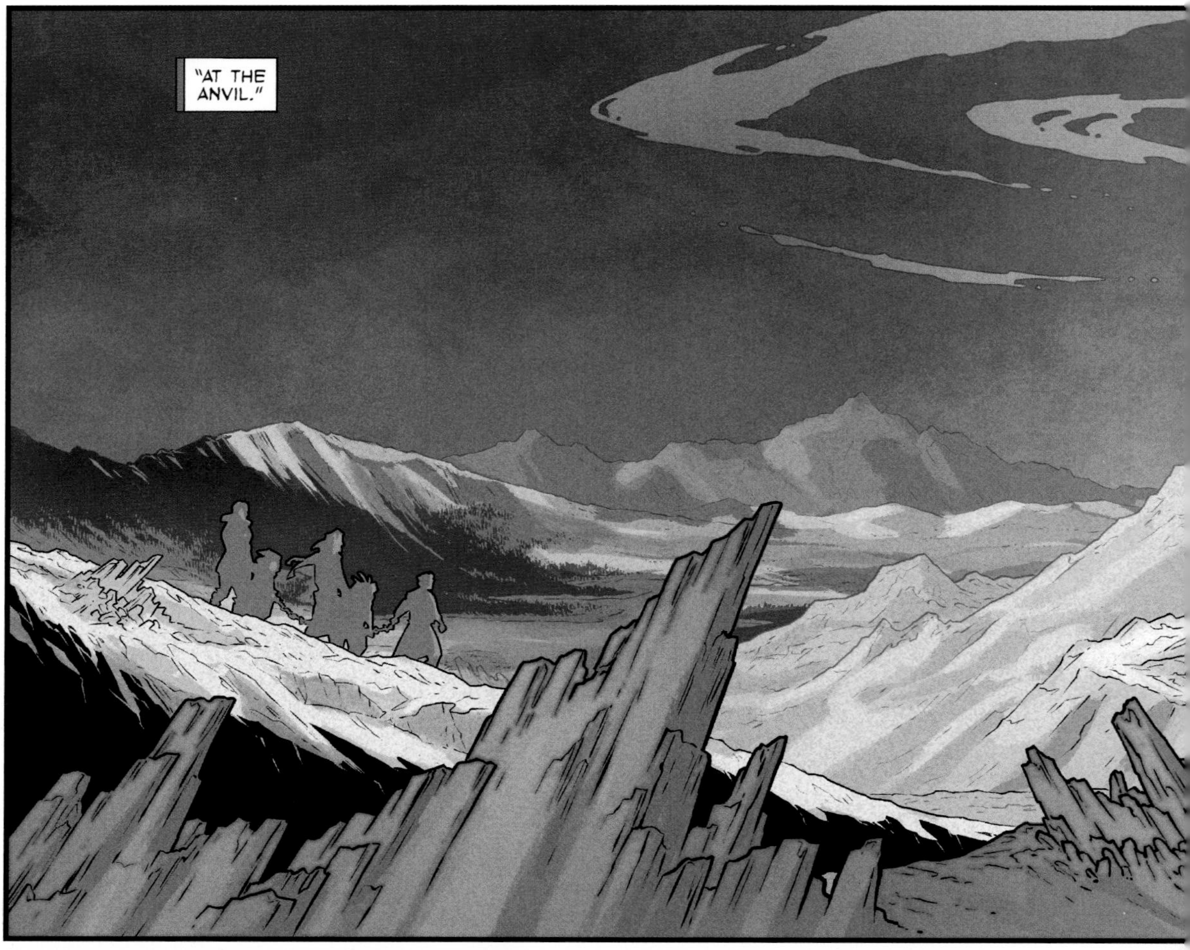
"AT THE ANVIL."

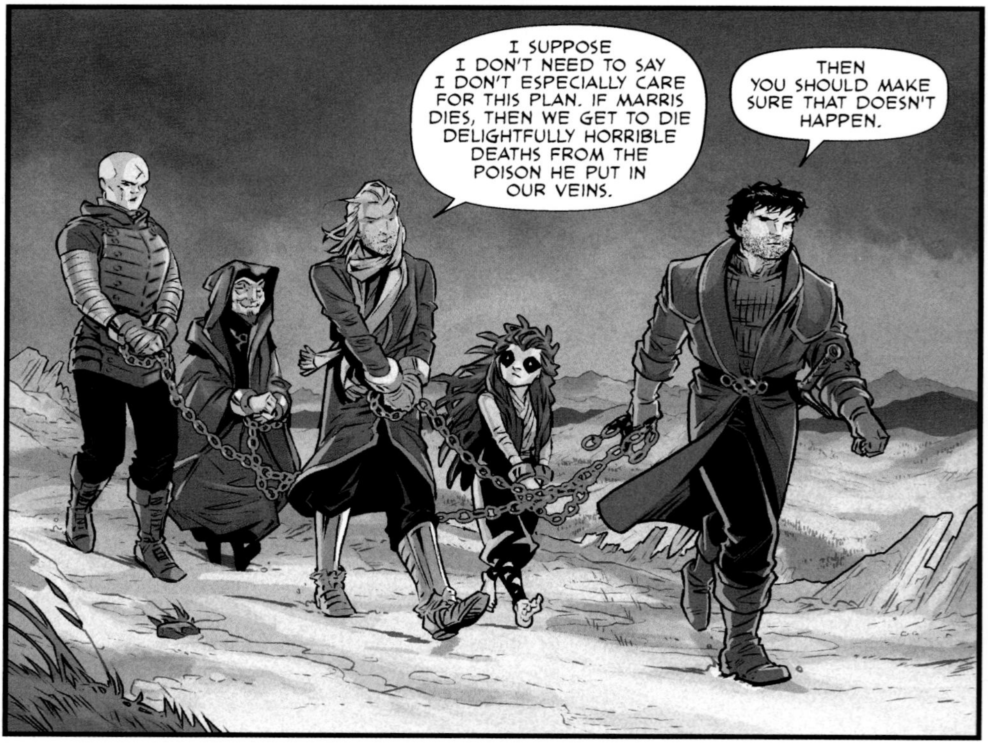
I SUPPOSE I DON'T NEED TO SAY I DON'T ESPECIALLY CARE FOR THIS PLAN. IF MARRIS DIES, THEN WE GET TO DIE DELIGHTFULLY HORRIBLE DEATHS FROM THE POISON HE PUT IN OUR VEINS.
THEN YOU SHOULD MAKE SURE THAT DOESN'T HAPPEN.

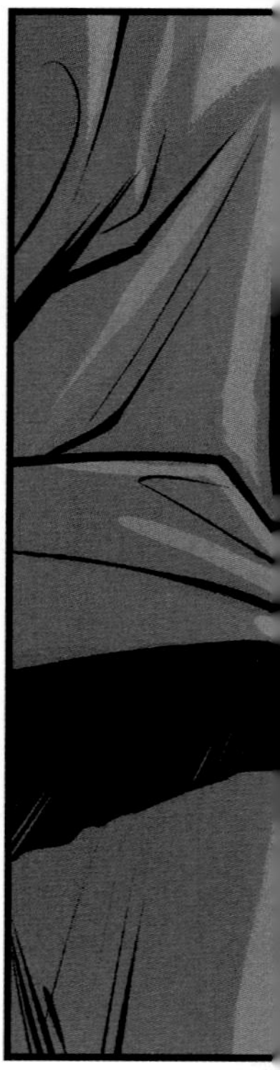

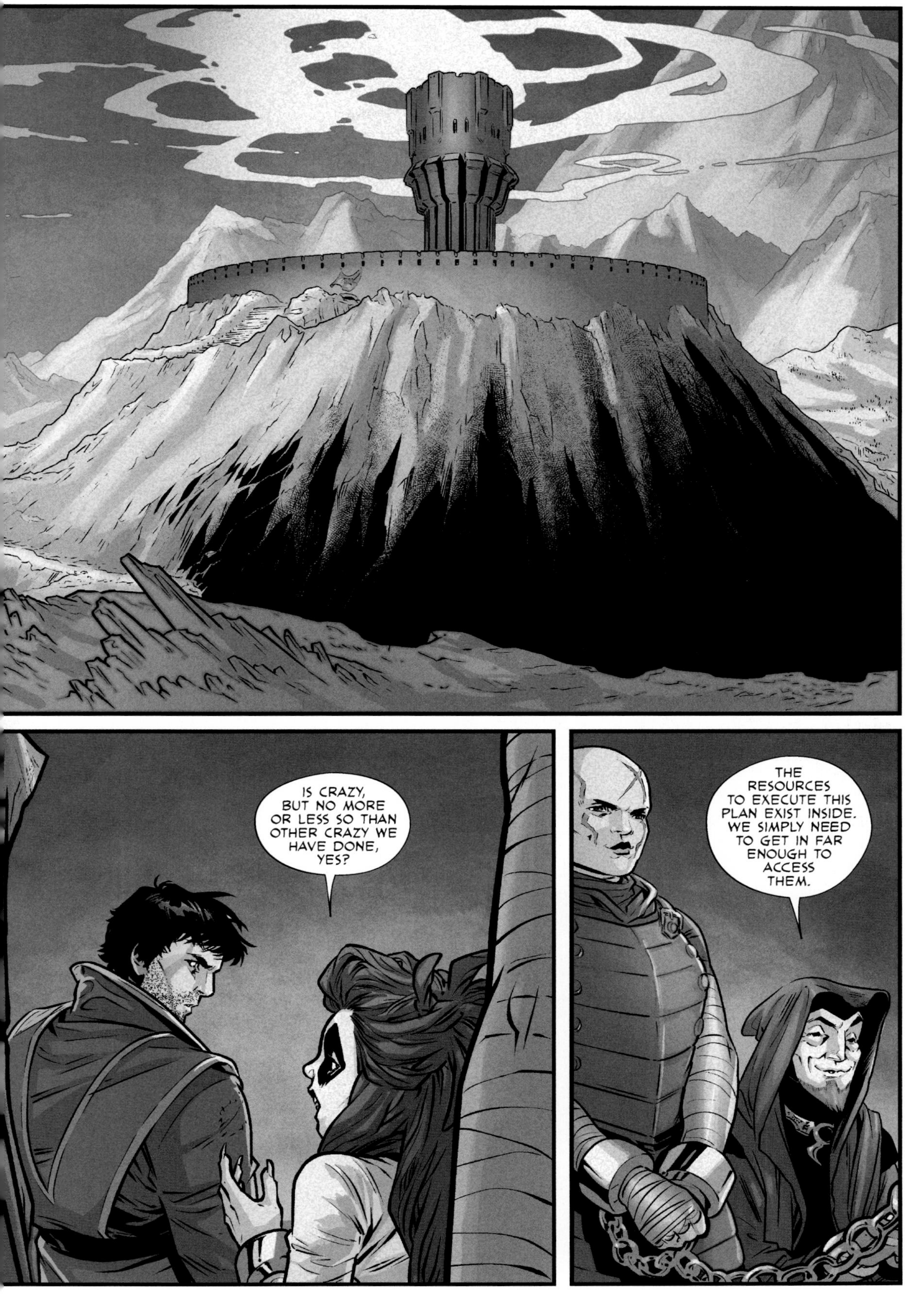
IS CRAZY, BUT NO MORE OR LESS SO THAN OTHER CRAZY WE HAVE DONE, YES?
THE RESOURCES TO EXECUTE THIS PLAN EXIST INSIDE. WE SIMPLY NEED TO GET IN FAR ENOUGH TO ACCESS THEM.

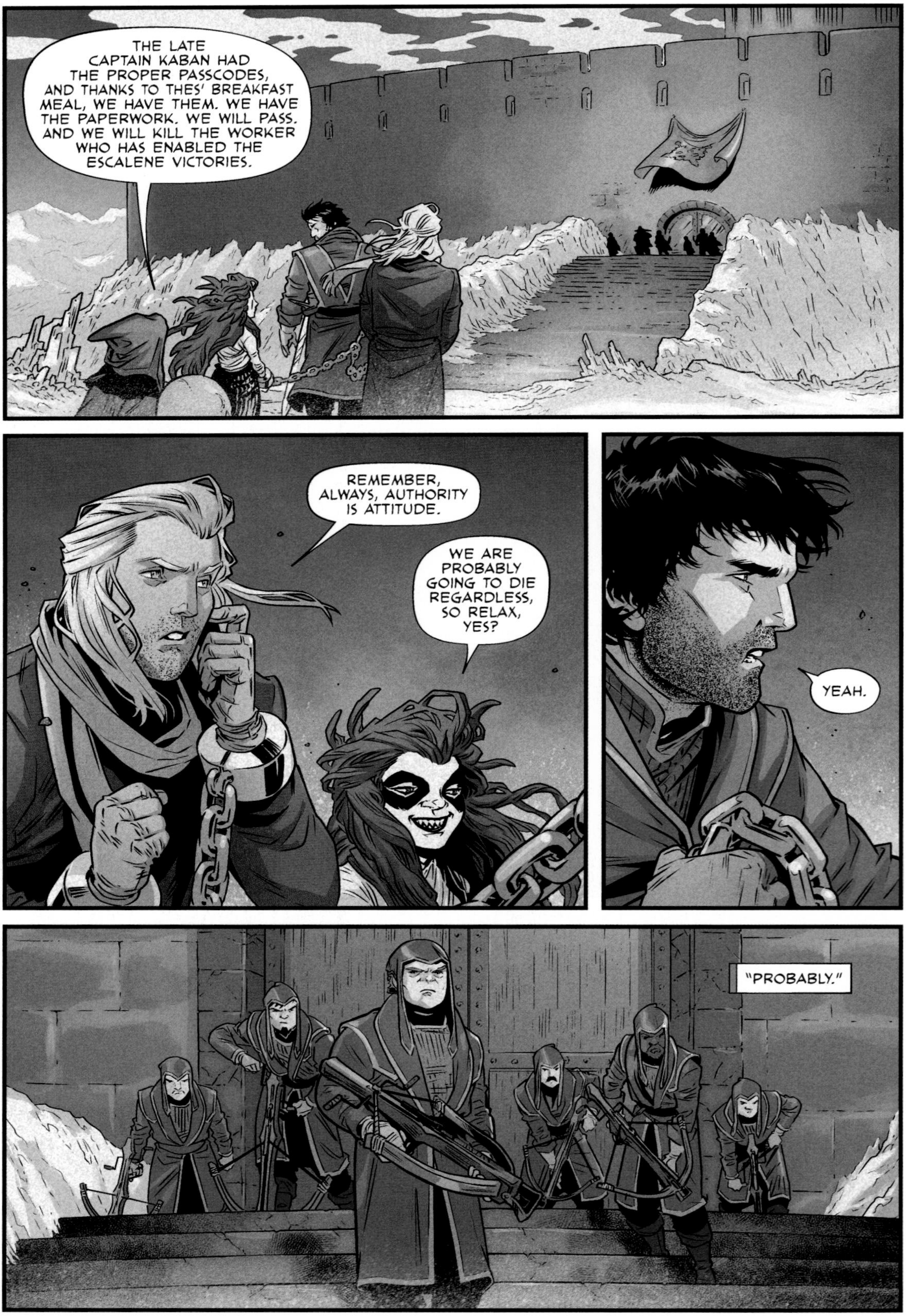
THE LATE CAPTAIN KABAN HAD THE PROPER PASSCODES, AND THANKS TO THES' BREAKFAST MEAL, WE HAVE THEM. WE HAVE THE PAPERWORK. WE WILL PASS. AND WE WILL KILL THE WORKER WHO HAS ENABLED THE ESCALENE VICTORIES.
REMEMBER, ALWAYS, AUTHORITY IS ATTITUDE.
WE ARE PROBABLY GOING TO DIE REGARDLESS, SO RELAX, YES?
YEAH.
"PROBABLY."

WHO THE FUCK ARE YOU?

I...I'M CAPTAIN KABAN. THESE PRISONERS WERE AT STRONGHOLD BREOUNT UNTIL THE FIRE.

PAPERS.

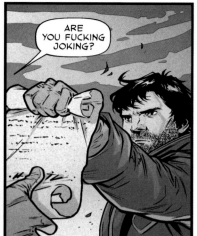

ARE YOU FUCKING JOKING?

THE PAPERS SHOULD ALL BE IN ORDER. THE PASSCODE IS BRILLIANT-FOREST-SEVEN-SEVEN. I...EVERYTHING SHOULD BE IN ORDER.

YEAH, WELL, IT ISN'T. THESE PAPERS LOOK LIKE A CHILD SIGNED THEM, WE HAVEN'T HAD ANY WORD ANYONE WAS COMING, AND I, FOR ONE, WOULD LIKE TO KNOW WHAT FUCKING ACCENT THAT IS YOU HAVE THERE, *CAPTAIN.*

IS NOT GOOD, THIS.

WHAT IS THE THIRD CODE OF THE STANDING ORDERS...

I...

PARAGRAPH C.

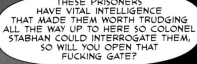

THE THIRD PARAGRAPH OF THE STANDING ORDERS IS THAT WHEN PRISONERS OF WAR ARE TAKEN, THEY ARE TO BE FED AND TREATED FOR ANY EXISTING WOUNDS, AND MY *ACCENT* IS BECAUSE I WAS ACTUALLY BORN IN ESCALENE, UNLIKE YOURS, WHICH I CAN ONLY ASSUME IS BECAUSE YOU WERE BORN WITH A MOUTH FULL OF SHIT.

THESE PRISONERS HAVE VITAL INTELLIGENCE THAT MADE THEM WORTH TRUDGING ALL THE WAY UP TO HERE SO COLONEL STABHAN COULD INTERROGATE THEM, SO WILL YOU OPEN THAT FUCKING GATE?

OPEN IT.

FUCK.

MY GOD.

YES...

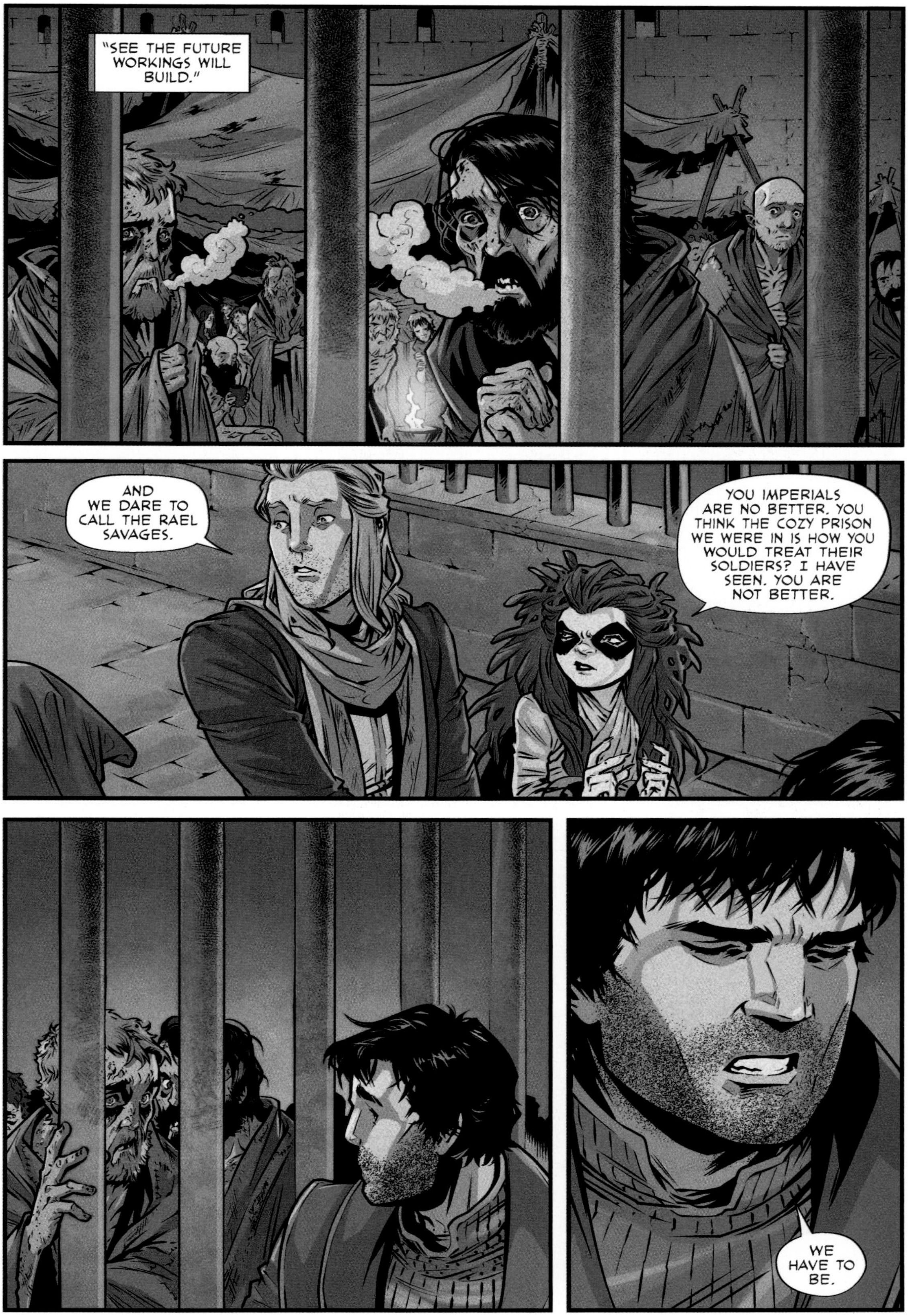
"SEE THE FUTURE WORKINGS WILL BUILD."
AND WE DARE TO CALL THE RAEL SAVAGES.
YOU IMPERIALS ARE NO BETTER. YOU THINK THE COZY PRISON WE WERE IN IS HOW YOU WOULD TREAT THEIR SOLDIERS? I HAVE SEEN. YOU ARE NOT BETTER.
WE HAVE TO BE.

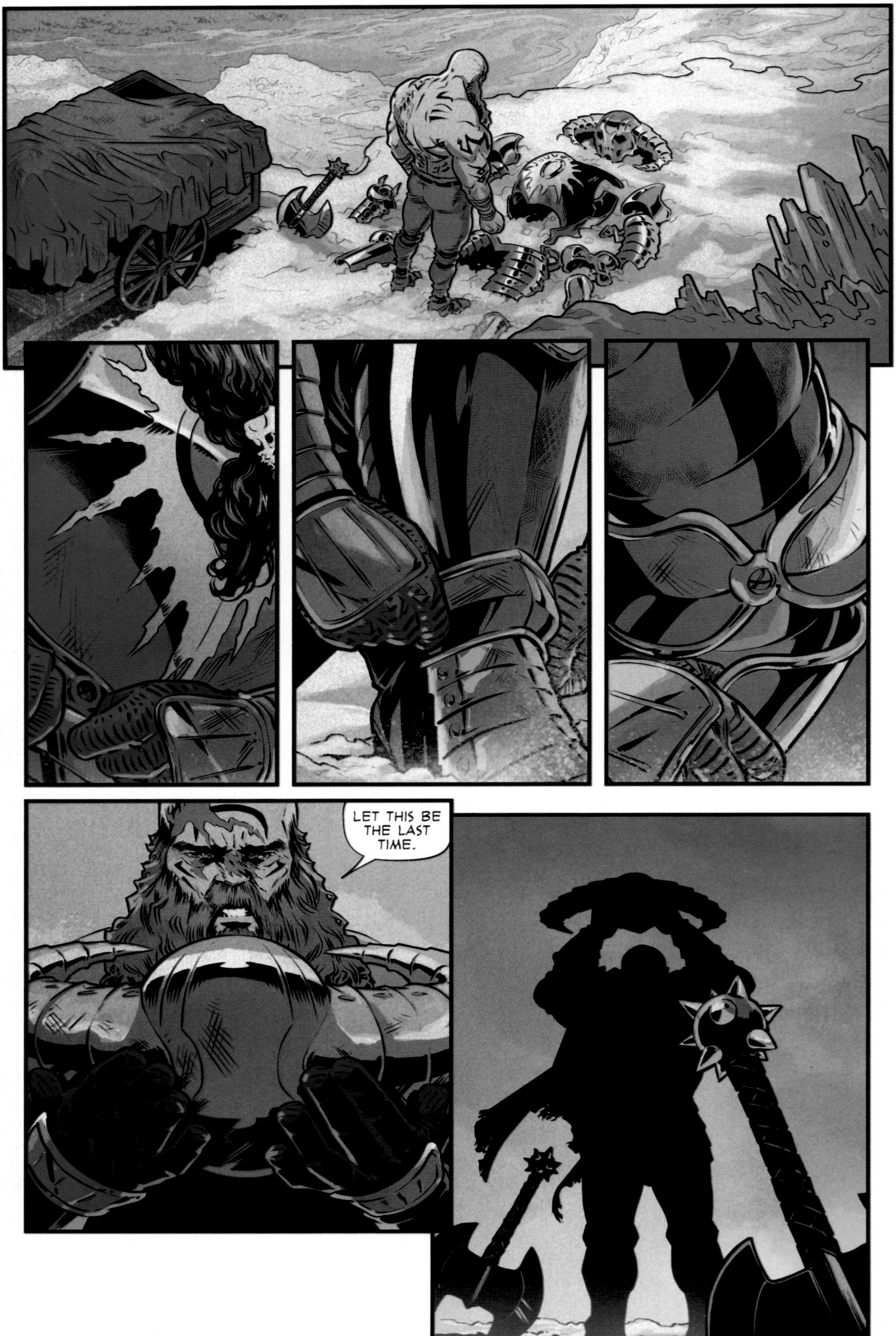
LET THIS BE THE LAST TIME.

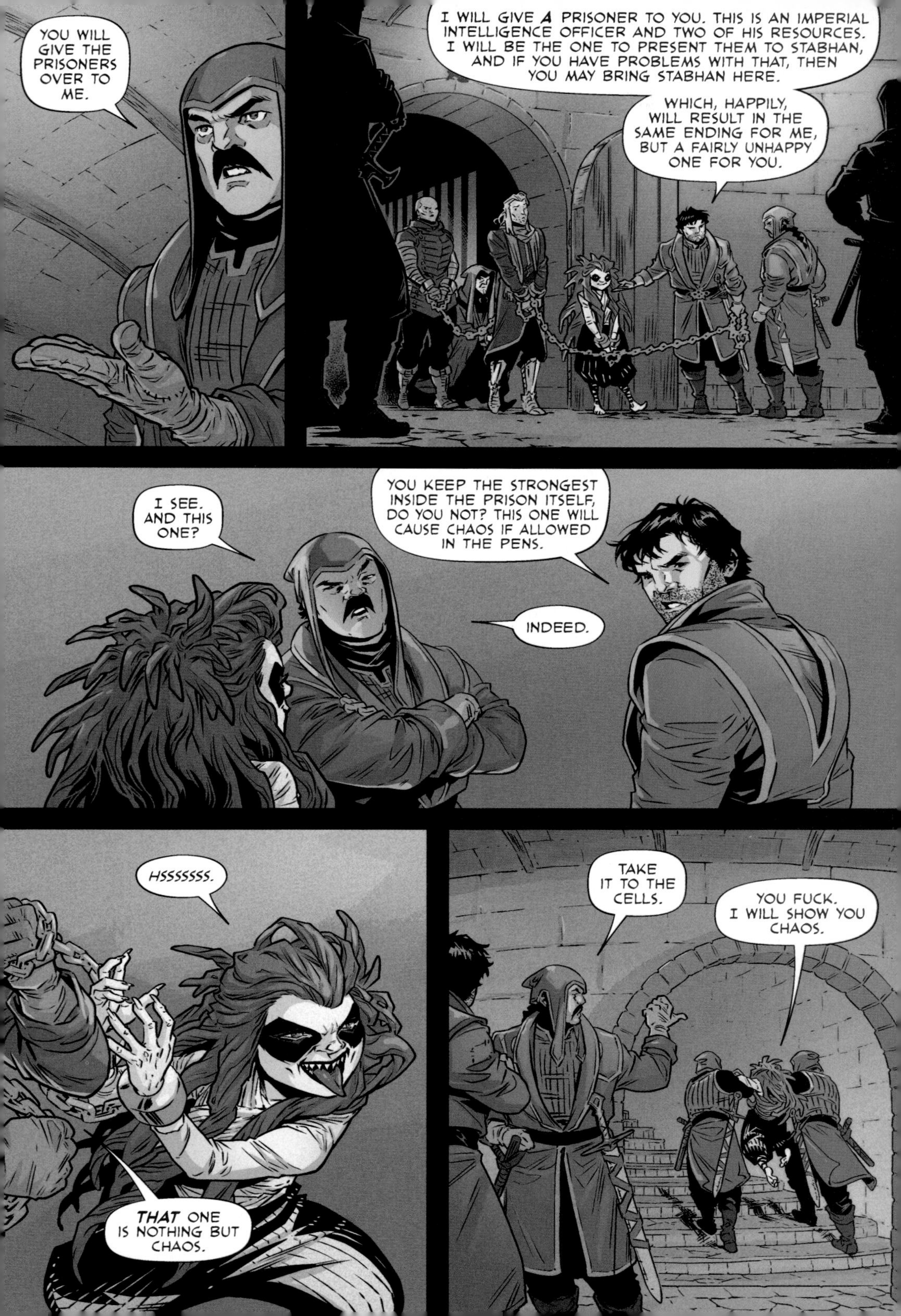
YOU WILL GIVE THE PRISONERS OVER TO ME.
I WILL GIVE A PRISONER TO YOU. THIS IS AN IMPERIAL INTELLIGENCE OFFICER AND TWO OF HIS RESOURCES. I WILL BE THE ONE TO PRESENT THEM TO STABHAN, AND IF YOU HAVE PROBLEMS WITH THAT, THEN YOU MAY BRING STABHAN HERE.
WHICH, HAPPILY, WILL RESULT IN THE SAME ENDING FOR ME, BUT A FAIRLY UNHAPPY ONE FOR YOU.
I SEE. AND THIS ONE?
YOU KEEP THE STRONGEST INSIDE THE PRISON ITSELF, DO YOU NOT? THIS ONE WILL CAUSE CHAOS IF ALLOWED IN THE PENS.
INDEED.
HSSSSSSS.
THAT ONE IS NOTHING BUT CHAOS.
TAKE IT TO THE CELLS.
YOU FUCK. I WILL SHOW YOU CHAOS.

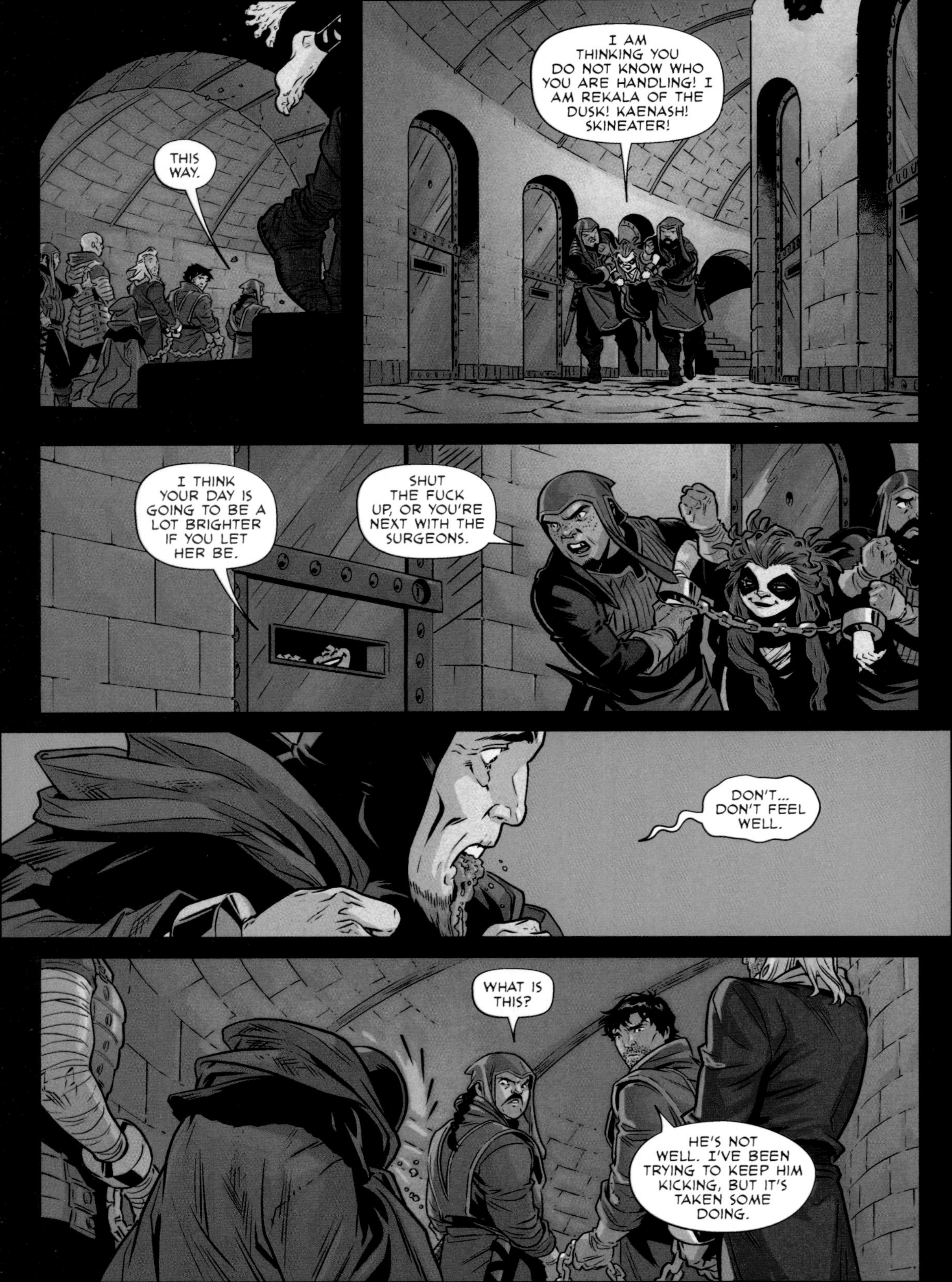
THIS WAY.
I AM THINKING YOU DO NOT KNOW WHO YOU ARE HANDLING! I AM REKALA OF THE DUSK! KAENASH! SKINEATER!
I THINK YOUR DAY IS GOING TO BE A LOT BRIGHTER IF YOU LET HER BE.
SHUT THE FUCK UP, OR YOU'RE NEXT WITH THE SURGEONS.
DON'T... DON'T FEEL WELL.
WHAT IS THIS?
HE'S NOT WELL. I'VE BEEN TRYING TO KEEP HIM KICKING, BUT IT'S TAKEN SOME DOING.

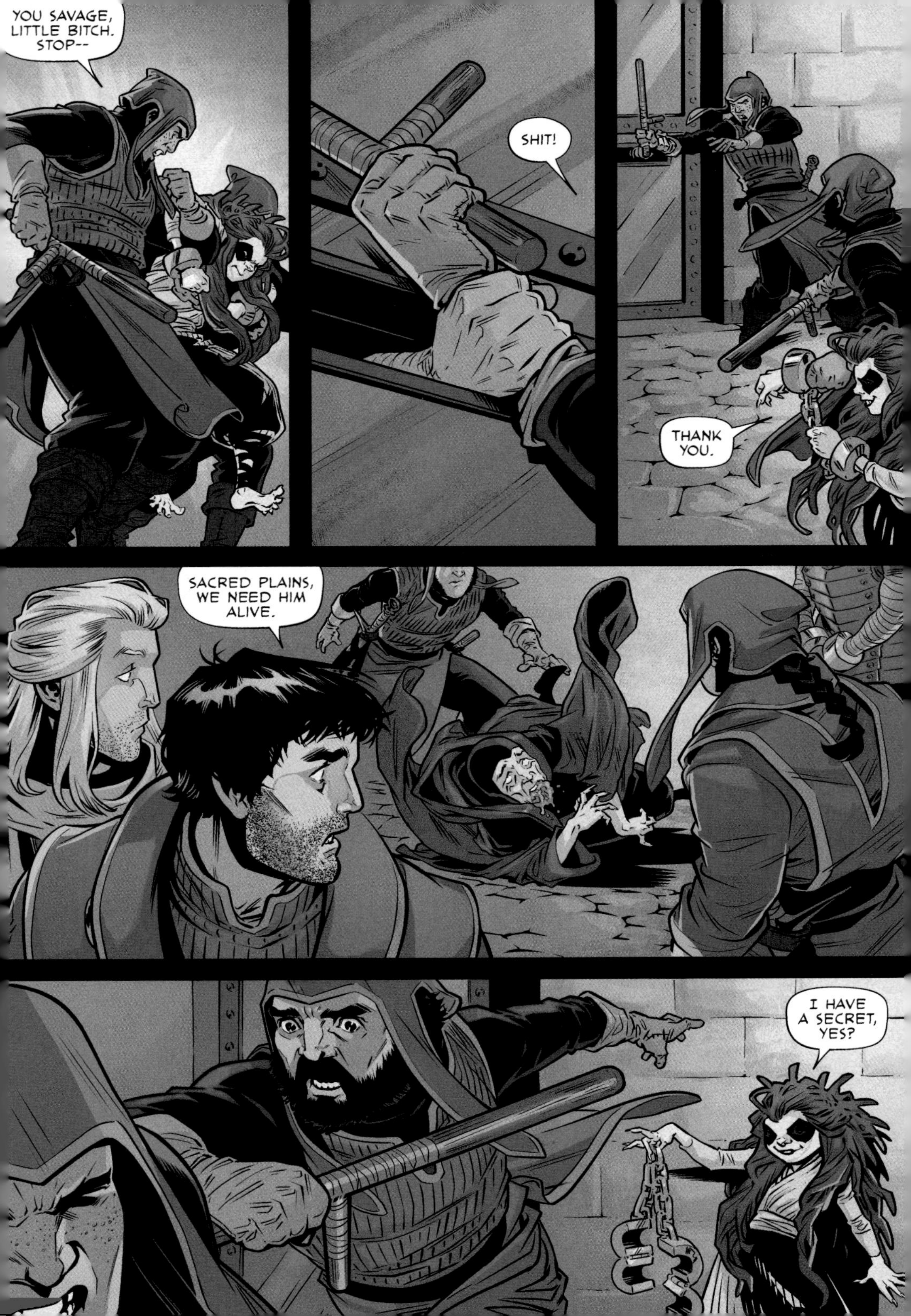
YOU SAVAGE, LITTLE BITCH. STOP--
SHIT!
THANK YOU.
SACRED PLAINS, WE NEED HIM ALIVE.
I HAVE A SECRET, YES?

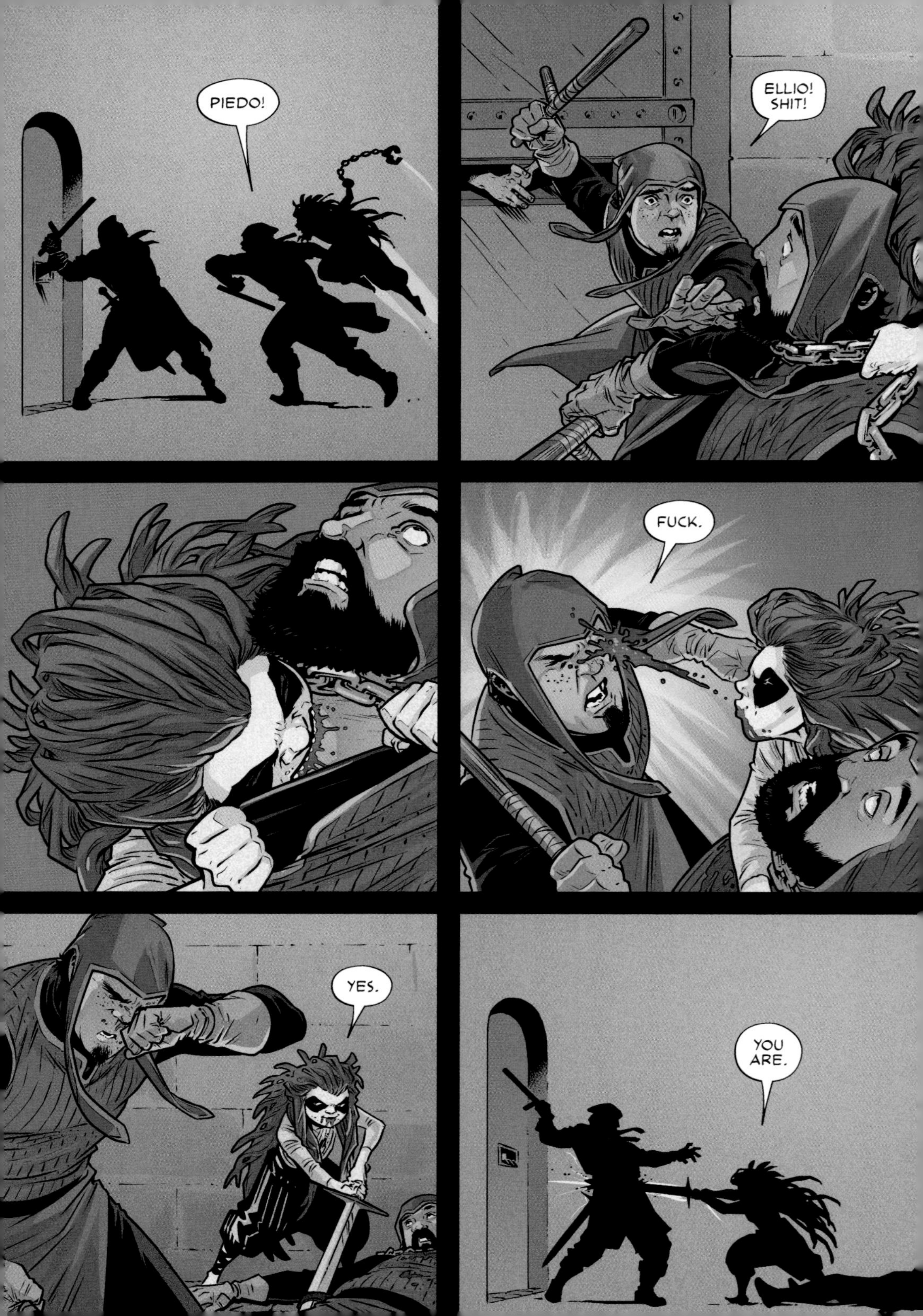
PIEDO!
ELLIO! SHIT!
FUCK.
YES.
YOU ARE.

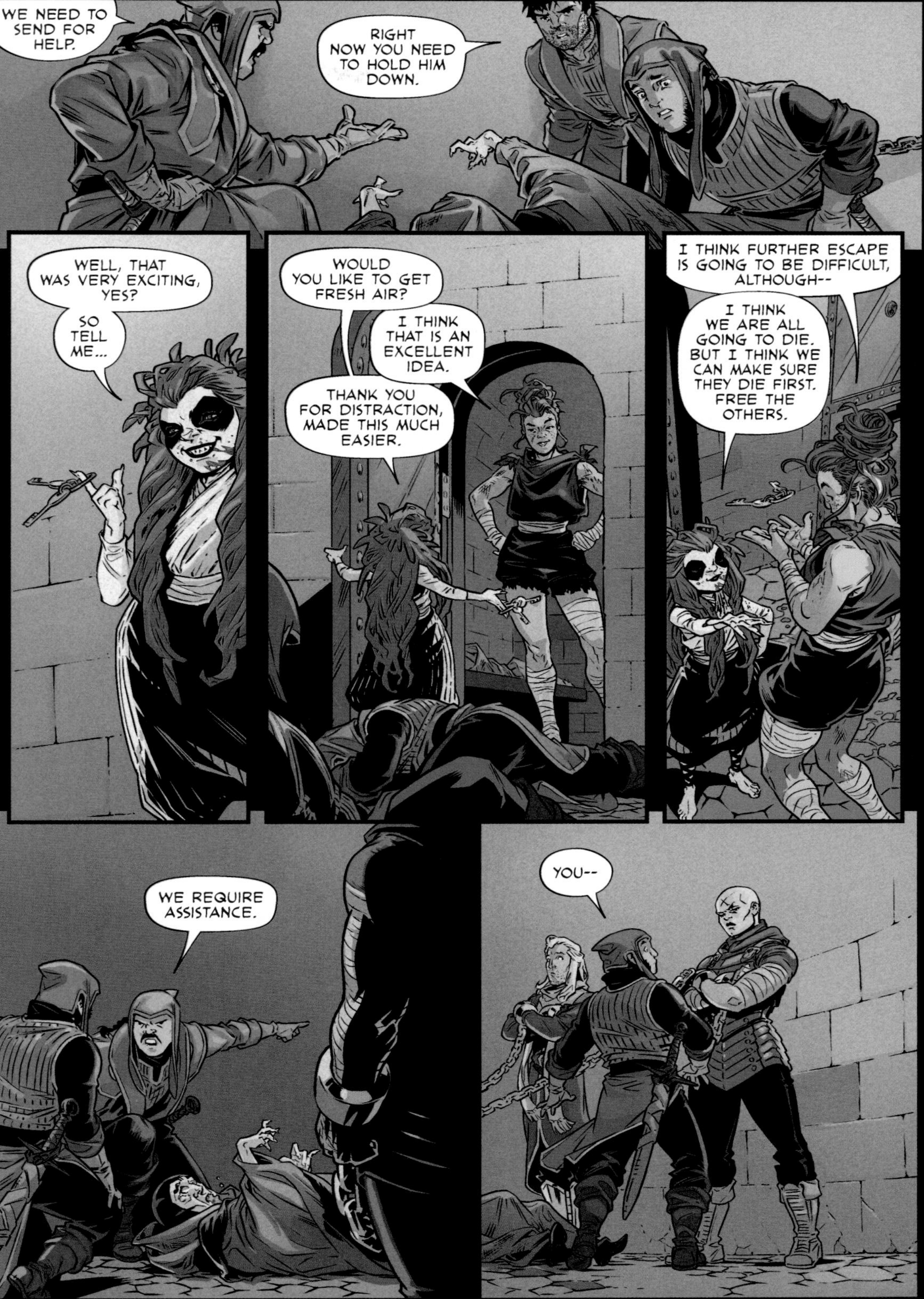
WE NEED TO SEND FOR HELP.
RIGHT NOW YOU NEED TO HOLD HIM DOWN.
WELL, THAT WAS VERY EXCITING, YES?
SO TELL ME...
WOULD YOU LIKE TO GET FRESH AIR?
I THINK THAT IS AN EXCELLENT IDEA.
THANK YOU FOR DISTRACTION, MADE THIS MUCH EASIER.
I THINK FURTHER ESCAPE IS GOING TO BE DIFFICULT, ALTHOUGH--
I THINK WE ARE ALL GOING TO DIE. BUT I THINK WE CAN MAKE SURE THEY DIE FIRST. FREE THE OTHERS.
WE REQUIRE ASSISTANCE.
YOU--

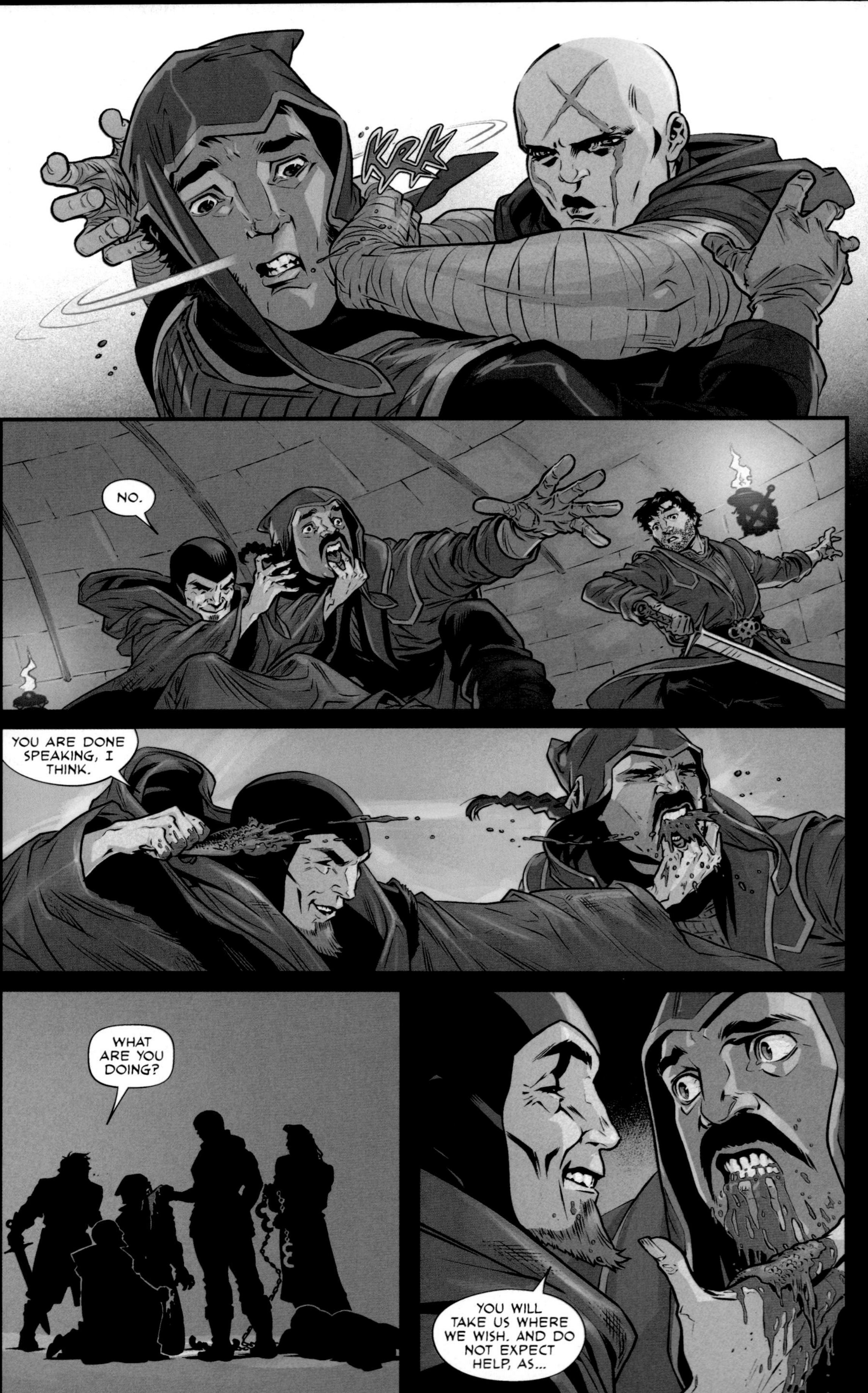
KRK
NO.
YOU ARE DONE SPEAKING, I THINK.
WHAT ARE YOU DOING?
YOU WILL TAKE US WHERE WE WISH. AND DO NOT EXPECT HELP, AS...

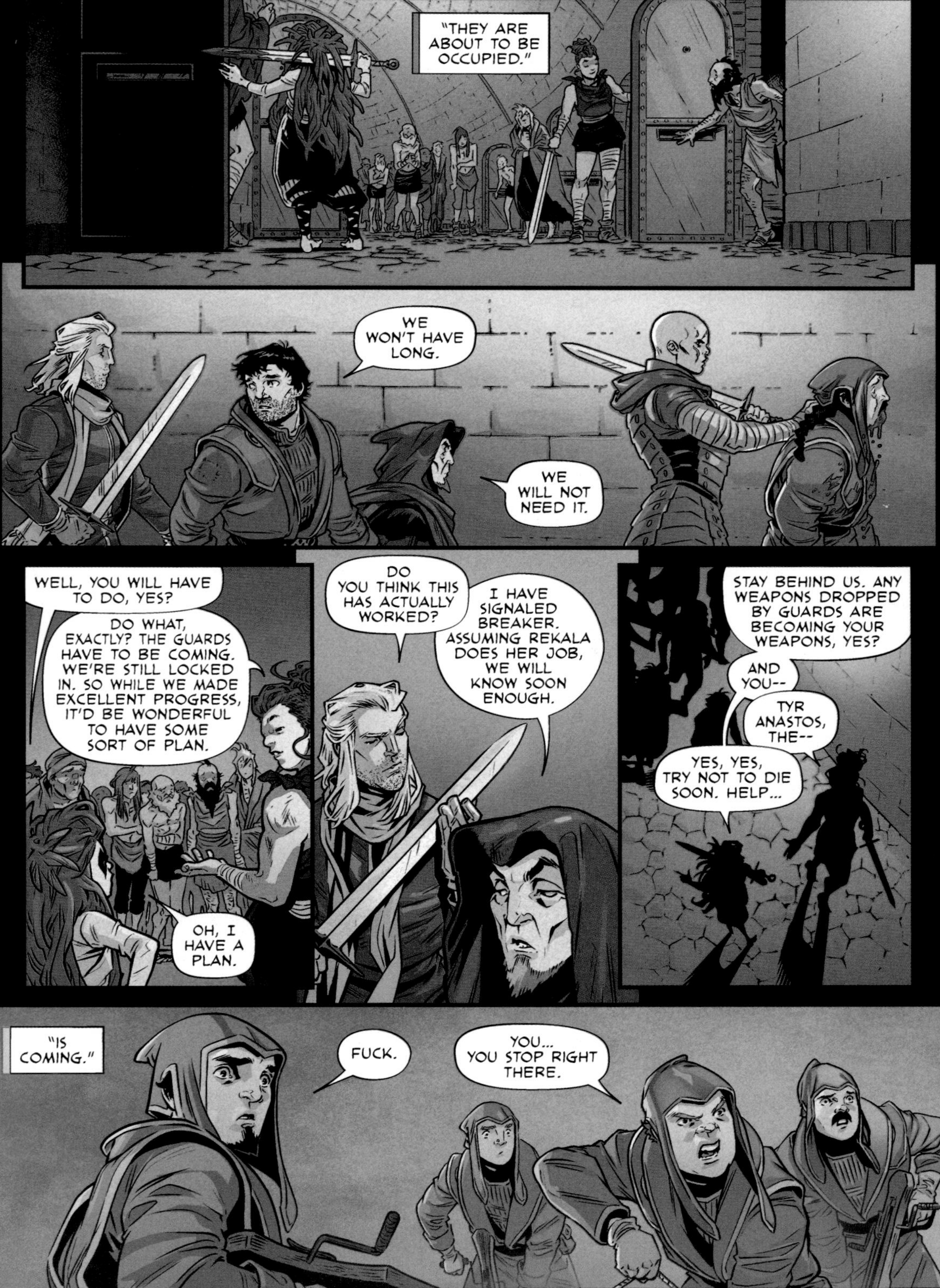
"THEY ARE ABOUT TO BE OCCUPIED."
WE WON'T HAVE LONG.
WE WILL NOT NEED IT.
WELL, YOU WILL HAVE TO DO, YES?
DO WHAT, EXACTLY? THE GUARDS HAVE TO BE COMING. WE'RE STILL LOCKED IN. SO WHILE WE MADE EXCELLENT PROGRESS, IT'D BE WONDERFUL TO HAVE SOME SORT OF PLAN.
OH, I HAVE A PLAN.
DO YOU THINK THIS HAS ACTUALLY WORKED?
I HAVE SIGNALED BREAKER. ASSUMING REKALA DOES HER JOB, WE WILL KNOW SOON ENOUGH.
STAY BEHIND US. ANY WEAPONS DROPPED BY GUARDS ARE BECOMING YOUR WEAPONS, YES?
AND YOU--
TYR ANASTOS, THE--
YES, YES, TRY NOT TO DIE SOON. HELP...
"IS COMING."
FUCK.
YOU... YOU STOP RIGHT THERE.

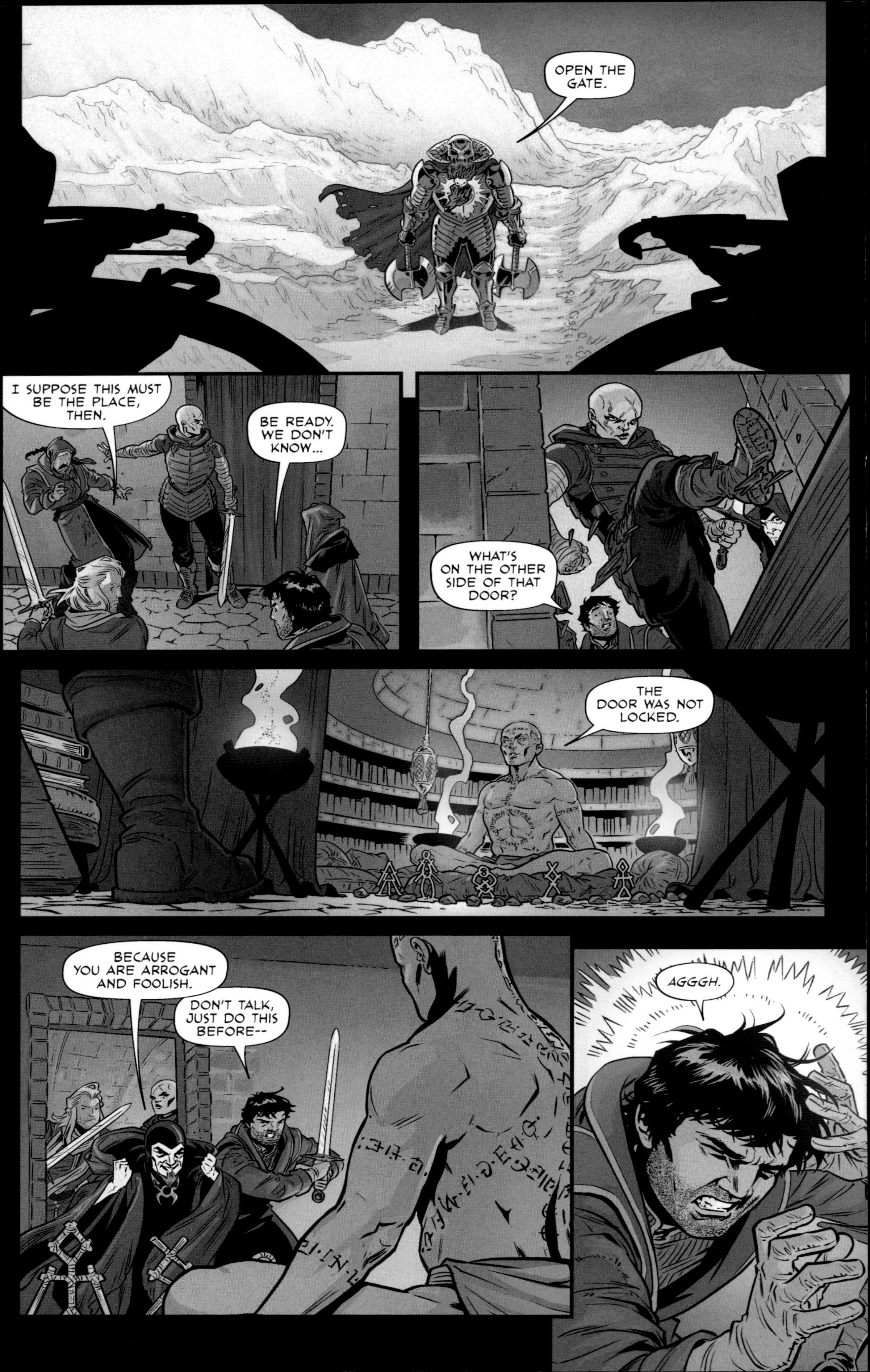
OPEN THE GATE.
I SUPPOSE THIS MUST BE THE PLACE, THEN.
BE READY. WE DON'T KNOW...
WHAT'S ON THE OTHER SIDE OF THAT DOOR?
THE DOOR WAS NOT LOCKED.
BECAUSE YOU ARE ARROGANT AND FOOLISH.
DON'T TALK, JUST DO THIS BEFORE--
AGGGH.

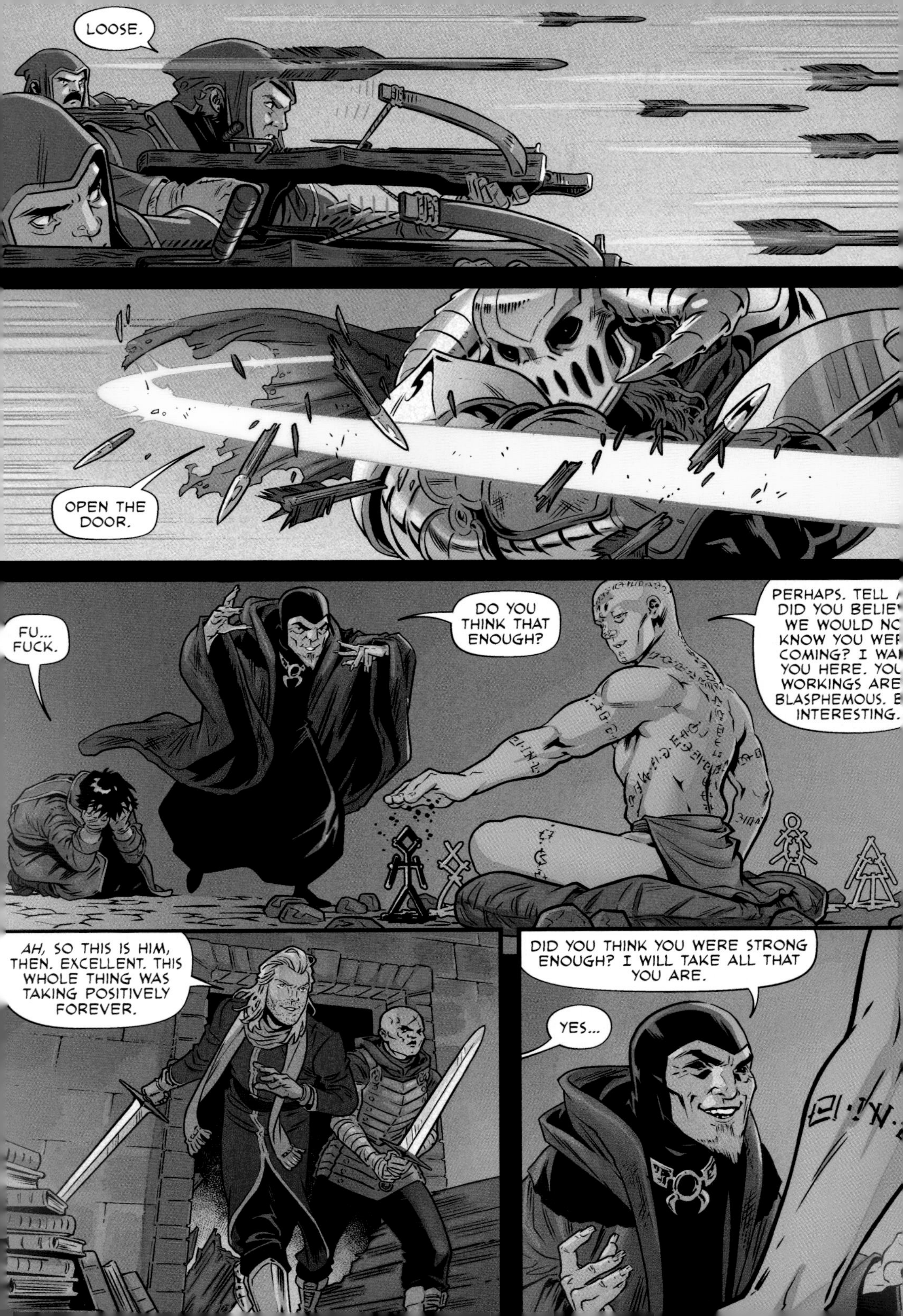
LOOSE.
OPEN THE DOOR.
FU... FUCK.
DO YOU THINK THAT ENOUGH?
PERHAPS. TELL DID YOU BELIE WE WOULD NO KNOW YOU WER COMING? I WA YOU HERE. YOU WORKINGS ARE BLASPHEMOUS. B INTERESTING.
AH, SO THIS IS HIM, THEN. EXCELLENT. THIS WHOLE THING WAS TAKING POSITIVELY FOREVER.
DID YOU THINK YOU WERE STRONG ENOUGH? I WILL TAKE ALL THAT YOU ARE.
YES...

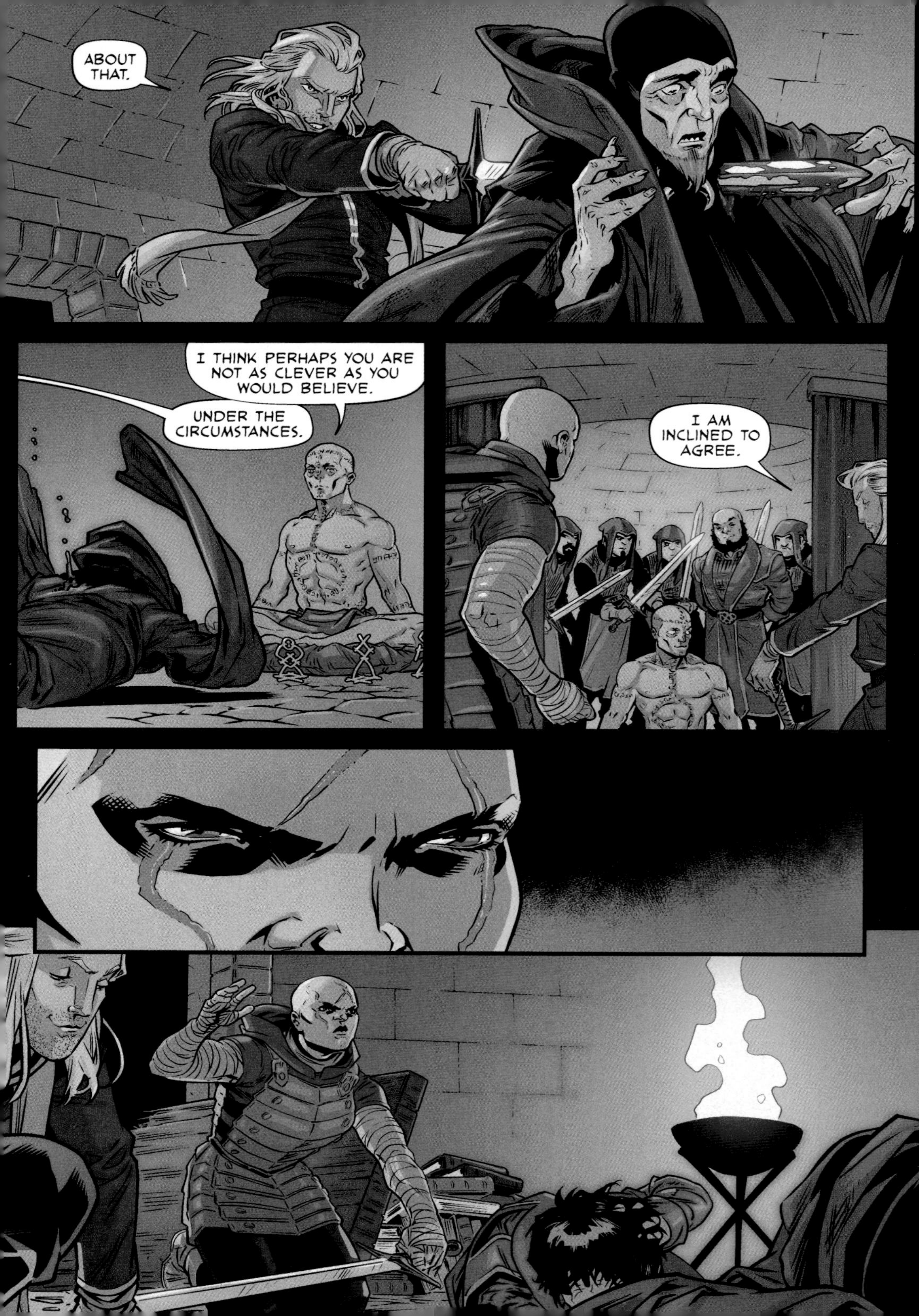
ABOUT THAT.
I THINK PERHAPS YOU ARE NOT AS CLEVER AS YOU WOULD BELIEVE.
UNDER THE CIRCUMSTANCES.
I AM INCLINED TO AGREE.

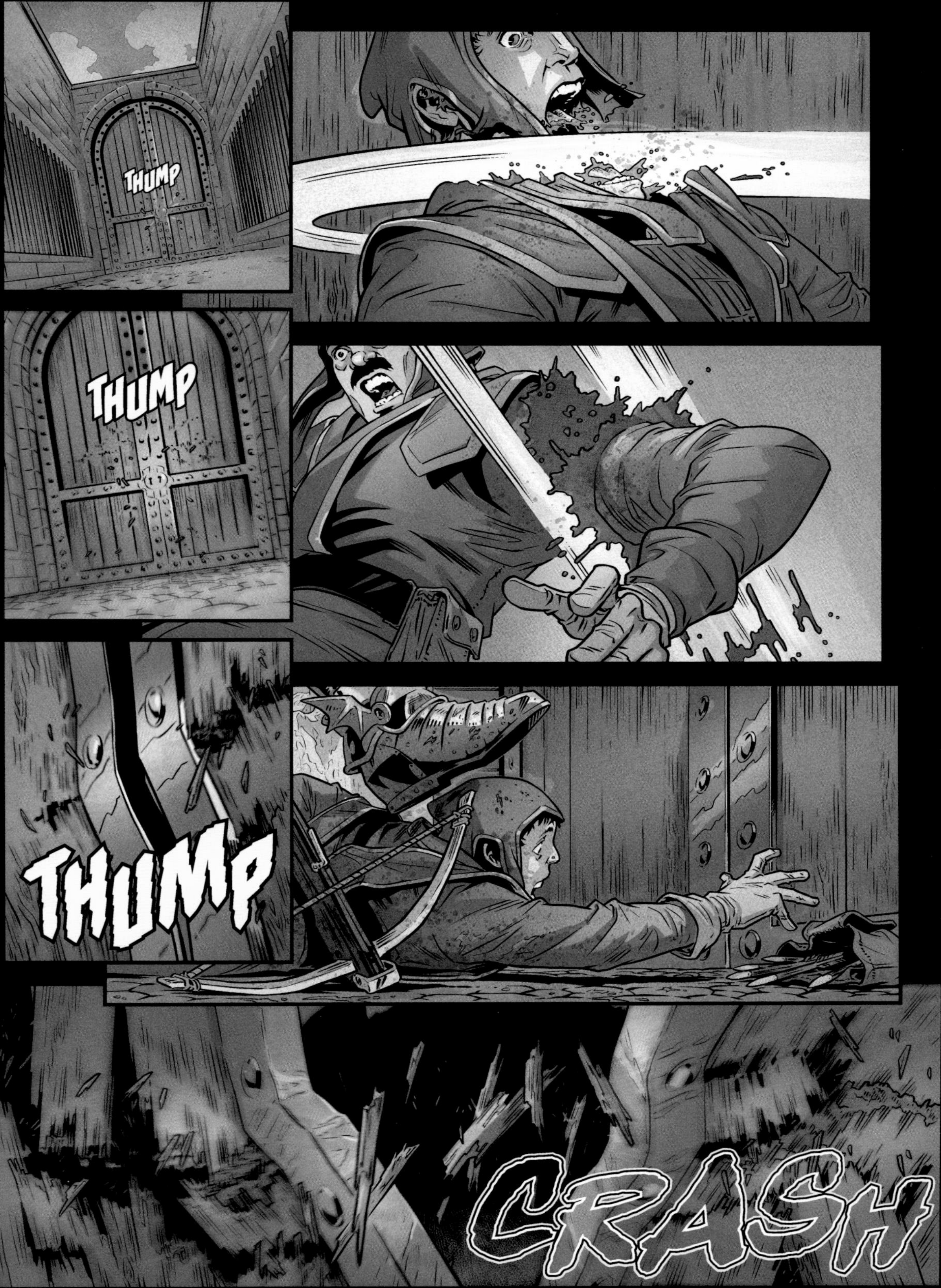
THUMP
THUMP
THUMP
CRASH

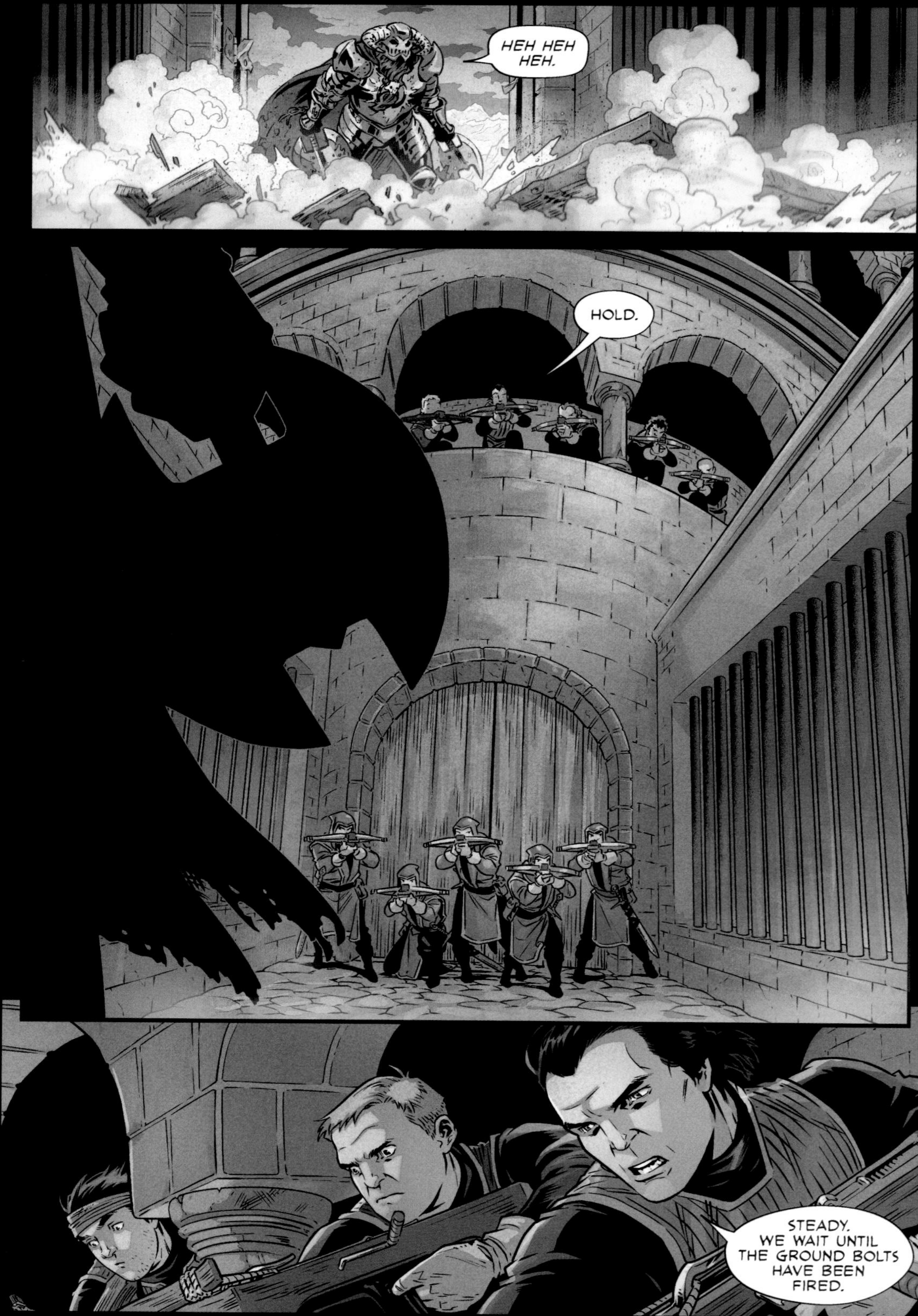
HEH HEH HEH.
HOLD.
STEADY. WE WAIT UNTIL THE GROUND BOLTS HAVE BEEN FIRED.

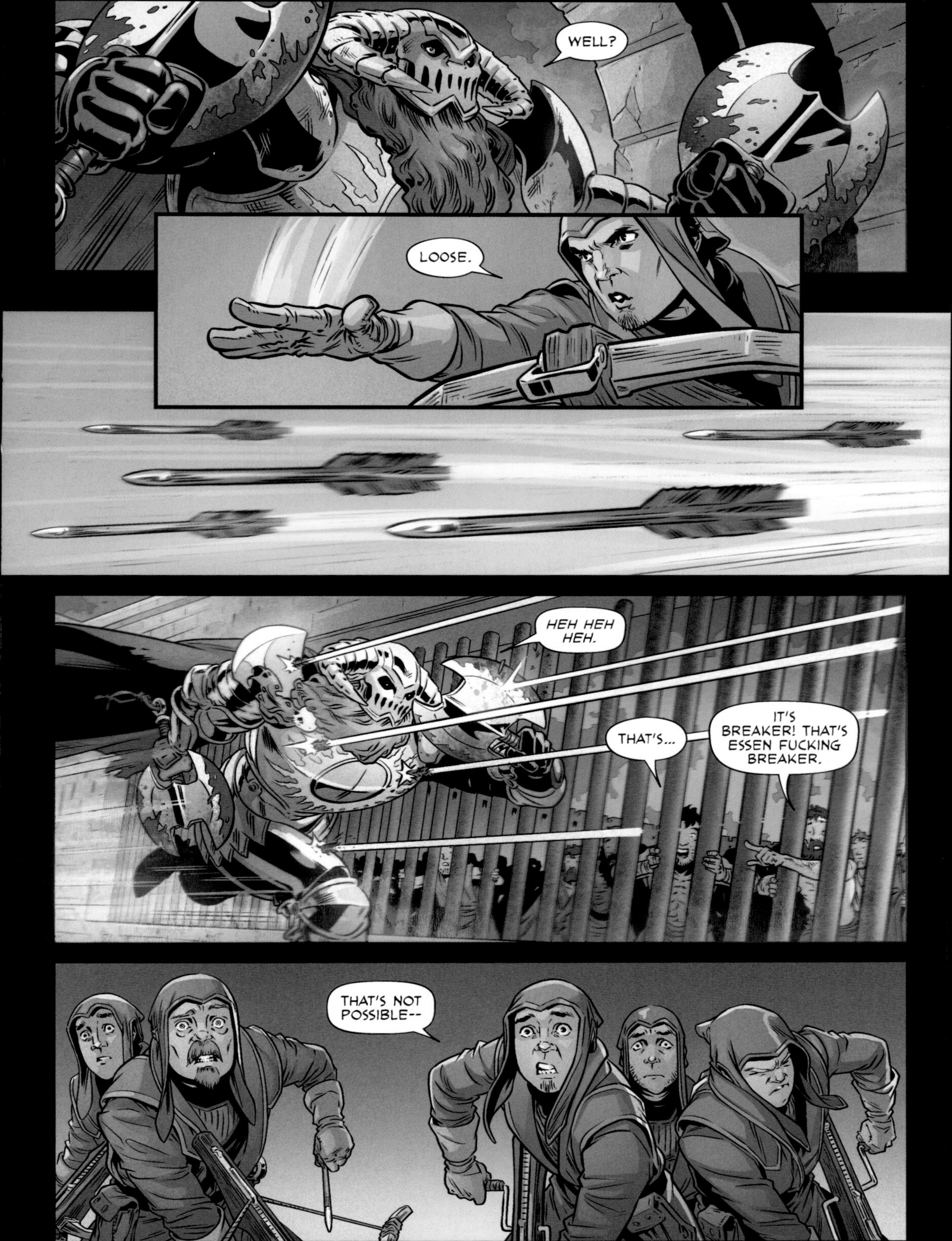
WELL?
LOOSE.
HEH HEH HEH.
THAT'S...
IT'S BREAKER! THAT'S ESSEN FUCKING BREAKER.
THAT'S NOT POSSIBLE--

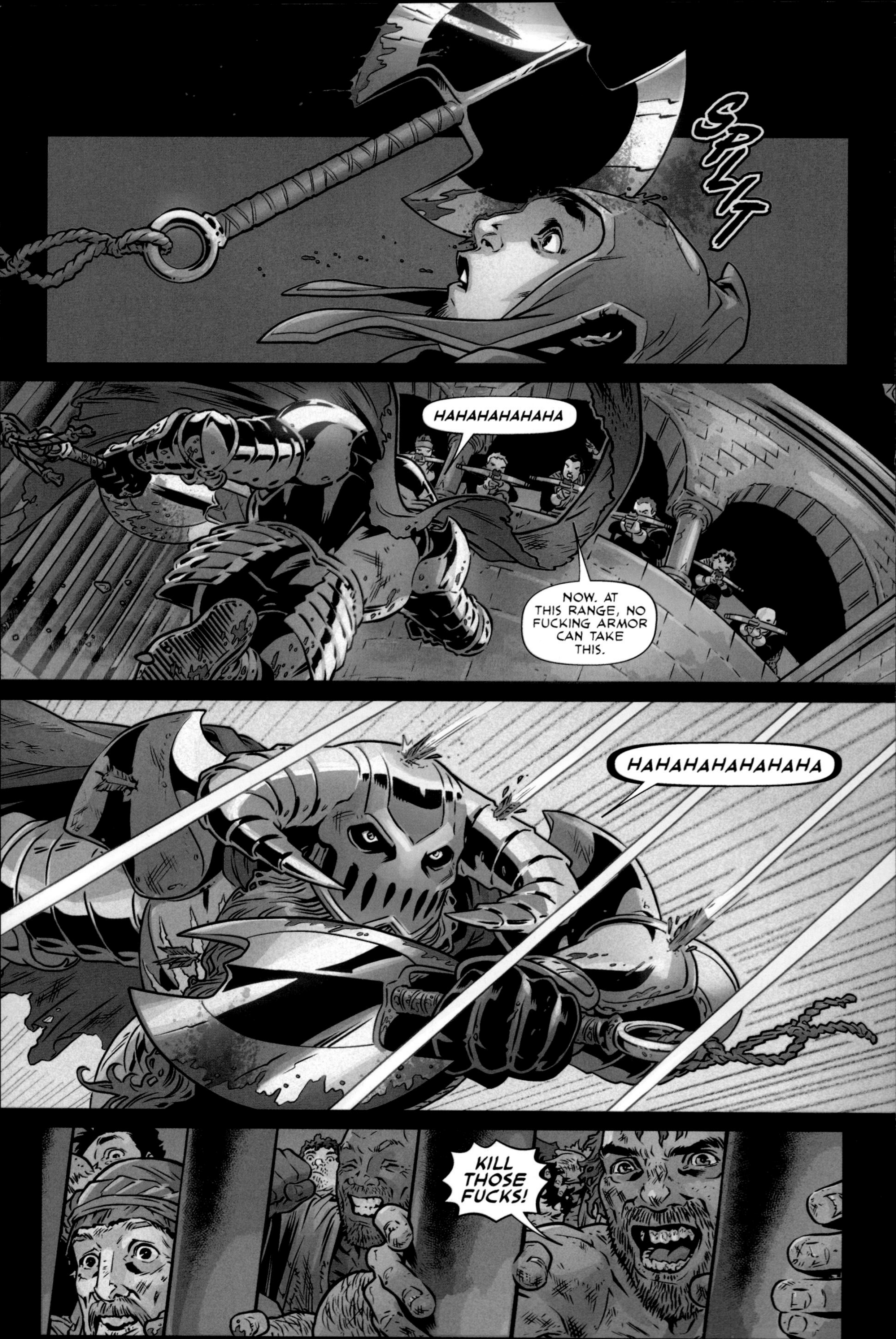
SPLIT
HAHAHAHAHAHA
NOW. AT THIS RANGE, NO FUCKING ARMOR CAN TAKE THIS.
HAHAHAHAHAHAHA
KILL THOSE FUCKS!

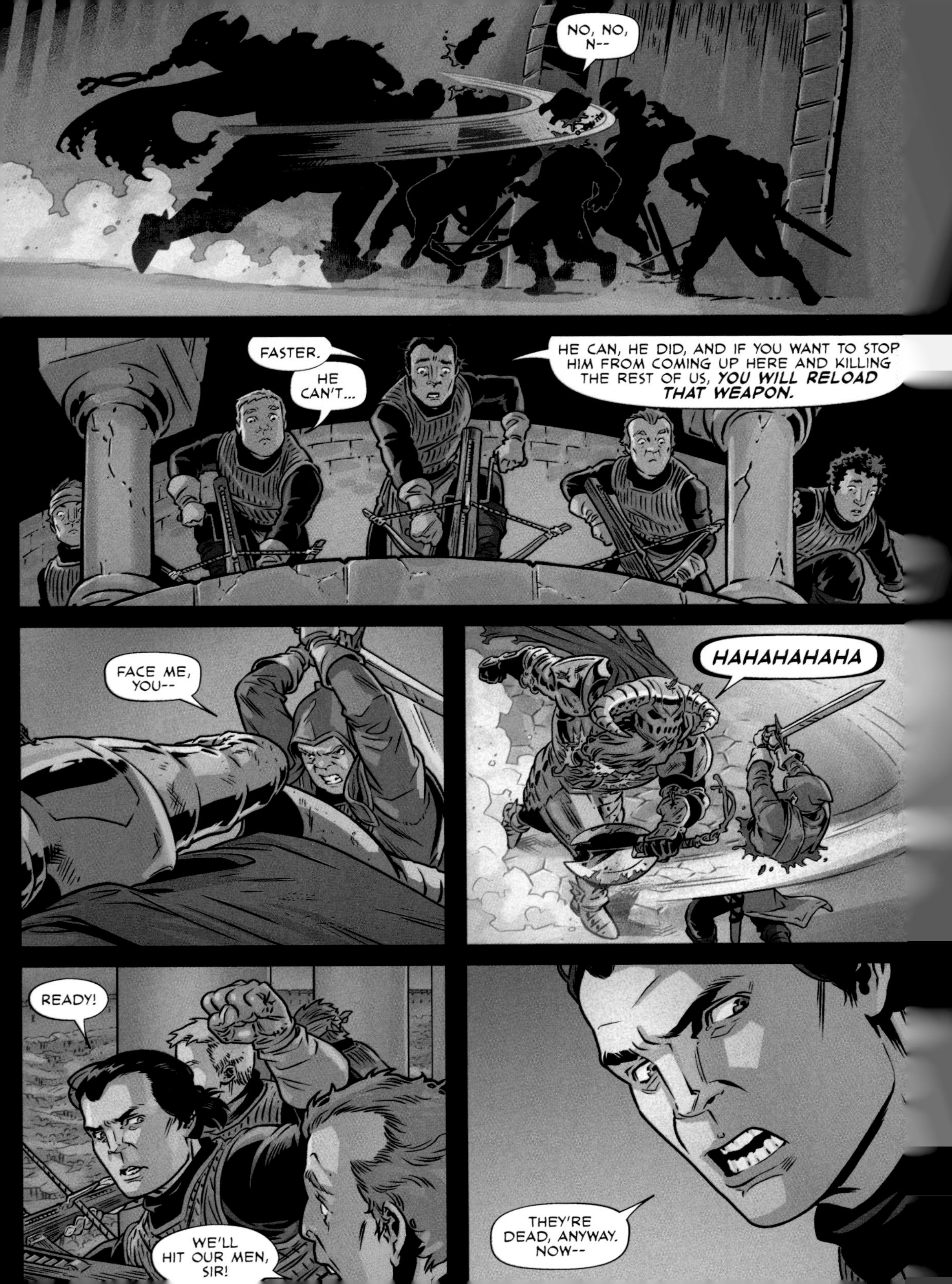
NO, NO, N--
FASTER.
HE CAN'T...
HE CAN, HE DID, AND IF YOU WANT TO STOP HIM FROM COMING UP HERE AND KILLING THE REST OF US, *YOU WILL RELOAD THAT WEAPON.*
FACE ME, YOU--
HAHAHAHAHA
READY!
WE'LL HIT OUR MEN, SIR!
THEY'RE DEAD, ANYWAY. NOW--

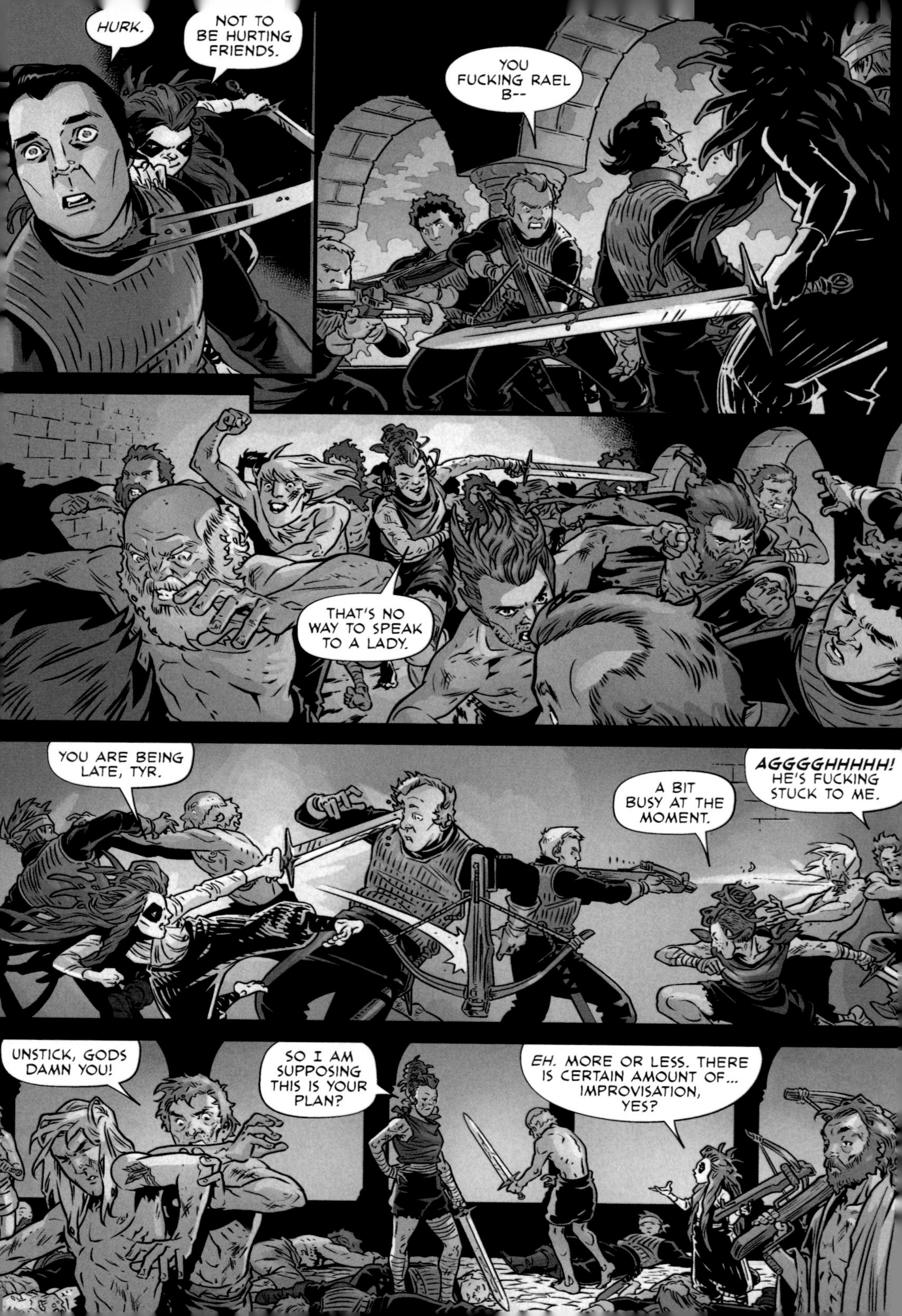
HURK.
NOT TO BE HURTING FRIENDS.
YOU FUCKING RAEL B--
THAT'S NO WAY TO SPEAK TO A LADY.
YOU ARE BEING LATE, TYR.
A BIT BUSY AT THE MOMENT.
AGGGGHHHHH! HE'S FUCKING STUCK TO ME.
UNSTICK, GODS DAMN YOU!
SO I AM SUPPOSING THIS IS YOUR PLAN?
EH. MORE OR LESS. THERE IS CERTAIN AMOUNT OF... IMPROVISATION, YES?

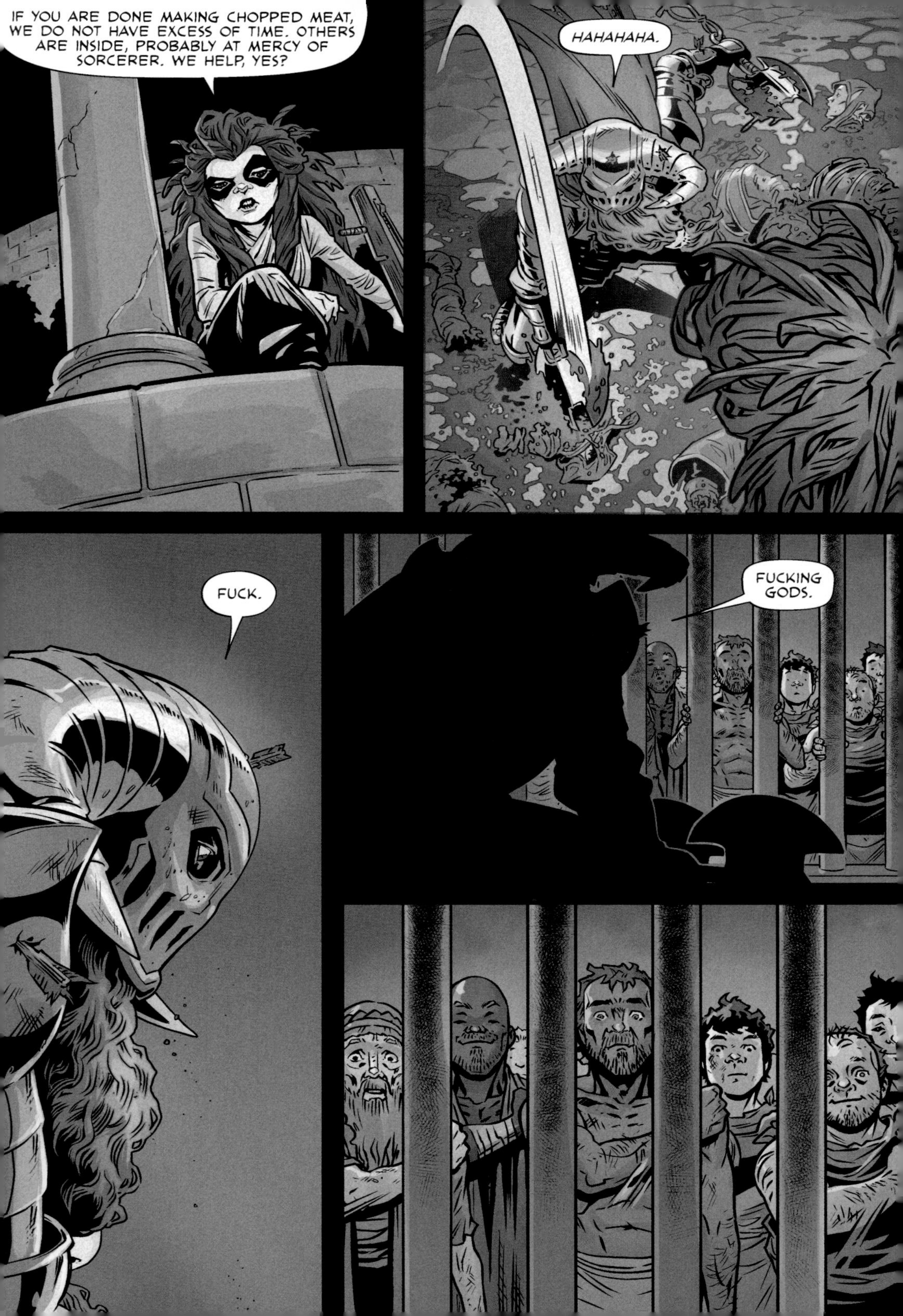
IF YOU ARE DONE MAKING CHOPPED MEAT, WE DO NOT HAVE EXCESS OF TIME. OTHERS ARE INSIDE, PROBABLY AT MERCY OF SORCERER. WE HELP, YES?
HAHAHAHA.
FUCK.
FUCKING GODS.

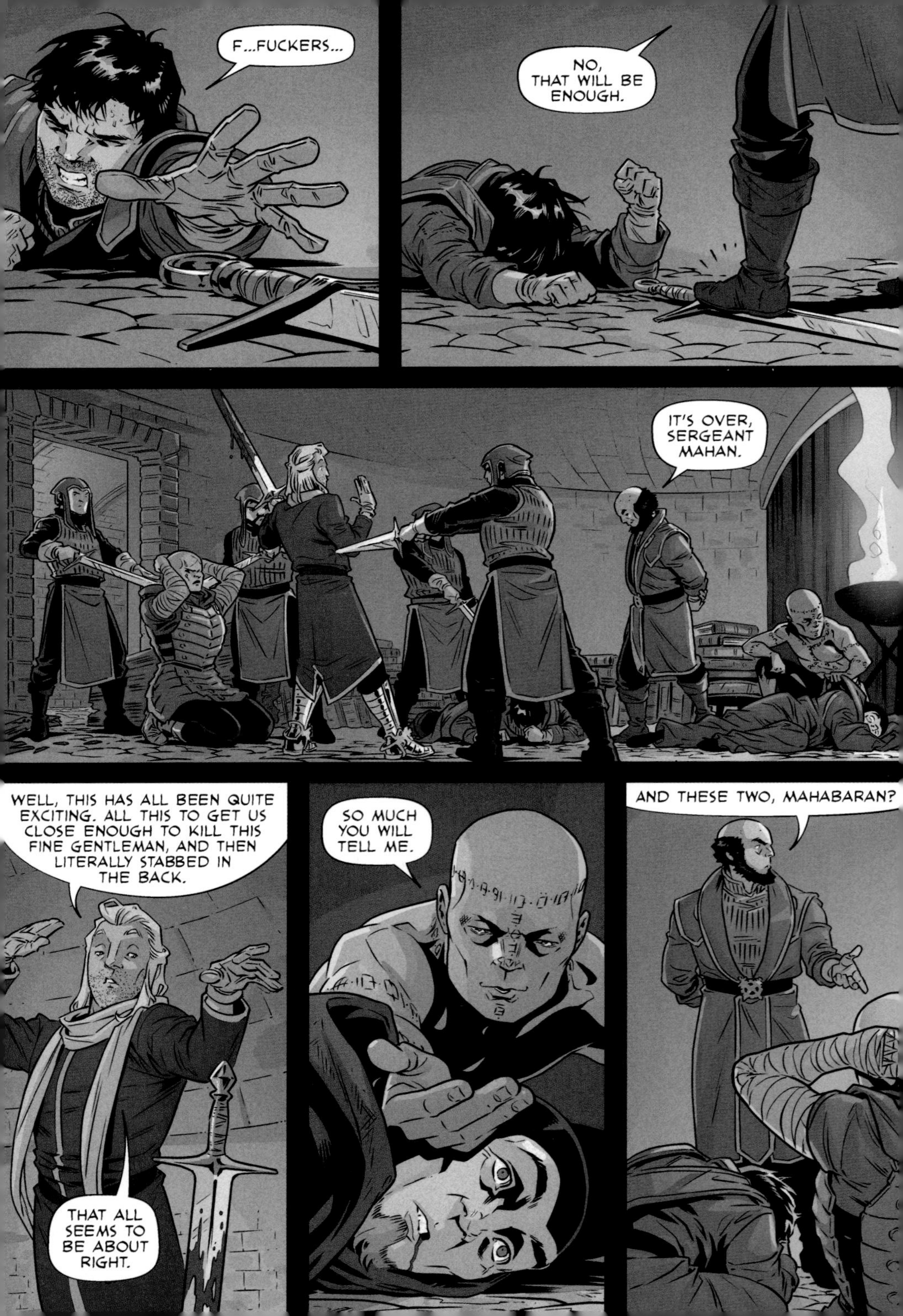
F...FUCKERS...
NO, THAT WILL BE ENOUGH.
IT'S OVER, SERGEANT MAHAN.
WELL, THIS HAS ALL BEEN QUITE EXCITING. ALL THIS TO GET US CLOSE ENOUGH TO KILL THIS FINE GENTLEMAN, AND THEN LITERALLY STABBED IN THE BACK.
THAT ALL SEEMS TO BE ABOUT RIGHT.
SO MUCH YOU WILL TELL ME.
AND THESE TWO, MAHABARAN?

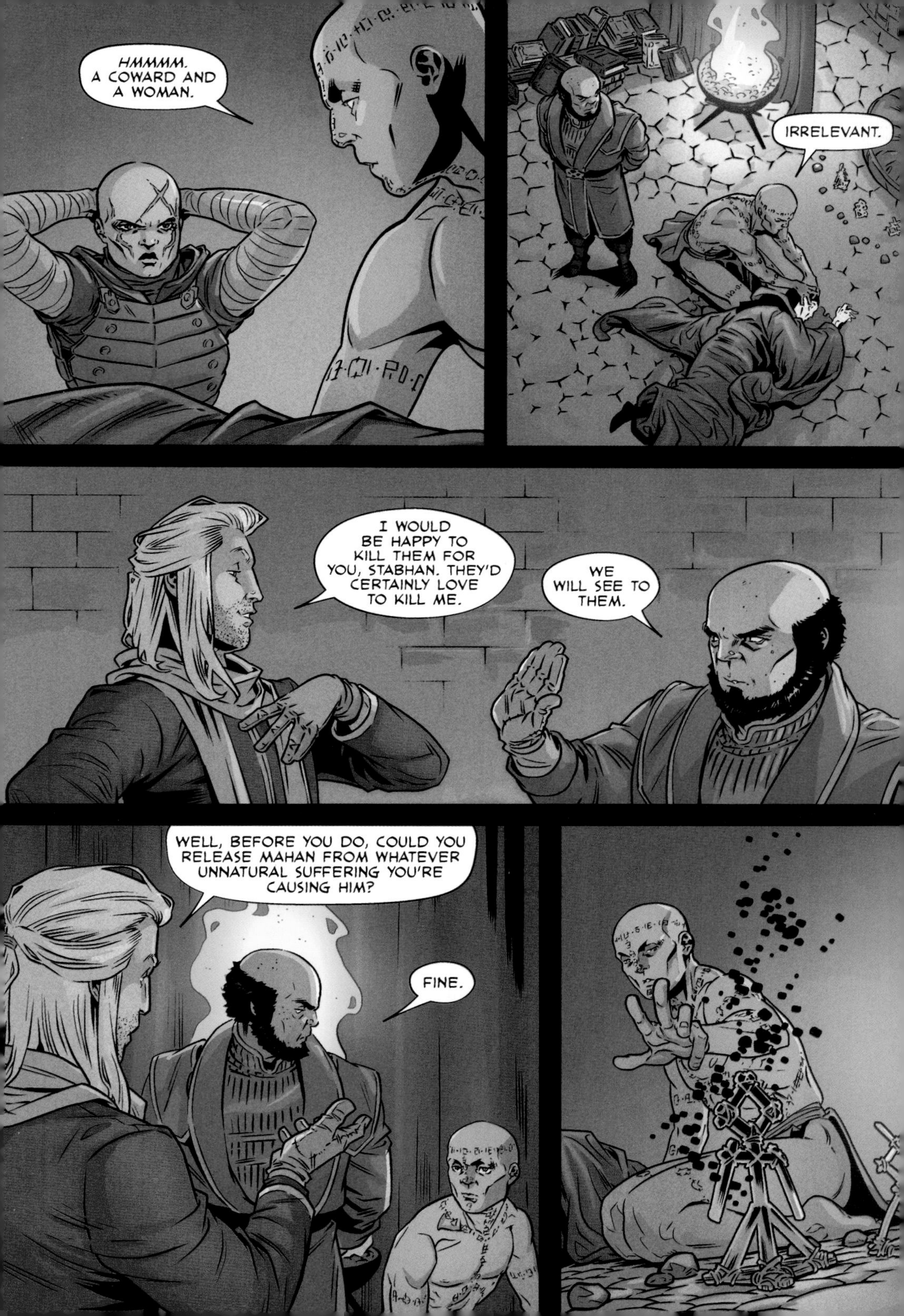
HMMMM. A COWARD AND A WOMAN.
IRRELEVANT.
I WOULD BE HAPPY TO KILL THEM FOR YOU, STABHAN. THEY'D CERTAINLY LOVE TO KILL ME.
WE WILL SEE TO THEM.
WELL, BEFORE YOU DO, COULD YOU RELEASE MAHAN FROM WHATEVER UNNATURAL SUFFERING YOU'RE CAUSING HIM?
FINE.

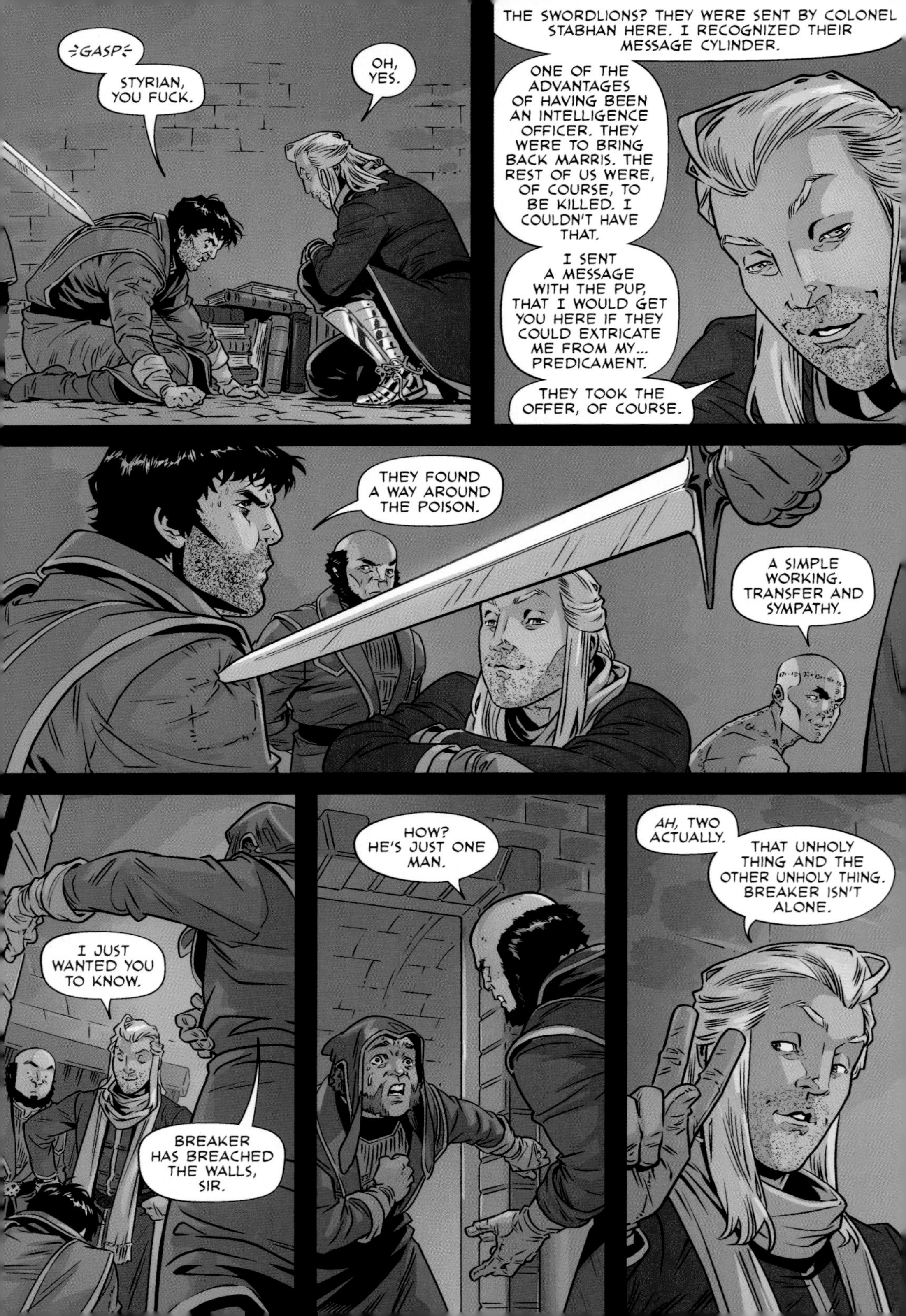

⇉GASP⇇
STYRIAN, YOU FUCK.
OH, YES.
THE SWORDLIONS? THEY WERE SENT BY COLONEL STABHAN HERE. I RECOGNIZED THEIR MESSAGE CYLINDER.
ONE OF THE ADVANTAGES OF HAVING BEEN AN INTELLIGENCE OFFICER. THEY WERE TO BRING BACK MARRIS. THE REST OF US WERE, OF COURSE, TO BE KILLED. I COULDN'T HAVE THAT.
I SENT A MESSAGE WITH THE PUP, THAT I WOULD GET YOU HERE IF THEY COULD EXTRICATE ME FROM MY... PREDICAMENT.
THEY TOOK THE OFFER, OF COURSE.
THEY FOUND A WAY AROUND THE POISON.
A SIMPLE WORKING. TRANSFER AND SYMPATHY.
I JUST WANTED YOU TO KNOW.
BREAKER HAS BREACHED THE WALLS, SIR.
HOW? HE'S JUST ONE MAN.
AH, TWO ACTUALLY.
THAT UNHOLY THING AND THE OTHER UNHOLY THING. BREAKER ISN'T ALONE.

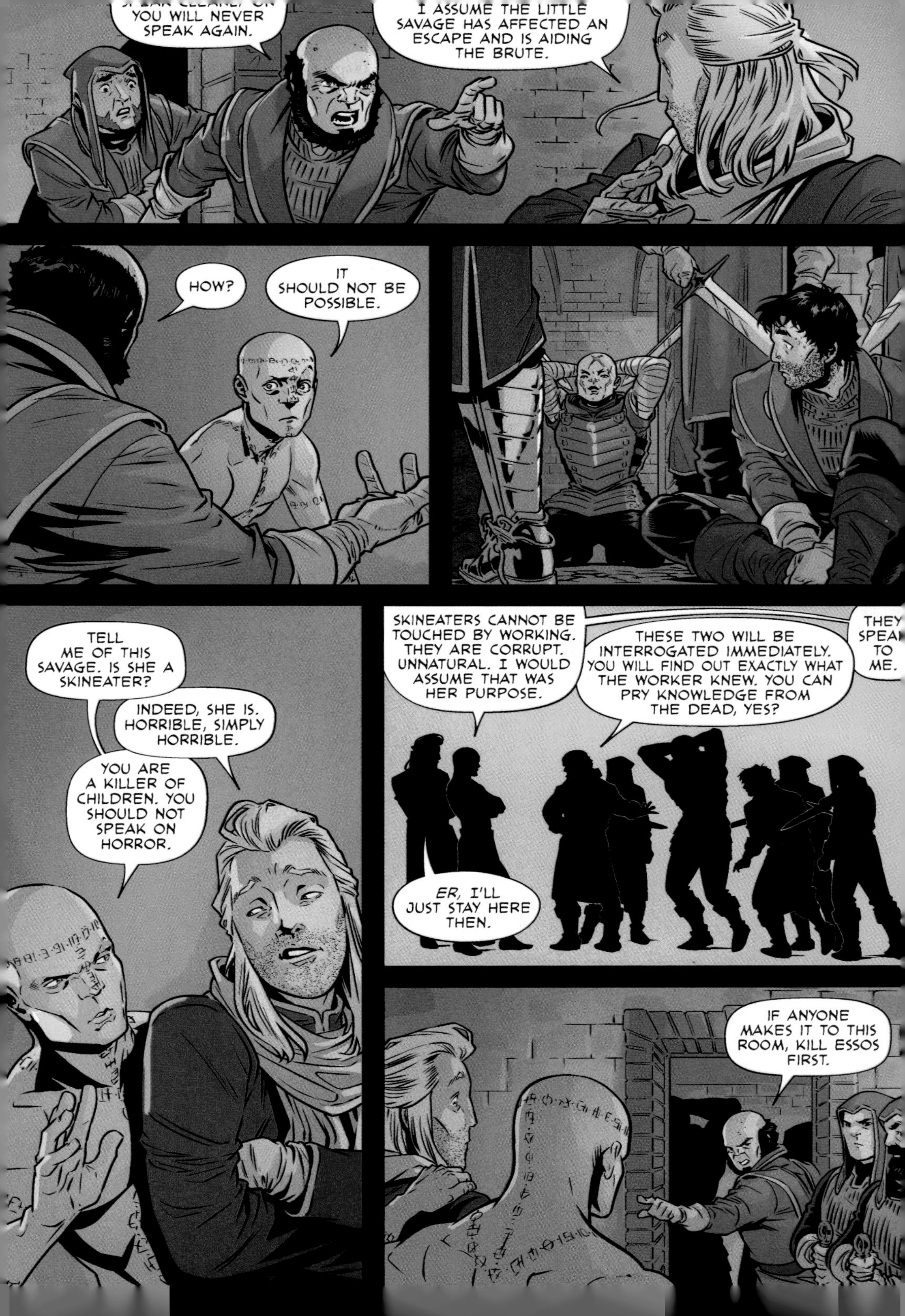

YOU WILL NEVER SPEAK AGAIN.
I ASSUME THE LITTLE SAVAGE HAS AFFECTED AN ESCAPE AND IS AIDING THE BRUTE.
HOW?
IT SHOULD NOT BE POSSIBLE.
TELL ME OF THIS SAVAGE. IS SHE A SKINEATER?
INDEED, SHE IS. HORRIBLE, SIMPLY HORRIBLE.
YOU ARE A KILLER OF CHILDREN. YOU SHOULD NOT SPEAK ON HORROR.
SKINEATERS CANNOT BE TOUCHED BY WORKING. THEY ARE CORRUPT. UNNATURAL. I WOULD ASSUME THAT WAS HER PURPOSE.
THESE TWO WILL BE INTERROGATED IMMEDIATELY. YOU WILL FIND OUT EXACTLY WHAT THE WORKER KNEW. YOU CAN PRY KNOWLEDGE FROM THE DEAD, YES?
ER, I'LL JUST STAY HERE THEN.
IF ANYONE MAKES IT TO THIS ROOM, KILL ESSOS FIRST.

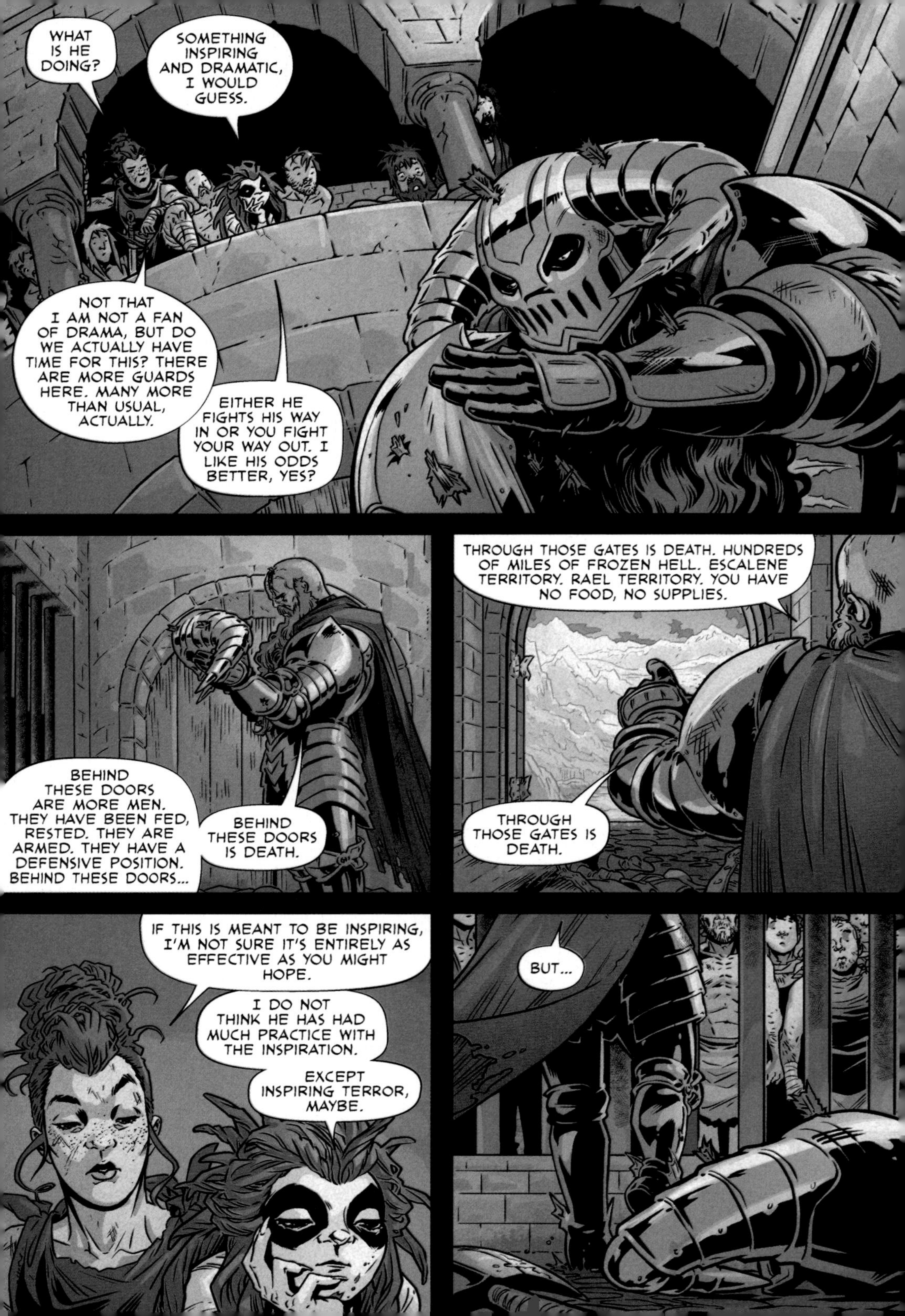
WHAT IS HE DOING?
SOMETHING INSPIRING AND DRAMATIC, I WOULD GUESS.
NOT THAT I AM NOT A FAN OF DRAMA, BUT DO WE ACTUALLY HAVE TIME FOR THIS? THERE ARE MORE GUARDS HERE. MANY MORE THAN USUAL, ACTUALLY.
EITHER HE FIGHTS HIS WAY IN OR YOU FIGHT YOUR WAY OUT. I LIKE HIS ODDS BETTER, YES?
BEHIND THESE DOORS ARE MORE MEN. THEY HAVE BEEN FED, RESTED. THEY ARE ARMED. THEY HAVE A DEFENSIVE POSITION. BEHIND THESE DOORS...
BEHIND THESE DOORS IS DEATH.
THROUGH THOSE GATES IS DEATH. HUNDREDS OF MILES OF FROZEN HELL. ESCALENE TERRITORY. RAEL TERRITORY. YOU HAVE NO FOOD, NO SUPPLIES.
THROUGH THOSE GATES IS DEATH.
IF THIS IS MEANT TO BE INSPIRING, I'M NOT SURE IT'S ENTIRELY AS EFFECTIVE AS YOU MIGHT HOPE.
I DO NOT THINK HE HAS HAD MUCH PRACTICE WITH THE INSPIRATION.
EXCEPT INSPIRING TERROR, MAYBE.
BUT...

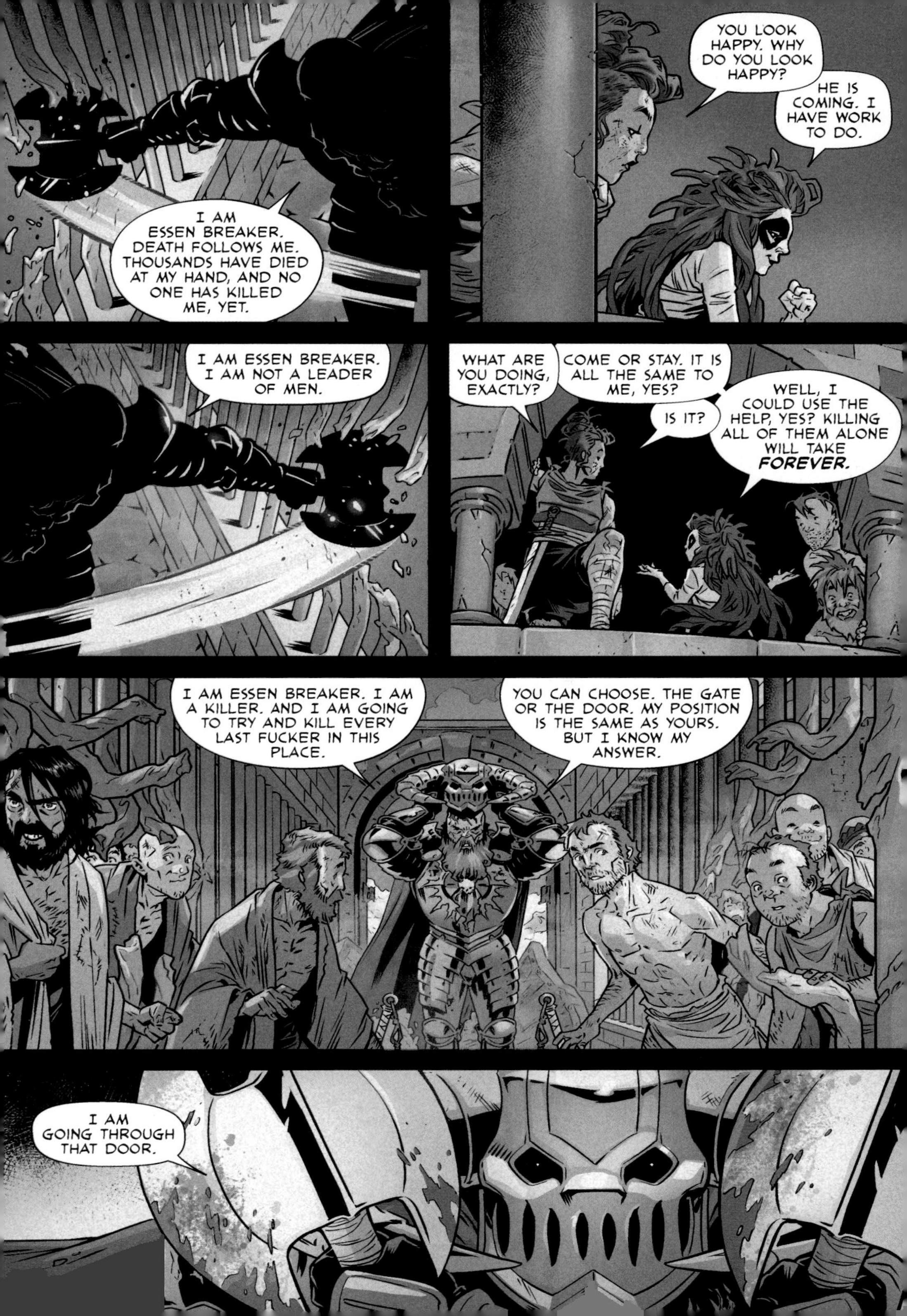
I AM ESSEN BREAKER. DEATH FOLLOWS ME. THOUSANDS HAVE DIED AT MY HAND, AND NO ONE HAS KILLED ME, YET.
YOU LOOK HAPPY. WHY DO YOU LOOK HAPPY?
HE IS COMING. I HAVE WORK TO DO.
I AM ESSEN BREAKER. I AM NOT A LEADER OF MEN.
WHAT ARE YOU DOING, EXACTLY?
COME OR STAY. IT IS ALL THE SAME TO ME, YES?
IS IT?
WELL, I COULD USE THE HELP, YES? KILLING ALL OF THEM ALONE WILL TAKE FOREVER.
I AM ESSEN BREAKER. I AM A KILLER. AND I AM GOING TO TRY AND KILL EVERY LAST FUCKER IN THIS PLACE.
YOU CAN CHOOSE. THE GATE OR THE DOOR. MY POSITION IS THE SAME AS YOURS. BUT I KNOW MY ANSWER.
I AM GOING THROUGH THAT DOOR.

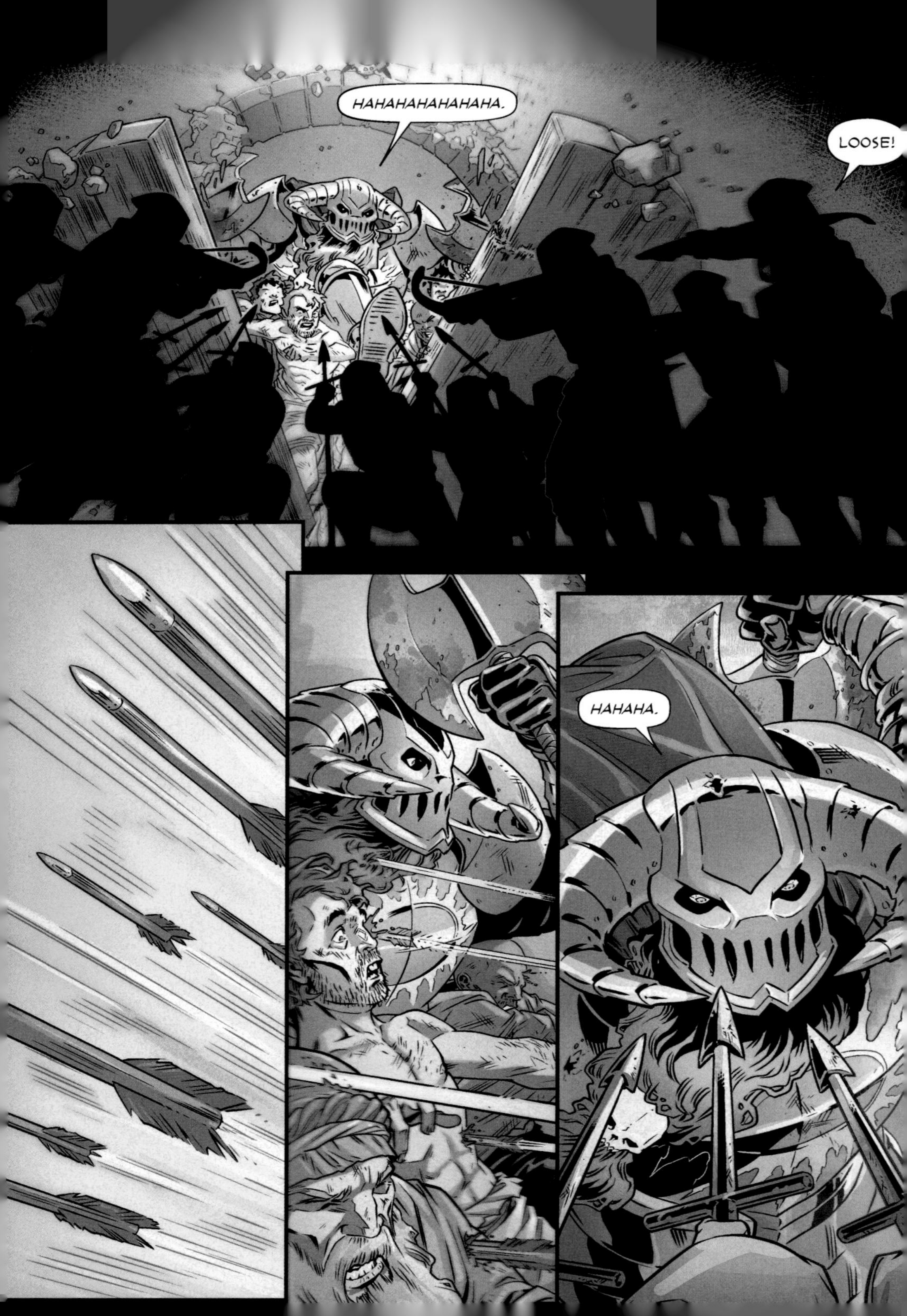
HAHAHAHAHAHAHA.
LOOSE!
HAHAHA.

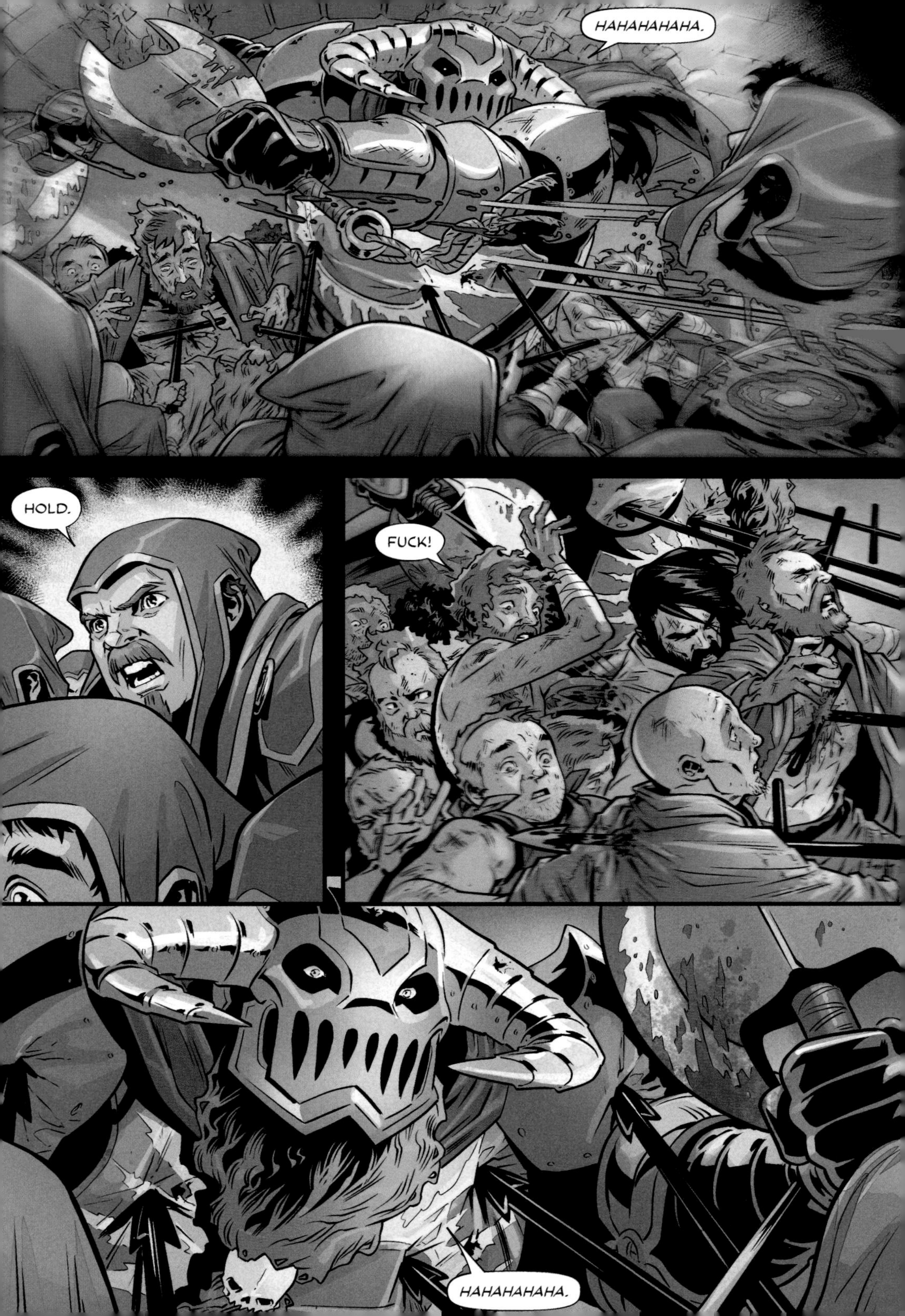
HAHAHAHAHA.
HOLD.
FUCK!
HAHAHAHAHA.

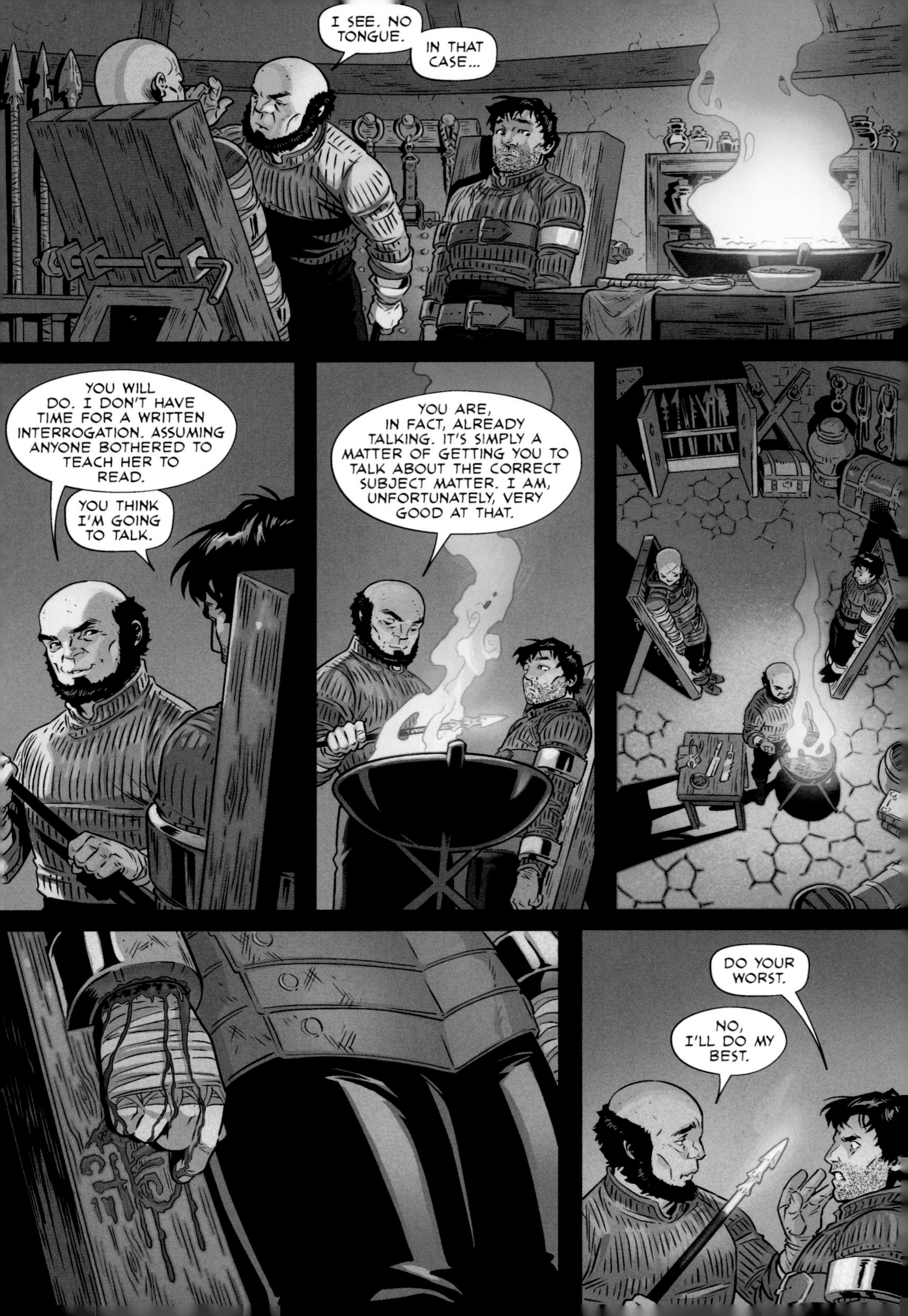
I SEE. NO TONGUE.
IN THAT CASE...
YOU WILL DO. I DON'T HAVE TIME FOR A WRITTEN INTERROGATION. ASSUMING ANYONE BOTHERED TO TEACH HER TO READ.
YOU THINK I'M GOING TO TALK.
YOU ARE, IN FACT, ALREADY TALKING. IT'S SIMPLY A MATTER OF GETTING YOU TO TALK ABOUT THE CORRECT SUBJECT MATTER. I AM, UNFORTUNATELY, VERY GOOD AT THAT.
DO YOUR WORST.
NO, I'LL DO MY BEST.

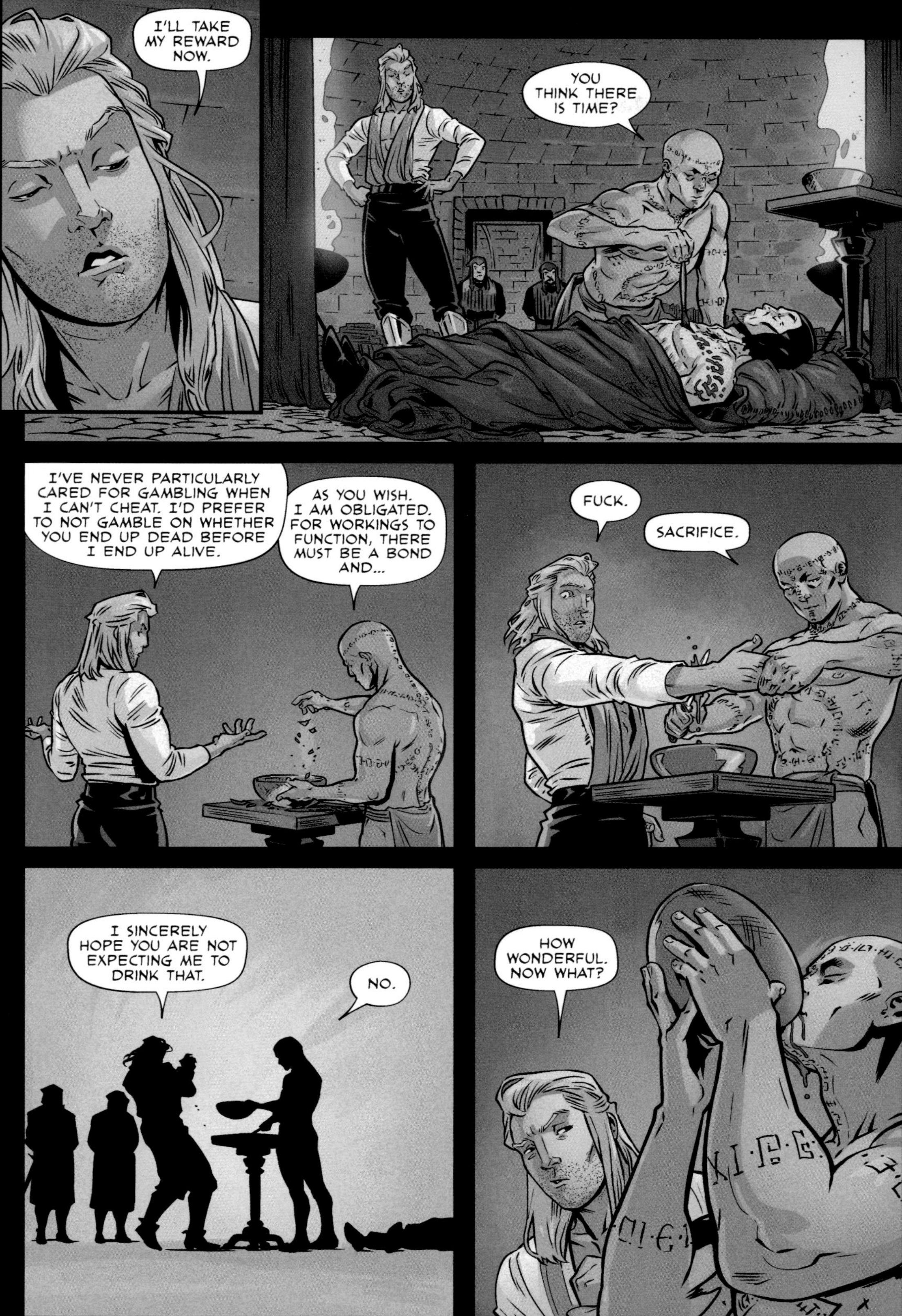

I'LL TAKE MY REWARD NOW.
YOU THINK THERE IS TIME?
I'VE NEVER PARTICULARLY CARED FOR GAMBLING WHEN I CAN'T CHEAT. I'D PREFER TO NOT GAMBLE ON WHETHER YOU END UP DEAD BEFORE I END UP ALIVE.
AS YOU WISH. I AM OBLIGATED. FOR WORKINGS TO FUNCTION, THERE MUST BE A BOND AND...
FUCK.
SACRIFICE.
I SINCERELY HOPE YOU ARE NOT EXPECTING ME TO DRINK THAT.
NO.
HOW WONDERFUL. NOW WHAT?

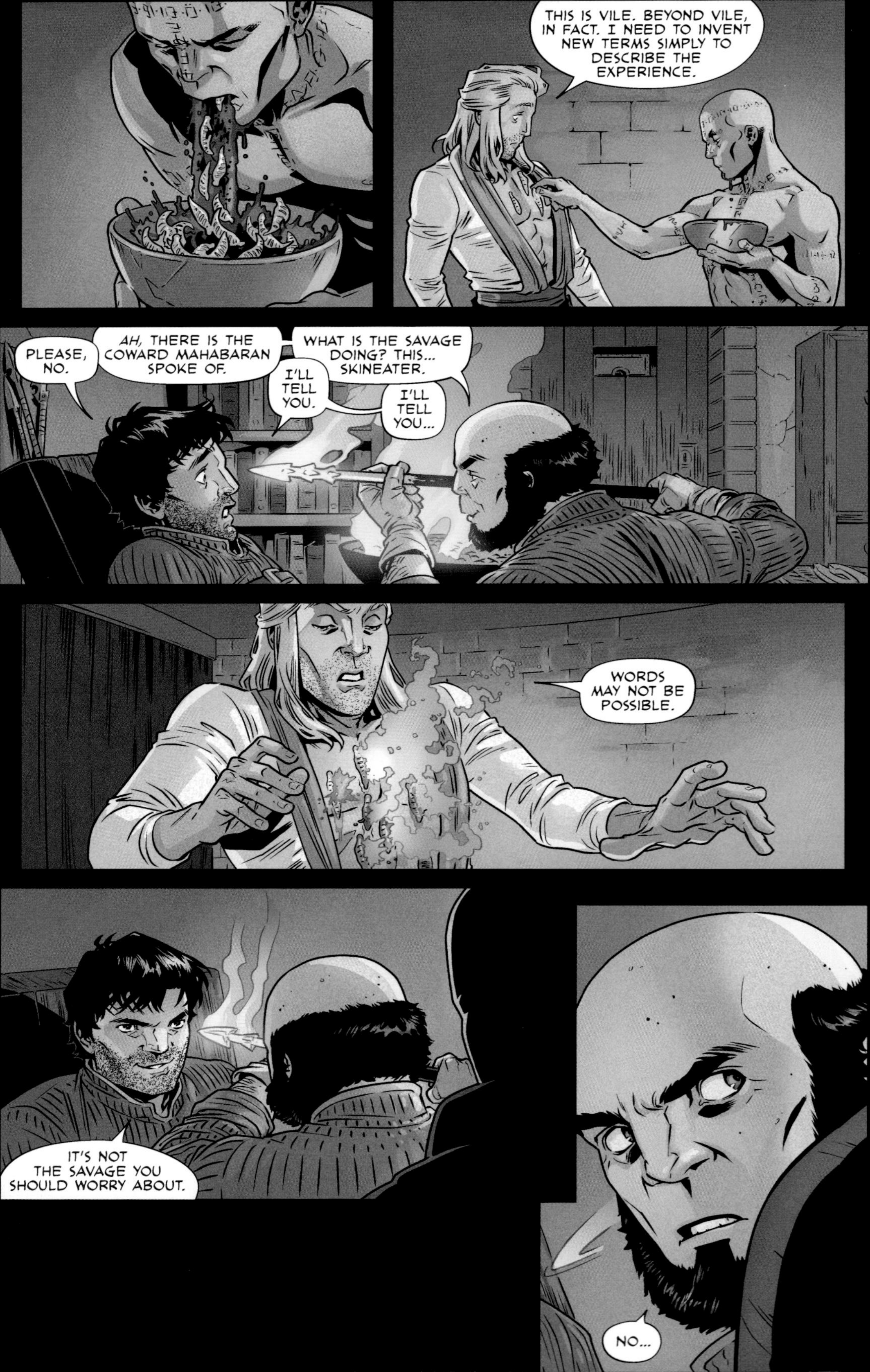
THIS IS VILE. BEYOND VILE, IN FACT. I NEED TO INVENT NEW TERMS SIMPLY TO DESCRIBE THE EXPERIENCE.
PLEASE, NO.
AH, THERE IS THE COWARD MAHABARAN SPOKE OF.
WHAT IS THE SAVAGE DOING? THIS... SKINEATER.
I'LL TELL YOU.
I'LL TELL YOU...
WORDS MAY NOT BE POSSIBLE.
IT'S NOT THE SAVAGE YOU SHOULD WORRY ABOUT.
NO...

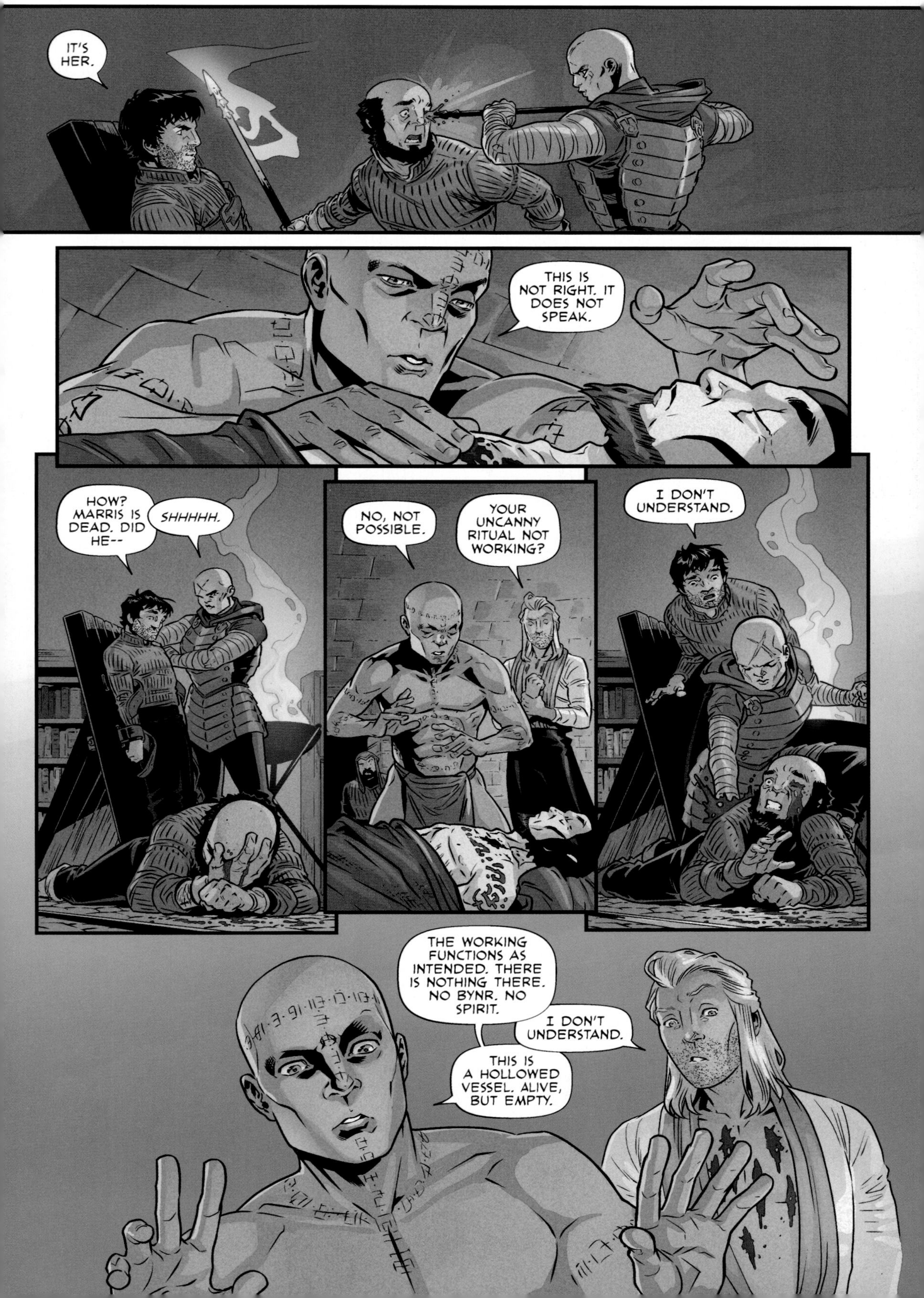
IT'S HER.
THIS IS NOT RIGHT. IT DOES NOT SPEAK.
HOW? MARRIS IS DEAD. DID HE--
SHHHHH.
NO, NOT POSSIBLE.
YOUR UNCANNY RITUAL NOT WORKING?
I DON'T UNDERSTAND.
THE WORKING FUNCTIONS AS INTENDED. THERE IS NOTHING THERE. NO BYNR. NO SPIRIT.
I DON'T UNDERSTAND.
THIS IS A HOLLOWED VESSEL. ALIVE, BUT EMPTY.

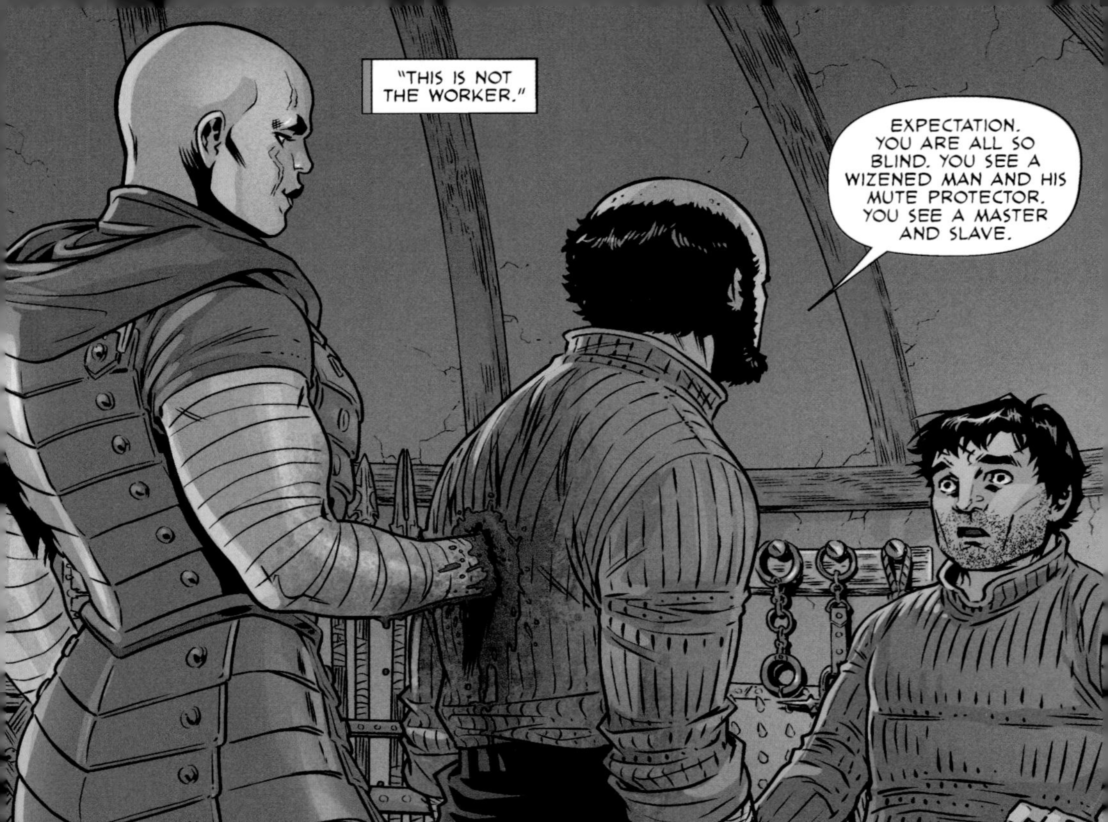
"THIS IS NOT THE WORKER."
EXPECTATION. YOU ARE ALL SO BLIND. YOU SEE A WIZENED MAN AND HIS MUTE PROTECTOR. YOU SEE A MASTER AND SLAVE.

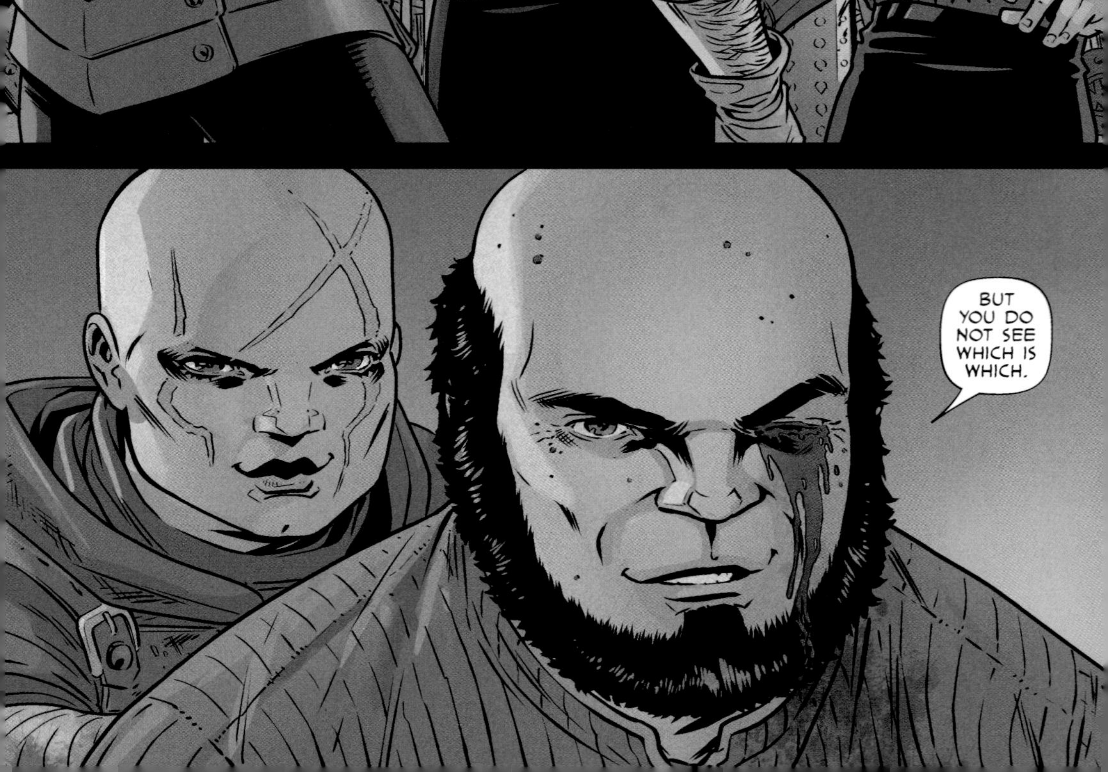
BUT YOU DO NOT SEE WHICH IS WHICH.

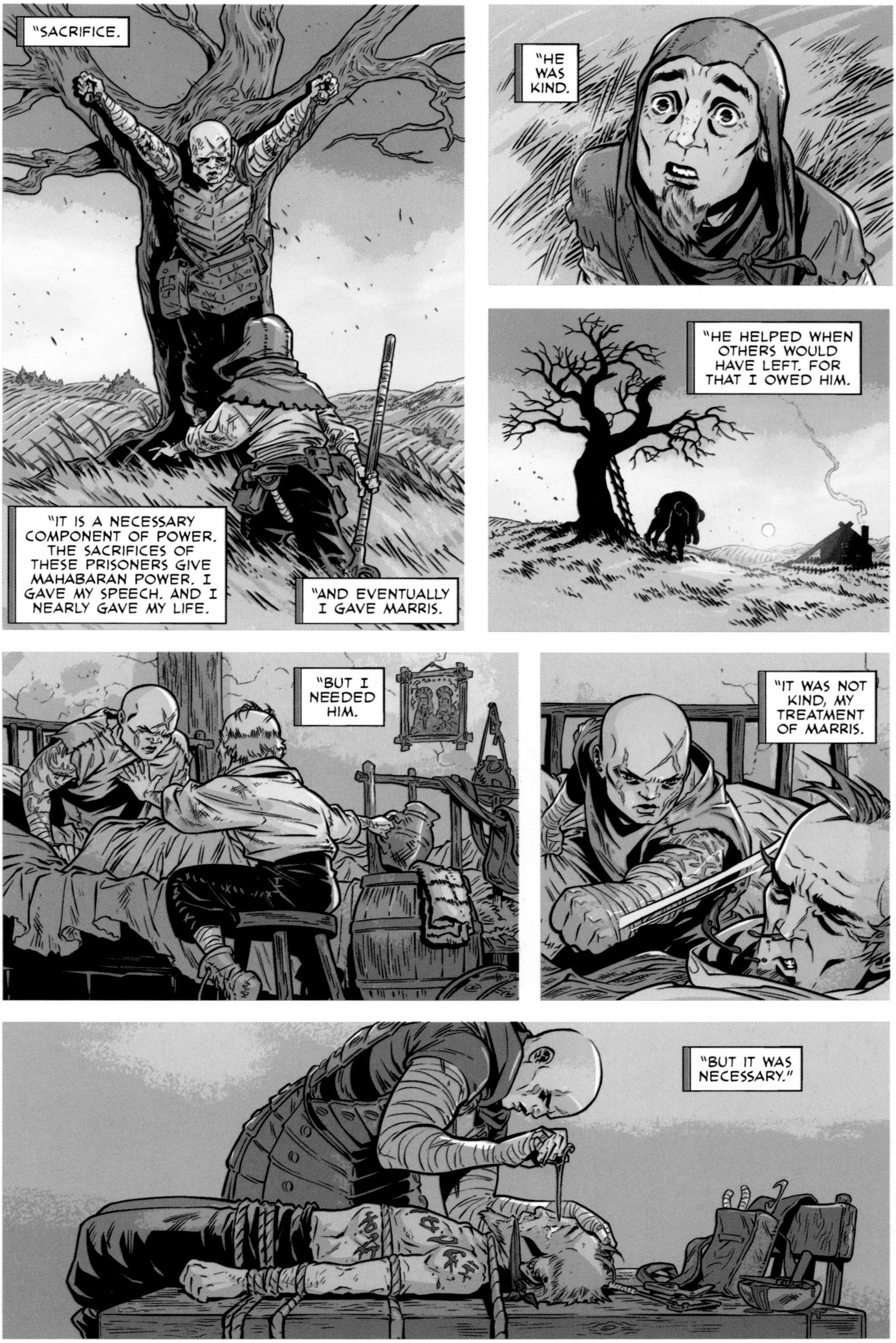
"SACRIFICE.
"IT IS A NECESSARY COMPONENT OF POWER. THE SACRIFICES OF THESE PRISONERS GIVE MAHABARAN POWER. I GAVE MY SPEECH. AND I NEARLY GAVE MY LIFE.
"AND EVENTUALLY I GAVE MARRIS.
"HE WAS KIND.
"HE HELPED WHEN OTHERS WOULD HAVE LEFT. FOR THAT I OWED HIM.
"BUT I NEEDED HIM.
"IT WAS NOT KIND, MY TREATMENT OF MARRIS.
"BUT IT WAS NECESSARY."

AS WAS THIS.

THIS ONE WILL NOT LAST. THIS IS A CRUDE WORKING. QUICK. MARRIS WAS STABLE. IT DIDN'T EVEN REQUIRE TOUCH, ALTHOUGH IT WAS EASIER WITH IT.

YOU. ALL OF THIS WAS YOU. THIS MISSION. YOU BROUGHT US HERE. YOU ACTED AS IF MARRIS WAS THE ONE IN CHARGE. WHY? WHY DO THIS?

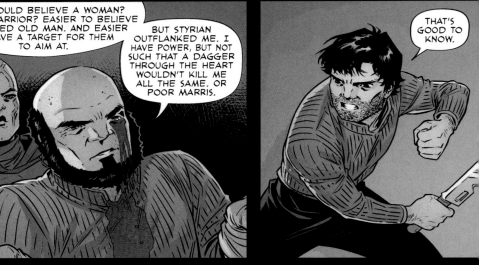

WHO WOULD BELIEVE A WOMAN? EVEN A WARRIOR? EASIER TO BELIEVE A WIZENED OLD MAN. AND EASIER TO HAVE A TARGET FOR THEM TO AIM AT.

BUT STYRIAN OUTFLANKED ME. I HAVE POWER, BUT NOT SUCH THAT A DAGGER THROUGH THE HEART WOULDN'T KILL ME ALL THE SAME. OR POOR MARRIS.

THAT'S GOOD TO KNOW.

YOU WOULD STRIKE ME DOWN, AT THE COST OF YOUR OWN LIFE? THERE'S POISON IN YOUR VEINS STILL.

I DON'T CARE IF I LIVE. YOUR POISON IS NOT WHY I CAME.

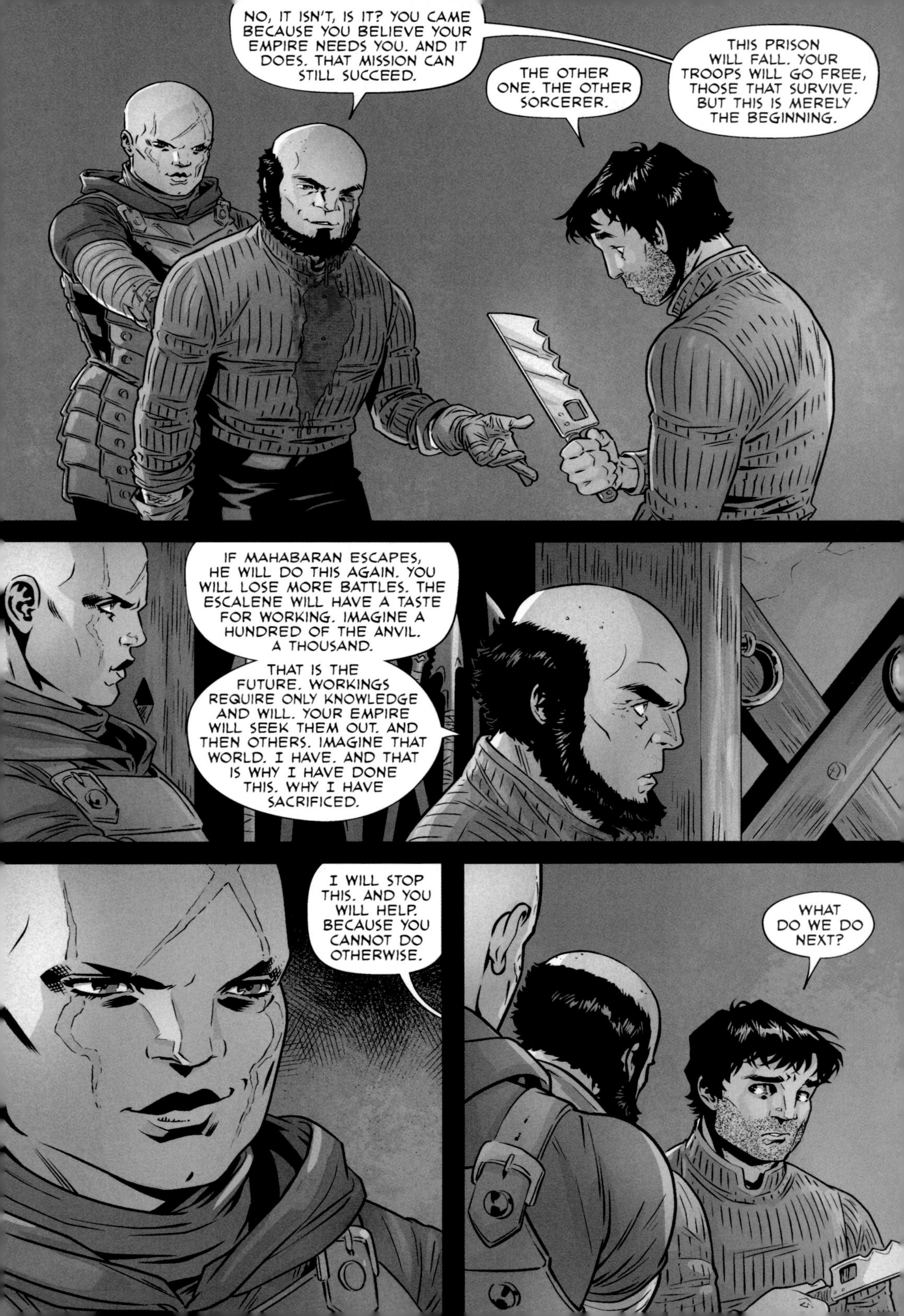
NO, IT ISN'T, IS IT? YOU CAME BECAUSE YOU BELIEVE YOUR EMPIRE NEEDS YOU. AND IT DOES. THAT MISSION CAN STILL SUCCEED.
THE OTHER ONE. THE OTHER SORCERER.
THIS PRISON WILL FALL. YOUR TROOPS WILL GO FREE, THOSE THAT SURVIVE. BUT THIS IS MERELY THE BEGINNING.
IF MAHABARAN ESCAPES, HE WILL DO THIS AGAIN. YOU WILL LOSE MORE BATTLES. THE ESCALENE WILL HAVE A TASTE FOR WORKING. IMAGINE A HUNDRED OF THE ANVIL. A THOUSAND.
THAT IS THE FUTURE. WORKINGS REQUIRE ONLY KNOWLEDGE AND WILL. YOUR EMPIRE WILL SEEK THEM OUT. AND THEN OTHERS. IMAGINE THAT WORLD. I HAVE. AND THAT IS WHY I HAVE DONE THIS. WHY I HAVE SACRIFICED.
I WILL STOP THIS. AND YOU WILL HELP. BECAUSE YOU CANNOT DO OTHERWISE.
WHAT DO WE DO NEXT?

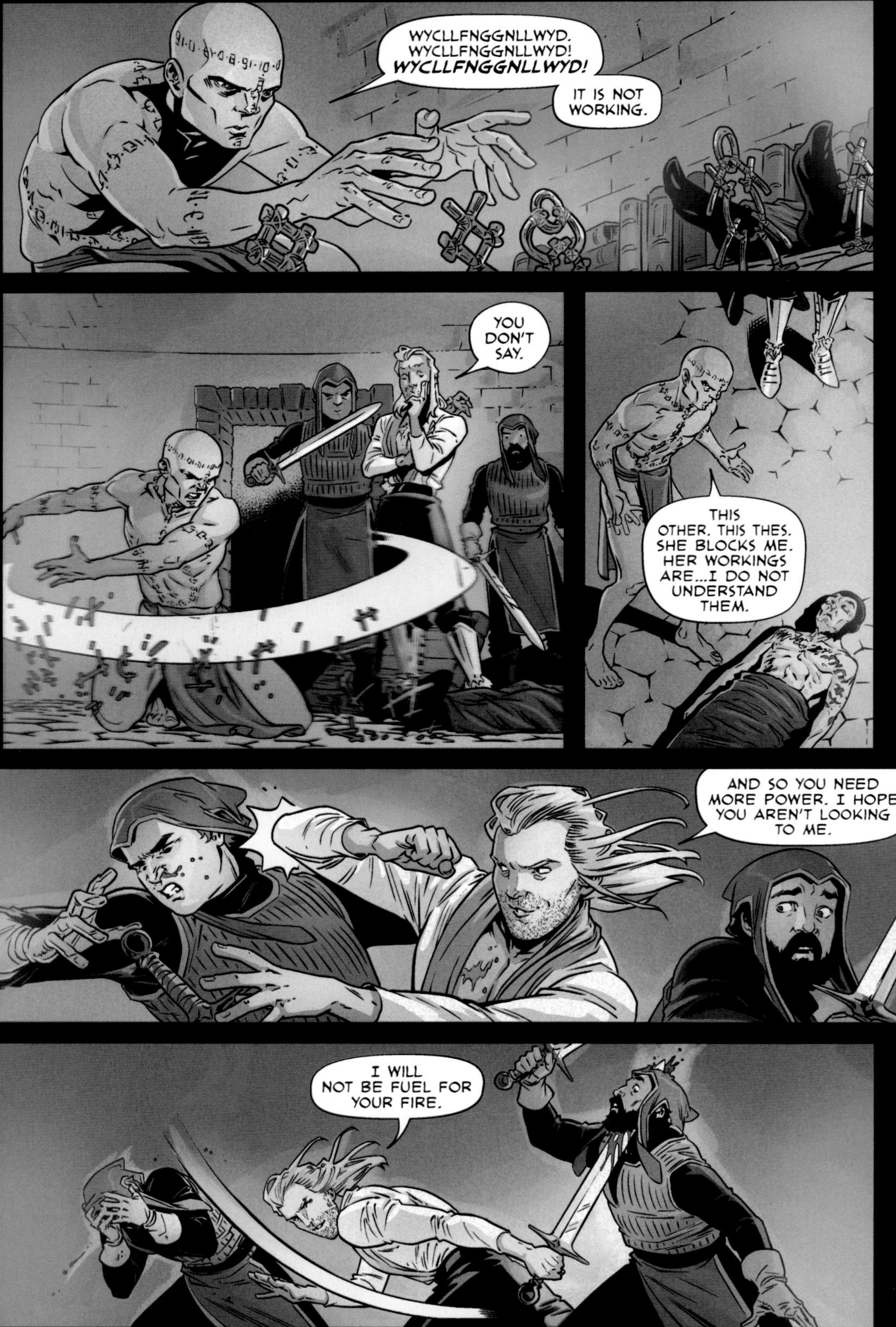
WYCLLFNGGNLLWYD. WYCLLFNGGNLLWYD! WYCLLFNGGNLLWYD!
IT IS NOT WORKING.
YOU DON'T SAY.
THIS OTHER. THIS THES. SHE BLOCKS ME. HER WORKINGS ARE...I DO NOT UNDERSTAND THEM.
AND SO YOU NEED MORE POWER. I HOPE YOU AREN'T LOOKING TO ME.
I WILL NOT BE FUEL FOR YOUR FIRE.

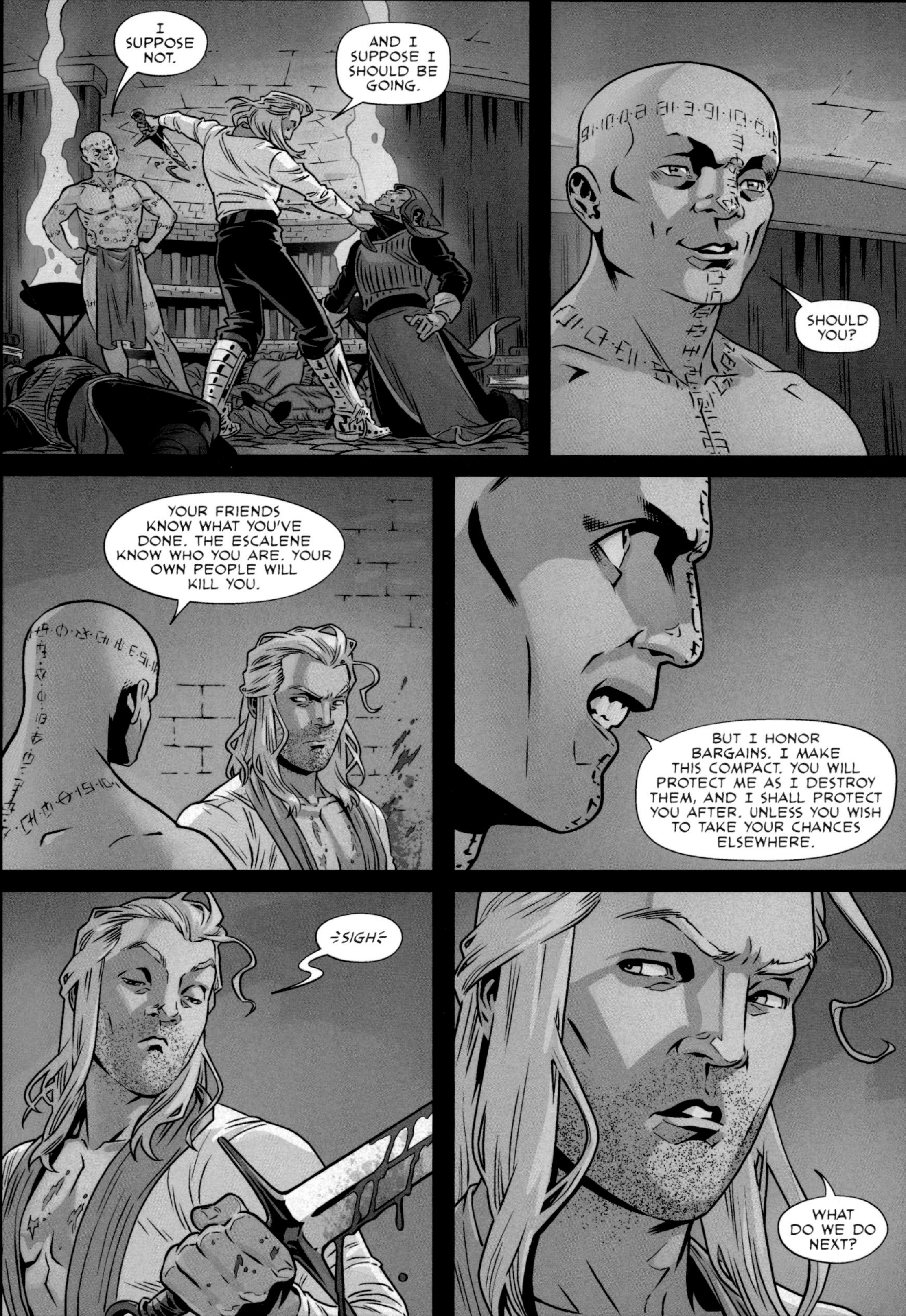
I SUPPOSE NOT.
AND I SUPPOSE I SHOULD BE GOING.
SHOULD YOU?
YOUR FRIENDS KNOW WHAT YOU'VE DONE. THE ESCALENE KNOW WHO YOU ARE. YOUR OWN PEOPLE WILL KILL YOU.
BUT I HONOR BARGAINS. I MAKE THIS COMPACT. YOU WILL PROTECT ME AS I DESTROY THEM, AND I SHALL PROTECT YOU AFTER. UNLESS YOU WISH TO TAKE YOUR CHANCES ELSEWHERE.
⁼SIGH⁼
WHAT DO WE DO NEXT?

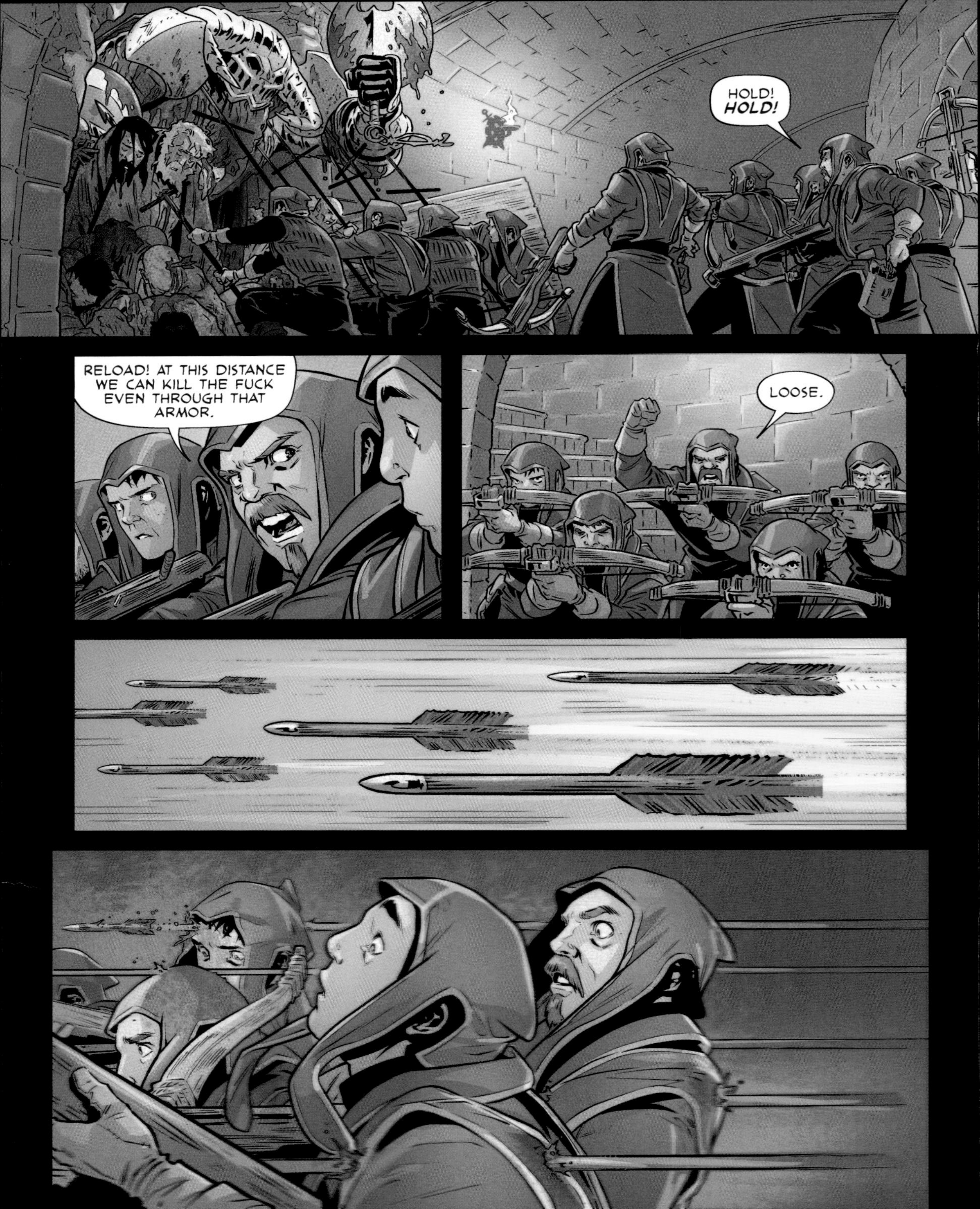
HOLD! HOLD!
RELOAD! AT THIS DISTANCE WE CAN KILL THE FUCK EVEN THROUGH THAT ARMOR.
LOOSE.

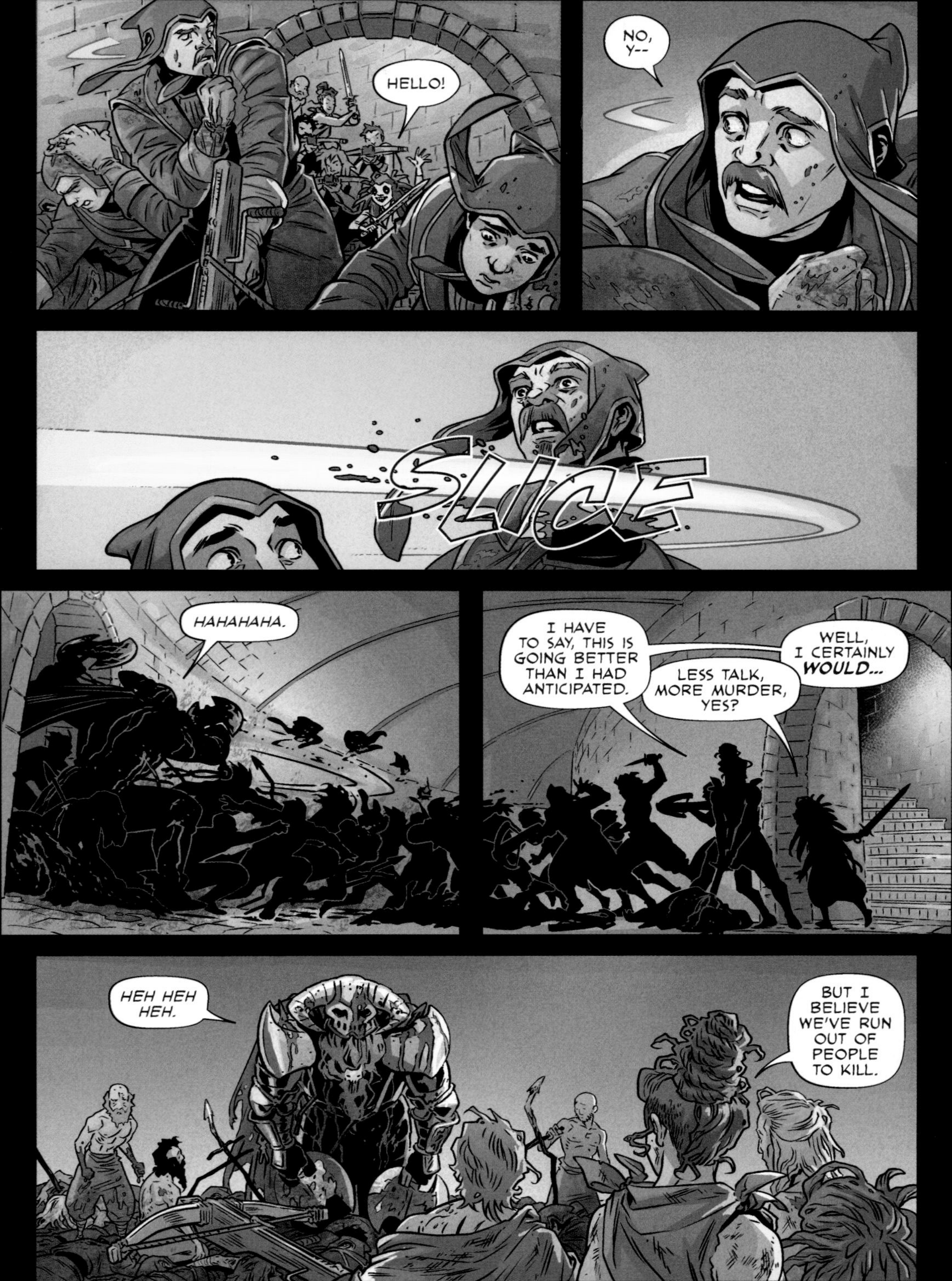
HELLO!
NO, Y--
SLICE
HAHAHAHA.
I HAVE TO SAY, THIS IS GOING BETTER THAN I HAD ANTICIPATED.
LESS TALK, MORE MURDER, YES?
WELL, I CERTAINLY WOULD...
HEH HEH HEH.
BUT I BELIEVE WE'VE RUN OUT OF PEOPLE TO KILL.

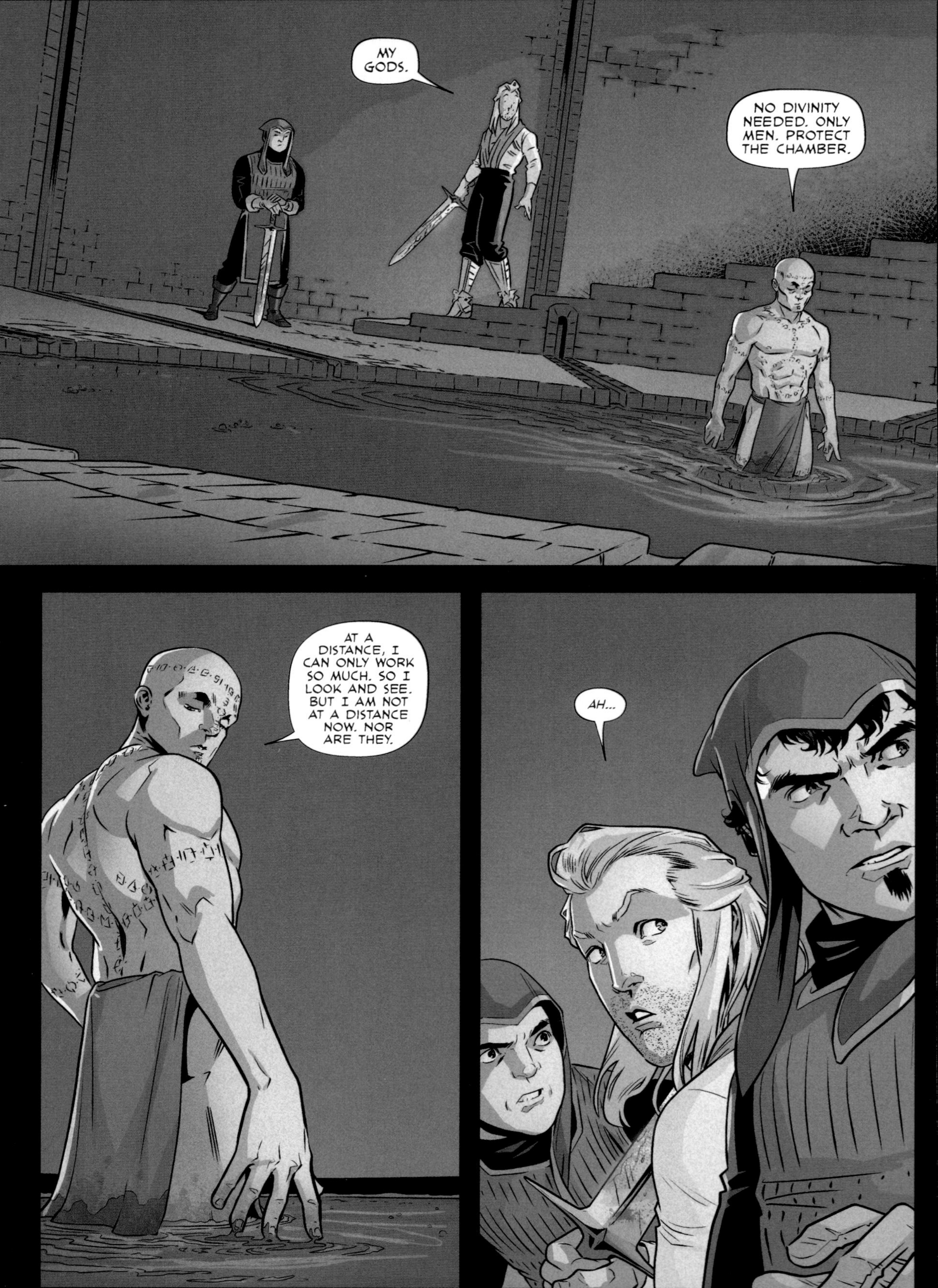
MY GODS.
NO DIVINITY NEEDED. ONLY MEN. PROTECT THE CHAMBER.
AT A DISTANCE, I CAN ONLY WORK SO MUCH. SO I LOOK AND SEE. BUT I AM NOT AT A DISTANCE NOW. NOR ARE THEY.
AH...

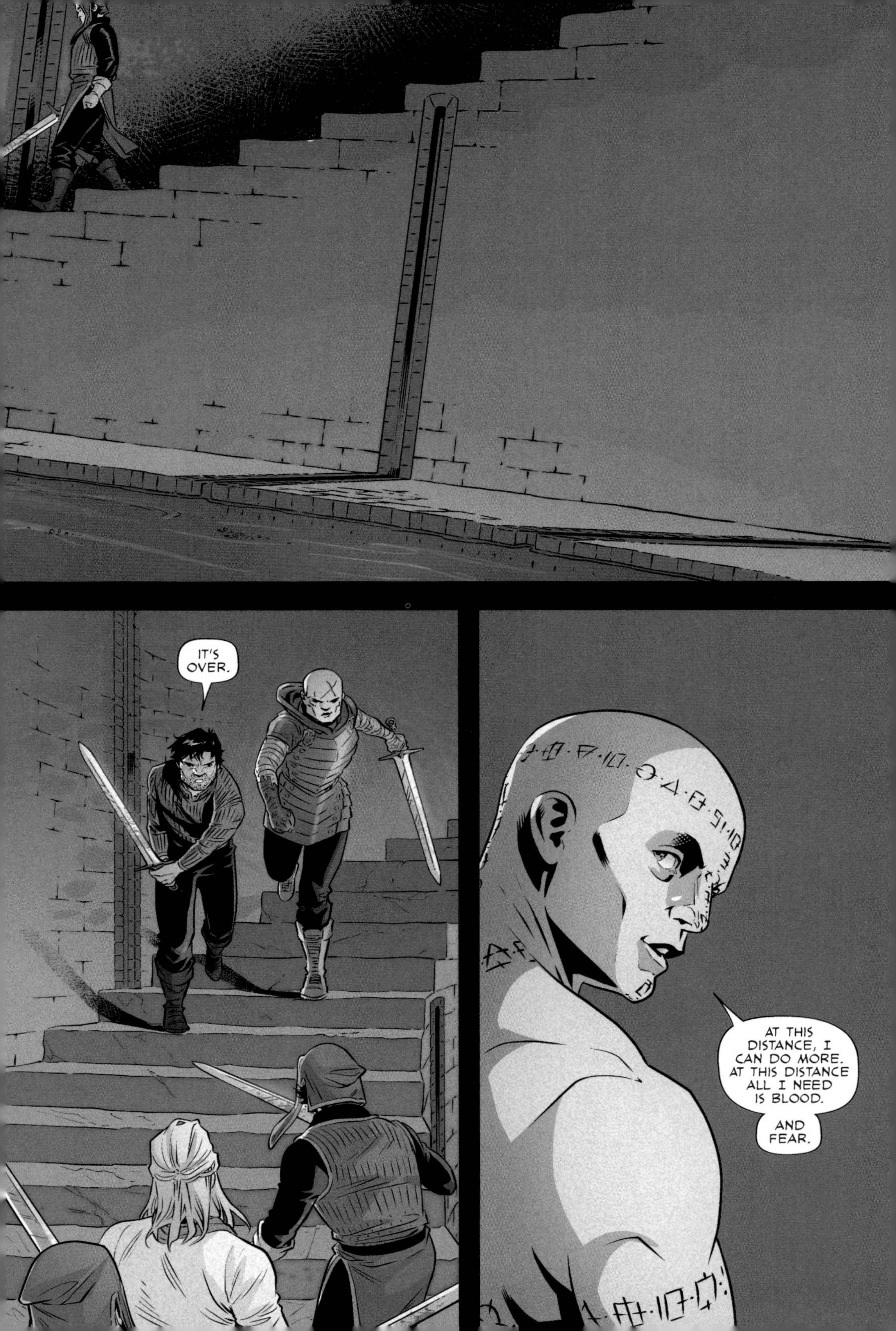
IT'S OVER.
AT THIS DISTANCE, I CAN DO MORE. AT THIS DISTANCE ALL I NEED IS BLOOD.
AND FEAR.

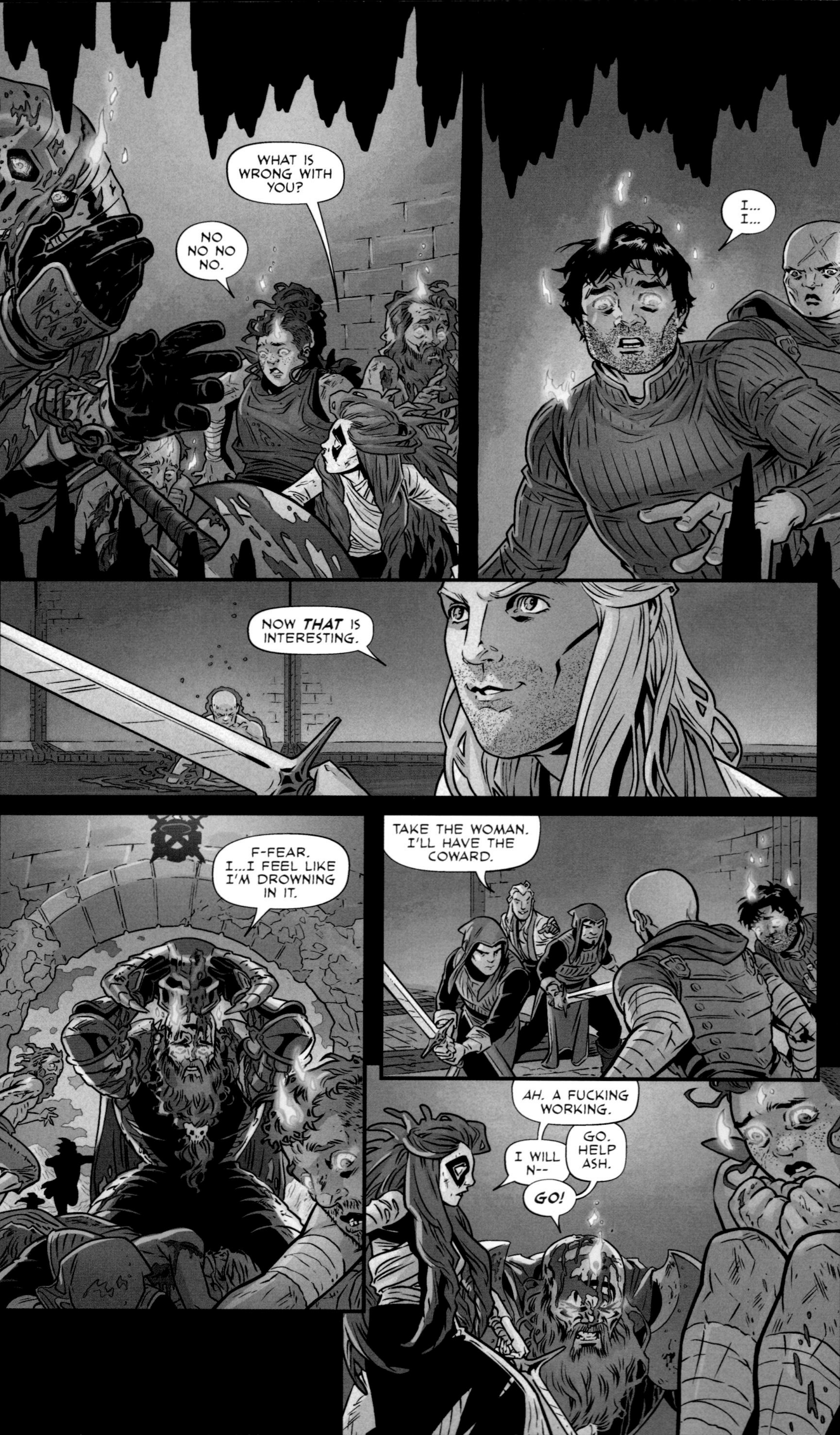
WHAT IS WRONG WITH YOU?
NO NO NO NO.
I... I...
NOW *THAT* IS INTERESTING.
F-FEAR. I...I FEEL LIKE I'M DROWNING IN IT.
TAKE THE WOMAN. I'LL HAVE THE COWARD.
AH. A FUCKING WORKING.
GO. HELP ASH.
I WILL N--
GO!

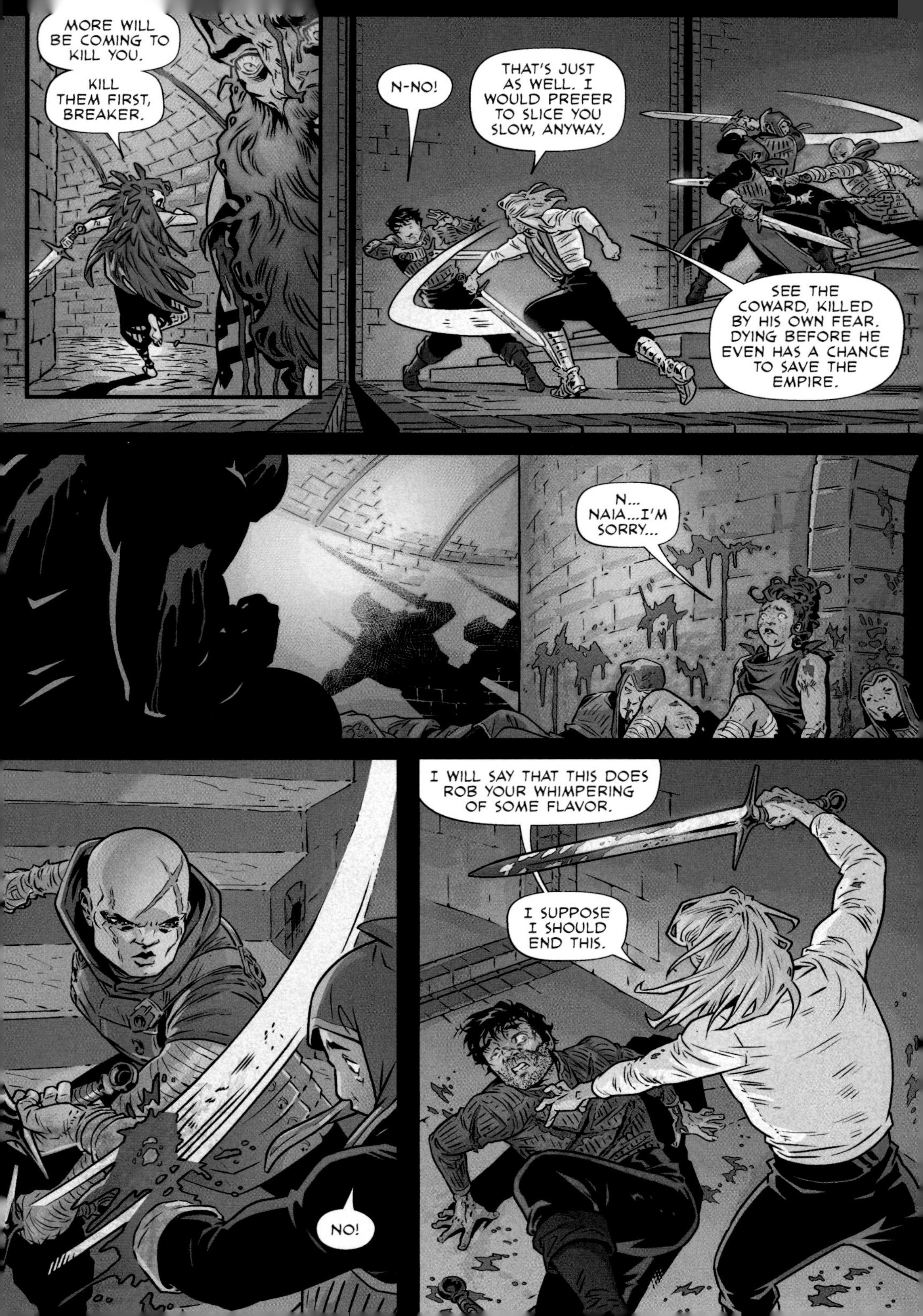

MORE WILL BE COMING TO KILL YOU.
KILL THEM FIRST, BREAKER.
N-NO!
THAT'S JUST AS WELL. I WOULD PREFER TO SLICE YOU SLOW, ANYWAY.
SEE THE COWARD, KILLED BY HIS OWN FEAR. DYING BEFORE HE EVEN HAS A CHANCE TO SAVE THE EMPIRE.
N... NAIA...I'M SORRY...
NO!
I WILL SAY THAT THIS DOES ROB YOUR WHIMPERING OF SOME FLAVOR.
I SUPPOSE I SHOULD END THIS.

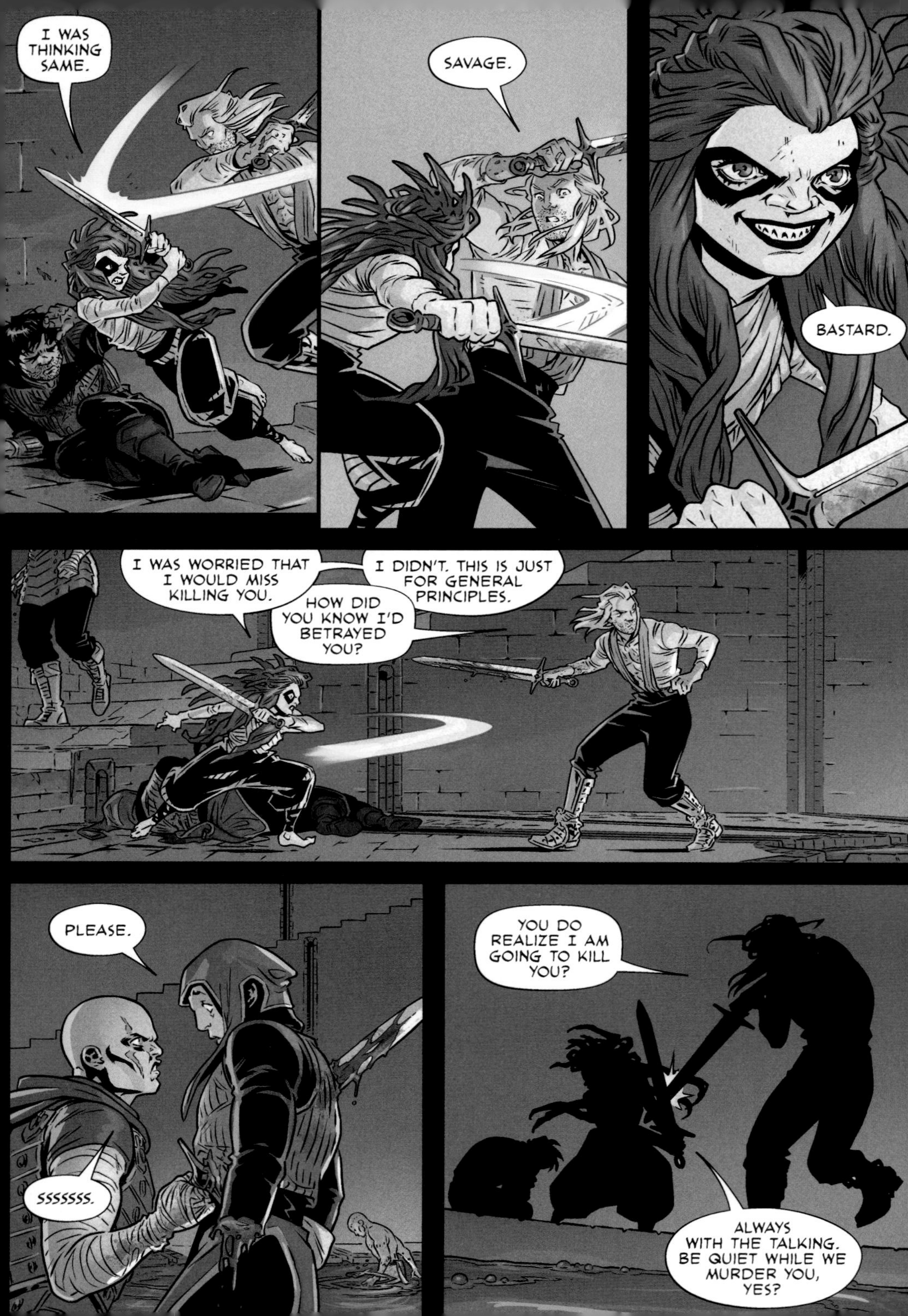
I WAS THINKING SAME.
SAVAGE.
BASTARD.
I WAS WORRIED THAT I WOULD MISS KILLING YOU.
I DIDN'T. THIS IS JUST FOR GENERAL PRINCIPLES.
HOW DID YOU KNOW I'D BETRAYED YOU?
PLEASE.
SSSSSSS.
YOU DO REALIZE I AM GOING TO KILL YOU?
ALWAYS WITH THE TALKING. BE QUIET WHILE WE MURDER YOU, YES?

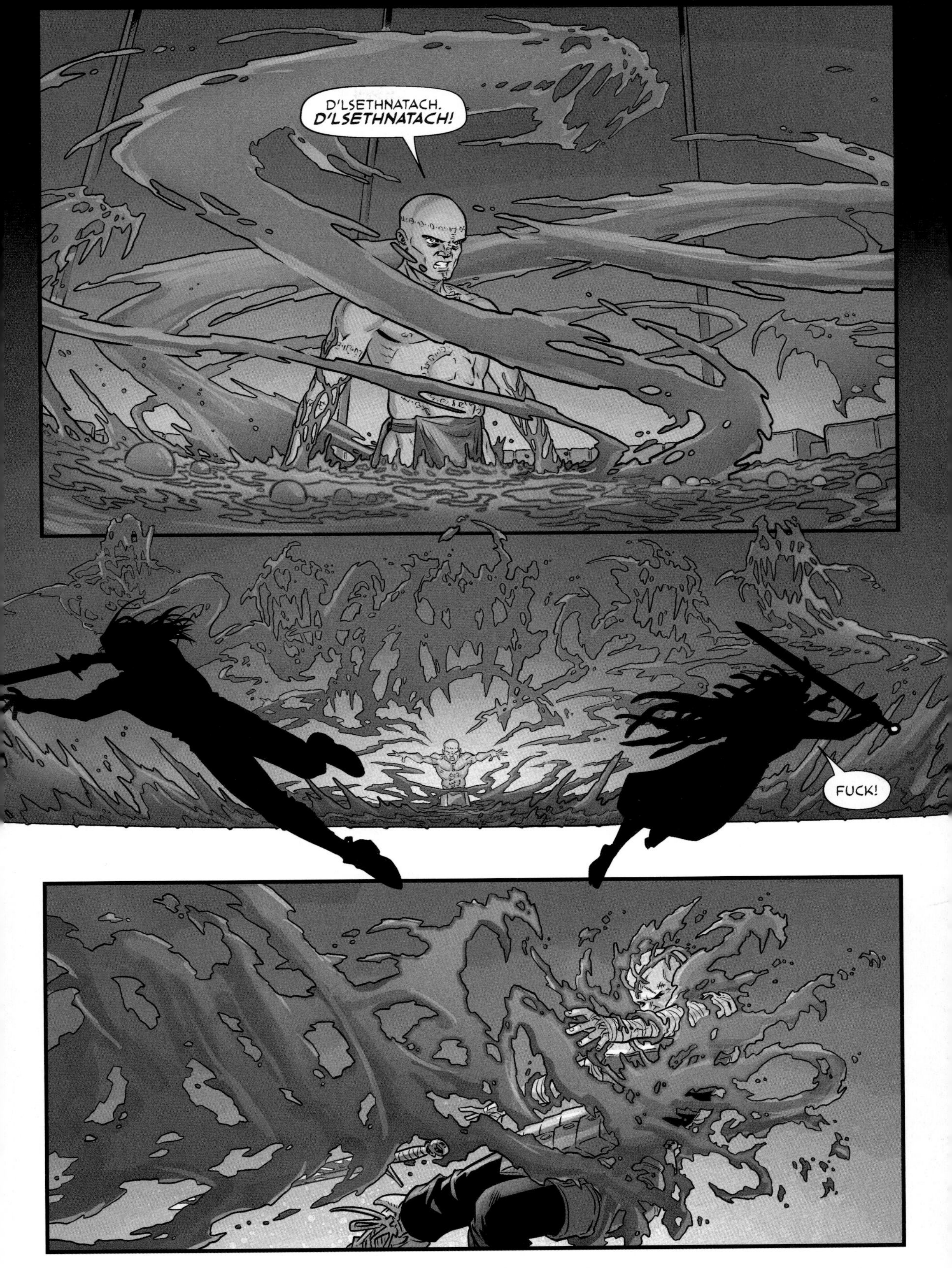
D'LSETHNATACH. D'LSETHNATACH!
FUCK!

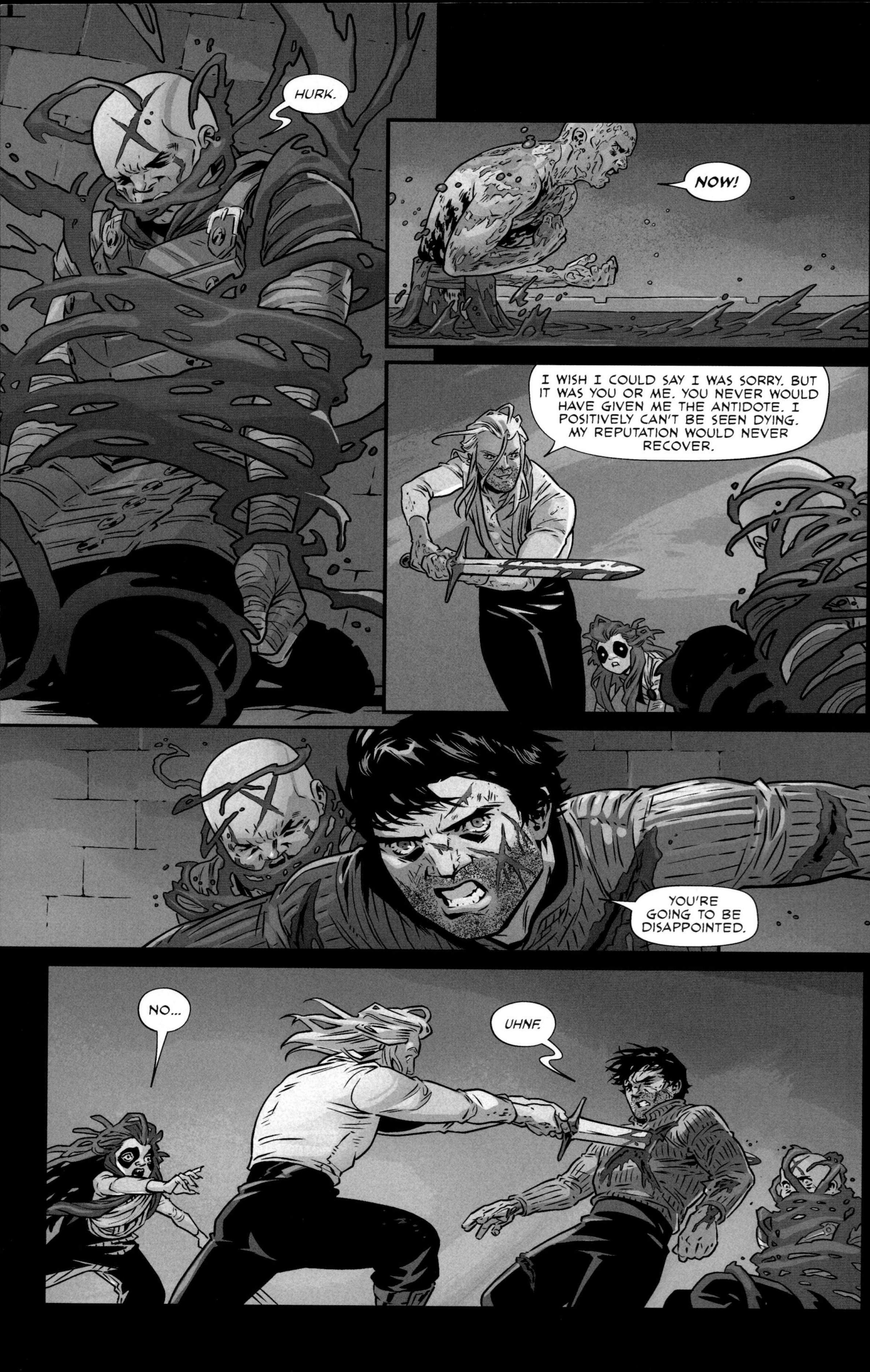
HURK.
NOW!
I WISH I COULD SAY I WAS SORRY. BUT IT WAS YOU OR ME. YOU NEVER WOULD HAVE GIVEN ME THE ANTIDOTE. I POSITIVELY CAN'T BE SEEN DYING. MY REPUTATION WOULD NEVER RECOVER.
YOU'RE GOING TO BE DISAPPOINTED.
NO...
UHNF.

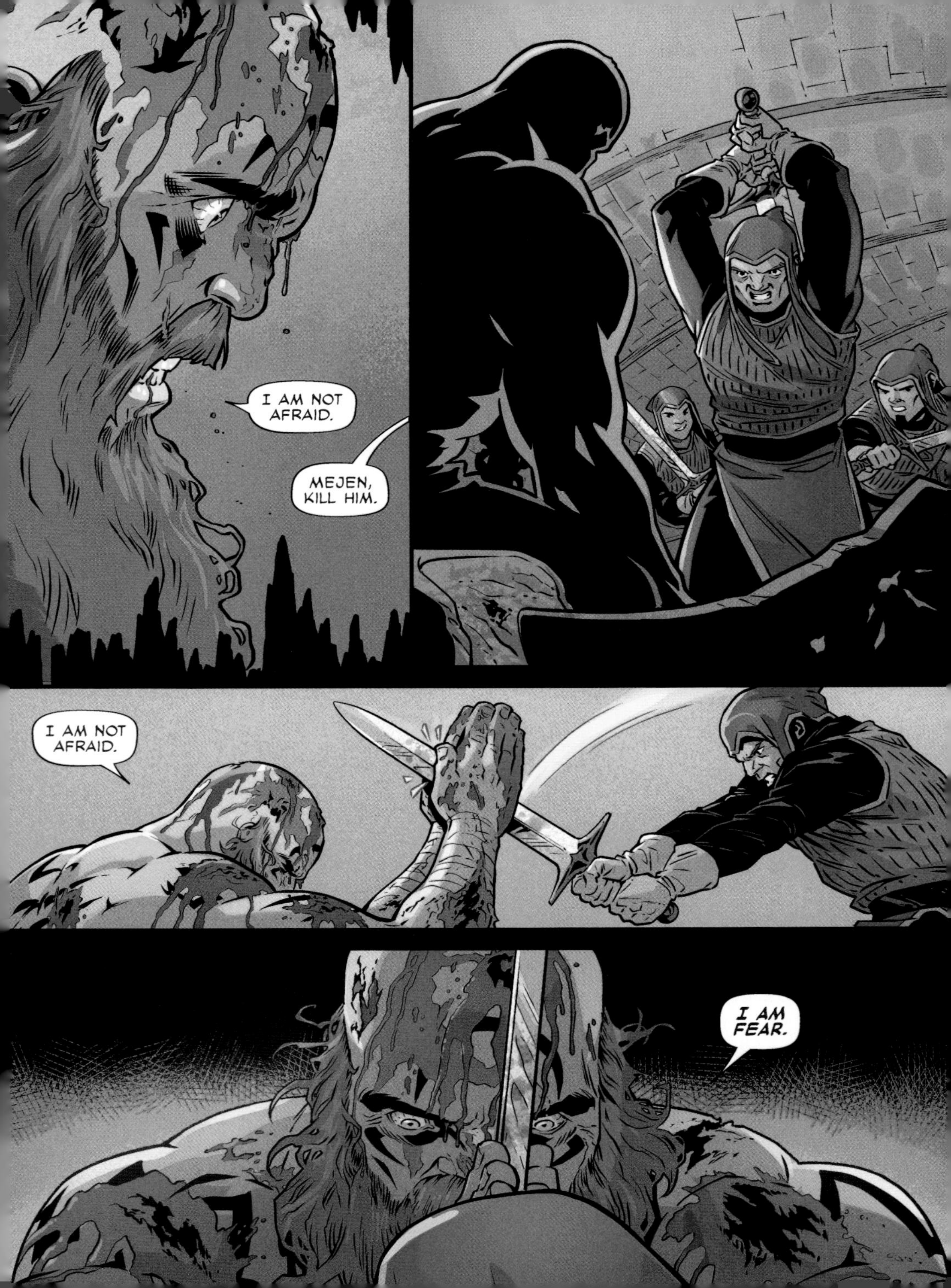
I AM NOT AFRAID.
MEJEN, KILL HIM.
I AM NOT AFRAID.
I AM FEAR.

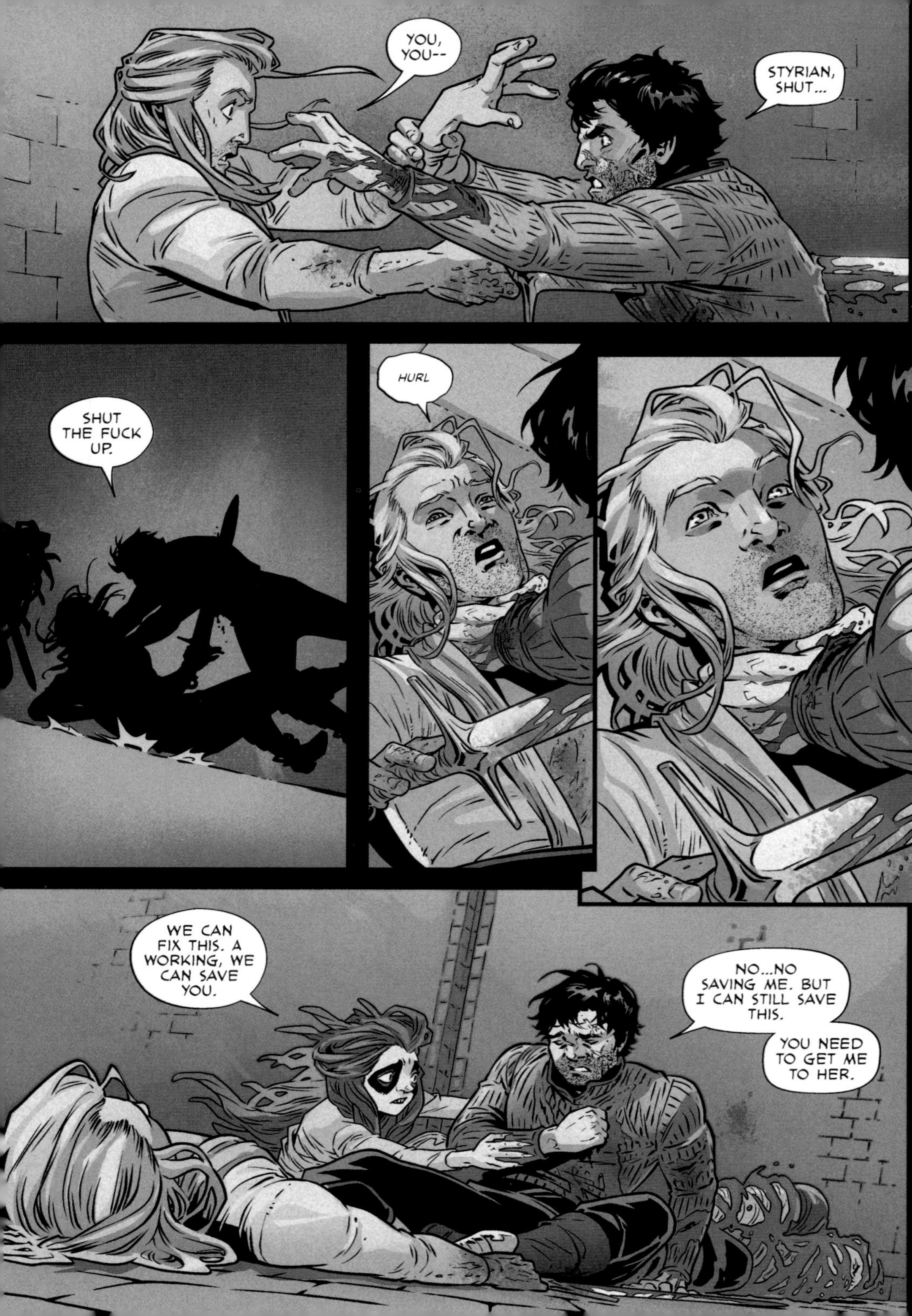
YOU, YOU--
STYRIAN, SHUT...
SHUT THE FUCK UP.
HURL
WE CAN FIX THIS. A WORKING, WE CAN SAVE YOU.
NO...NO SAVING ME. BUT I CAN STILL SAVE THIS.
YOU NEED TO GET ME TO HER.

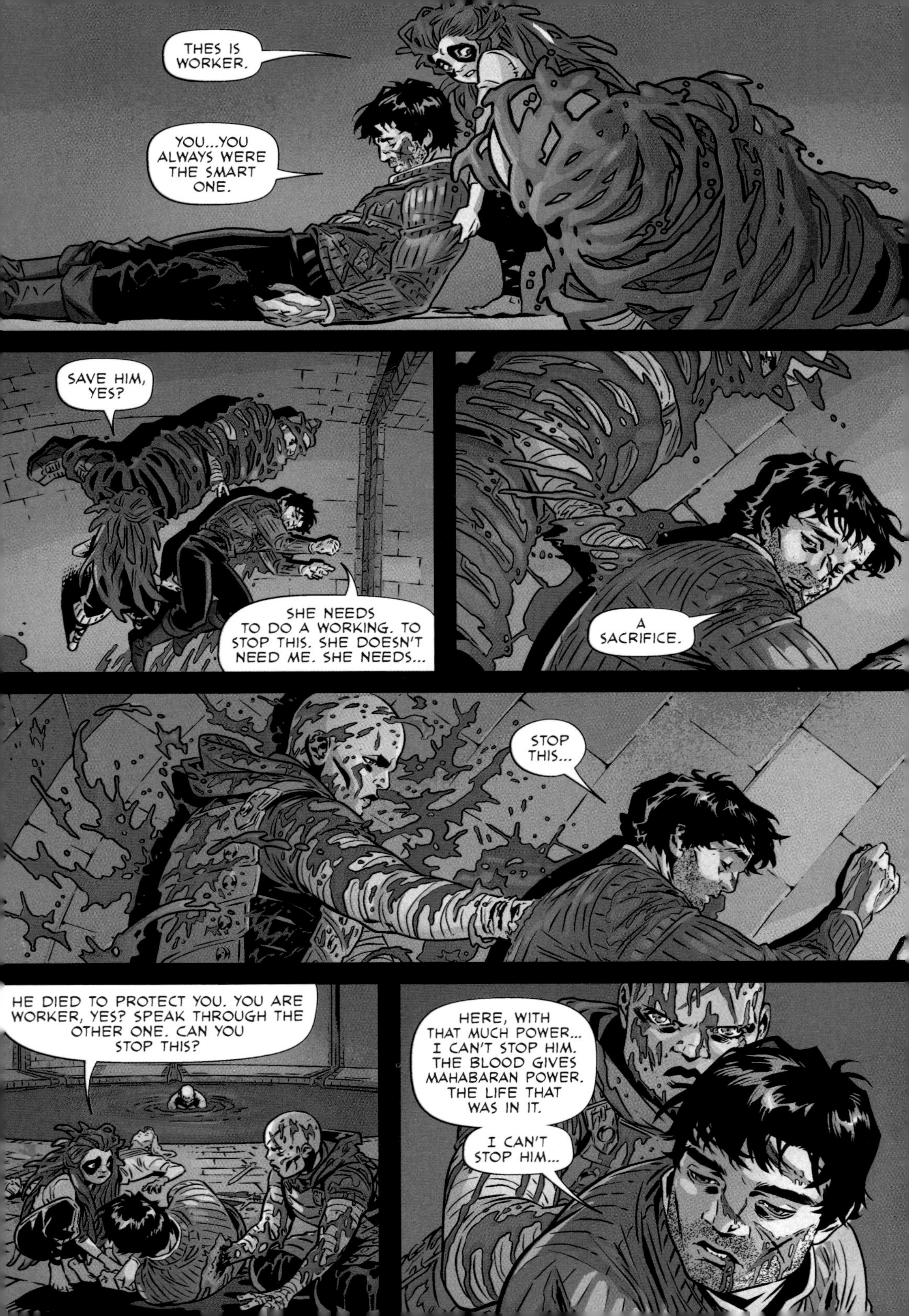
THES IS WORKER.
YOU...YOU ALWAYS WERE THE SMART ONE.
SAVE HIM, YES?
SHE NEEDS TO DO A WORKING. TO STOP THIS. SHE DOESN'T NEED ME. SHE NEEDS...
A SACRIFICE.
STOP THIS...
HE DIED TO PROTECT YOU. YOU ARE WORKER, YES? SPEAK THROUGH THE OTHER ONE. CAN YOU STOP THIS?
HERE, WITH THAT MUCH POWER... I CAN'T STOP HIM. THE BLOOD GIVES MAHABARAN POWER. THE LIFE THAT WAS IN IT.
I CAN'T STOP HIM...

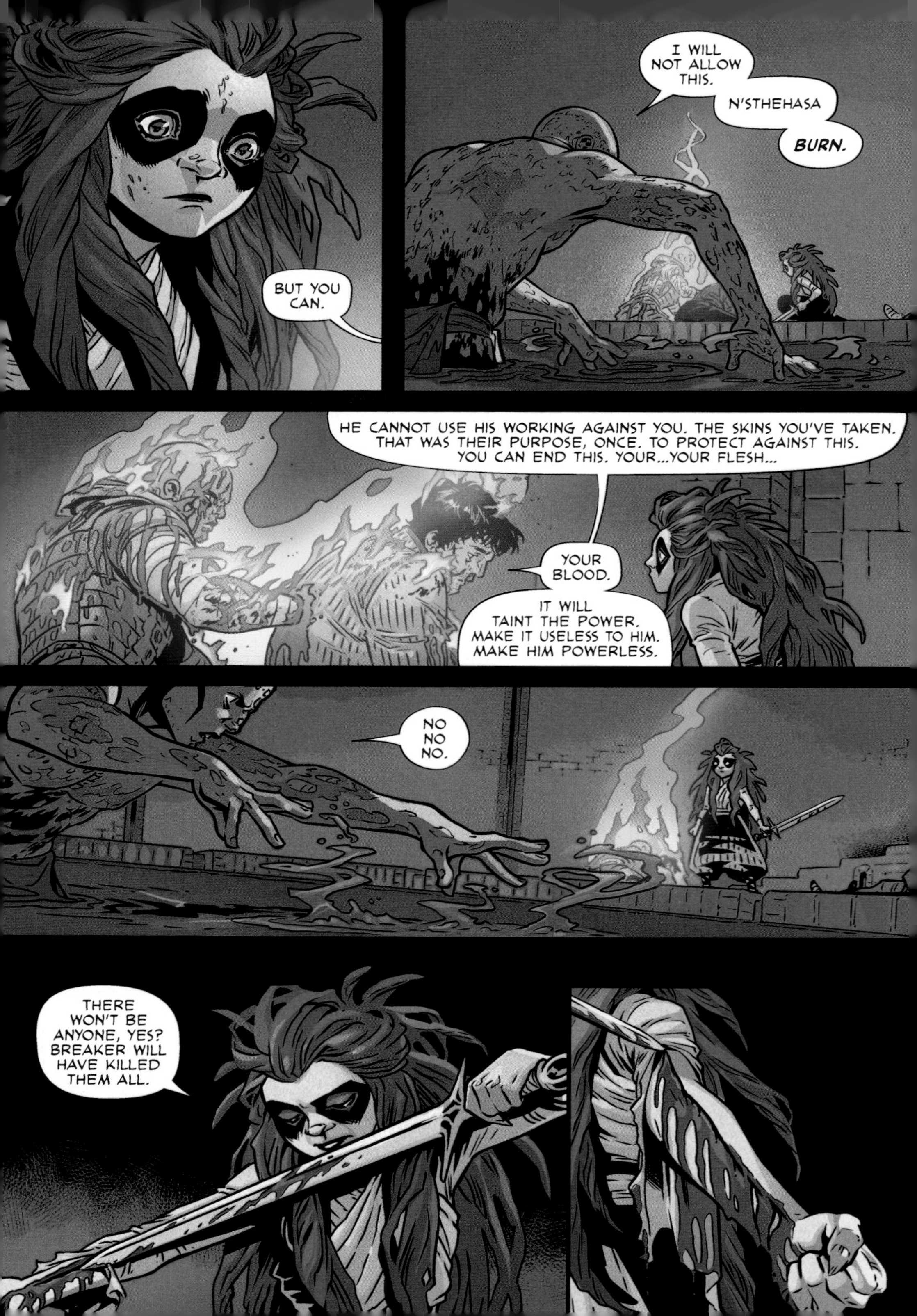
BUT YOU CAN.
I WILL NOT ALLOW THIS.
N'STHEHASA
BURN.
HE CANNOT USE HIS WORKING AGAINST YOU. THE SKINS YOU'VE TAKEN. THAT WAS THEIR PURPOSE, ONCE. TO PROTECT AGAINST THIS. YOU CAN END THIS. YOUR...YOUR FLESH...
YOUR BLOOD.
IT WILL TAINT THE POWER. MAKE IT USELESS TO HIM. MAKE HIM POWERLESS.
NO NO NO.
THERE WON'T BE ANYONE, YES? BREAKER WILL HAVE KILLED THEM ALL.

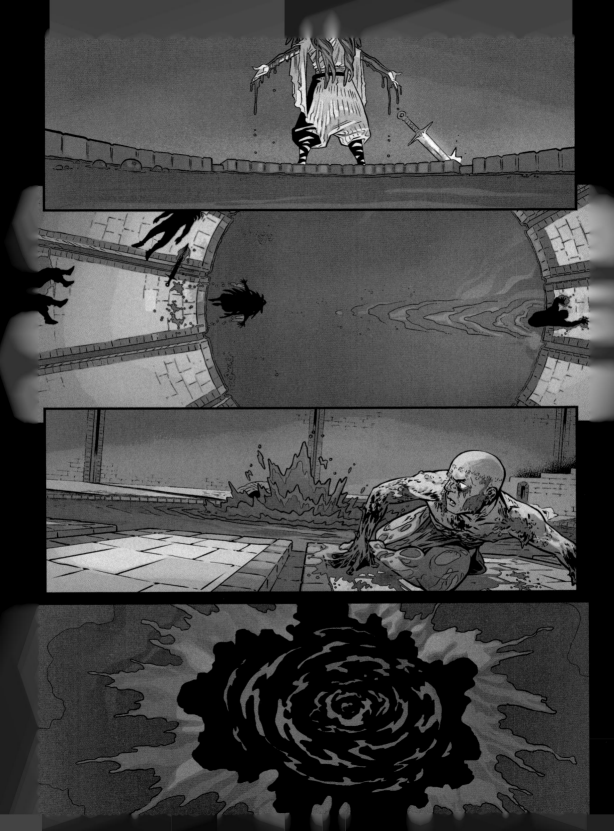

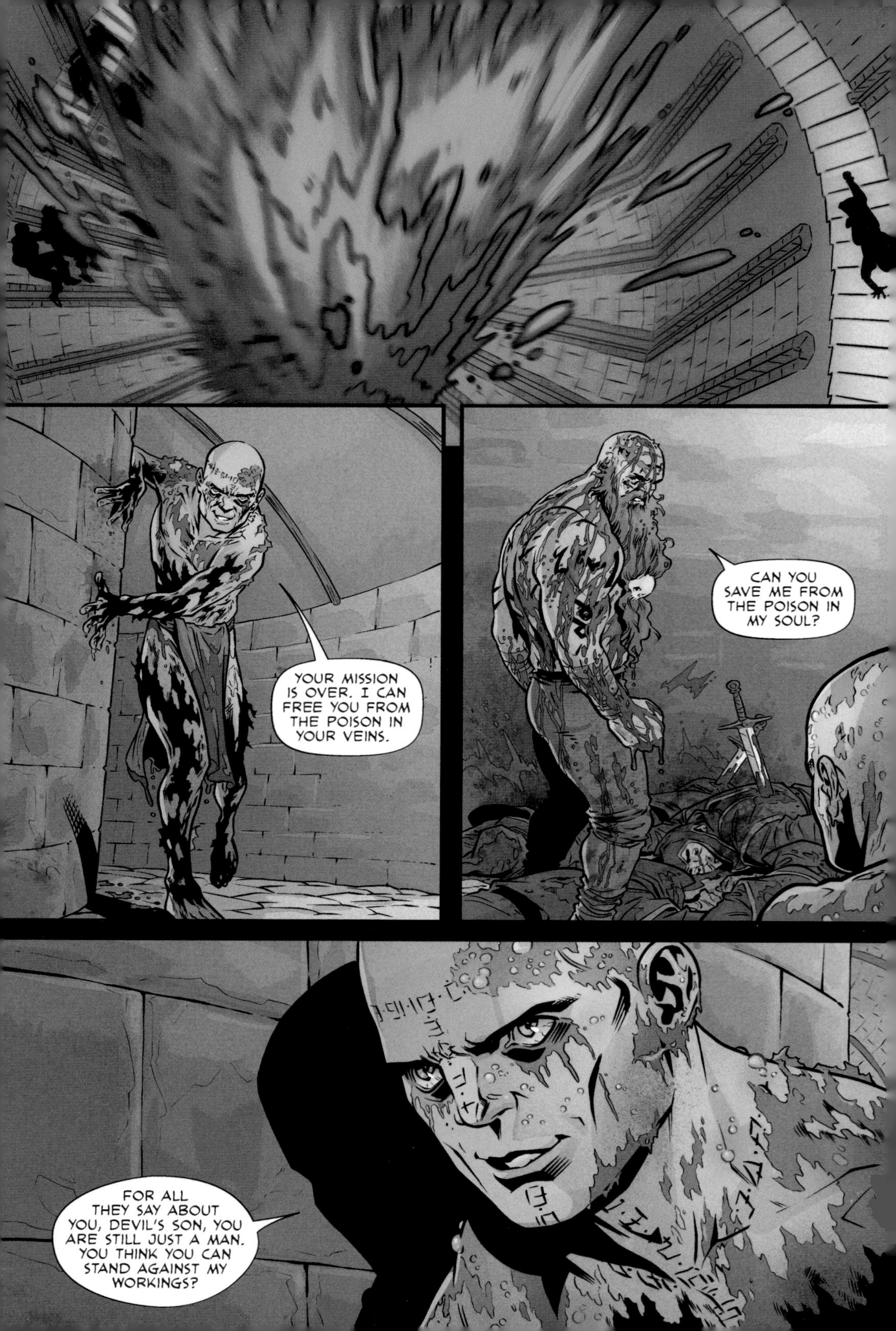
YOUR MISSION IS OVER. I CAN FREE YOU FROM THE POISON IN YOUR VEINS.
CAN YOU SAVE ME FROM THE POISON IN MY SOUL?
FOR ALL THEY SAY ABOUT YOU, DEVIL'S SON, YOU ARE STILL JUST A MAN. YOU THINK YOU CAN STAND AGAINST MY WORKINGS?

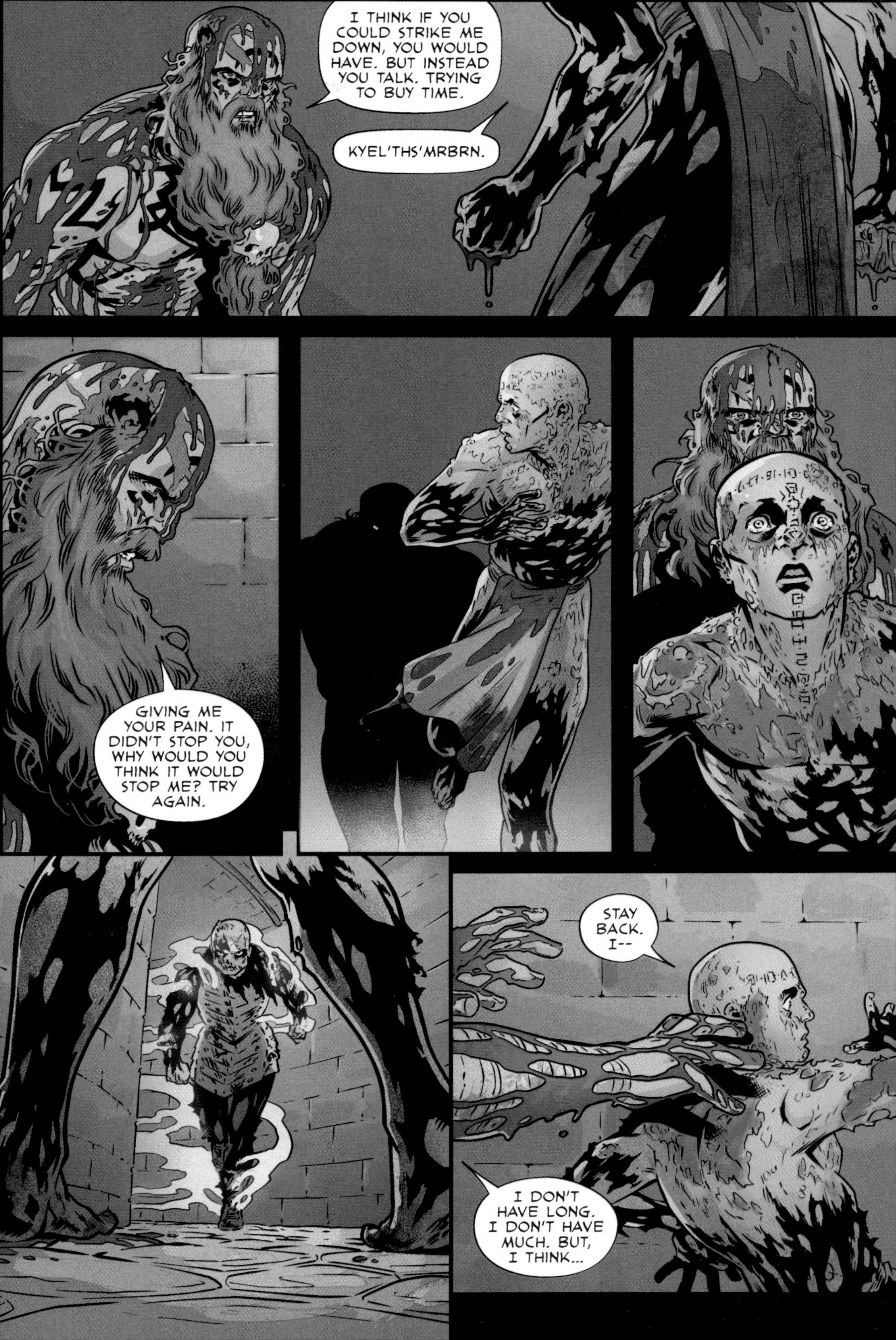
I THINK IF YOU COULD STRIKE ME DOWN, YOU WOULD HAVE. BUT INSTEAD YOU TALK. TRYING TO BUY TIME.
KYEL'THS'MRBRN.
GIVING ME YOUR PAIN. IT DIDN'T STOP YOU, WHY WOULD YOU THINK IT WOULD STOP ME? TRY AGAIN.
STAY BACK. I--
I DON'T HAVE LONG. I DON'T HAVE MUCH. BUT, I THINK...

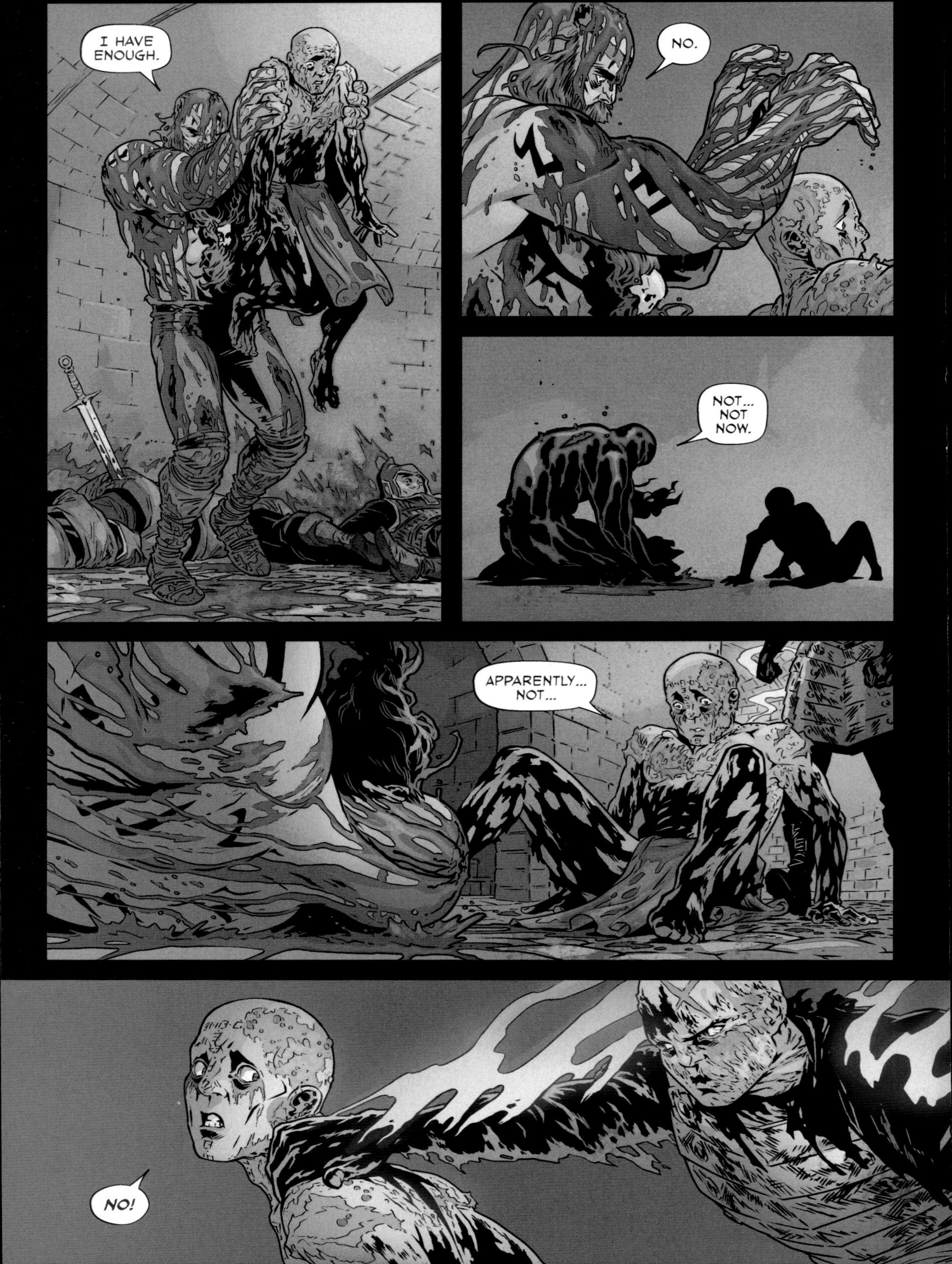
I HAVE ENOUGH.
NO.
NOT... NOT NOW.
APPARENTLY... NOT...
NO!

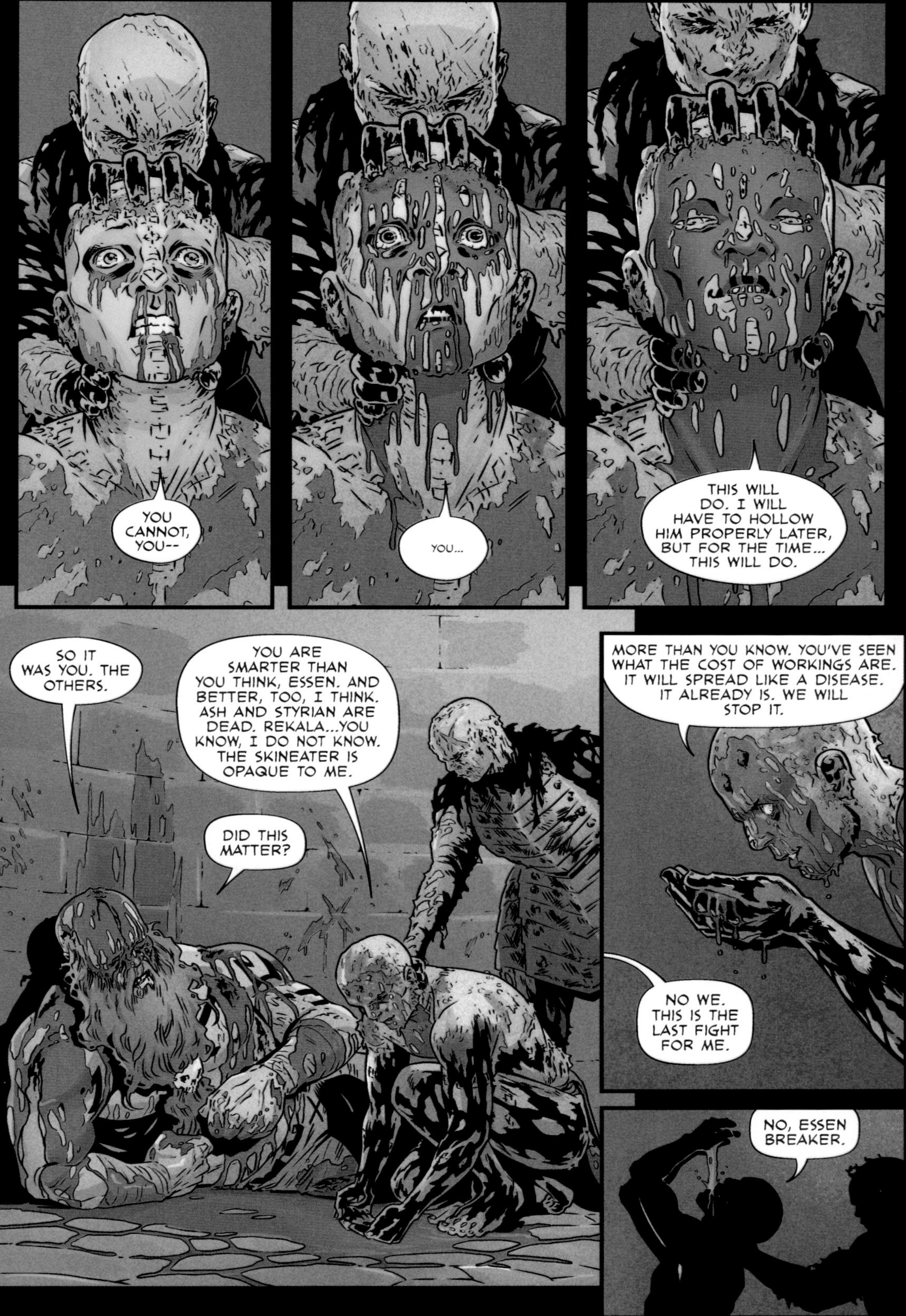
YOU CANNOT, YOU--
YOU...
THIS WILL DO. I WILL HAVE TO HOLLOW HIM PROPERLY LATER, BUT FOR THE TIME... THIS WILL DO.
SO IT WAS YOU. THE OTHERS.
YOU ARE SMARTER THAN YOU THINK, ESSEN. AND BETTER, TOO, I THINK. ASH AND STYRIAN ARE DEAD. REKALA...YOU KNOW, I DO NOT KNOW. THE SKINEATER IS OPAQUE TO ME.
DID THIS MATTER?
MORE THAN YOU KNOW. YOU'VE SEEN WHAT THE COST OF WORKINGS ARE. IT WILL SPREAD LIKE A DISEASE. IT ALREADY IS. WE WILL STOP IT.
NO WE. THIS IS THE LAST FIGHT FOR ME.
NO, ESSEN BREAKER.

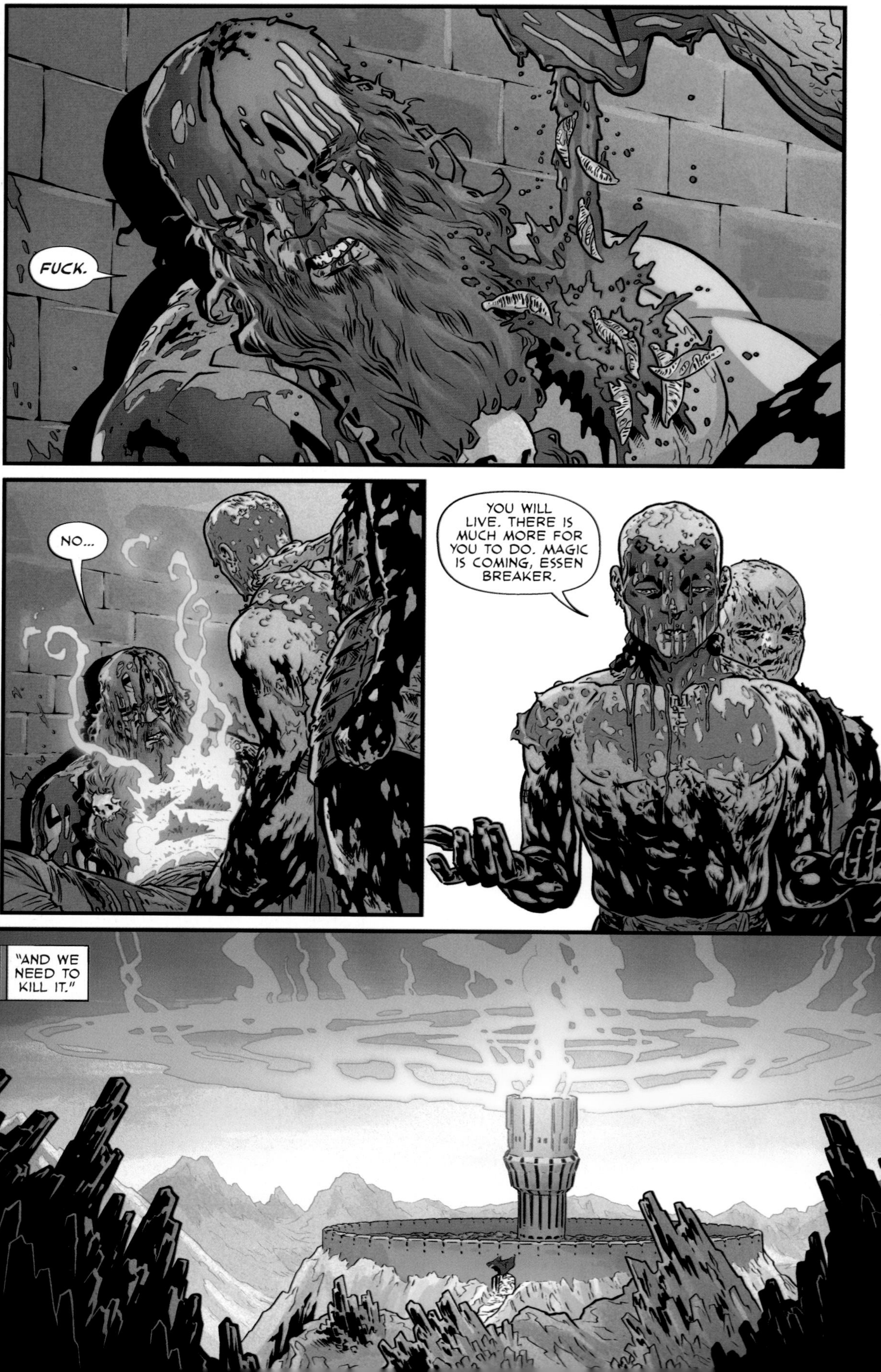
FUCK.
NO...
YOU WILL LIVE. THERE IS MUCH MORE FOR YOU TO DO. MAGIC IS COMING, ESSEN BREAKER.
"AND WE NEED TO KILL IT."

TO BE CONTINUED

COVER GALLERY

BECKY CLOONAN
Portrait Covers

REBEKAH ISAACS
Wanted Cover

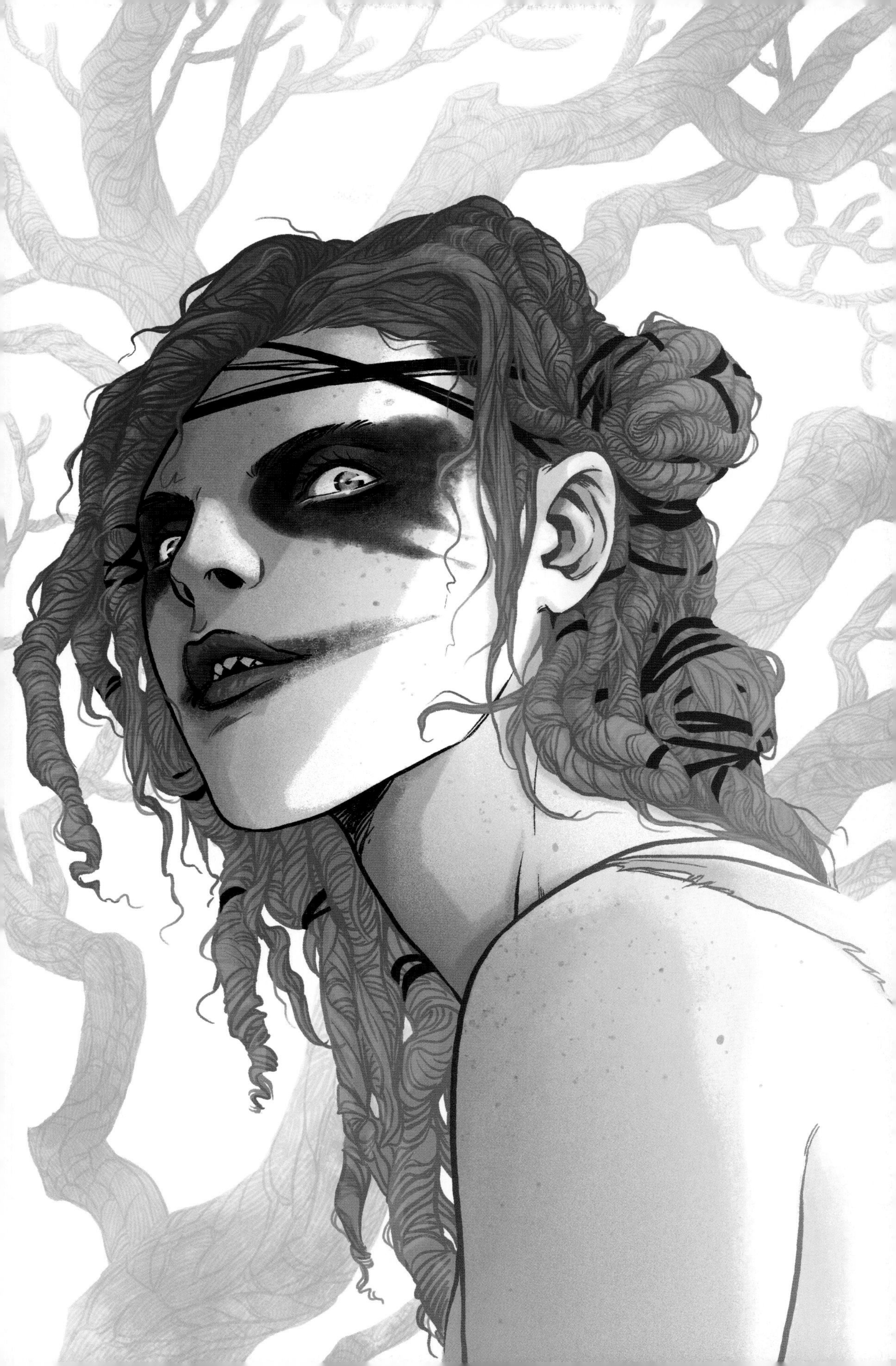

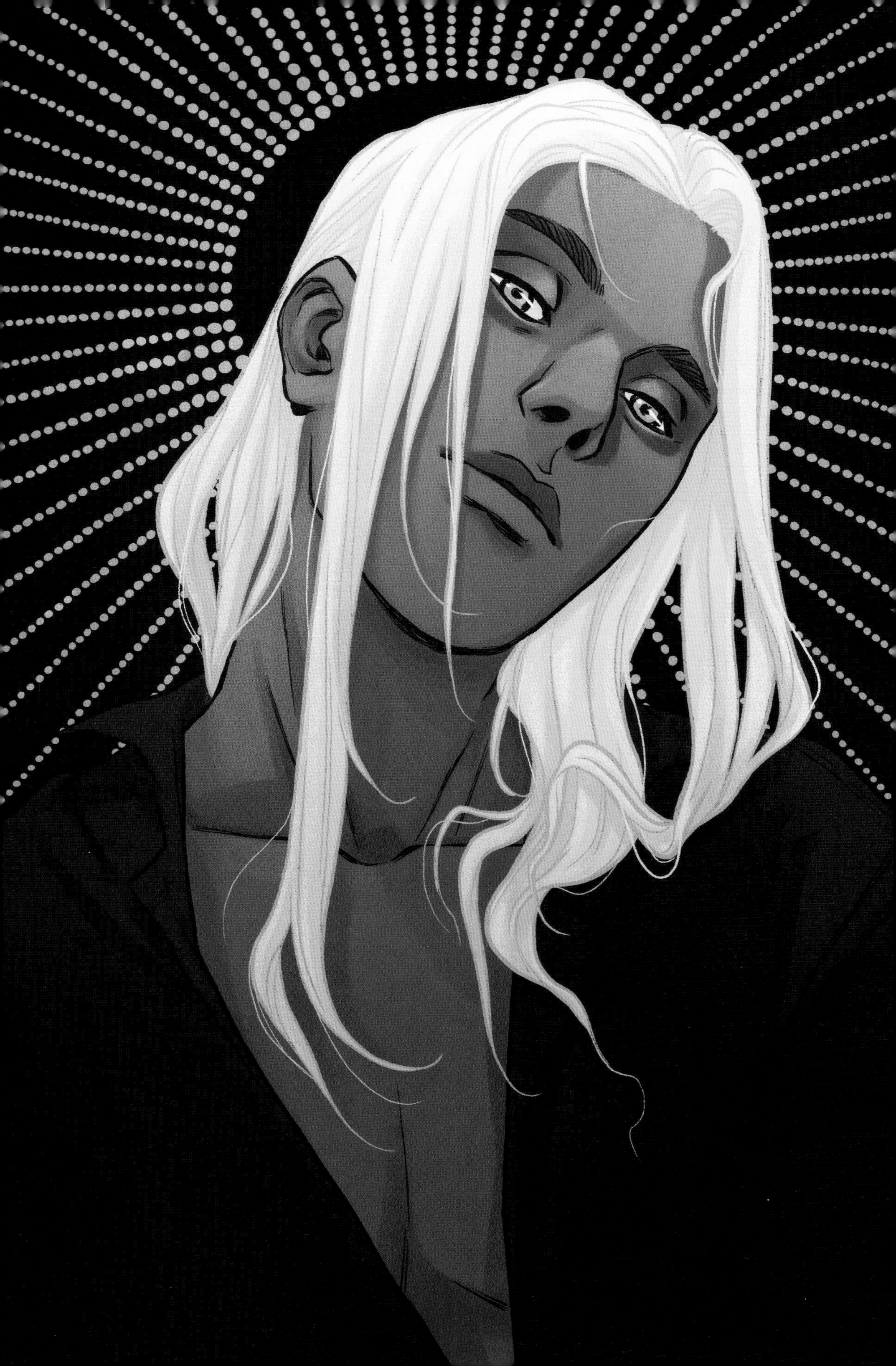

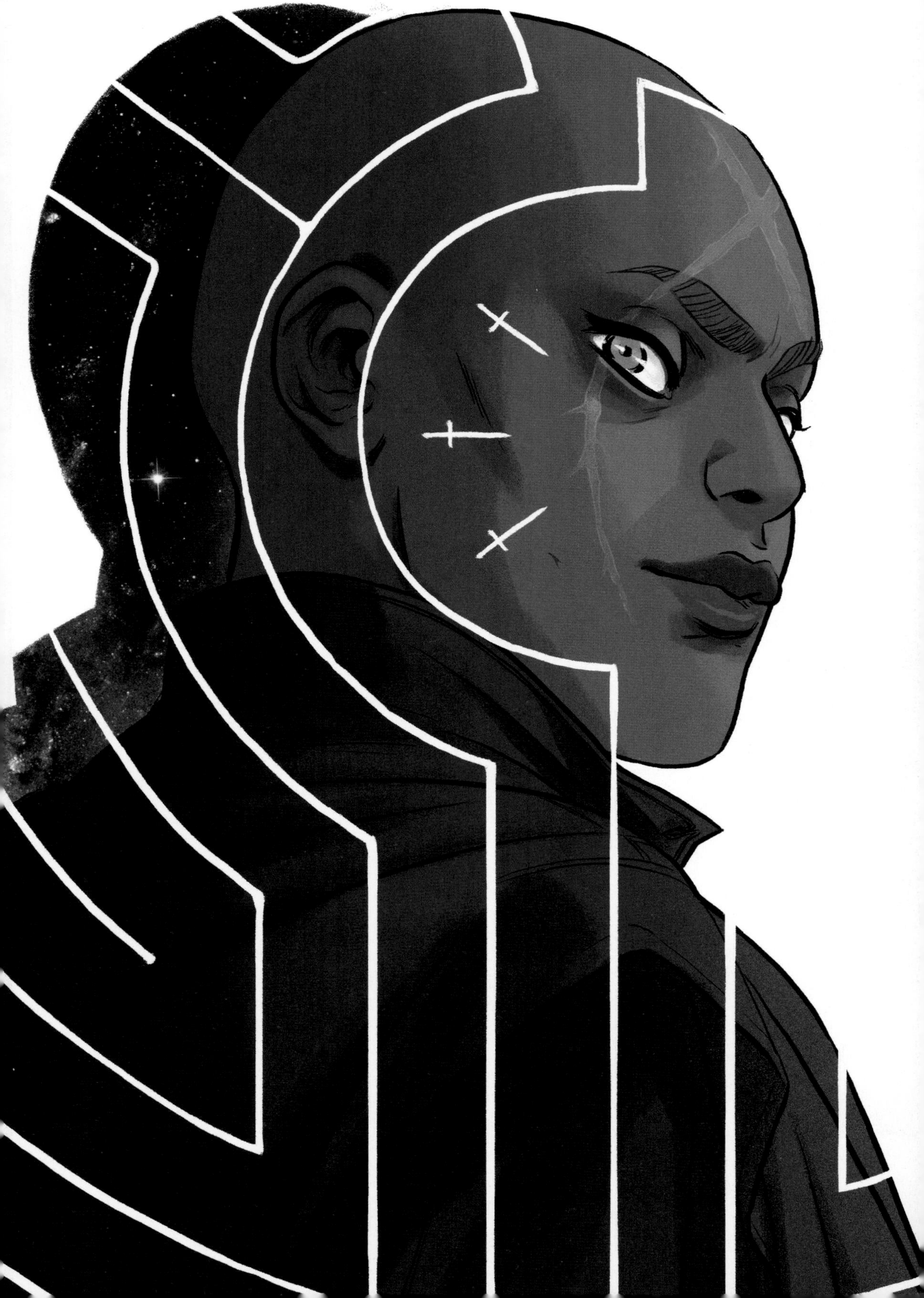

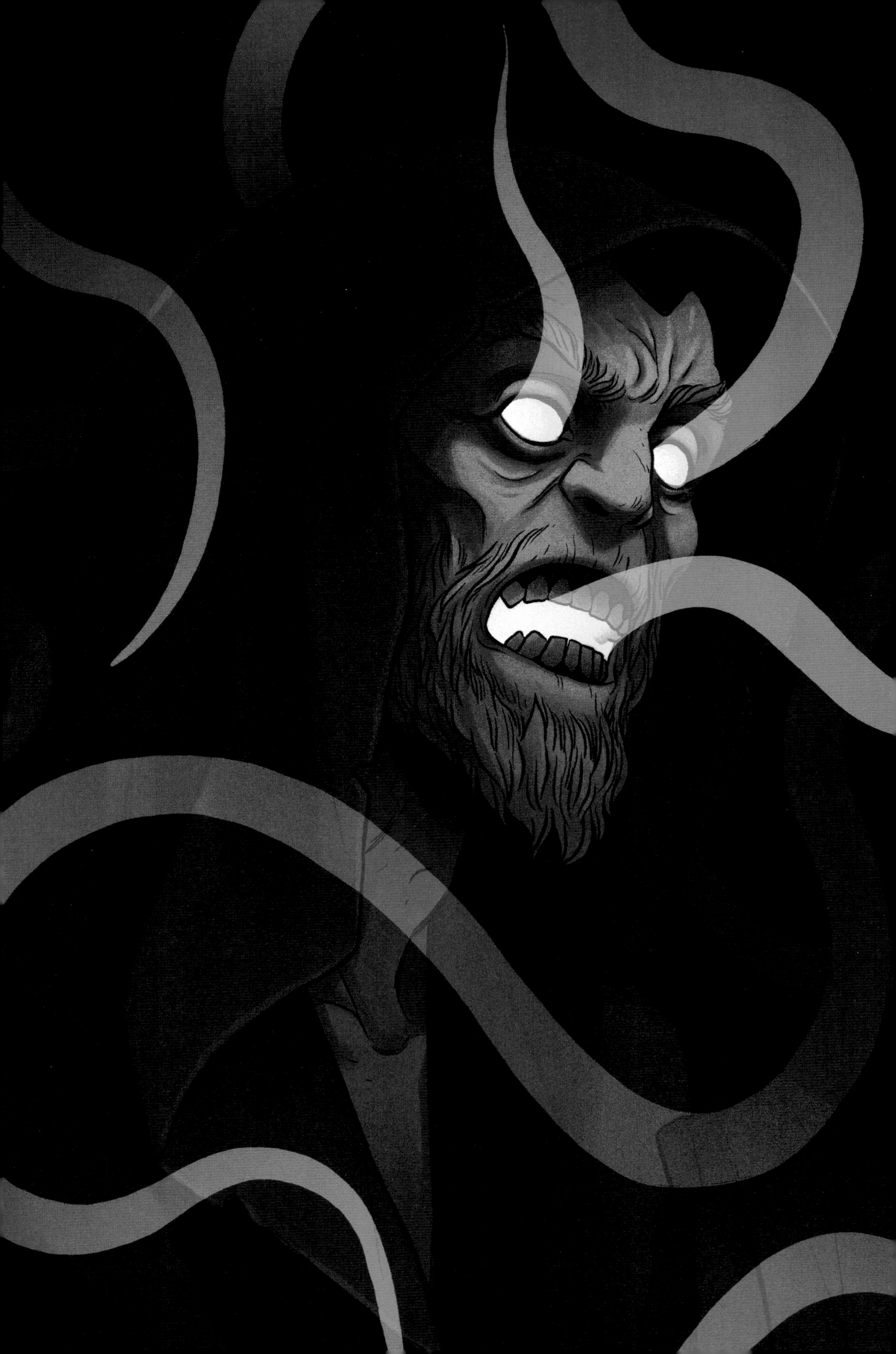

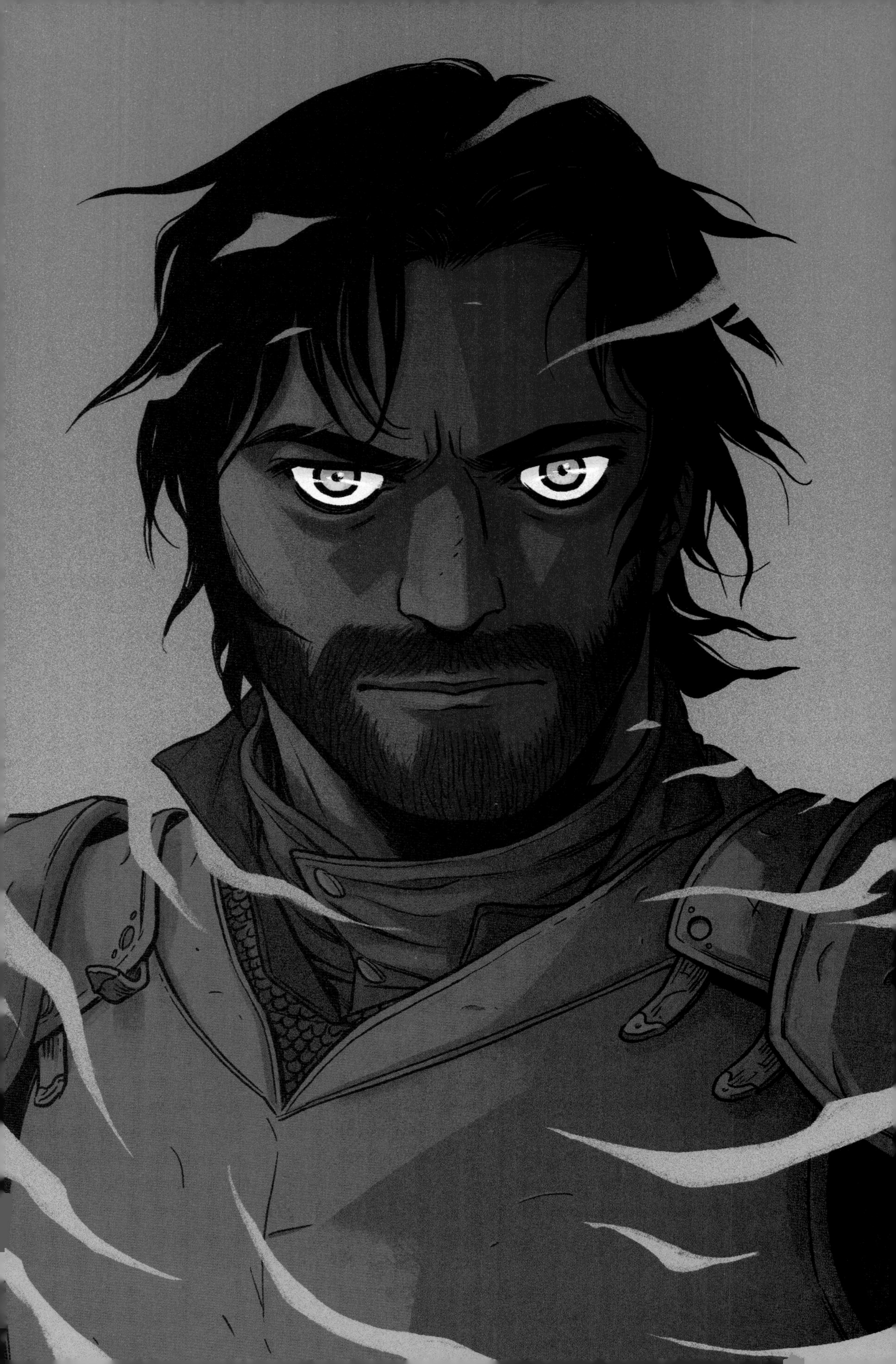

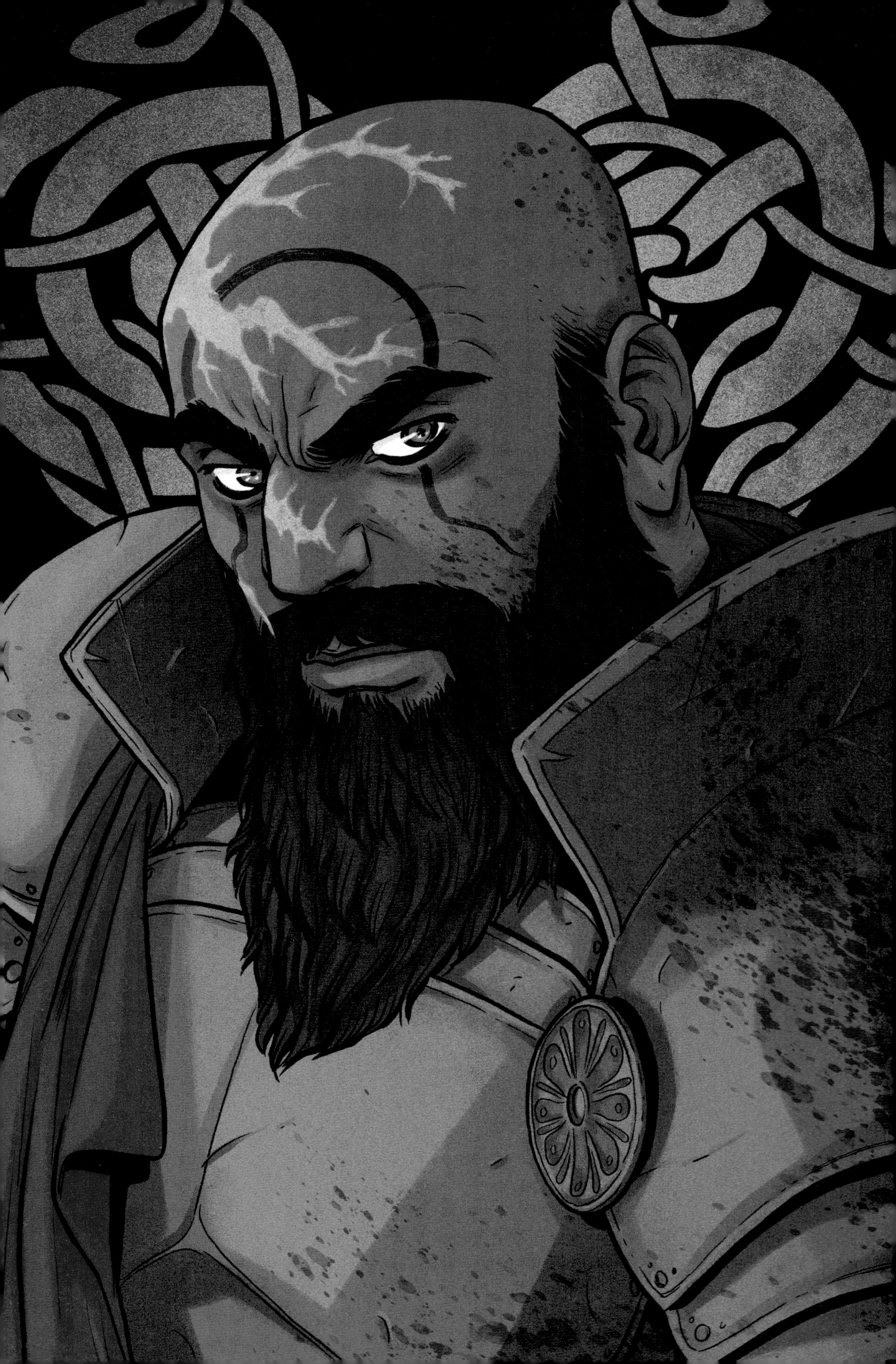

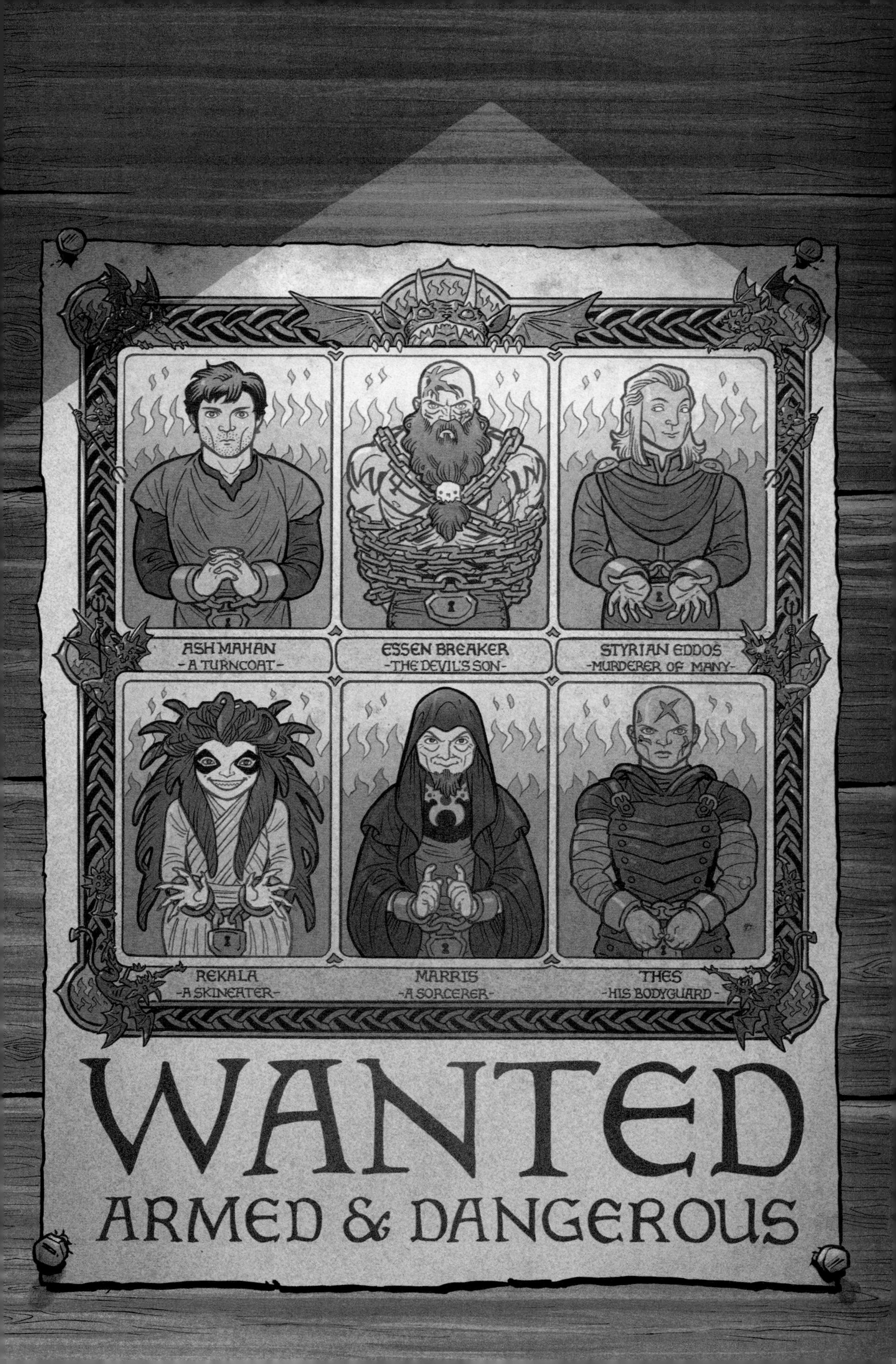
ASH MAHAN
- A TURNCOAT -
ESSEN BREAKER
-THE DEVIL'S SON-
STYRIAN EDDOS
-MURDERER OF MANY-
REKALA
-A SKINEATER-
MARRIS
-A SORCERER-
THES
-HIS BODYGUARD-
WANTED
ARMED & DANGEROUS

"SACRIFICE...

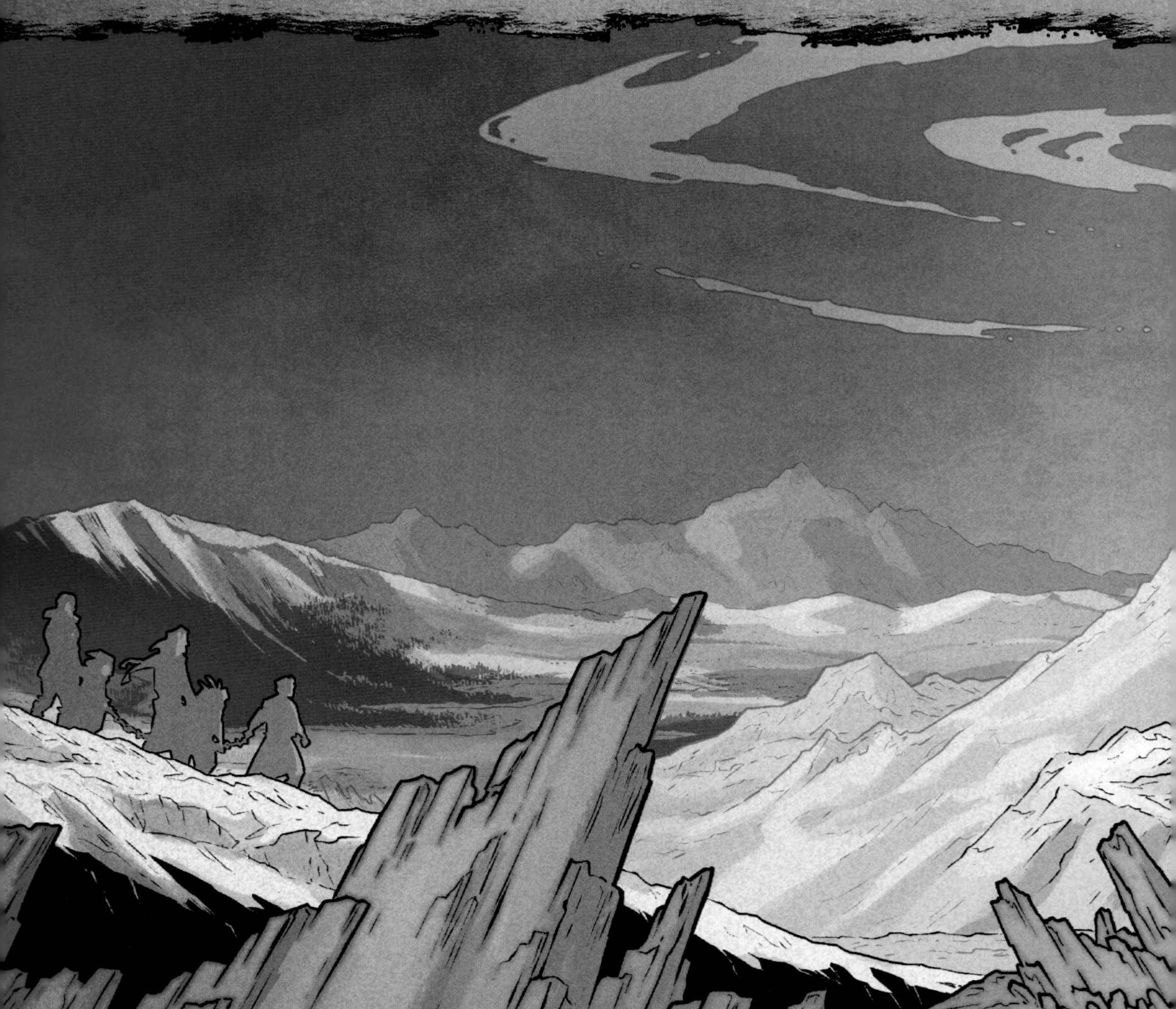

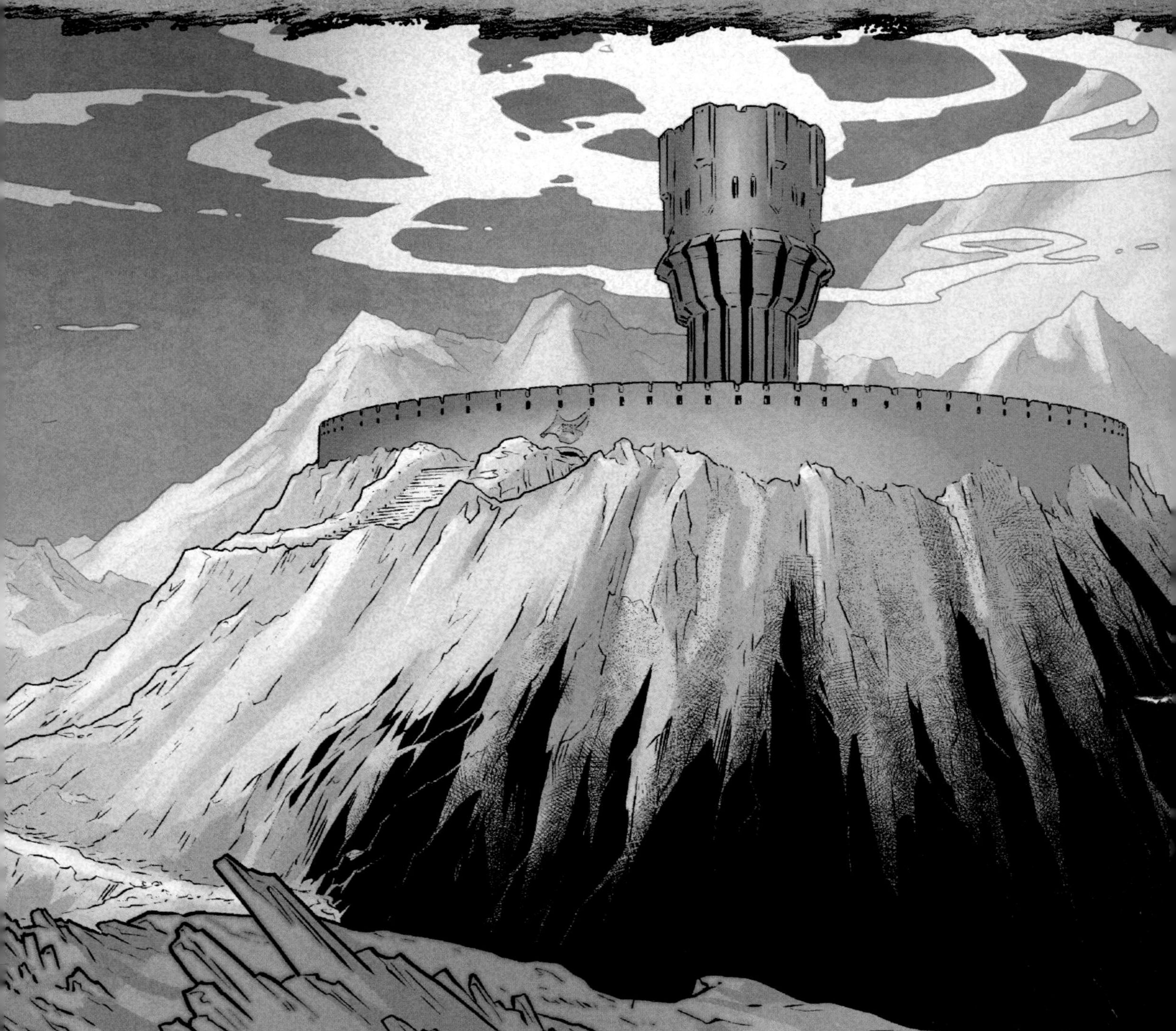

A NECESSARY
COMPONENT OF POWER."

For more tales from **ROBERT KIRKMAN and SKYBOUND**

DANIEL WARREN JOHNSON
MIKE SPICER
MURDER FALCON

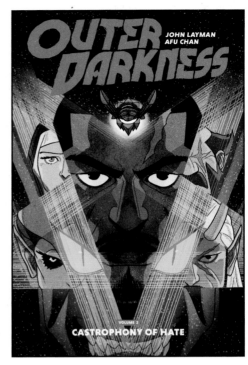

MURDER FALCON TP
ISBN: 978-1-5343-1235-7
$19.99

OUTER DARKNESS
JOHN LAYMAN
AFU CHAN
VOLUME 2
CASTROPHONY OF HATE

VOL. 1: EACH OTHER'S THROATS
ISBN: 978-1-5343-1210-4
$16.99

VOL. 2: CASTROPHANY OF HATE
ISBN: 978-1-5343-1370-5
$16.99

BIRTHRIGHT
LIVE BY THE SWORD

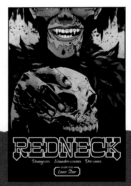

VOL. 1: HOMECOMING TP
ISBN: 978-1-63215-231-2
$9.99

VOL. 2: CALL TO ADVENTURE TP
ISBN: 978-1-63215-446-0
$12.99

VOL. 3: ALLIES AND ENEMIES TP
ISBN: 978-1-63215-683-9
$12.99

VOL. 4: FAMILY HISTORY TP
ISBN: 978-1-63215-871-0
$12.99

VOL. 5: BELLY OF THE BEAST TP
ISBN: 978-1-5343-0218-1
$12.99

VOL. 6: FATHERHOOD TP
ISBN: 978-1-53430-498-7
$14.99

VOL. 7: BLOOD BROTHERS TP
ISBN: 978-1-5343-1053-7
$14.99

VOL. 8: LIVE BY THE SWORD TP
ISBN: 978-1-5343-1368-2
$14.99

ROBERT KIRKMAN
LORENZO DE FELICI
ANNALISA LEONI
OBLIVION SONG
CHAPTER THREE

CHAPTER ONE
ISBN: 978-1-5343-0642-4
$9.99

CHAPTER TWO
ISBN: 978-1-5343-1057-5
$16.99

CHAPTER THREE
ISBN: 978-1-5343-1326-2
$16.99

BY KIRKMAN & AZACETA
OUTCAST

VOL. 1: A DARKNESS SURROUNDS HIM
ISBN: 978-1-6321-5053-0
$9.99

VOL. 2: A VAST AND UNENDING RUIN
ISBN: 978-1-6321-5448-4
$14.99

VOL. 3: THIS LITTLE LIGHT
ISBN: 978-1-6321-5693-8
$14.99

VOL. 4: UNDER DEVIL'S WING
ISBN: 978-1-5343-0050-7
$14.99

VOL. 5: THE NEW PATH
ISBN: 978-1-5343-0249-5
$16.99

VOL. 6: INVASION
ISBN: 978-1-5343-0751-3
$16.99

VOL. 7: THE DARKNESS GROWS
ISBN: 978-1-5343-1239-5
$16.99

REDNECK
Lone Star

VOL. 1: DEEP IN THE HEART TP
ISBN: 978-1-5343-0331-7
$16.99

VOL. 2: THE EYES UPON YOU TP
ISBN: 978-1-5343-0665-3
$16.99

VOL. 3: LONGHORNS TP
ISBN: 978-1-5343-1050-6
$16.99

VOL. 4: LONE STAR TP
ISBN: 978-1-5343-1367-5
$16.99